GREAT
BRITISH
SHORT
STORIES

GREAT BRITISH SHORT STORIES

Selected by the Editors of
The Reader's Digest

With an introduction by J. B. Priestley

VOLUME ONE

The Reader's Digest Association
London, Sydney, Cape Town

FIRST EDITION 1974
REPRINTED 1995, 1996

Published by
THE READER'S DIGEST ASSOCIATION LIMITED
Berkeley Square House, Berkeley Square, London W1X 6AB

The stories in this volume are used by permission of
and special arrangement with the holders of the respective copyrights.
(For further information see pages 370-1.)

ISBN 0-276-42199-X (Volume 1)
ISBN 0-276-42201-5 (2-volume pack)

Printed and bound by William Clowes Ltd, Great Britain

Contents

Introduction

by

J. B. PRIESTLEY
(1894-1984)

W HEN I first went through the list of writers to be included in this volume, I discovered that I had known—many as casual acquaintances, some as friends—over half of them. Remembering these men and women, I could not help wondering at the extraordinary variety of talents, temperaments, characters, a wide-ranging collection of short stories could offer us. No other anthology of fiction, unless it ran into many volumes and weighed several pounds, could offer the same fascinating variety. Here the short story scores easily.

Moreover, as a form it allows—indeed, it encourages—its writers to be different. They can do what pleases them best. They can be blood-chilling, coolly satirical, sympathetic and pathetic, comical, simple and straightforward or most elaborately ingenious: no rule binds them—except that they must retain our interest and not go on too long. Here I will make a personal point. I am fond of reading detective stories in bed. But too many of these have been padded out to book-length when in fact they would have been far more effective as longish short stories.

One reason for this padding-out has been the disappearance in this country of magazines specializing in good short stories. The chief of these was the old *Strand Magazine*, probably at its best between the 1890's and the earlier 1920's. As a boy I had an attic bedroom next to the lumber room, where there were piles of old magazines that I used to plunder for bed-reading. I remember sharply how I terrified myself with the very Sherlock Holmes story, *The Speckled Band*, that has been chosen for this anthology.

Not as popular entertainment but as a highbrow literary form, the short story, I believe, enjoyed its greatest success, claiming most critical attention, in the 1920's. Those were the days when the famous short stories of Chekhov, a tremendous influence, were being translated and appearing in volume after volume. Writers like Katherine Mansfield and Stacy Aumonier (who both died in the 1920's) made their reputations entirely on short stories. As early as 1923 Elizabeth Bowen, afterwards to achieve great distinction as a novelist, began her career with a volume of short stories, *Encounters*, which, she told me more than once later, I was the first person to praise in print. Then there were one or two men who made a name simply by producing anthologies of short stories, not to be compared, however, in length, breadth, catholic taste, with the one we have here. Finally, Professors of the Short Story actually made their appearance in some American universities.

Though observation and memory play considerable parts in the creative processes of writers, I imagine that few good short stories, like those collected here, have been directly based on actual people and events. In this matter the notable exception is Somerset Maugham. Though I knew Maugham and, unlike some of my colleagues, always found him friendly and appreciative, I said of him that every time he published a volume of short stories he closed a continent for any further visits. It was his habit for some years to travel to far distant places, to sit up with district commissioners or lonely planters and listen carefully to their gossip and accounts of local scandals. Out of these he would create, again very carefully, his highly successful short stories, occasionally to the distress of the persons involved in those old scandals. But I am sure his dubious method was exceptional.

Now I began by pointing out what a variety of talents, temperaments, characters, a collection like this offers us. But to these we must add short-story techniques, which are as varied as their authors. To illustrate this point, also to encourage readers to make their own analyses, instead of hurrying all round the table of contents for the most obvious examples, I will briefly examine stories that turn up in the first quarter of the list. So here goes.

Miss Bracegirdle does her Duty (Stacy Aumonier). It has action of a kind but is really based on character—or, to be more accurate, a certain type of character. Miss Bracegirdle is the timid ladylike English spinster, but when it comes to the crunch she shows us that she can be patiently resourceful—therefore a character story. *Patience* (Nigel Balchin) depends neither on character nor atmosphere but owes everything to its final surprise twist in the narrative. A good example of the limited but very ingenious short story.

The Avenging Chance (Anthony Berkeley) is a brilliantly clever whodun-it, with devices often imitated since. But please note that while, as I said earlier, many detective novels have been padded-out short stories,

10

in this particular instance we might have welcomed a rather longer account of the detective at work. *Running Wolf* (Algernon Blackwood): no character build-up but plenty of atmosphere and with Algernon Blackwood's usual stealthy approach to an occult theme.

The Demon Lover (Elizabeth Bowen) is a little gem that combines everything—character, with Mrs. Drover; the atmosphere of the deserted wartime house; economic narration; and a final twist when we are no longer expecting it. *The Hammer of God* (G. K. Chesterton): it is easy to enjoy the Father Brown stories, often ingeniously worked out. But it is hard to *believe* in them. They are happening in a Chestertonian world, not quite this one. However, we may be tired of this one.

The Higgler (A. E. Coppard): no suspense and no surprises here. Coppard's strong appeal comes from a certain density and richness, half-poetic, half-humorous, in his narrative style and atmosphere. His short stories are like condensed novels. *Parson's Pleasure* (Roald Dahl) shows us a rather leisurely character study—that of the artful but contemptible Mr. Boggis—which explodes into ironic action in its final scene. It must not be confused with stories, like the one by Balchin, that depend entirely upon surprise twists.

Finally, two very different stories by successful contemporary writers. *Winter's Morning* (Len Deighton), taking us to the First World War air battles, is closely packed, as this author's work always is, with highly realistic detail, properly researched. He offers it with a certain suggestion of brutality, as if he were not emotionally committed (though he is), that is as effective here as it is in his longer tales. *The Gifts of War* (Margaret Drabble), in sharpest contrast to *Winter's Morning*, compels us to enter the minds and hearts of an adoring mother and of a girl in love, then very skilfully brings these two women into a dramatic confrontation— in a toy department, of all places! It is quite unlike any other story we have examined, it is very good indeed—and new to me, so that I owe our editors my thanks.

By playing fair and simply taking these stories as they came along, I hope I have demonstrated the astonishing variety of temperaments, techniques, methods, skills, we can find here, and I also hope that some readers will follow my example as they first enjoy and then analyse all the stories that follow these. But my time and space are up. If I went on, I would be like a man standing at the door of a party and holding up its guests by telling them how everybody in the house is dressed. So now I stand aside. Walk in, dear reader, and enjoy yourself!

1974

MARGERY ALLINGHAM

1904-1966

Her long marriage and the rural contentment of much
of her life contrasted oddly with the world of crime and its
detection that she chose to write about. But devoted
research was her forte, backed by tireless ingenuity and
a divertingly cheerful acceptance of life's seamier side.

Evidence in Camera

THERE ARE PEOPLE who might consider
Chippy Wager unethical and others who go
a great deal further. At the time I am telling
you about he was on the *Cormorant*, which is
not that paper's real name, but why make
enemies if you don't have to? He was, and is
of course, a photographer; one of those boys
who shoot through a cop's legs and jump on
to the running-board of the limousine so that
you can see the Society bride in tears as she
takes her first cold look at the man she's got.
They pay those lads plenty, but Chippy had
uses for money, mainly liquid, and he made another income on the side
by taking photographs privately of practically everything from the
Mayor and Corporation to the local beauty queen. He made time for
these activities when there was none, and used the *Cormorant*'s excellent
equipment, but, as he said, he had to drink.

We both went down to St. Piers for the fifth murder. I was on the old
Post at the time, and when I say 'we' went I mean among others. The
Southern Railway put on one excursion train for the Press and another
for the police.

The story was simple and, if you like that sort of thing, good. You
probably remember it. It rated about as much space as an election and
by the time the body of the fifth victim, Mrs. Lily Clarke, was found at
St. Piers it was practically the one subject of conversation in the bars.

13

Briefly, someone was killing off middle-aged redheads in seaside towns. There had been a summer of it. In May Mrs. Wild was killed in Whichbourne, in June Mrs. Garrard at Turnhill Bay, and by July the murderer had got round to Southwharf and had attended to a Mrs. Jelf. In August he chose a fashionable resort and strangled Mrs. Ginger Hollis, just outside the polo ground at Prinny's Plage, and in September there was this latest affair at St. Piers.

In all five instances the details were astonishingly similar. Each victim was respectable, homely in appearance, in the habit of letting rooms to visitors, and either naturally or artificially auburn-haired. Each woman was found strangled in a secluded place in the open air, with her untouched handbag beside her. Each woman lost some trifling ornament, such as a cheap earring, a gold clasp from a chain bracelet, a locket containing edelweiss, and once, in Mrs. Hollis's case, a small silver button with a regimental crest on it.

Not once was any trace of the murderer seen either before or after the crime, and by the time the St. Piers news came through the police were savage while the Press were on the verge of being bored. There was still plenty to write about but nothing new. The *Cormorant* and its sisters, who had worked themselves up to screaming hysterics in July, were showing signs of exhaustion, and even the heavies, like ourselves and the *World*, were falling back on such items as the slayer's preference for the new moon.

From my own purely personal point of view the thing was becoming a nightmare and the principal reason for that was Chippy. I had first met him when I travelled down to Whichborne in May. On that occasion there were seventeen of us in a carriage which might have held ten without active inconvenience, and although he was the last to arrive he was in a corner seat with only myself atop of him before the journey was half way over. I do not know how he did this. My impression is that there was a jolt in a tunnel and that when we came out into the light there he was, slung with cameras, sitting just underneath me.

I suppose I must bring myself to describe him. He is a small thin rag of a man with a surprisingly large square head in which, somewhere low down in front, has been inserted the bright predatory face of an evil child. Whenever I think of him, which is as seldom as possible, I receive a mental picture of white lashes on red lids and a row of widely spaced uneven teeth barred in a 'Have you got anything *I* want?' smile.

His is hardly one of the dressy professions but I have seen even his confrères blench when confronted by some of his ensembles. Peterson, my opposite number on the *World*, who interests himself in these matters, insists that the man finds his clothes lying about in hotel bedrooms. It may be so. At any rate, when I first saw him he was certainly wearing jodhpurs, carefully tailored for a larger and even more curiously shaped leg, a green cardigan buttoning on the wrong side, and a new cheap sports coat adorned by a single gigantic beer-stain. Every pocket, one frankly marsupial, bulged strangely rather than dangerously, and he carried as much gear as a paratrooper.

I remember my conversation with him on that occasion. I had pulled back my sleeve to glance at the time and he prodded me in the back.

"That's a good watch," he said. "Ever had it photographed?"

I said that strange as it might seem to him such a notion had never entered my head.

"It's wise," he assured me seriously. "In case you ever have it pinched, see? Gives the busies something to go on? I'll do it for you when we get in. It won't cost you more than half a bar. You're married, of course. Got any kids?"

I told him no, and he seemed hurt.

"Kids make good pictures," he explained. "Kids and dogs. Got a dog?"

Again I had to disappoint him.

"Pity," he said. "What a pal, eh? What a pal. You might pick one up down here. There's a chap only five miles out who breeds Irish wolfhounds. I'll put you on to him and we'll take a spool. Surprise the wife, eh?"

I escaped from him as soon as I could but everything was against me. The news, what there was of it, broke late and the town was packed. By the time I realised that I should have to stay there was no accommodation in the place. I was resigning myself to a bench on the front when I ran into Chippy just before closing time in the back bar of the Queen's. He was in the same predicament, having, so he said, had to waste time photographing a cotton magnate and his fifth wife who were having their second honeymoon in the King's Suite at the Grand. He was not worrying, however, and when they turned us out he produced an old friend who was the manager of a flea-ridden little pub in a back street. He fixed us up with two cots in an attic, for which I paid, and I let Chippy take a photograph of my watch, rewarding him, as far as I remember, with fourteen shillings and sixpence in cash for three excellent prints.

After that I was doomed. The man became an incubus, haunting me as I drank furtively in corners or hunted our murderer with one eye, so to speak, behind me lest I myself should be waylaid. I do agree with Peterson that I am free, adult, and a member of a profession which ought at least to be able to look after itself, and I could once I suppose have got rid of him with brutality and the fishy eye, but I could not bring myself to do it. He was so fearful, so unmitigatedly awful that he

15

fascinated me. Some unsuspected masochism in my nature compelled me to be at least half civil to him, and then of course he was often so infuriatingly useful. There was a rumour that he was lucky, but that explanation did him less than justice. He was indefatigable and his curious contacts and side jobs sometimes provided him with most useful breaks, as for instance when he nipped down to Whichborne station to oblige a man who wanted a shot of his greyhound and got instead a very fine one of the Yard's Chief Inspector Tizer getting off the train at a time when no one was sure if the local police had appealed to H.Q. and if so who was going to be sent.

By the time the murderer had got round to St. Piers Chippy was most anxious that the homicidal nut should be apprehended and the case finished. His reason was personal and typical and I happened to know about it because he had confided it to me one night at Prinny's Plage, when he had hounded me down to a hostelry which I felt fairly confident not even he had heard of. I can see him now, pointing to the brewer's almanac which hung on the varnished match-boarding of the bar wall.

"Look, chum," he said, his filthy forefinger tracing out the dates, "next new moon is September sixteen, isn't it? Don't think I'm complaining about that. It'll still be summer then and the seaside suits me. But what about the month after? New moon October fourteen. I don't want anything awkward to happen then, do I?"

I made a point of never giving him encouragement and I said nothing, knowing perfectly well I should not silence him.

"October fourteen." He was indignant. "The Distillers Livery Company conference begins on the fourteenth. Fancy missing that. What a tragedy, eh? What a tragedy!"

That was in August. We were all expecting the September murder, although naturally there was no way of telling where it was going to crop up. When the news broke just too late for the edition which everybody was holding for it in a shamefaced way, it was very nearly anticlimax. As Peterson said, there would have been almost more news value in the story if it hadn't occurred. No one was pleased. The livelier dailies had planted men at most of the larger southern watering places but no one had thought of St. Piers, cheap and respectable, out on the mud-flats of the estuary. We had a local correspondent there, as we had in every town in the country. The last thing he had sent us, according to the book, was an account of a stork which a coachload of machine-shop operatives had seen flying inland one evening in June the previous year. According to his story, the phenomenon had caused wild excitement in the town. It appeared to be that sort of place.

I managed to avoid Chippy going down but I saw his back disappearing into the Railway Tavern as I picked up a taxi at the station.

I was glad of the respite, for the newsflash which had come in was so familiar in its wording—'Body of well-nurtured woman found strangled. Lonely woodland. Auburn-haired. Chief Inspector Tizer hurrying to scene'—that I felt a wave of pure nausea at the prospect of having to deal with him as well.

St. Piers was much as I had feared. At first it is only the light and the faint smell of iodine which warns the newcomer that the coast is at hand, but towards the front, where the architecture veers towards Victorian Moorish, a faded ocean licks a dun-coloured strand and the shops sell coloured buckets and sticks of sweet rock and crested china to take home.

I found our local correspondent, a tobacconist called Cuffley, in his shop on the parade. He was waiting for me on the step, every hair in his moustache electrified with excitement. He had leapt to the job, had been on the spot soon after the body had been discovered, and had had a word with the inevitable small boy who had given the first alarm. He had even written a short piece which began, as I remember, '*Mad Killer Visits St. Piers at Last.* A baleful sun rose early this morning over the municipally maintained woodland behind the Kursaal and must have shone down unheeding for quite a space on the ghastly, blue, contorted lips of a respected local resident . . .' However, he had got the victim's name and address for me and had written it down in block caps on the back of one of his trade cards: MRS. LILY CLARKE, KNOLE, SEAVIEW AVENUE. It was the same sort of name and the same sort of address as all the others in the long weary business, and when he told me with delight that he had recognized a relation of the dead woman among his customers, and had gone to the length of having her waiting for me in the little room behind the shop, I knew before I saw her exactly the kind of gal I was going to find. The sameness of all five cases was slightly unnerving. I recognized at once both the horror and the dreadful secret enjoyment she was finding in it. I had seen it often that summer.

Her story, too, was a fifth variation of a tale I had heard four times already. Like her predecessors, Mrs. Clarke had been a widow. She had not dyed her hair exactly but she had touched it up. She had not taken in lodgers in the ordinary way, being much too refined. But yes, on occasions she had obliged. The idea of her going for a walk at night with a man she did not know! Well, if the situation had not been so tragic the relation would have had to laugh, she would really.

I asked the question I had grown used to asking. "Was she a nice woman? Did you like her?" I was prepared for the girl's hesitation and the faint uneasiness, the anxiety to speak well of the dead. I remembered comments on the other women. "She had a temper." "You would not call her exactly generous." "She liked her own way." "She could be very nice when she wanted to."

17

This time Mr. Cuffley's customer, in speaking of Mrs. Clarke, said something which seemed to me to sum up them all.

"Oh, she was all for herself," she said grimly and shut her mouth like a vice.

At Sub-Divisional Police Headquarters there was no information of a startling character. Mrs. Clarke had met her death at some time before midnight and in the process she had not been robbed. Fifteen pounds in treasury notes had been found in the mock-crocodile handbag which still hung from her arm. The sergeant in charge spoke of the negligence of the criminal in this respect with an amazement which bordered upon indignation. The only blessed thing she had lost, he said regretfully, was a silver tassel which had hung from the old-fashioned silver brooch she wore in her lapel, and, of course, her life.

As in all the earlier crimes there was absolutely no suspect. There were no visitors staying at Knole, Seaview Avenue, and so far no one had come forward to report having seen the woman out with a stranger.

I sent my story off and took a tram to the Kursaal. Half the town appeared to have the same idea and I joined a stream of consciously casual strollers advancing purposefully up a threadbare path between ragged ill-used trees. The body had been found in a dusty glade where cartons and little scraps of paper grew instead of anemones. The spot needed no signpost. The police had got their screens up and I could see Tizer's hunched shoulders appearing above one of them.

The sightseers stood around at a police-prescribed distance and here again nothing was new. In the last few months reams had been written about the avid, open-mouthed defectives who had come to stare at the last couch of each of the victims, and here as far as I could see they all were once more. I felt certain I had seen the dreary man with the fascinated blue eyes and the watch-chain full of darts medals at every road accident, case of illness in the street, or mere surface reconstruction at which I had had the misfortune to be present. The adolescent girl with the weeping baby brother was familiar, too, and as for the plump middle-aged man with the broad smile he could not possibly have known he was wearing, I was sure I had seen him, or someone darned like him, grinning at the scene of every catastrophe in my experience. They were all standing about, looking and hoping, God knew what for. One group, which contained at least one collapsible perambulator, appeared to be thinking of picnicking.

I had a word with Tizer, who was not pleased to see me and had nothing to tell me. He is never sanguine and by this time his gloom was painful. I came away feeling nearly as sorry for him as I was for myself.

The Press was there in force and I walked down the hill with Peterson. We came on Chippy at the turning where the path divides. He was busy, as usual, and appeared to be taking a photograph of a holiday trio, two plump blondes in tight slacks and brassieres, with a flushed lout wriggling between them. There could be only one explanation of the performance and I was gratified if surprised to see he had the grace not to notice me.

"Grafters and buskers on fairgrounds call it 'mug-faking', I believe," observed Peterson as we turned into the White Lion. "What does he charge them? Half a dollar? It's an interesting comment on the price of whisky." He has an acid little voice.

For the rest of the week the case dragged on. We had our hopes raised by several false alarms. Tizer thought he had a lead and went scampering to St. Leonards with a trail of us behind him, but the chase led nowhere. Everybody did what they could. The *Cormorant* tried to start a stink against the police. The tame psychiatrists wrote more articles for the Sundays. Somebody asked a question in the House and the Yard sent a second Chief Inspector down. Middle-aged women everywhere began to give themselves airs.

From our point of view it was all very dull. The weather turned cold and three of the best hotels ran out of scotch. I saw Chippy now and again but he did not worry me. He was picking up plenty of work, I gathered, and, if his glazed eyes in the evenings were any guide, appeared to find it profitable.

He had a new friend, I was interested to see. So far I have not mentioned Chippy's friends. A natural distaste and embarrassment has prevented me from enlarging on them. It is one of his major disadvantages that he always seems to discover a local drinking companion who matches, if not exceeds, the man himself in pure unpresentableness. On this occasion he had chummed up with the fat man I had seen grinning at the scene of the crime, or if it was not he it was someone very like him. God knows what he was by profession, a bookmaker's tout perhaps, or a traveller in something unmentionable. I had nothing against him save that if I had seen but the soles of his feet through a grating, or the top of his hat from a bus, I should have known unerringly that he was a fellow for whom I should never have the slightest possible use. He had crumbs in the creases of his blue serge waistcoat, he dribbled his beer when he drank, his voice was hoarse and coarse and negligible, and the broad vacant grin never left his face.

Chippy went about with him most of the time and I was grateful for my release. I was agitating the office for my recall by the Saturday and should have left, I think, by the Sunday had not I made a sudden startling discovery. Chippy was trying to avoid not only me but every other newspaperman in the town. At first I could not bring myself to believe it, but having ceased to hide from him I suddenly found I saw very little of him, and then that Sunday morning we met face to face on the steps of the Grand. In the normal way it would have been I who had become wooden-faced and evasive and he who pursued me to insist on the morning snifter, but today he slunk from me and for the first time in my life I thought I saw him discomposed. I even stood looking after him as he shuffled off, his harness clumping round his shanks, but it was not until I was drinking with Peterson and one or two others some fifteen minutes later that the truth occurred to me. Someone had asked if Chippy had gone since he had not seen him lately, while somebody else observed that he too had noticed a singular freshness in the atmosphere.

Peterson defended him at once with all that charity of his which is far more lethal than straight attack, and I stood quite still looking at the big calendar over the bar.

Of course. I could not think why I had not realized it before. For Chippy, time was growing pretty short.

I was so anxious that Peterson, whom I love like a brother and who knows me nearly as well, should not cotton on to my idea that I wasted several valuable minutes in what I hope was misleading casualness before I drifted off, ostensibly to phone my wife. From that moment I hunted Chippy as he had never hunted me and it was not too easy an undertaking, since, as I have said, the place was stiff with pressmen and I was more than anxious not to raise any general hue and cry. Anything he had I was willing to share, but, until my wire was safely sent, not with the world.

I hunted carefully and systematically like a peasant woman going through a shawl for a flea, and for the best part of the day I was fighting a conviction that he had vanished into air. But just before six, when I was growing desperate, I suddenly saw him, still festooned with cameras, stepping ashore from a so-called pleasure steamer which had been chugging a party round the bay for the best part of three hours. The other people looked to me like the same crowd who had tramped up to the wood behind the Kursaal the day after the body was found. The adolescent girl with the baby brother was certainly there, and so was Chippy's buddy of the moment, the man with the smile.

From that moment I do not think I lost sight of him or them either. Shadowing them was comparatively simple. The whole party moved, it seemed by instinct, to the nearest hostelry and from there in due course they moved to the next. So it went on throughout the whole evening, when the lights first came out yellow in the autumn haze and, too, when they shone white against the quickening dark.

I do not know when he first became aware that I was behind him. I think it was on the second trip up the Marine Boulevard, where the bars are so thick that no serious drinking time is lost in transit. I met his

20

eyes once and he hesitated but did not nod. He had a dreadful group round him. The man with the smile was still there and so was a little seedy man with a cap and a watch-chain, and two plump blondes in slacks. I recognized them all and none of them, if I make myself clear. After that I could feel him trying to shake me off, but he was hampered and I was, I think, a fraction more sober than he. There must have been a bar on the boat.

After a while I realized that he was going somewhere in particular, heading somewhere definitely if obliquely, like a wasp to its nest. His red eyes wandered to the clock more and more often, I noticed, and his moves from pub to pub seemed quicker and more frequent.

Then I lost him. The party must have split. At any rate I found myself following one of the blondes and a sailor who I felt was new to me, unless of course it was not the same blonde but another just like her. I was in the older and dirtier part of the town and closing time, I felt with dismay, could not possibly be far off. For some time I searched in a positive panic, diving into every lighted doorway and pushing every swinging door. As far as I remember I neglected even to drink and it may be it was that which saved me.

At any rate I came finally to a big ugly old-fashioned drinking house on a corner. It was as large and drab and inviting as a barn and in the four-ale bar, into which I first put my head, there was no one at all but a little blue-eyed seedy man wearing a flat cap and a watch-chain weighted with medals. He was sitting on a bench close to the counter, drinking a pint with the quiet absorption of one who has been doing just that for the last two hours. I glanced at him sharply but there was no way of telling if he had been the same man who had been with Chippy's party. It was not that I am unobservant, but such men exist not in hundreds but in thousands in every town on or off the coast, and there was nothing distinctive about this one. Also, he was alone.

I turned away and would have passed on down the street, when I noticed that there was a second frontage to the building. I put my head in the first door I came to and saw Chippy's back. He was leaning on the bar, which was small and temporarily unattended, the landlord having moved further along it to the adjoining room. At first I thought he was alone, but on coming into the room I saw his smiling friend reclining on a narrow bench which ran along the inner wall. He was still beaming but the vacancy of his broad face was intensified, if one can say such a thing, and I knew he must have ceased to hear anything Chippy was telling him long ago. Chippy was talking. He always talks when he's drunk, not wanderingly nor thickly but with the low intensity some people find unnerving. He was in full flight now. Soft incisive words illustrated by the sharp gestures of one hand—the other, after all, was

21

supporting him—flowed from him in a steady forceful stream. I had to go very close up behind him to hear what he was saying.

"Trapped," he whispered to his friend's oblivion. "Trapped for life by a woman with a sniff and a soul so mean—so *mean*—so *MEAN*..." He turned and looked at me. "Hullo," he said.

I remember I had some idea that in that condition of his I could fool him that I'd either been there all the time or was not there at all, I forget which. Anyway I certainly stood looking at him in surprise without speaking. The thing that surprised me was that he had his old Rolleiflex, the thing he used for close inside work, hanging round his neck with the sight-screens, or whatever they call them, up ready for action.

He returned my stare with friendliness at first, but I saw caution creep across his eyes, tomcat fashion, and presently he made an effort.

"Goodbye," he said.

The barman saved me answering him by bustling back, wiping the wood and thrusting a can at me all in one motion. He rattled the money I gave him in the till and waddled off again after nodding to Chippy in a secret important way I entirely misunderstood.

"She was mean, was she?" I ventured, mumbling into my beer.

"As hell," Chippy agreed and his red eyes wandered up to look over my shoulder. "Come in, son," he said softly.

A pallid youth was hesitating in the doorway and he came forward at once, a long cardboard roll held out before him like a weapon. He was white with excitement, I thought, and I did not suppose it was at the sight of us.

"Dad said you was to have these and he'd see you tomorrow."

I could see by the way Chippy took the parcel that it was important, but he was so casual, or so drunk, that he almost dropped it, and did scatter some of the coins that he gave the boy. He carried them in handfuls in his jacket pocket, apparently.

As soon as the kid had gone, Chippy tore the paper off the roll and I could see it consisted of four or five huge blown-up prints, but he did not open them out, contenting himself with little squints at each corner, and I could see nothing.

The smiling man on the bench moved but did not rise. His eyes were tightly shut but he continued to grin. Chippy looked at him for some time before he suddenly turned to me.

"He's canned," he said. "Canned as a toot. I've been carting him round the whole week to have someone safe to talk to, and now look at him. Never mind. Listen to me. Got imagination?"

"Yes," I assured him flatly.

"You'll need it," he said. "Listen. He was young, a simple ordinary friendly kid like you or I were, and he came to the seaside on his holiday.

22

Only one week's holiday in the year." He paused for the horror to sink in. "One week, and she caught him. God! Think of it!"

I looked at the smiling man on the bench and I must have been a little whistled myself, for I saw no incongruity in the tale.

"He was *ordinary*!" shouted Chippy suddenly. "So ordinary that he might be you or me."

I did not care for that and I spoke sharply.

"His wife caught him, you say?"

"No." He lowered his voice to the intense stage again. "Her mother. The landlady. She worked it. Twisted him." He made a peculiar bending movement with his two hands. "You know, said things. Made suggestions. Forced it. He had to marry the girl. Then he had hell. Couldn't afford it. Got nagged night and day, day and night. Got him down."

He leant towards me and I was aware of every one of his squat uneven teeth.

"He grew old," he said. "He lost his job. Got another, buying old gold. Used to go round buying old gold for a little firm in the Ditch who kept him skint. It went on for years and years. Years and years. And more years. A long time. Then it happened. He began to see her."

"Who?" I demanded. "His wife?"

"No, no." Chippy was irritated. "She'd left him, taken all he had, sold the furniture and scarpered with another poor mug. That was years ago. No, he began to see the mother."

"Good God," I said, "and she was red-haired, I suppose?"

"And mean," he told me solemnly. "Mean as hell."

I was trembling so much I had to put my beer down.

"Look here, Chippy," I began, "why wasn't he spotted? Why didn't *she* spot him?"

He took me by the coat collar.

"Imagination," he whispered at me. "Use it. Think. He married the girl in nineteen-twelve, but this year he began to see the mother as she used to be."

Our heads were very close together over the bar and his soft urgent voice poured the story at me.

"He's been travelling round the coast for years buying old gold. Everybody knows him and nobody notices him. Millions of women recognize him when he taps at their doors and very often they sell him little things. But he was ill last winter, had pleurisy, had to go into hospital. Since he's been out he's been different. The past has come back to him. He's been remembering the tragedy of his life." He wiped his mouth and started again.

"In May he saw her. At first she looked like a woman he knew called Mrs. Wild, but as they were talking her face changed and he recognized

23

her. He knew just what to do. He told her he'd had a bargain he didn't feel like passing on to his firm. Said he'd got a ring cheap and if she'd meet him he'd show it to her and maybe sell it to her for the same money he paid for it. He knew it was a tale she would fall for because he knew just how mean she was. She went because she'd known him for years coming round to the door, and she didn't tell anybody because she thought she was doing something shady, see?"

"And when he got her alone he killed her?" I whispered.

"Yes." Chippy's voice held an echoed satisfaction. "Paid her out at last. He went off happy as an old king and felt freed and content and satisfied until June, when he went to Turnhill Bay and knocked all unsuspecting at a door in a back street and—*saw her again*."

I wiped my forehead and stood back from him.

"And at Southwharf, and at Prinny's Plage?" I began huskily.

"That's right. And now St. Piers," said Chippy. "Whenever there's a new moon."

It was at this precise moment that the smiling drunk on the bench opened his eyes and sat straight up abruptly, as drunks do, and then with a spurt set out at a shambling trot for the door. He hit the opening with a couple of inches to spare and was sucked up by the night. I yelled at Chippy and started after him, pausing on the threshold to glance back.

Chippy leant there against the bar, looking at me with fishlike unintelligence. I could see he was hopeless and the job was mine. I plunged out and saw the smiling man about fifty yards down the street. He was conspicuous because he kept to the middle of the road and was advancing at a perfectly extraordinary trot which had a skip or a gallop in it at every two or three yards, as if he were jet-propelled. I was not in sprinting form myself, but I should certainly have caught him and broken my heart if I had not tripped over a grating thirty feet from the pub door.

It was as I was getting up that I looked over my shoulder and saw Chief Inspector Tizer and the local Super, together with a couple of satellites, slip quietly across the road. It was just enough to make me stone-cold sober and I slid back in behind the police just before they closed the door.

Chippy was standing at the bar with Tizer on one side of him and the local man on the other. The five blown-up prints were spread out on the wood and everyone was so engrossed in them that I came quietly up behind and saw everything over Chippy's own head.

They were five three-quarter length portraits of the same man. Each one had been taken out of doors in a gaping crowd, and on each print a mid-section was heavily circled with process-white. In each case, within the circle was a watch-chain hung with darts medals and other small decorations, which might easily have been overlooked had not attention thus been called to them. In the first portrait the watch-chain carried two medals and a cheap silver earring. In the second a gold clasp from a chain bracelet had been added. In the third a small locket. In the fourth a silver button. And in the fifth there hung beside the rest an ugly little tassel from an old-fashioned brooch.

Tizer, who is one of those men who look as if they have been designed by someone who was used to doing bison, put a fist as big as a ham on Chippy's little shoulder.

"You're trying to tell me you only noticed this yesterday and you had the astounding luck to find the earlier photographs in your file?" His tone was pretty ugly, I thought, but Chippy shrugged himself free. Like myself he was sober enough now.

"I *am* lucky," he said coldly, "and observant." He glanced at the bartender who was fidgeting in the archway where the counter ran through into the other room. "Ready, George?"

"Yes, he's still there, Mr. Wager. I've slipped round and shut the doors on him. He's sitting very quiet, just drinking his beer."

He lifted the flap and the police moved forward in a body. Chippy turned to me.

"Poor little blob," he said. "He's quite happy now, you see, till next new moon."

"When you will be otherwise engaged, I seem to remember," I said acidly.

He glanced at me with a sudden smile and adjusted his camera.

"That's right," he said. "There's sympathy in this business but no sentiment. Wait just a minute while I get the arrest."

STACY AUMONIER

1887–1928

Born the son of a sculptor and brought up to be a painter,
he was destined for a future in the arts, but it was his wit as
a raconteur and not his skill with a brush that enabled him to
fulfil himself during a sadly short life. Today he is remembered
for his novels and gently humorous short stories.

Miss Bracegirdle does her Duty

"THIS IS THE room, madame."

"Ah, thank you . . . thank you."

"Does it appear satisfactory to madame?"

"Oh, yes, thank you . . . quite."

"Does madame require anything further?"

"Er—if not too late, may I have a hot bath?"

"*Parfaitement*, madame. The bathroom is at the end of the passage on the left. I will go and prepare it for madame."

"There is one thing more . . . I have had a very long journey. I am very tired. Will you please see that I am not disturbed in the morning until I ring."

"Certainly, madame."

Millicent Bracegirdle was speaking the truth—she *was* tired. In the sleepy cathedral town of Easingstoke, from which she came, it was customary for every one to speak the truth. It was customary, moreover, for every one to lead simple, self-denying lives—to give up their time to good works and elevating thoughts. One had only to glance at little Miss Bracegirdle to see that in her were epitomized all the virtues and ideals of Easingstoke. Indeed, it was the pursuit of duty which had brought her to the Hôtel de l'Ouest at Bordeaux on this summer's night. She had travelled from Easingstoke to London, then without a break to Dover, crossed that horrid stretch of sea to Calais, entrained for Paris,

26

where she of necessity had to spend four hours—a terrifying experience —and then had come on to Bordeaux, arriving at midnight. The reason of this journey being that someone had to come to Bordeaux to meet her young sister-in-law, who was arriving the next day from South America. The sister-in-law was married to a missionary in Paraguay, but the climate not agreeing with her, she was returning to England. Her dear brother, the dean, would have come himself, but the claims on his time were so extensive, the parishioners would miss him so . . . it was clearly Millicent's duty to go.

She had never been out of England before, and she had a horror of travel, and an ingrained distrust of foreigners. She spoke a little French —sufficient for the purposes of travel and for obtaining any modest necessities, but not sufficient for carrying on any kind of conversation. She did not deplore this latter fact, for she was of opinion that French people were not the kind of people that one would naturally want to have conversation with; broadly speaking, they were not quite 'nice', in spite of their ingratiating manners.

The dear dean had given her endless advice, warning her earnestly not to enter into conversation with strangers, to obtain all information from the police, railway officials—in fact, any one in an official uniform. He deeply regretted to say that he was afraid that France was not a country for a woman to travel about in *alone* . . . There were loose, bad people about, always on the look-out . . . He really thought perhaps he ought not to let her go. It was only by the utmost persuasion, in which she rather exaggerated her knowledge of the French language and character, her courage, and indifference to discomfort, that she managed to carry the day.

She unpacked her valise, placed her things about the room, tried to thrust back the little stabs of homesickness as she visualized her darling room at the deanery. How strange and hard and unfriendly seemed these foreign hotel bedrooms—heavy and depressing, no chintz and lavender and photographs of . . . all the dear family, the dean, the nephews and nieces, the interior of the cathedral during harvest festival, no samplers and needlework or coloured reproductions of the paintings by Marcus Stone. Oh dear, how foolish she was! What did she expect?

She disrobed and donned a dressing-gown; then, armed with a sponge-bag and towel, she crept timidly down the passage to the bathroom, after closing her bedroom door and turning out the light. The gay bathroom cheered her. She wallowed luxuriously in the hot water, regarding her slim legs with quiet satisfaction. And for the first time since leaving home there came to her a pleasant moment—a sense of enjoyment in her adventure. After all, it *was* rather an adventure, and her life had been peculiarly devoid of it. What queer lives some people

27

must live, travelling about, having experiences! How old was she? Not really old—not by any means. Forty-two? Forty-three? She had shut herself up so. She hardly ever regarded the potentialities of age. As the world went, she was a well-preserved woman for her age. A life of self-abnegation, simple living, healthy walking and fresh air, had kept her younger than these hurrying, pampered city people.

Love? yes, once when she was a young girl . . . he was a schoolmaster, a most estimable kind gentleman. They were never engaged—not actually, but it was a kind of understood thing. For three years it went on, this pleasant understanding and friendship. He was so gentle, so distinguished and considerate. She would have been happy to have continued in this strain for ever. But there was something lacking. Stephen had curious restless lapses. From the physical aspect of marriage she shrunk—yes, even with Stephen, who was gentleness and kindness itself. And then one day . . . one day he went away—vanished, and never returned. They told her he had married one of the country girls—a girl who used to work in Mrs. Forbes's dairy—not a very nice girl, she feared, one of these fast, pretty, foolish women. Heigho! well, she had lived that down, destructive as the blow appeared at the time. One lives everything down in time. There is always work, living for others, faith, duty . . . At the same time she could sympathize with people who found satisfaction in unusual experiences.

There would be lots to tell the dear dean when she wrote to him on the morrow; nearly losing her spectacles on the restaurant car; the amusing remarks of an American child on the train to Paris; the curious food everywhere, nothing simple and plain; the two English ladies at the hotel in Paris who told her about the death of their uncle—the poor man being taken ill on Friday and dying on Sunday afternoon, just before tea-time; the kindness of the hotel proprietor who had sat up for her; the prettiness of the chambermaid. Oh, yes, every one was really very kind. The French people, after all, were very nice. She had seen nothing—nothing but was quite nice and decorous. There would be lots to tell the dean to-morrow.

Her body glowed with the friction of the towel. She again donned her night attire and her thick, woollen dressing-gown. She tidied up the bathroom carefully in exactly the same way she was accustomed to do at home, then once more gripping her sponge-bag and towel, and turning out the light, she crept down the passage to her room. Entering the room she switched on the light and shut the door quickly. Then one of those ridiculous things happened—just the kind of thing you would expect to happen in a foreign hotel. The handle of the door came off in her hand.

She ejaculated a quiet "Bother!" and sought to replace it with one hand, the other being occupied with the towel and sponge-bag. In doing this she behaved foolishly, for thrusting the knob carelessly against the steel pin—without properly securing it—she only succeeded in pushing the pin farther into the door and the knob was not adjusted. She uttered another little "Bother!" and put her sponge-bag and towel down on the floor. She then tried to recover the pin with her left hand, but it had gone in too far.

"How very foolish!" she thought, "I shall have to ring for the chambermaid—and perhaps the poor girl has gone to bed."

She turned and faced the room, and suddenly the awful horror was upon her. *There was a man asleep in her bed!*

The sight of that swarthy face on the pillow, with its black tousled hair and heavy moustache, produced in her the most terrible moment of her life. Her heart nearly stopped. For some seconds she could neither think nor scream, and her first thought was: "I mustn't scream!"

She stood there like one paralysed, staring at the man's head and the great curved hunch of his body under the clothes. When she began to think she thought very quickly, and all her thoughts worked together. The first vivid realization was that it wasn't the man's fault; it was *her* fault. *She was in the wrong room.* It was the man's room. The rooms were identical, but there were all his things about, his clothes thrown carelessly over chairs, his collar and tie on the wardrobe, his great heavy boots and the strange yellow trunk. She must get out somehow, anyhow.

She clutched once more at the door, feverishly driving her finger-nails into the hole where the elusive pin had vanished. She tried to force her fingers in the crack and open the door that way, but it was of no avail. She was to all intents and purposes locked in—locked in a bedroom in a strange hotel alone with a man . . . a foreigner . . . *a Frenchman!* She must think. She must think . . . She switched off the light. If the light was off he might not wake up. It might give her time to think how to act. It was surprising that he had not awakened. If he *did* wake up, what would he do? How could she explain herself? He wouldn't believe her. No one would believe her. In an English hotel it would be difficult enough, but here where she wasn't known, where they were all foreigners and consequently antagonistic . . . merciful heavens!

She *must* get out. Should she wake the man? No, she couldn't do that. He might murder her. He might . . . Oh, it was too awful to contemplate! Should she scream? Ring for the chambermaid? But no, it would be the same thing. People would come rushing. They would find her there in the strange man's bedroom after midnight—she, Millicent Bracegirdle, sister of the Dean of Easingstoke! Easingstoke!

Visions of Easingstoke flashed through her alarmed mind. Visions of the news arriving, women whispering around tea-tables: "Have you heard, my dear? . . . Really no one would have imagined! Her poor brother! He will of course have to resign, you know, my dear. Have a little more cream, my love."

Would they put her in prison? She might be in the room for the purpose of stealing or . . . She might be in the room for the purpose of breaking every one of the ten commandments. There was no explaining it away. She was a ruined woman, suddenly and irretrievably, unless she could open the door. The chimney? Should she climb up the chimney? But where would that lead to? And then she visualized the man pulling her down by her legs when she was already smothered in soot. Any moment he might wake up . . .

She thought she heard the chambermaid going along the passage. If she had wanted to scream, she ought to have screamed before. The maid would know she had left the bathroom some minutes ago. Was she going to her room? Suddenly she remembered that she had told the chambermaid that she was not to be disturbed until she rang the next morning. That was something. Nobody would be going to her room to find out that she was not there.

An abrupt and desperate plan formed in her mind. It was already getting on for one o'clock. The man was probably a quite harmless commercial traveller or business man. He would probably get up about seven or eight o'clock, dress quickly, and go out. She would hide under his bed until he went. Only a matter of a few hours. Men don't look under their beds, although she made a religious practice of doing so herself. When he went he would be sure to open the door all right. The handle would be lying on the floor as though it had dropped off in the night. He would probably ring for the chambermaid or open it with a penknife. Men were so clever at those things. When he had gone she would creep out and steal back to her room, and then there would be no necessity to give any explanation to any one. But heavens! What an experience! Once under the white frill of that bed she would be safe till the morning. In daylight nothing seemed so terrifying.

With feline precaution she went down on her hands and knees and crept toward the bed. What a lucky thing there was that broad white frill! She lifted it at the foot of the bed and crept under. There was just sufficient depth to take her slim body. The floor was fortunately carpeted all over, but it seemed very close and dusty. Suppose she coughed or sneezed! Anything might happen. Of course . . . it would be much more difficult to explain her presence under the bed than to explain her presence just inside the door. She held her breath in suspense. No sound came from above, but under this frill it was difficult to hear anything. It was almost more nerve-racking than hearing everything . . . listening for signs and portents. This temporary escape in any case would give her time to regard the predicament detachedly.

Up to the present she had not been able to visualize the full significance of her action. She had in truth lost her head. She had been like a wild animal, consumed with the sole idea of escape . . . a mouse or a cat would do this kind of thing—take cover and lie low. If only it hadn't all happened *abroad!* She tried to frame sentences of explanation in French, but French escaped her. And then—they talked so rapidly, these people. They didn't listen. The situation was intolerable. Would she be able to endure a night of it?

At present she was not altogether uncomfortable, only stuffy and . . . very, very frightened. But she had to face six or seven or eight hours of it—perhaps even then discovery in the end! The minutes flashed by as she turned the matter over and over in her head. There was no solution. She began to wish she had screamed or awakened the man. She saw now that that would have been the wisest and most politic thing to do; but she had allowed ten minutes or a quarter of an hour to elapse from the moment when the chambermaid would know that she had left the bathroom. They would want an explanation of what she had been doing in the man's bedroom all that time. Why hadn't she screamed before?

She lifted the frill an inch or two and listened. She thought she heard the man breathing but she couldn't be sure. In any case it gave her more air. She became a little bolder, and thrust her face partly through the frill so that she could breathe freely. She tried to steady her nerves by concentrating on the fact that—well, there it was. She had done it. She must make the best of it. Perhaps it would be all right after all.

"Of course I shan't sleep," she kept on thinking, "I shan't be able to. In any case it will be safer not to sleep. I must be on the watch."

She set her teeth and waited grimly. Now that she had made up her mind to see the thing through in this manner she felt a little calmer. She almost smiled as she reflected that there would certainly be something to tell the dear dean when she wrote to him to-morrow. How would he take it? Of course he would believe it—he had never doubted a single word that she had uttered in her life—but the story would sound so . . . preposterous. In Easingstoke it would be almost impossible to envisage such an experience. She, Millicent Bracegirdle, spending a night under a strange man's bed in a foreign hotel! What would those women think? Fanny Shields and that garrulous old Mrs. Rushbridger? Perhaps . . . yes, perhaps it would be advisable to tell the dear dean to let the story go no further. One could hardly expect Mrs. Rushbridger to . . . not make implications . . . exaggerate.

Oh, dear! What were they all doing now? They would be all asleep, every one in Easingstoke. Her dear brother always retired at ten-fifteen. He would be sleeping calmly and placidly, the sleep of the just . . . breathing the clear sweet air of Sussex, not this—oh, it *was* stuffy! She felt a great desire to cough. She mustn't do that. Yes, at nine-thirty all the servants summoned to the library—a short service—never more than fifteen minutes, her brother didn't believe in a great deal of ritual— then at ten o'clock cocoa for every one. At ten-fifteen bed for every one. The dear sweet bedroom with the narrow white bed, by the side of which she had knelt every night as long as she could remember—even in her dear mother's day—and said her prayers.

Prayers! Yes, that was a curious thing. This was the first night in her life's experience that she had not said her prayers on retiring. The situation was certainly very peculiar . . . exceptional, one might call it. God would understand and forgive such a lapse. And yet after all, why . . . what was to prevent her saying her prayers? Of course she couldn't kneel in the proper devotional attitude, that would be a physical impossibility; nevertheless, perhaps her prayers might be just as efficacious . . . if they came from the heart. So little Miss Bracegirdle curved her body and placed her hands in a devout attitude in front of her face and quite inaudibly murmured her prayers under the strange man's bed.

"Our Father which art in heaven, Hallowed be Thy name. Thy kingdom come. Thy will be done in earth as it is in heaven; Give us this day our daily bread. And forgive us our trespasses . . ."

Trespasses! Yes, surely she was trespassing on this occasion, but God would understand. She had not wanted to trespass. She was an unwitting sinner. Without uttering a sound she went through her usual prayers in her heart. At the end she added fervently:

"Please God protect me from the dangers and perils of this night."

Then she lay silent and inert, strangely soothed by the effort of praying. "After all," she thought, "it isn't the attitude which matters— it is that which occurs deep down in us."

For the first time she began to meditate—almost to question—church forms and dogma. If an attitude was not indispensable, why a building, a ritual, a church at all? Of course her dear brother couldn't be wrong, the church was so old, so very old, its root deep buried in the story of human life, it was only that . . . well, outward forms *could* be misleading. Her own present position for instance. In the eyes of the world she had, by one silly careless little action, convicted herself of being the breaker of every single one of the ten commandments.

She tried to think of one of which she could not be accused. But no— even to dishonouring her father and mother, bearing false witness, stealing, coveting her neighbour's . . . husband! That was the worst thing of all. Poor man! He might be a very pleasant honourable married gentleman with children and she—she was in a position to compromise him! Why hadn't she screamed? Too late! Too late!

It began to get very uncomfortable, stuffy, but at the same time draughty, and the floor was getting harder every minute. She changed her position stealthily and controlled her desire to cough. Her heart was beating rapidly. Over and over again recurred the vivid impression of every little incident and argument that had occurred to her from the moment she left the bathroom. This must, of course, be the room next to her own. So confusing, with perhaps twenty bedrooms all exactly alike on one side of a passage—how was one to remember whether one's number was 115 or 116?

Her mind began to wander idly off into her schooldays. She was always very bad at figures. She disliked Euclid and all those subjects about angles and equations—so unimportant, not leading anywhere. History she liked, and botany, and reading about strange foreign lands, although she had always been too timid to visit them. And the lives of great people, *most* fascinating—Oliver Cromwell, Lord Beaconsfield, Lincoln, Grace Darling—*there* was a heroine for you—General Booth, a great, good man, even if a little vulgar. She remembered dear old Miss Trimming talking about him one afternoon at the vicar of St. Bride's garden party. She was *so* amusing. She . . . *Good heavens!*

Almost unwittingly, Millicent Bracegirdle had emitted a violent sneeze!

It was finished! For the second time that night she was conscious of her heart nearly stopping. For the second time that night she was so paralysed with fear that her mentality went to pieces. Now she would hear the man get out of bed. He would walk across to the door, switch on the light, and then lift up the frill. She could almost see that fierce moustached face glaring at her and growling something in French. Then he would thrust out an arm and drag her out. And then? O God in heaven! What then? . . .

"I shall scream before he does it. Perhaps I had better scream now. If he drags me out he will clap his hand over my mouth. Perhaps chloroform . . ."

But somehow she could not scream. She was too frightened even for that. She lifted the frill and listened. Was he moving stealthily across the carpet? She thought—no, she couldn't be sure. Anything might be happening. He might strike her from above—with one of those heavy boots perhaps. Nothing seemed to be happening, but the suspense was intolerable. She realized now that she hadn't the power to endure a night of it. Anything would be better than this—disgrace, imprisonment, even death. She would crawl out, wake the man, and try and explain as best she could.

She would switch on the light, cough, and say: "*Monsieur!*"

Then he would start up and stare at her.

Then she would say—what should she say?

"*Pardon, monsieur, mais je——*" What on earth was the French for 'I have made a mistake'.

"*J'ai tort. C'est, la chambre*—er—incorrect. *Voulez-vous*—er——"

What was the French for 'door-knob', 'let me go'?

It didn't matter. She would turn on the light, cough and trust to luck. If he got out of bed, and came toward her, she would scream the hotel down . . .

The resolution formed, she crawled deliberately out at the foot of the bed. She scrambled hastily toward the door—a perilous journey. In a few seconds the room was flooded with light. She turned toward the bed, coughed, and cried out boldly:

"*Monsieur!*"

Then, for the third time that night, little Miss Bracegirdle's heart all but stopped. In this case the climax of the horror took longer to develop, but when it was reached, it clouded the other two experiences into insignificance.

The man on the bed was dead!

She had never beheld death before, but one does not mistake death. She stared at him bewildered, and repeated almost in a whisper:

"*Monsieur! . . . Monsieur!*"

Then she tiptoed toward the bed. The hair and moustache looked extraordinarily black in that grey, wax-like setting. The mouth was slightly open, and the face, which in life might have been vicious and sensual, looked incredibly peaceful and far away. It was as though she were regarding the features of a man across some vast passage of time, a being who had always been completely remote from mundane pre-occupations.

When the full truth came home to her, little Miss Bracegirdle buried her face in her hands and murmured:

"Poor fellow . . . poor fellow!"

For the moment her own position seemed an affair of small consequence. She was in the presence of something greater and more all-pervading. Almost instinctively she knelt by the bed and prayed.

For a few moments she seemed to be possessed by an extraordinary calmness and detachment. The burden of her hotel predicament was a gossamer trouble—a silly, trivial, almost comic episode, something that could be explained away.

But this man—he had lived his life, whatever it was like, and now he was in the presence of his Maker. What kind of man had he been?

Her meditations were broken by an abrupt sound. It was that of a pair of heavy boots being thrown down by the door outside. She started, thinking at first it was someone knocking or trying to get in. She heard the 'boots', however, stumping away down the corridor, and the realization stabbed her with the truth of her own position. She mustn't stop there. The necessity to get out was even more urgent.

To be found in a strange man's bedroom in the night is bad enough, but to be found in a dead man's bedroom was even worse. They could accuse her of murder, perhaps. Yes, that would be it—how could she possibly explain to these foreigners? Good God! They would hang her. No, guillotine her, that's what they do in France. They would chop her head off with a great steel knife. Merciful heavens! She envisaged herself standing blindfold, by a priest and an executioner in a red cap, like that man in the Dickens story—what was his name? . . . Sydney Carton, that was it, and before he went on the scaffold he said:

"It is a far, far better thing that I do than I have ever done."

But no, she couldn't say that. It would be a far, far worse thing that she did. What about the dear dean? Her sister-in-law arriving alone from Paraguay to-morrow? All her dear people and friends in Easingstoke? Her darling Tony, the large grey tabby cat? It was her duty not to have her head chopped off if it could possibly be avoided. She could do no good in the room. She could not recall the dead to life. Her only mission was to escape. Any minute people might arrive. The chambermaid, the boots, the manager, the gendarmes . . . Visions of gendarmes arriving armed with swords and note-books vitalized her almost exhausted energies. She was a desperate woman. Fortunately now she had not to worry about the light. She sprang once more at the door and tried to force it open with her fingers. The result hurt her and gave her pause. If she was to escape she must *think*, and think intensely. She mustn't do anything rash and silly, she must just think and plan calmly.

She examined the lock carefully. There was no keyhole, but there was a slip-bolt, so that the hotel guest could lock the door on the inside, but it couldn't be locked on the outside. Oh, why didn't this poor dear dead man lock his door last night? Then this trouble could not have happened. She could see the end of the steel pin. It was about half an inch down the hole. If any one was passing they must surely notice the handle sticking out too far the other side! She drew a hairpin out of her hair and tried to coax the pin back, but she only succeeded in pushing it a little farther in. She felt the colour leaving her face, and a strange feeling of faintness come over her.

She was fighting for her life, she mustn't give way. She darted round the room like an animal in a trap, her mind alert for the slightest crevice of escape. The window had no balcony and there was a drop of five stories to the street below. Dawn was breaking. Soon the activities of the hotel and the city would begin. The thing must be accomplished before then.

She went back once more and stared at the lock. She stared at the dead man's property, his razors, and brushes, and writing materials, pens and pencils and rubber and sealing-wax . . . Sealing-wax!

Necessity is truly the mother of invention. It is in any case quite certain that Millicent Bracegirdle, who had never invented a thing in her life, would never have evolved the ingenious little device she did, had she not believed that her position was utterly desperate. For in the end this is what she did. She got together a box of matches, a candle, a bar of sealing-wax, and a hairpin. She made a little pool of hot sealing-wax, into which she dipped the end of the hairpin. Collecting a small blob on the end of it she thrust it into the hole, and let it adhere to the end of the steel pin. At the seventh attempt she got the thing to move. It took her just an hour and ten minutes to get that steel pin back into the room, and when at length it came far enough through for her to grip it with her finger-nails, she burst into tears through the sheer physical tension of the strain. Very, very carefully she pulled it through, and holding it firmly with her left hand she fixed the knob with her right, then slowly turned it. The door opened!

The temptation to dash out into the corridor and scream with relief was almost irresistible, but she forbore. She listened; she peeped out. No one was about. With beating heart, she went out, closing the door inaudibly. She crept like a little mouse to the room next door, stole in and flung herself on her bed. Immediately she did so it flashed through her mind that *she had left her sponge-bag and towel in the dead man's room!*

In looking back upon her experience she always considered that that second expedition was the worst of all. She might have left the sponge-bag and towel there, only that the towel—she never used hotel towels—had neatly inscribed in the corner 'M.B'.

With furtive caution she managed to retrace her steps. She re-entered the dead man's room, reclaimed her property, and returned to her own. When this mission was accomplished she was indeed wellnigh spent. She lay on her bed and groaned feebly. At last she fell into a fevered sleep . . .

It was eleven o'clock when she awoke and no one had been to disturb her. The sun was shining, and the experiences of the night appeared a dubious nightmare. Surely she had dreamt it all?

With dread still burning in her heart she rang the bell. After a short interval of time the chambermaid appeared. The girl's eyes were bright with some uncontrollable excitement. No, she had not been dreaming. This girl had heard something.

"Will you bring me some tea, please?"

"Certainly, madame."

The maid drew back the curtains and fussed about the room. She was under a pledge of secrecy, but she could contain herself no longer.

Suddenly she approached the bed and whispered excitedly: "Oh, madame, I have promised not to tell . . . but a terrible thing has happened. A man, a dead man, has been found in room 117—a guest. Please not to say I tell you. But they have all been there, the gendarmes, the doctors, the inspectors. Oh, it is terrible . . . terrible."

The little lady in the bed said nothing. There was indeed nothing to say. But Marie Louise Lancret was too full of emotional excitement to spare her.

"But the terrible thing is—— Do you know who he was, madame? They say it is Boldhu, the man wanted for the murder of Jeanne Carreton in the barn at Vincennes. They say he strangled her, and then cut her up in pieces and hid her in two barrels which he threw into the river . . . Oh, but he was a bad man, madame, a terrible bad man . . . and he died in the room next door . . . suicide, they think; or was it an attack of the heart? . . . Remorse, some shock perhaps . . . Did you say a *café complet*, madame?"

"No, thank you, my dear . . . just a cup of tea . . . strong tea . . ."

"*Parfaitement*, madame."

The girl retired, and a little later a waiter entered the room with a tray of tea. She could never get over her surprise at this. It seemed so—well, indecorous for a man—although only a waiter—to enter a lady's bedroom. There was no doubt a great deal in what the dear dean said. They were certainly very peculiar, these French people—they had most peculiar notions. It was not the way they behaved at Easingstoke. She got farther under the sheets, but the waiter appeared quite indifferent to the situation. He put the tray down and retired.

When he had gone she sat up and sipped her tea, which gradually warmed her. She was glad the sun was shining. She would have to get up soon. They said that her sister-in-law's boat was due to berth at one o'clock. That would give her time to dress comfortably, write to her brother, and then go down to the docks. Poor man! So he had been a murderer, a man who cut up the bodies of his victims . . . and she had spent the night in his bedroom! They were certainly a most—how could she describe it?—people. Nevertheless she felt a little glad that at the end she had been there to kneel and pray by his bedside. Probably nobody else had ever done that. It was very difficult to judge people . . . Something at some time might have gone wrong. He might not have murdered the woman after all. People were often wrongly convicted. She herself . . . If the police had found her in that room at three o'clock that morning . . . It is that which takes place in the heart which counts. One learns and learns. Had she not learnt that one can pray just as effectively lying under a bed as kneeling beside it? . . . Poor man!

She washed and dressed herself and walked calmly down to the

37

writing-room. There was no evidence of excitement among the other hotel guests. Probably none of them knew about the tragedy except herself. She went to a writing-table, and after profound meditation wrote as follows:

My dear Brother,

I arrived late last night after a very pleasant journey. Every one was very kind and attentive, the manager was sitting up for me. I nearly lost my spectacle case in the restaurant car! But a kind old gentleman found it and returned it to me. There was a most amusing American child on the train. I will tell you about her on my return. The people are very pleasant, but the food is peculiar, nothing *plain and wholesome*. I am going down to meet Annie at one o'clock. How have you been keeping, my dear? I hope you have not had any further return of the bronchial attacks.

Please tell Lizzie that I remembered in the train on the way here that that large stone jar of marmalade that Mrs. Hunt made is behind those empty tins in the top shelf of the cupboard next to the coach-house. I wonder whether Mrs. Butler was able to come to evensong after all? This is a nice hotel, but I think Annie and I will stay at the 'Grand' to-night, as the bedrooms here are rather noisy. Well, my dear, nothing more till I return. Do take care of yourself. Your loving sister,

Millicent.

Yes, she couldn't tell Peter about it, neither in the letter nor when she went back to him. It was her duty not to tell him. It would only distress him; she felt convinced of it. In this curious foreign atmosphere the thing appeared possible, but in Easingstoke the mere recounting of the fantastic situations would be positively . . . indelicate. There was no escaping that broad general fact—she had spent a night in a strange man's bedroom. Whether he was a gentleman or a criminal, even whether he was dead or alive, did not seem to mitigate the jar upon her sensibilities, or rather it would not mitigate the jar upon the peculiarly sensitive relationship between her brother and herself. To say that she had been to the bathroom, the knob of the door-handle came off in her hand, she was too frightened to awaken the sleeper or scream, she got under the bed—well, it was all perfectly true. Peter would believe her, but—one simply could not conceive such a situation in Easingstoke deanery. It would create a curious little barrier between them, as though she had been dipped in some mysterious solution which alienated her. It was her duty not to tell.

She put on her hat, and went out to post the letter. She distrusted an hotel letter-box. One never knew who handled these letters. It was not a proper official way of treating them. She walked to the head post office in Bordeaux.

The sun was shining. It was very pleasant walking about amongst these queer excitable people, so foreign and different-looking—and the cafés already crowded with chattering men and women, and the flower stalls, and the strange odour of—what was it? Salt? Brine? Charcoal? . . . A military band was playing in the square . . . very gay and moving. It was all life, and movement, and bustle . . . thrilling rather.

"I spent a night in a strange man's bedroom."

Little Miss Bracegirdle hunched her shoulders, murmured to herself, and walked faster. She reached the post office and found the large metal plate with the slot for letters and 'R.F.' stamped above it. Something official at last! Her face was a little flushed—was it the warmth of the day or the contact of movement and life?—as she put her letter into the slot. After posting it she put her hand into the slot and flicked it round to see that there were no foreign contraptions to impede its safe delivery. No, the letter had dropped safely in. She sighed contentedly and walked off in the direction of the docks to meet her sister-in-law from Paraguay.

ENID BAGNOLD

1889–1981

Her childhood was spent in the West Indies; later she served as a nurse and ambulance driver in World War I. During the twenties she was a member of the so-called "Bohemian" and artistic circles of her day. She turned to writing after her marriage and is best known for her story of a race-horse, *National Velvet*, which was later to become a popular film. She was the author of many successful plays, novels and short stories.

The Amorous Ghost

IT WAS FIVE o'clock on a summer morning. The birds, who had woken at three, had long scattered about their duties. The white, plain house, blinkered and green-shuttered, stood four-square to its soaking lawns, and up and down on the grass, his snow-boots planting dark blots on the grey dew, walked the owner. His hair was uncombed, he wore his pyjamas and an overcoat, and at every turn at the end of the lawn he looked up at a certain window, that of his own and his wife's bedroom, where, as on every other window on the long front, the green shutters lay neatly back against the wall and the cream curtains hung down in heavy folds.

The owner of the house, strangely and uncomfortably on his lawns instead of in his bed, rubbed his chilly hands and continued his tramp. He had no watch on his wrist, but when the stable clock struck six he entered the house and passing through the still hall he went up to his bathroom. The water was luke-warm in the taps from the night before, and he took a bath. As he left the bathroom for his dressing-room he heard the stirring of the first housemaid in the living-room below, and at seven o'clock he rang for his butler to lay out his clothes.

As the same thing had happened the day before, the butler was half prepared for the bell; yawning and incensed but ready dressed.

"Good morning," said Mr. Templeton rather suddenly. It was a greeting which he never gave, but he wished to try the quality of his voice. Finding it steady he went on, and gave an order for a melon from the greenhouse.

For breakfast he had very little appetite, and when he had finished the melon he unfolded the newspaper. The door of the dining-room opened, and the parlourmaid and housemaid came in and gave him their notice. "A month from to-day, sir," repeated the parlourmaid to bridge the silence that followed.

"It's nothing to do with me," he said in a low voice. "Your mistress is coming home to-night. You must tell her of these things."

They left the room.

"What's the matter with those girls?" said Mr. Templeton to the butler who came in.

"They haven't spoken to me, sir," said the butler untruly; "but I gather there has been an upset."

"Because I chose to get up early on a summer morning?" asked Mr. Templeton with an effort.

"Yes, sir. And there were other reasons."

"Which were?"

"The housemaid," said the butler with detachment, as though he were speaking of the movements of a fly, "has found your bedroom, sir, strewn with clothes."

"With my clothes?" said Mr. Templeton.

"No, sir."

Mr. Templeton sat down. "A nightgown?" he said weakly, as though appealing for human understanding.

"Yes, sir."

"More than one?"

"Two, sir."

"Good God!" said Mr. Templeton, and walked to the window whistling shakily.

The butler cleared the table quietly and left the room.

"There's no question about it," said Mr. Templeton under his breath. "She was undressing . . . behind the chair."

After breakfast he walked down his two fields and through a wood with the idea of talking to Mr. George Casson. But George had gone to London for the day, and Mr. Templeton, faced with the polish on the front door, the polish on the parlourmaid, and the sober look of the *Morning Post* folded on the hall table, felt that it was just as well that he had not after all to confide his incredible story. He walked back again, steadied by the air and exercise.

"I'll telephone to Hettie," he decided, "and make sure that she is coming to-night." He rang up his wife, told her that he was well, that all was well, and heard with satisfaction that she was coming down that night after her dinner-party, catching the eleven-thirty, arriving at twelve-fifteen at the station.

"There is no train before at all," she said. "I sent round to the station to see, and owing to the strike they run none between seven-fifteen and eleven-thirty."

"Then I'll send the car to the station and you'll be here at half-past twelve. I may be in bed, as I'm tired."

"You're not ill?"

"No. I've had a bad night."

It was not until the afternoon, after a good luncheon and a whisky-and-soda, that Mr. Templeton went up to his bedroom to have a look at it. The cream curtains hung lightly blowing in the window. By the fire-place stood a high, wing, grandfather chair upholstered in patterned rep. Opposite the chair and the fire-place was the double bed, in one side of which Mr. Templeton had lain working at his papers the night before. He walked up to his chair, put his hands in his pockets, and stood looking down at it. Then he crossed to the chest of drawers and drew out a drawer. On the right-hand side were Hettie's vests and chemises, neatly pressed and folded. On the left was a pile, folded but not pressed, of Hettie's nightgowns. Mr. Templeton noted the crumples and creases on the silk.

"Evidence, evidence," he said, walking to the window, "that something happened in this room after I left it this morning. The maids believe they found a strange woman's nightgowns crumpled on the floor. As a matter of fact they are Hettie's nightgowns. I suppose a doctor would say I'd done it myself in a trance."

"Two nights ago?" he thought, looking again at the bed. It seemed a week. The night before last as he lay working, propped up on pillows and cushions and his papers spread over the bed, he had glanced up, absorbed, at two o'clock in the morning and traced the pattern on the grandfather chair as it stood facing the empty grate with its back towards him, just as he had left it, when he had got into bed. It was then that he had seen the two hands hanging idly over the back of the chair as though an unseen owner were kneeling in the seat. His eyes stared, and a cold fear wandered down his spine. He sat without moving and watched the hands.

Ten minutes passed, and the hands were withdrawn quickly as though the occupant of the chair had silently changed its position.

Still he watched, propped, stiffening, on his pillows, and as time went on he fought the impression down. "Tired," he said. "One's read of it. The brain reflecting something." His heart quietened, and cautiously he settled himself a little lower and tried to sleep. He did not dare straighten the litter of papers around him, but with the light on he lay there till the dawn lit the yellow paint on the wall. At five he got up, sleepless, his eyes still on the back of the grandfather chair, and without his dressing-gown or slippers he left the room. In the hall he found an overcoat and his warm snow-boots behind a chest and unbolting the front door he tramped the lawn in the dew.

On the second night (*last* night) he had worked as before. So completely had he convinced himself after a day of fresh air that his previous night's experience had been the result of his own imagination, his eyesight and his mind hallucinated by his work, that he had not even remembered (as he had meant to do) to turn the grandfather chair with its seat towards him. Now, as he worked in bed, he glanced from time to time at its patterned and concealing back, and wished vaguely that he had thought to turn it round.

He had not worked more than two hours before he knew that there was something going on in the chair.

"Who's there?" he called. The slight movement he had heard ceased for a moment, then began again. For a second he thought he saw a hand shoot out at the side, and once he could have sworn he saw the tip of a mound of fair hair showing over the top. There was a sound of scuffling in the chair, and some object flew out and landed with a bump on the floor below the field of his vision. Five minutes went by, and after a fresh scuffle a hand shot up and laid a bundle, white and stiff, with what seemed a small arm hanging, on the back of the chair.

Mr. Templeton had had two bad nights and a great many hours of emotion. When he grasped that the object was a pair of stays with a suspender swinging from them, something bumped unevenly in his heart, a million black motes like a cloud of flies swam in his eyeballs; he fainted.

He woke up, and the room was dark, the light off, and he felt a little sick. Turning in bed to find comfort for his body, he remembered that he had been in the middle of a crisis of fear. He looked about him in the dark, and saw again the dawn on the curtains. Then he heard a chink by the washstand, several feet nearer to his bed than the grandfather chair. He was not alone; the thing was still in the room.

By the faint light from the curtains he could just see that his visitor was by the washstand. There was a gentle clinking of china and a sound of water, and dimly he could see a woman standing.

"Undressing," he said to himself, "washing."

His gorge rose at the thought that came to him. Was it possible that the woman was coming to bed? It was that thought that had driven him with a wild rush from the room, and sent him marching for a second time up and down his grey and dewy lawns.

"And now," thought Mr. Templeton as he stood in the neat bedroom in the afternoon light and looked around him, "Hettie's got to believe in the unfaithful or the supernatural."

He crossed to the grandfather chair, and taking it in his two hands was about to push it on to the landing. But he paused. "I'll leave it where it is to-night," he thought, "and go to bed as usual. For both our sakes I must find out something more about all this."

Spending the rest of the afternoon out of doors, he played golf after tea, and eating a very light dinner he went to bed. His head ached badly from lack of sleep, but he was pleased to notice that his heart beat steadily. He took a couple of aspirin tablets to ease his head, and with a light novel settled himself down in bed to read and watch. Hettie would arrive at half-past twelve, and the butler was waiting up to let her in. Sandwiches, nicely covered from the air, were placed ready for her on a tray in a corner of the bedroom.

It was now eleven. He had an hour and a half to wait. "She may come at any time," he said (thinking of his visitor). He had turned the grand-father chair towards him, so that he could see the seat.

Quarter of an hour went by, and his head throbbed so violently that he put the book on his knees and altered the lights, turned out the brilliant reading lamp, switched on the light which illuminated the large face of the clock over the mantelpiece so that he sat in shadow. Five minutes later he was asleep.

He lay with his face buried in the pillow, the pain still drumming in his head, aware of his headache even at the bottom of his sleep. Dimly he heard his wife arrive, and murmured a hope to himself that she would not wake him. A slight movement rustled around him as she entered the room and undressed, but his pain was so bad that he could not bring himself to give a sign of life, and soon, while he clung to his half-sleep, he felt the bedclothes gently lifted and heard her slip in beside him.

Feeling chilly he drew his blanket closer round him. It was as though a draught was blowing about him in the bed, dispelling the mists of sleep and bringing him to himself. He felt a touch of remorse at his lack of welcome, and putting out his hand he sought his wife's beneath the sheet. Finding her wrist his fingers closed round it. She too was cold, strange, icy, and from her stillness and silence she appeared to be asleep.

"A cold drive from the station," he thought, and held her wrist to warm it as he dozed again. "She is positively chilling the bed," he murmured to himself.

He was awakened by a roar beneath the window and the sweep of a light across the wall of the room. With amazement he heard the bolts shoot back across the front door. On the illuminated face of the clock over the fire-place he saw the hands standing at twenty-seven minutes past twelve. Then Mr. Templeton, still gripping the wrist beside him, heard his wife's clear voice in the hall below.

NIGEL BALCHIN

1908-1970

By training, a scientist, he turned his analytical mind to studying people and writing about them. He once said, "As a writer, whatever happens to me can be turned to advantage." While traumatic experiences certainly engendered novels such as *The Small Back Room*, happier memories must have inspired this urbane short story.

Patience

MY SHARE of the meal had been some whitebait, some cheese and a cup of coffee. The bill was for four pounds, three and sixpence.

"You once told me that the last proprietor of this place was executed," I said rather bitterly. "It wasn't by any chance for highway robbery?"

My Uncle Charles shook his head. "No —just ordinary murder. The circumstances were not uninteresting. I will tell you about it some time." He sighed. "If I were a younger man, with less knowledge of the world," he said sadly, "I suppose I should be offering to pay the bill, or at least to split it with you."

"Why?" I said, astonished.

"On the grounds that I have won some money. I won twenty-five pounds at the Marshalls at bridge last night."

"Well, it's very decent of you . . ."

"But you and I know," said my Uncle Charles firmly, "that to win a sum of that kind can be the height of misfortune. I do not know the Marshalls well, and have only played with them a couple of times before. But they are a pair of quietly incompetent performers who, properly nursed, would have meant a steady two or three pounds a week to me for the next ten years. As it is, having lost twenty-five pounds in an

45

evening, they will never ask me there again. I tried hard to avoid it. But when I doubled their final ludicrous slam bid in an effort to save them, they merely re-doubled. They made two tricks and I went out into the night. The thing may or may not end in a divorce between them. It is certainly the end of bridge with them for me."

"You believe in small profits and steady returns?"

"It is the only possible principle nowadays, in any form of gambling which involves skill. When the Duchess of Devonshire was prepared to lose £50,000 at a sitting, it was different. But at a mere five shillings a hundred, one must be prepared to consider one's winnings as a modest pension rather than as the making of a fortune."

"Nobody can afford to play high nowadays."

"Nobody ever could." My Uncle Charles smiled gently to himself. "I have, in fact, taken part in a game of cards which ended in one of the players writing a cheque for eight hundred pounds, and he certainly could not afford it. But even so, it was, in a way, an illustration of my point that to win may be disastrous and to lose profitable."

"I don't quite follow you."

My Uncle Charles glanced round the restaurant. "You have paid the bill," he said. "If you were to order two more brandies, now, it is possible, though not likely, that they will forget to charge you for them. In the meantime, I will clarify my last statement."

"I HAVE NEVER been enthusiastic about the French Riviera which, to me, is a place to which all the people I want to avoid go in order to meet each other. I cannot now recall why, some twenty-five years ago, I spent some time at Nice; and the whole incident is made even more baffling by the fact that I appear to have been staying in a hotel. But it was certainly in the bar of a hotel in Nice that I first met Mr. Brander Heavistone. We were sitting at adjoining tables, and were inadvertently introduced by a waiter who spilt a tray of drinks over the pair of us. Mr. Heavistone was not a difficult man to get to know, and by the time we had mopped ourselves up and had made sure that none of the liquid had gone on his companion's dress, he was ordering replacements for all the three of us. Mr. Heavistone was a middle-aged American who wore the type of rather thick spectacles that magnify the eyes of the wearer. He was a quiet, soft-spoken man with a rather slow, courteous manner. The English have a maddening habit of assuming that all Americans of this type are Southerners. In fact, Mr. Heavistone came from Detroit, and I think he had made his money, of which there appeared to be a good deal, in some offshoot of the automobile industry.

"His companion, whom he introduced as Miss Tracey, was obviously English. In fact, in both appearance and manner, she might have sat for a very flattering portrait of The English Girl. I guessed her age at about twenty-five. She had light brown hair, very fine blue eyes, lovely skin, and very nice manners. I must say that as casual acquaintances to pick up in a bar in Nice, they were both exceptionally pleasant. How they had first met, I never knew, but they did not know one another very well. Perhaps somebody had spilt a tray of drinks over them somewhat earlier. We spent a pleasant half-hour together and then parted.

"Mr. Heavistone was staying in the hotel and so was I, and during the next few days I saw him several times, and exchanged a few words. On a couple of occasions, Miss Tracey was with him, and during this time I learnt that she lived in a villa just outside the town with her father, who was a retired soldier. From what she said I inferred that they were not well-off, and merely lived in the South of France because of her father's health. She seemed to worry a good deal about the fact that her father was bored and rather lonely, and one evening she asked me to come out to the villa with Mr. Heavistone and herself to meet him. Mr. Heavistone, I gathered, had been there a couple of times before. I had nothing to do, she was a very attractive girl, and I liked both her and Heavistone, so I was glad to accept.

"The villa was a couple of miles to the east of the town, and very much as I expected—comfortable, pleasant, but quite unpretentious. Colonel Tracey more or less completed the picture—a tall, handsome man of about sixty with closely cut iron-grey hair and a bearing of quiet dignity. He was playing patience when we arrived, and I gathered from his daughter that he spent many hours doing so. I am no expert at patience, and did not recognize the form of the game he was playing; but Heavistone did, and insisted that he should finish it. However, the game came out in a few minutes, and the Colonel then joined us, and we sat and chatted very pleasantly. It was obvious that the Colonel and his daughter were devoted to one another, and one could not help feeling that it was a slightly pathetic household in which the elderly man and the young girl both worried a good deal about the other, without the means to do much about it.

"Colonel Tracey and Heavistone talked a good deal about patience, of which they were both fond, and in the course of conversation I was asked if I played. When I said that I did not play patience but was fond of other card games, I saw the Colonel's face light up. He seemed to hesitate for a moment, and I saw him glance almost guiltily at his daughter. Then he said: 'Do you play poker?'

"'Yes.'

"'Do you, Mr. Heavistone?'

"'I have done, Colonel.'

"'Then we must make up a little school one evening.' He looked at

47

his daughter defiantly. 'I hardly ever get a chance to play poker now, and I'm very fond of it. That would be nice, wouldn't it, Leo?'

"Miss Tracey smiled and said, 'Of course,' without, I thought, much enthusiasm. But the Colonel insisted on going on and arranging for us to come out and play two evenings later. He was obviously delighted at the prospect, and when we were leaving he reminded us both in turn of the engagement.

"By now Mr. Heavistone and I were on terms of considerable friendship, and it was our habit to meet in the bar most evenings before dinner. The evening after our visit to the Colonel's villa we were sitting there when Miss Tracey entered. We, of course, rose to greet her and offered her a drink. She accepted and sat down with us, but it was not difficult to see that she was nervous and ill at ease. After a very few minutes' rather laboured conversation Heavistone happened to mention that we should be seeing her the following evening. Miss Tracey hesitated for a moment and then said bluntly: 'Yes. I—I want to talk to you about that. In fact to be quite frank that's what I came here about this evening. I hoped you'd be here and . . . Would you mind if I asked you something?'

"Heavistone said: 'Why sure. Go ahead.'

"She looked at her glass and twirled it by the stem. 'It's about Daddy and—playing poker.'

"I said gently: 'You don't like him to play, do you?'

"'How did you know that?' she said sharply.

"'I saw your face when he proposed it.'

"'It's not that I don't like him to *play*,' she said slowly. 'In fact I like him to, because he does love it and he's very lonely, and doesn't have much fun. It's just . . .' she looked up, and the blue eyes were very worried. 'Well, frankly, I'm always scared that he'll lose more than he can afford.'

"'Does he tend to lose?' said Heavistone.

"'Oh, not particularly. He says he's a very good player and I dare say he is. But once or twice when he's played with people, he's told me after the sort of amounts they were playing for, and I've wondered what would have happened if—if he *had* lost. You see, the poor old darling hasn't a cent except his pension and . . . Once he played and won two hundred pounds in an evening. He was terribly pleased and being Daddy, went straight off and spent it on me, which was very nice, of course. But I couldn't help wondering what would have happened if he'd *lost* the two hundred. He'll never listen to me. He just laughs and says he's too good a player to lose too much. But surely even the best of players do have runs of bad luck . . .?'

"'They do,' I said with feeling.

" 'They certainly do,' said Mr. Heavistone.

" 'So what I wanted to ask you,' said Leonora, 'was whether you'd mind not—not playing for much to-morrow. I've no right to ask you, and it may make it awfully dull for you. But you've both been very kind, and I thought perhaps you wouldn't mind . . .' There were tears in her eyes.

"Mr. Heavistone gave her a gentle pat on the arm. 'Don't you worry,' he said in his soft, slow drawl. 'We'll watch it, won't we, Charles?'

" 'Of course.'

" 'Only he'll try to make you play for a lot. He always does.'

"I said: 'I never play for more than I can afford, and that's practically nothing.'

" 'I can't honestly say that,' said Mr. Heavistone, smiling, 'but I certainly never like to play for enough to make any difference to anybody present. And that goes if we play for matches.'

"She said: 'Oh no—you'll have to play for *something* otherwise he'll be hurt. But just—not an awful lot.'

" 'Be all right if he lost ten pounds?'

" 'Yes. Quite. But not—not much more than that.'

" 'O.K.,' said Mr. Heavistone. 'Then we know where we are.'

"She gave us both a small and rather pathetic smile. 'Mind you, he mustn't ever know I asked you. He'd be . . . I don't know what he'd do.'

" 'That's all right,' said Mr. Heavistone. 'Hell, we understand, Leo. Have another drink.'

"She said: 'No, thank you. I've got to get back and see to Daddy's dinner. Good-bye and thank you very much. See you to-morrow.'

"When she had gone Mr. Heavistone said: 'Now that's a nice girl.'

" 'Yes. As a matter of fact if the old boy does like to bang it up I'm glad she told us. Otherwise it might have been a bit awkward.'

" 'I doubt the Colonel'd come to much harm, my poker being the way it is. He's probably pretty good. He's certainly a smart patience player.'

" 'Can you be a smart patience player? I thought it was pure chance.'

" 'Well it is and it isn't. But I'd say the Colonel would be all right. Still, you never know. Something might have gone wrong, and anyhow I wouldn't like that little girl to worry. Might have been awkward, as you say.'

" 'I wasn't really thinking of him so much as of me.'

"Mr. Heavistone eyed me. 'Why?'

" 'Well, I very rarely play cards for much money. And certainly not with anybody I don't know—even if it's somebody like the Colonel.'

"Mr. Heavistone smiled his gentle smile. 'Nor me,' he said. 'So now we can all play a shilling limit just for the hell of it.'

"IN THE EVENT, we didn't play a shilling limit the following evening, but it was certainly a very harmless game. Leonora did not play, but there was a fourth man about whom I can now remember absolutely nothing except that he spoke English like an Italian. As his daughter had prophesied, the Colonel made a couple of attempts to get the stakes to a more interesting level, but when he got no support from Heavistone or me he did not press it. I fancy Leonora had been lecturing him. He struck me as a good player, but not exceptionally so. He was one of those people who go a trifle exaggeratedly calm and expressionless when they bluff, which is an elementary fault, but one which very few people can spot in themselves. However, on the evening, he won about a couple of pounds, and so did I. Mr. Heavistone lost about three pounds. He was a poor player and obviously had not played the game much. It was not an exciting evening, but it was pleasant enough and the Colonel obviously enjoyed it immensely. On the way home Mr. Heavistone said: 'Well I hope the old boy goes out to-morrow and buys Leo a box of candy with his winnings.'

"THIS WAS THE pattern of several evenings that followed. Usually the vague Italian person made a fourth, and on one occasion there were five of us. The Colonel always made some effort to get us to play for real money, but never pressed it when we objected. On the whole, being a reasonable player, he usually won; but in the whole of the three or four occasions we went there I doubt if anybody was more than ten pounds up or down. Mr. Heavistone never said so, but I think he was a trifle bored by the whole business. He did not really like poker much, and would have been happier just to sit and talk to Leonora—as, indeed, I should. But the Colonel liked his game of poker, and on one occasion when we tried playing bridge instead, he clearly felt that it was a waste of valuable time. It was all very peaceful and pleasant if a trifle dull, and so it remained right up until the fatal evening when M. de Grouchy called.

"Four of us were playing as usual—the Colonel, Mr. Heavistone, the Italian and myself. The only unusual thing about the occasion was that Mr. Heavistone, whose game had improved considerably with practice, had been winning. He may have won thirty shillings. Leonora had left the room a few minutes before. We had just finished a hand, when she returned and said: 'Daddy—here's M. de Grouchy.' She said it as though something delightful had happened, but there was something in her face that told me that it wasn't delightful at all. The Colonel, however, seemed genuinely pleased and jumped up saying, 'Well well—just the man we want,' and proceeded to introduce us.

"Presumably, from his name and his appearance, M. de Grouchy was a Frenchman. He was a slim, rather dapper, youngish man with very sleek black hair and a sallow skin. But his English was absolutely perfect, and if he had an accent at all it was very faintly American.

"I cannot say I took to M. de Grouchy at first sight. I noticed that he greeted the Colonel with considerably less warmth than the Colonel showed towards him; and though what he said was polite enough, there was something slightly insolent in his smile and his manner. While he was being introduced to Heavistone, I caught Leonora's eye and she gave me a quick, anxious shake of the head. For a moment I didn't understand what she was trying to say. But it soon became clear.

"De Grouchy was saying: '. . . I happened to be in Nice, and thought I'd just drop in to see if there was any chance of my revenge.'

" 'You couldn't have come at a better time,' said the Colonel. He turned to us. 'Last time de Grouchy was here I trimmed him properly. Two hundred pounds, wasn't it?'

" 'Something like that,' said de Grouchy, with his smile. 'But you will admit Colonel, that the cards ran for you.'

" 'Oh yes. Up to a point anyhow.' The Colonel smiled at him. 'But the cards always *do* run for the good player, you know.'

" 'That's exactly what I want to see,' said de Grouchy. He walked over to the table and flicked some cards through his fingers. 'Well— am I allowed to come in?'

"The Italian said quickly: 'You will take my place, sir. I have to go.'

"The Colonel started to protest but the Italian was already bowing to Leonora. He was a remarkably imperceptible little man, and he simply faded himself out of the room firmly, neatly and rapidly. I had a strong impression that he had tried this party before and didn't propose to try it again. As Leonora went out with him the Colonel said: 'Never mind, we're four which is always a nice game.' I glanced at Heavistone and he at me. The same thought, of course, had occurred to both of us. If the Colonel had taken two hundred pounds off de Grouchy the last time he had been there, he could hardly offer him a hand in a game where, with a bit of luck, he might win thirty shillings. We had promised Leonora to keep the game small, and I for one didn't particularly relish a big game with a character like de Grouchy, Heavistone who wasn't a good player, and the Colonel to worry about. On the other hand, we could hardly refuse to play, particularly now the Italian had ducked out.

"The Colonel said briskly: 'Well come along, here's de Grouchy panting to give us the money. Let's get going.' He moved towards the table.

"Heavistone said in his quiet way: 'Look, gentlemen, I don't want to spoil the fun, but I'm a small timer at this game, and so's my friend.'

" 'Oh come,' said the Colonel. 'It won't hurt us to bang it up a bit for once.' His eyes were shining with pleasure and excitement. 'We've all been good boys for a long time. Here's a chance to make some cigar money.'

" 'It may not hurt you, sir, but it might hurt me. I'm a poor player as you know.'

" 'You're right in the middle of a streak of luck. Come on—you can't let me down, Heavistone.'

"Leonora had come back and was sitting by the fire very tense and upright. Her face was rather pale.

"I started to say: 'Well, I agree with Heavistone . . .' when de Grouchy cut in.

" 'But surely there is no problem,' he said, with the smile that made one want to kick him. 'You and I wish to play poker, Colonel. If these gentlemen do not wish to trust their skill or their luck against us, we can do one of two things. We can play for points, the points between us having a rather higher value, when we come to settle, than the points between them, or between us and them. Or we can play an ordinary game in which, after all, anybody can always throw in his cards if he feels that the risks are becoming excessive.'

"There was no answer to that—particularly said as he said it. I glanced at Leonora and saw her give a tiny helpless shrug of the shoulders and sink wearily back in her chair. Heavistone had gone slightly red at de Grouchy's tone. He hesitated for a moment and then said coldly: 'Very well, Colonel. If you wish it. I only hope I don't spoil your game.' He sat down and so did I.

"It wasn't a very happy start to the game and it didn't continue very happily. De Grouchy made no secret of the fact that he was after the Colonel—and not in any friendly way. And the Colonel knew it and liked it. Heavistone stuck to his guns and played very small, so that he was hardly ever in the game, which was a pity, since his streak of luck was continuing. I compromised. For a while I felt my way very carefully, and during that time I came to two conclusions—that de Grouchy was a first-class player and that the Colonel was a far worse one playing high than he was when playing our friendly game where there was no money in it. In fact, I didn't like the look of it at all.

"As the cards fell, the first half-hour was slightly farcical, since Heavistone and I, who weren't seriously in the game, held very good cards, and de Grouchy and the Colonel, who were panting to cut one another's throats, held nothing at all. Even they weren't prepared to go very far on a pair of tens, which was the sort of thing that took the pots—usually after Heavistone had thrown in three aces. Eventually I got tired of it and took ten pounds off de Grouchy, holding a full house to his three kings. When he saw my hand he smiled thinly and said:

'Only a full house? I thought you must have at least fours to be as reckless as that.'

"After that things began to warm up a bit, as he and the Colonel began to get more cards; and right from the start de Grouchy had the edge on him. It wasn't that he was particularly lucky, though he had what little luck was going. It was mainly that he was simply the better player, and that he could spot the Colonel's over-expressionless bluff every time. I had a few cracks at him myself and on balance was slightly up. But he never went very high with me, and once the Colonel was out he barely pretended to be interested. After the first hour I should say he was about fifty pounds up on the Colonel, and a few down to me. Then he had a very good patch and cleaned up a couple of big pots, so that by about eleven o'clock he'd certainly had his revenge for his two hundred pounds, and a bit over.

"I was getting more and more unhappy, and so was Heavistone. We were both remembering what Leonora had said. 'If he'd lost two hundred instead of winning it, I don't know what would have happened.' The Colonel himself seemed much less worried than we were. Perhaps a bit of the sparkle had gone out of him, but he certainly wasn't acting like a man who had lost enough to matter to him.

"At eleven o'clock Heavistone looked at his watch and said: 'Well, gentlemen, I hate to break up a good party but . . .'

"The Colonel said: 'Oh come now, Heavistone—we can't let this fellow get away with it. It's only eleven o'clock.'

"I said: 'I'm a bit weary myself.'

" 'What are you worrying about, Charles? You're winning.'

"De Grouchy said: 'I am, of course, at everybody's disposal. But last time—on which occasion I was losing—we broke up at four.'

" 'Well, if you think *I'm* going on till four in the morning, sir, you're wrong,' said Heavistone. It was the nearest to an acid remark that I ever heard him make to anybody.

"The Colonel sighed and said: 'They've got no stamina these people, have they, de Grouchy? Look Heavistone, I tell you what—give it another hour and then we'll stop. At twelve sharp.'

" 'I don't really want to, Colonel.'

" 'But you must give me a chance to take it back from this fellow. It's been running all his way for the last hour, and now it ought to even out.'

"Mr. Heavistone hesitated and looked at me. But I had nothing to offer. If there was any truth in what Leonora had said, the Colonel was pretty well in already. If he wanted to try to get himself out, at the risk of going in further, one could hardly stop him. Heavistone said helplessly: 'All right. Twelve sharp then,' and on we went.

"If the previous hour had been worrying, the last hour was a nightmare; for de Grouchy went straight into as big a run of luck as I have ever seen. It wasn't only that he held good cards, but that they were always *just* good enough, and at poker that can be heartbreaking. I can even remember an actual occasion when they both held a full house, de Grouchy's being Queens and sevens, and the Colonel's being Knaves and fives. It was all like that, and there was nothing we could do but sit and watch it. The Colonel didn't play badly. In fact the more he lost the better and more calmly he seemed to play. But there was nothing he could do about it. There was nothing anybody could have done about it. He had reasonable cards—even good ones. He played them reasonably and he lost practically every hand. By midnight, he must have owed de Grouchy at least five hundred pounds.

"As we threw the cards in at five-to-twelve Heavistone looked at his watch and said: 'Well—that's that.'

"The Colonel smiled and said: 'The verdict of the umpires is that there's time for one more over.' He was still as calm as ever. If the strain was telling, it merely made his face look rather older than usual.

"De Grouchy said: 'In which he hopes to hit many runs.' He was obviously proud of his knowledge of English colloquialism. Nobody else said anything, and the Colonel dealt.

"My cards, I remember, were of no interest. I had a pair of sixes, and drew one more six. Heavistone told me afterwards that he had a pair of Queens and a pair of fours. Neither was the sort of hand which was very relevant in the circumstances. But from the very outset, de Grouchy and the Colonel went out against one another. De Grouchy called for two cards and the Colonel took one, and then the fun began. I was pretty sure from the start of it that the Colonel held fours of something, and for a long time my guess was that de Grouchy had a full house. But he went on with complete confidence and eventually I began to wonder. He must guess that the Colonel held fours, after drawing one card. The question was whether he had drawn the four of something or whether he was bluffing—or indeed whether they both were."

My Uncle Charles paused and tapped the ash off his cigar. I noticed that his hand was trembling slightly. "I have implied," he said, "that the Colonel was not really a very good player. In justice to him, I must say that in his place I should have done exactly what he did. He was a lot of money down, and on his cards he had the right to think he had caught de Grouchy at last. In fact, his nerves held rather better than the other man's, and when eventually de Grouchy raised to three hundred pounds to see him, he was still raising with the air of a man who will do so indefinitely. The Colonel put down four kings and de Grouchy smiled and put down four aces.

"There was a moment's pause and then Mr. Heavistone said: 'Christ!'

"The Colonel smiled and said: 'There's no justice. Moral—never play against the run of the cards.'

"De Grouchy said: 'You *worried* me. I thought you'd picked up the Joker to four.' It was the only thing he said in the course of the evening with no unpleasant edge in it.

"I said nothing, having nothing in particular to say. After a few moments the Colonel gathered up the cards as though he was not altogether sure what he was doing and said: 'Well well—a pleasant game, if mildly disastrous. Add up, will you?' He turned to Leonora who was still sitting staring into the fire. 'Darling, bring me my cheque book, will you?' She brought it, and the end of it was that he made out a cheque for eight hundred and thirty odd pounds and gave it to de Grouchy and she stood and watched him. He was an elderly man, but I noticed that he signed the cheque without a tremor, and turned and smiled at her in a crooked way. I had been sorry for the Colonel before, that evening, but that was the moment I really disliked.

"Heavistone and I were silent in the car going back to Nice, but I remember saying: 'What will the old boy do now? I doubt if he's got eight hundred pounds in the world.'

"Mr. Heavistone was silent for a moment and then said with sudden and rather startling bitterness: 'No, sir. But he's got a daughter.'

"TO SAY THAT I lay awake that night worrying about Colonel Tracey's losses would be an exaggeration. I am constitutionally incapable of lying awake at night worrying about anybody's troubles, including my own. But I must confess that I felt very unhappy about the whole affair. Whilst nobody could very well hold Heavistone and myself responsible, the fact remained that Leonora had more or less committed the Colonel to our care, and we had sat by, however excusably, and let him do exactly the thing that she had most feared. I was forcibly reminded of a time when, as an undergraduate, I had been given charge of the only son of a widowed mother on Boat Race night, and at four o'clock the following morning had been forced to lay the body on her door-step, ring the bell, and run. I was therefore embarrassed, though not at all surprised, when Leonora walked into the lounge of the hotel on the following morning when I was drinking my morning coffee. Mr. Heavistone, unfortunately, had not yet appeared.

"I said all the obvious things—how sorry I was, how unfortunate it had all been, how we had seen no obvious way out, and so on. I then braced myself for the reproaches.

"In this, however, I had underestimated Leonora. She apologized for having given us what she felt must have been a very unpleasant evening, pointed out rather bitterly that it was no responsibility of ours if the Colonel would do these things, and thanked us for our efforts to stop him. She then smiled in a rather strained way and said: 'What I want from you is some advice. What do I do now?'

" 'He can't afford to lose the money?'

" 'He not only can't afford it—he hasn't got it.'

" 'He gave de Grouchy a cheque.'

" 'Anybody can write cheques. He hasn't *got* eight hundred pounds.'

" 'You're sure?'

" 'Absolutely. He's got one hundred and seven pounds, three and eightpence in that account, and the monthly bills are due in a week. When that rat de Grouchy tries to cash that cheque the bank will refuse it, and Daddy will then talk some nonsense about his honour and shoot himself. Or say he will.' She picked up a couple of lumps of sugar and began to roll them as if they were dice. 'I don't understand about male honour,' she said bitterly. 'It seems that you can play cards for money that ought to pay the tradesmen, or that you haven't got, and as long as you win you're still a gentleman. But if you lose you're a cad and ought to shoot yourself. Is being a gentleman being lucky, or just not being found out?'

"I said: 'Either or both.'

" 'Well anyhow, how do I lay hands on seven hundred and fifty pounds in the next few hours? Have *you* got seven hundred and fifty?"

" 'No, my dear.'

" 'I thought not. Nobody ever has.'

" 'Does that villa belong to you?'

" 'No. We only rent it.'

" 'Anything you can sell? Jewellery or anything?'

" 'There's my watch. And my necklace that was Mummy's. They're worth a bit, but not as much as that.' She flicked one of the lumps of sugar away impatiently. 'The maddening thing is that in about six months I get a thousand pounds.'

" 'How?'

" 'Under my aunt's will. When I'm twenty-five. But that isn't till December.'

" 'You might borrow on it.'

" 'Yes. But not by midday to-day which is about the latest it's likely to be any good.' She suddenly gave a slightly hysterical giggle. 'Where's Uncle Heavistone? He must have seven hundred and fifty pounds he wouldn't miss.'

" 'I shouldn't think so. He's only here on holiday. But you might ask him.'

" 'Hardly.'

" 'Why not?'

" 'How could I?'

" 'You asked me.'

" 'Only for fun.' She smiled wryly. 'I can hardly go round asking casual acquaintances to pay Daddy's betting losses when I've no security or . . .'

" 'How about your aunt's will?'

" 'But why should he, anyhow?'

" 'I've never seen why anybody should lend anybody money. But in my experience they often do.'

"She hesitated. 'You really think he might?'

" 'If he's got it. He was very put out about the whole thing.'

"Leonora sat for a moment in silence. Then she glanced at her watch and sat up. 'Right,' she said quietly. 'It is now ten-thirty. I shall go and try to borrow seven hundred and fifty pounds off Mr. Heavistone, if I can find him . . .' She paused. 'You—you wouldn't like to come with me, Charles? I haven't got a lot of experience of this sort of thing.' "

My Uncle Charles paused. "There were tears in her eyes," he said pensively. "I have already said that they were very blue eyes. We found Mr. Heavistone on the terrace."

"AS ONE WHO has borrowed a good deal of money in his time, I am perennially interested in the psychology of the touchee. The experienced borrower, of course, knows his man. He knows whether the poor wretch, in an agony of embarrassment, will mutter 'Of course, old man, of course' and press the money into his hand; or whether he will settle for half the amount requested; or whether he will say with artificial firmness that he never lends money but will willingly give it you; or whether he will produce the money and take the opportunity of offering a few words of advice. All these, and many others, are the common coin of borrowing, and in my experience these pitiful defensive techniques are not greatly affected by the sum involved. But I must say that I have never seen anybody borrow five pounds, let alone seven hundred and fifty, as quickly as Leonora borrowed it off Mr. Heavistone. The thing, in fact, struck me as mildly indecent. Mr. Heavistone was sitting in a deck-chair on the terrace. I said, with painful jocularity, 'Hallo, Heavistone. Here's Leonora, who wants to borrow some money off you.'

"Mr. Heavistone got up and said: 'Money? How much, my dear?'

"Leonora looked at him and smiled but she couldn't say anything so I said: 'Oh—about seven hundred and fifty.'

" 'Pounds or dollars or what?'

" 'Pounds.'

"Mr. Heavistone made a mental calculation and clicked his tongue. 'In that case,' he said, 'I shall have to go up to my room. I don't carry that much with me.'

"He was gone about five minutes. When he came down he handed Leonora a thick bundle of notes and said: 'It's in dollars, but maybe it doesn't matter. It's money.'

"Leonora looked at the notes for a moment, and then she stepped forward and kissed Mr. Heavistone on the cheek and turned and ran away. She didn't say anything.

"Mr. Heavistone stood and looked after her and after a while he said: 'I dare say. But what's my chance of ever seeing that back?'

"I said: 'She's got some money coming to her.'

" 'So what?'

" 'I should think she'll pay you back.'

"Mr. Heavistone said: 'Why seven fifty? The Colonel dropped over eight hundred.'

" 'She says there's a hundred in the bank.'

"Mr. Heavistone was still looking in the direction in which Leonora had gone. 'Gee,' he said softly, 'there are some pretty good people about. You know I wouldn't care a lot if I never saw that back.' "

My Uncle Charles paused and then suddenly whipped round at me and said: "Have I told you this story before?"

"No," I said.

He shook his head. "I can't think why not. One of the most terrifying aspects of growing old is this sudden conviction—usually entirely justified—that one has told people things before. But however—for the next two days I saw nothing of Mr. Heavistone or Leonora, being involved in a visit along the coast. I still don't know what induced me, when returning to Nice on the third day, to go somewhat out of my way to visit the Colonel's villa. Nor why, as soon as I saw it, before I had left my car, I knew it was empty. Perhaps (who knows) some vestige of the brains I was born with had really remained with me throughout the whole affair. I like to think so, and to point to the fact that on the whole transaction I personally was in pocket to the extent of some fourteen pounds.

"But this is beside the immediate point, which was that the Colonel and Leonora had gone, that they had been gone a couple of days, and that no one appeared to know their next address, and that probably Mr. Heavistone's money had gone too. As I was driven back to Nice, I kept thinking of Mr. Heavistone's face as he looked after Leonora, and I must confess I felt slightly sick. You must remember that I was a good deal younger then than I am now. Indeed, I remember going into the bar and having a large brandy before I went to see Mr.

Heavistone, merely because I was not looking forward to telling him what had happened.

"Mr. Heavistone was in his room playing patience. I think the game must have been at a rather critical stage, because he put another card down and considered for a moment before he looked round at me with the curious magnified eyes. 'Hallo,' he said, 'still here? I thought you'd gone.'

"I said: 'No. I've been along the coast. Look here, Heavistone, I'm sorry but I'm afraid I've got a shock for you. We've been swindled.'

" 'We?'

" 'Well, you have, at least.'

" 'Who by?'

" 'The Colonel and his daughter. They've bolted.'

"Mr. Heavistone took another card from the pack, considered it, and put it down with a little grunt. 'She isn't his daughter,' he said gently, 'she's his wife. Come to that, he isn't a Colonel.'

" 'How d'you know?'

" 'You find these things out—after.'

" 'Did you know they'd gone?'

" 'I thought they would be.' He turned and looked at me and gave a little chuckle. 'Tell you the truth, sir, when you didn't show up yesterday, I thought you'd be gone too.'

" 'I! . . . Why?'

" 'Well, think it over. She was so embarrassed, that poor girl, that she couldn't ask for the money. *You* had to come and . . .'

"I said: 'My God!'

" 'Though mind you,' said Mr. Heavistone, 'I wasn't sure about you, any more than about the Italian. Now he may have been in it or he may not. But I doubt it, because then they would have to split the money four ways instead of three.'

" 'You mean de Grouchy was in it?'

" 'Sure. He had star billing, didn't he?'

"I sat down rather limply and said: 'When did you tumble to all this?'

" 'The first time you and I went out there, sir.'

" 'Then why on earth did you give her the money?'

"Mr. Heavistone shook his head. 'I hope they don't try to spend that money. The top note was twenty bucks all right. I thought it had been worth that, and maybe the Colonel can buy her a box of candy with it. But the rest cost five dollars the lot at a shop in Madison Avenue. I had a lot more but I gave it to a con man in Paris. They make it for conjurers for that trick where they keep pulling thousands of dollars out of a hat.' He shook his head again. 'It's surprising how few folks in Europe know about what proper American money looks like. You'd think they would by now. They've had enough of it.'

"I said: 'Either I've been so slow that I ought to be in a home, or else you've been damned quick. *How* did you spot it?'

" 'Well, you don't play patience. You ought to play patience. It's a great game. Now the Colonel was a smart patience player.'

" 'So you said.'

" 'Yes. Well the first twice I went out there with the girl, the Colonel was playing patience; and he was playing a sort of patience called Mrs. Kitchner's Ramp, which very few people play. And what is more, sir, he got it out both times. Now I don't know much about poker, as you've seen, but I know a lot about patience, and if you get Mrs. Kitchner's Ramp out once every six months you're lucky. So when you and I went there and he got it out again just conveniently so as to come and talk to us, I knew the Colonel was a smart man with cards, and that they came when he called them.'

" 'Then why . . .?'

" 'Why didn't he take us in the ordinary way? Well think it over, sir. I doubt you'd have played him for three thousand dollars, nice as he was. You said you wouldn't to me. Nor would I. Nor would anybody. So the way it went was to build up a big story through the girl, and then have a big loss to a four-letter man like de Grouchy and then it was easy.'

"I said: 'I must have my head attended to. But even now, there's one bit I don't see. Why on earth *should* he cheat himself at patience?'

"Mr. Heavistone smiled. 'If you'd played patience, you wouldn't ask that question, sir. More people cheat at patience than at anything else.' He pointed to the table. 'Now look at this. If that last card I turned up had been a nine, then it would have come out. The next card in the deck *is* a nine. And I haven't got a game out for a fortnight. See what I mean?' Mr. Heavistone sighed and gathered up the cards. 'Maybe the Colonel just played patience to give him practice with his trick decks. It takes a lot of practice to be as good as that. Or maybe he was like the rest of us and liked to win. After all, he always had to lose when it came to the big hand, and you can see that could be dull, sir.' "

H.E. BATES

1905–1974

During World War II he wrote the famous Flying Officer X stories;
more recently he created the inimitable Larkin family. He remained
popular throughout a prolific career and, although his reputation
is international, he is considered among the most "English" of
writers—some of his best work being inspired by a deep,
nostalgic love of his native countryside.

The Little Fishes

 MY UNCLE SILAS was very fond
of fishing. It was an occupation
that helped to keep him from thinking too much about work and also
about how terribly hard it was.

If you went through the bottom
of my Uncle Silas's garden, past
the gooseberry bushes, the rhubarb
and the pigsties, you came to a
path that went alongside a wood
where primroses grew so richly in spring that they blotted out the floor
of oak and hazel leaves. In summer wild strawberries followed the
primroses and by July the meadows beyond the wood were frothy with
meadow-sweet, red clover and the seed of tall soft grasses.

At the end of the second meadow a little river, narrow in parts and
bellying out into black deep pools in others, ran along between willows
and alders, occasional clumps of dark high reeds and a few wild crab
trees. Some of the pools, in July, would be white with water lilies, and
snakes would swim across the light flat leaves in the sun. Moorhens
talked to each other behind the reeds and water rats would plop suddenly
out of sight under clumps of yellow monkey flower.

Here in this little river, my Uncle Silas used to tell me when I was a
boy, "the damn pike used to be as big as hippopotomassiz."

"Course they ain't so big now," he would say. "Nor yit the tench.
Nor yit the perch. Nor yit the——"

61

"Why aren't they so big?"

"Well I'm a-talkin' about fifty years agoo. Sixty year agoo. Very near seventy years agoo."

"If they were so big then," I said, "all that time ago, they ought to be even bigger now."

"Not the ones we catched," he said. "They ain't there."

You couldn't, as you see from this, fox my Uncle Silas very easily, but I was at all times a very inquisitive, persistent little boy.

"How big were the tench?" I said.

"Well, I shall allus recollect one as me and Sammy Twizzle caught," he said. "Had to lay it in a pig trough to carry home."

"And how big were the perch?"

"Well," he said, rolling his eye in recollection, in that way he had of bringing the wrinkled lid slowly down over it, very like a fish ancient in craftiness himself, "I don' know as I can jistly recollect the size o' that one me and Arth Sugars nipped out of a September morning one time. But I do know as I cleaned up the back fin and used it for a horse comb for about twenty year."

"Oh! Uncle Silas," I would say, "let's go fishing! Let's go and see if they're still as big as hippopotomassiz!"

But it was not always easy, once my Uncle Silas had settled under the trees at the end of the garden on a hot July afternoon, to persuade him that it was worth walking across two meadows just to see if the fish were as big as they used to be.

Nevertheless I was, as I say, a very inquisitive, persistent little boy and finally my Uncle Silas would roll over, take the red handkerchief off his face and grunt:

"If you ain't the biggest whittle-breeches I ever knowed I'll goo t'Hanover. Goo an' git the rod and bring a bit of dough. They'll be no peace until you do, will they?"

"Shall I bring the rod for you too?"

"*Rod?*" he said. "For *me. Rod?*" He let fall over his eyes a tremulous bleary fish-like lid of scorn. "When me and Sammy Twizzle went a-fishin', all we had to catch 'em with wur we bare hands and a drop o' neck-oil."

"What's neck-oil?"

"Never you mind," he said. "You git the rod and I'll git the neck-oil."

And presently we would be walking out of the garden, past the wood and across the meadows; I carrying the rod, the dough and perhaps a piece of carraway cake in a paper bag, my Uncle Silas waddling along in his stony-coloured corduroy trousers, carrying the neck-oil.

Sometimes I would be very inquisitive about the neck-oil, which was often pale greenish-yellow, rather the colour of cowslip, or perhaps of parsnips, and sometimes purplish-red, rather the colour of elder-berries, or perhaps of blackberries or plums.

On one occasion I noticed that the neck-oil was very light in colour, almost white, or perhaps more accurately like straw-coloured water.

"Is it a new sort of neck-oil you've got?" I said.

"New flavour."

"What is it made of?"

"Taters."

"And you've got two bottles today," I said.

"Must try to git used to the new flavour."

"And do you think," I said, "we shall catch a bigger fish now that you've got a new kind of neck-oil?"

"Shouldn't be a bit surprised, boy," he said, "if we don't git one as big as a donkey."

That afternoon it was very hot and still as we sat under the shade of a big willow, by the side of a pool that seemed to have across it an oiled black skin broken only by minutest winks of sunlight when the leaves of the willow parted softly in gentle turns of air. "This is the place where me and Sammy tickled that big 'un out," my Uncle Silas said.

"The one you carried home in a pig trough?"

"That's the one."

I said how much I too should like to catch one I could take home in a pig trough and my Uncle Silas said:

"Well, you never will if you keep whittlin' and talkin' and ompolodgin' about." My Uncle Silas was the only man in the world who ever used the word ompolodgin'. It was a very expressive word and when my Uncle Silas accused you of ompolodgin' it was a very serious matter. It meant that you had buttons on your bottom and if you didn't drop it he would damn well ding your ear.

"You gotta sit still and wait and not keep fidgetin' and very like in another half-hour you'll see a big 'un layin' aside o' that log. But not if you keep ompolodgin'! See?"

"Yes, Uncle."

"That's why I bring the neck-oil," he said. "It quiets you down so's you ain't a-whittlin' and a-ompolodgin' all the time."

"Can I have a drop of neck-oil?"

"When you git thirsty," my Uncle Silas said, "there's that there spring in the next medder."

After this my Uncle Silas took a good steady drink of neck-oil and settled down with his back against the tree. I put a big lump of paste on my hook and dropped it into the pool. The only fish I could see in the pool were shoals of little silver tiddlers that flickered about a huge fallen willow log a yard or two upstream or came to play inquisitively about my little white and scarlet float, making it quiver up and down like the trembling scraps of sunlight across the water.

Sometimes the bread paste got too wet and slipped from the hook and I quietly lifted the rod from the water and put another lump on the hook. I tried almost not to breathe as I did all this and every time I took the rod out of the water I glanced furtively at my Uncle Silas to see if he thought I was ompolodgin'.

Every time I looked at him I could see that he evidently didn't think so. He was always far too busy with the neck-oil.

I suppose we must have sat there for nearly two hours on that hot windless afternoon of July, I not speaking a word and trying not to breathe as I threw my little float across the water, my Uncle Silas never uttering a sound either except for a drowsy grunt or two as he uncorked one bottle of neck-oil or felt to see if the other was safe in his jacket pocket. All that time there was no sign of a fish as big as a hippopotamus or even of one you could take home in a pig trough and all the time my Uncle Silas kept tasting the flavour of the neck-oil, until at last his head began to fall forward on his chest. Soon all my bread paste was gone and I got so afraid of disturbing my Uncle Silas that I scotched my rod to the fallen log and walked into the next meadow to get myself a drink of water from the spring.

The water was icy cold from the spring and very sweet and good and I wished I had brought myself a bottle too, so that I could fill it and sit back against a tree, as my Uncle Silas did, and pretend that it was neck-oil. Ten minutes later, when I got back to the pool, my Uncle Silas was fast asleep by the tree trunk, one bottle empty by his side and the other still in his jacket pocket. There was, I thought, a remarkable expression on his face, a wonderful rosy fogginess about his mouth and nose and eyes.

But what I saw in the pool, as I went to pick my rod from the water, was a still more wonderful thing. During the afternoon the sun had moved some way round and under the branches of the willow, so that now, at the first touch of evening, there were clear bands of pure yellow light across the pool.

In one of these bands of light, by the fallen log, lay a long lean fish, motionless as a bar of steel, just under the water, basking in the evening sun.

When I woke my Uncle Silas he came to himself with a fumbling start, red eyes only half open, and I thought for a moment that perhaps he would ding my ear for ompolodgin'. "But it's as big as a hippopotamus," I said. "It's as big as the one in the pig trough."

"Wheer, boy? Wheer?"

When I pointed out the fish, my Uncle Silas could not, at first, see it lying there by the log. But after another nip of neck-oil he started to focus it correctly.

"By Jingo, that's a big 'un," he said. "By Jingo, that's a walloper."

"What sort is it?"

"Pike," he said. "Git me a big lump o' paste and I'll dangle it a-top of his nose."

"The paste has all gone."

"Then give us a bit o' carraway and we'll tiddle him up wi' that."

"I've eaten all the carraway," I said. "Besides, you said you and Sammy Twizzle used to catch them with your hands. You said you used to tickle their bellies——"

"Well, that wur——"

"Get him! Get him! Get him!" I said. "He's as big as a donkey!"

Slowly, and with what I thought was some reluctance, my Uncle Silas heaved himself to his feet. He lifted the bottle from his pocket and took a sip of neck-oil. Then he slapped the cork back with the palm of his hand, wiped his lips with the back of his hand and put the bottle back in his pocket.

"Now you stan' back," he said, "and dammit, don't git ompolodgin'!"

I stood back. My Uncle Silas started to creep along the fallen willow-log on his hands and knees. Below him, in the band of sunlight, I could see the long dark lean pike, basking.

For nearly two minutes my Uncle Silas hovered on the end of the log. Then slowly he balanced himself on one hand and dipped his other into the water. Over the pool it was marvellously, breathlessly still and I knew suddenly that this was how it had been in the good great old days, when my Uncle Silas and Sammy Twizzle had caught the mythical mammoth ones, fifty years before.

"God A'mighty!" my Uncle Silas suddenly yelled. "I'm a-gooing' over!" My Uncle Silas was indeed gooin' over. Slowly, like a turning spit, the log started heeling, leaving my Uncle Silas half-slipping, half-dancing at its edge, like a man on a greasy pole.

In terror I shut my eyes. When I opened them and looked again my Uncle Silas was just coming up for air, yelling "God A'mighty, boy, I believe you ompolodged!"

I thought for a moment he was going to be very angry with me. Instead he started to cackle with crafty, devilish, stentorian laughter, his wet lips dribbling, his eyes more fiery than ever under the dripping water, his right hand triumphant as he snatched it up from the stream.

"Jist managed to catch it, boy," he yelled and in triumph he held up the bottle of neck-oil.

And somewhere downstream, startled by his shout, a whole host of little tiddlers jumped from the water, dancing in the evening sun.

HILAIRE BELLOC

1870–1953

The brilliant son of a French barrister, great-nephew of no less than four of Napoleon's generals, he was educated in England. Although probably best-known today for his children's *Cautionary Tales* ("Henry King", who died from chewing little bits of string), he was also a distinguished Liberal M.P., novelist, critic and historian.

The Apprentice

29th January (or, as we should say, 10th February) 1649

Charles I was executed on this day, upon a scaffold outside the second window on the north of Whitehall Banqueting Hall, at four in the afternoon.

MEN WERE WELL into the working week; it was a Tuesday and apprentices were under the hard eyes of their masters throughout the City of London and in the rarer business places that elbowed the great palaces along the Strand. The sky was overcast and the air distastefully cold, nor did anything in the landscape seem colder than the dark band of the river under those colourless and lifeless January clouds.

Whether it were an illusion or a reality, one could have sworn that there was a sort of silence over the houses and on the families of the people; one could have sworn that men spoke in lower tones than was their custom, and that the streets were emptier. The trial and the sentence of the King had put all that great concourse of men into the very presence of Death.

The day wore on; the noise of the workmen could be heard at the scaffold by Whitehall; one hour was guessed at and then another; rumours and flat assertions were busy everywhere, especially among the young, and an apprentice to a harness-maker in the Water Lane, near

66

Essex House, knew not what to believe. But he was determined to choose his moment and to slip away lest he should miss so great a sight. The tyranny of the army kept all the city in doubt all day long, and allowed no news; none the less, from before noon there had begun a little gathering of people in Whitehall, round the scaffold at which men were still giving the last strokes of the hammer. Somewhat after noon a horseshoe of cavalry assembled in their long cloaks and curious tall civilian hats; they stood ranked, with swords drawn, all round the platform. Their horses shifted uneasily in the cold.

The harness-maker's apprentice found his opportunity; his master was called to the door for an order from Arundel House, and the lad left his bench quickly, just as he was, without hat or coat, in the bitter weather, and darting through the side door ran down through the Water Gate and down its steps to the river. The tide was at the flood and his master's boat lay moored. He cast her off and pulled rapidly up the line of gardens, backing water when he came to the public stairs just beyond Whitehall. Here he quickly tied the painter and ran up breathless to Whitehall Gate, fearing he might have missed his great expectation. He was in ample time.

It was perhaps half-past three o'clock when he got through the gate and found himself in the press of people. Far off to the left, among the soldiery that lined the avenue from the park to the Mall, and so to St. James's, a continuous roll of drums burdened the still air.

The crowd was not very large, but it filled the space from the gate to the scaffold and a little beyond, save where it was pressed outward by the ring of cavalry. It did not overflow into the wide spaces of the park, though these lay open to Whitehall, nor did it run up towards Charing Cross beyond the Banqueting Hall.

The apprentice was not so tall as the men about him; he strained and elbowed a little to see, and he was sworn at. He could make out the low scaffold, a large platform all draped in black, with iron staples, and a railing round it; it covered the last three blank windows of Whitehall, running from the central casement until it met the brick house at the north end of the stonework; there the brickwork beneath one of the windows had been taken out so as to give access through it from the floor within to the scaffold on the same level without; and whispers round told the apprentice, though he did not know how much to trust them, that it was through this hasty egress that the King would appear. Upon the scaffold itself stood a group of men, two of them masked, and one of the masked ones, of great stature and strong, leant upon the axe with his arms crossed upon the haft of it. A little block, barely raised above the floor of the platform, he could only see by leaping on tiptoe, catching it by glimpses between the heads of his neighbours or the

67

shoulders of the cavalry guard; but he noticed in those glimpses how very low it was, and saw, ominous upon it, two staples driven as though to contain the struggler. Before it, so that one kneeling would have his face toward the palace and away from the crowd, was a broad footstool covered with red velvet, and making a startling patch upon all that expanse of black baize.

It was cold waiting; the motionless twigs of the small bare trees in the park made it seem colder still. The three-quarters struck in the new clock behind him upon Whitehall Gate, but as yet no one had appeared.

In a few moments, however, there was a movement in the crowd, heads turning to the right, and a corresponding backing of the mounted men to contain the first beginnings of a rush, for the commanders of the army feared, while they despised, the popular majority of London; and the wealthy merchants, the allies of the army, had not joined this common lot. This turning of faces towards the great blank stone wall of the palace was caused by a sound of many footsteps within. The only window not masked with stone, the middle window, was that upon which their gaze universally turned. They saw, passing it very rapidly, a group of men within; they were walking very sharply along the floor (which was here raised above the level of the window itself and cut the lower panes of it); they were hurrying towards the northern end of the great Banqueting Hall. It was but a moment's vision, and again they appeared in the open air through the broken brickwork at the far end of the stone façade.

For a moment the apprentice saw clearly the tall King, his face grown old, his pointed beard left full, his long features not moved. The great cloak that covered him, with the Great Star of the Garter upon the left shoulder, he drew off quickly and let fall into the hands of Herbert. He wore no hat; he stepped forward with precision towards the group of executioners, and a little murmur ran through the crowd.

The old bishop, moving his limbs with difficulty, but suppliant and attendant upon his friend, stood by in an agony. He helped the King to pull off his inner coat until he stood conspicuous in the sky-blue vest beneath it, and round his neck a ribbon and one ornament upon it, a George carved in onyx. This also he removed and gave to the bishop, while he took from his hands a little white silken cap and fixed it firmly upon his long and beautiful hair. From beneath the sky-blue of his garment, at the neck and at the wrists, appeared frills of exquisite linen and the adornment of lace. He stood for a few moments praying, then turned and spoke as though he were addressing them all. But the apprentice, though he held his breath, and strained to hear, as did all others about him, could catch no separate word, but only the general sound of the King's voice speaking. The movement of the horses, the occasional striking of a hoof upon the setts of the street, the distance, covered that voice. Next, Charles was saying something to the masked man, and a moment later he was kneeling upon the footstool. The apprentice saw him turn a moment and spread his arms out as an example of what he next should do; he bent him toward the block—it was too low; he lay at full length, and the crowd lifted and craned to see him in this posture.

The four heavy strokes of the hour struck and boomed in the silence. The hands of the lying figure were stretched out again, this time as a final signal, and right up in the air above them all the axe swung, white against the grey sky, flashed and fell.

In a moment the group upon the scaffold had closed round, a cloth was thrown, the body was raised, and among the hands stretched out to it were the eager and enfeebled hands of the bishop, trembling and still grasping the George.

A long moan or wail, very strange and dreadful, not very loud, rose from the people now that their tension was slackened by the accomplishment of the deed. And at once from the north and from the south, with such ceremony as is used to the conquered, the cavalry charged right through, hacking and dispersing these Londoners and driving them every way.

THE APPRENTICE dodged and ran, his head full of the tragedy and bewildered, his body in active fear of the horses that pursued flying packets of the crowd down the alley-ways of the offices and palace buildings.

He went off by a circuitous way to find, not his master's house after such an escapade, but his mother's, where she lived beyond St. Martin's.

The dusk did not long tarry; as it gathered and turned to night small flakes of snow began to fall and lie upon the frozen ground.

ARNOLD BENNETT

1867–1931

He began his career in the legal profession—a strange choice,
perhaps, in view of his troublesome stammer. At any rate, he soon
turned to journalism and writing, where he scored signal successes with
his *Old Wives' Tale*, and his harshly realistic stories of the Five Towns,
centres of the northern pottery industry.

Death, Fire and Life

MR. CURTENTY lay in
bed in the winter morn-
ing darkness, and re-
flected upon the horrible
injustice of destiny. Mr.
Curtenty was a most respectable gentleman—indeed, a connection of
the celebrated Jos Curtenty of Longshaw, and, be it admitted, a great
deal more dignified than Jos ever was. He had never done anything
wrong; his conscience was sinless. In sixty years his dignity and his
respectability had not been even compromised. He could, and he did,
look everybody unyieldingly in the face. By nature and long practice he
was intensely proud and independent. All the world addressed him as
'Mr.' Once he had lost a situation through his employer omitting
the 'Mr.' Of course he had not openly resented the omission, for he
was not a fool, but the omission had put him in a frame of mind favourable to quarrelling, and a quarrel about some trifle had ensued. Nevertheless he had soon obtained a new situation, which unhappily he had
lost through the death of the new employer.

Since that disaster—now rather more than a year ago—he had been
workless, and therefore wageless. Society seemed to blame him for
being sixty years old. The fact that he had no particular trade also
counted against him. He had always had posts such as watchman, door-
keeper, timekeeper, inspector—posts which meant doing nothing with
dignity. Hence no doubt his feeling of superiority to people who
actually did things.

70

Somehow he could scarce hide this feeling—even from his daughter's husband, who secretly resented it. Jim Crowther was a young miner living at Longshaw, and in the opinion of Mr. Curtenty, Jim's wife, Harriet, had married beneath her. Mr. Curtenty was mistaken in supposing that he had concealed this opinion from Jim and Harriet. Every week he disliked Jim and Harriet more and more, because they were contributing to his subsistence. They were not so crude in their methods of charity as to give him money direct. Certainly not. Such clumsiness would have made an everlasting breach between the two generations. Mr. Curtenty knew naught, officially, of any help. Only it invariably happened that when Mr. Curtenty had not a shilling, Mrs. Curtenty had ten shillings or so, which she produced as it were, apologetically. Mr. Curtenty was diplomatic enough never to enquire whence she had obtained the money. Thus the twelve lean months had run precariously and unsatisfactorily on.

But a crisis was now upon Mr. Curtenty. For his wife had told him that Harriet had told her that Jim had told Harriet that Mrs. Curtenty could go and live with the Crowthers at Longshaw if she liked, and Mr. Curtenty too. And little by little Mr. Curtenty was given to understand that either he must submit to this humiliation—or starve. Well, Mr. Curtenty had his pride, and he swore to himself that he would not submit to it. He simply could not imagine himself as a helpless pauper dependent in the home of his son-in-law. He conveyed his decision to Mrs. Curtenty, and the next thing he heard was that if he wouldn't go she would! Ah! He saw well enough that the notion was to force him into submission! As if anybody could force him into submission!

Two days previously, it being then a Wednesday, Mr. Curtenty had been informed that Mrs. Curtenty would migrate to Longshaw at the end of the week, Saturday. It was now Friday. The supreme catastrophe was indeed shaping. All his life Mr. Curtenty had worried about the future, and his relatives and acquaintances had laughed at him for worrying. But was he not justified by the event? Had he ever been wrong? They twitted him about being miserly. He was not miserly. He had always been careful, and was he not now justified of his carefulness also? Financially, there was the matter of the Post Office Savings Bank account. They did not positively accuse him of keeping a private hoard in the Post Office Savings Bank; but they hinted at it, and no amount of denials by him would stop their hints.

His ear caught a *puffpuff-puffpuff*, the same being the first irregular coughings of the engine of Clayhanger's Steam-Printing Works, which extended from Duck Bank down the opposite side of the lane. These coughings were Mr. Curtenty's morning clock—he had no other, nor watch either. Soon followed the sound of sirens from different parts of the town of Bursley. The hour was seven. Mr. Curtenty slid out of bed from his wife's side, and began with deliberation to dress. He did everything with deliberation. He even looked for work—when he looked for it—with deliberation. (But he had an idea that work ought to look for him.) His nature demanded that he should always have plenty of time in front of him. Time was the basis of dignity; hurry was the enemy of dignity. The first part of his dressing he did in the dark. Then he lit a candle, behind the bed's head, and with a morsel of blacking and an old stumpy brush he softly cleaned his boots—or such poor fragments of them as were left to clean.

A miserable small room, but the totality of Mr. Curtenty's home! Once he had rented a whole house, and could walk from one room to another and go upstairs and downstairs and still be at home . . . A few pitiable bits of furniture, including the little oil-stove on which his wife cooked their so-called meals! Once she had held sway over a whole kitchen-range.

In a dignified way he was sorry for his young and ingenuous, quietly grumbling wife. Not really young, for she was the mother of a mother! But he, at thirty, had married her at nineteen, and to him she had always remained curiously young. There she lay, on the verge of fifty, and looking to the impartial observer more than her age—she had had a wearing life—but to him, in her tranquil, pathetic sleep, she seemed rather like a girl, foolish, feckless, helpless. Yes, he was sorry for her . . . So she intended on the morrow to migrate to her daughter's at Longshaw, whether he went or not! Unless he yielded she meant to leave him—leave him to his own devices. It had come to that.

On the old tin tray was just enough bread, and dripping, and bits of cured fish to last them till the next morning. Thenceforward, the fiat had been issued from Longshaw, there were to be no more supplies. And then what? He knew that his wife was wondering, and Harriet was wondering, and Jim was wondering what the obstinate, secretive old man would do—what would happen. He alone knew what would happen.

When he had laced his boots under the candle, and combed his hair, he extinguished the candle and finished his toilet in the dark. But the dark was now twilight; the earth was revolving as usual, and in its revolution baring Bursley to the dawn. Mr. Curtenty buttoned his greenish jacket, tied an antique woollen muffler round his collarless neck, put on his cap, and went forth into Woodisun Lane.

He knew he would be too early. He always was too early. He paced smartly but with dignity about Duck Square. A huge tram, packed with people who had work and were going off to do it, rumbled past the Wesleyan chapel down Duck Bank towards Hanbridge. Mr. Curtenty stamped his feet into the pavement and rubbed his hands, for January mornings are always dank and chill in the Five Towns. Yet while doing this he pretended with dignity not to feel the cold. At last he descried the postman, and returned to the front door of the cottage in which he occupied one room; and he received the postman majestically on the doorstep.

"Good morning," said the genial postman.

"Good morning to you," said Mr. Curtenty, grandly, and took from the postman a small blue official envelope.

In the privacy of the cottage stairs he opened the envelope. Its contents were quite in order: an authority to withdraw the sum of two shillings from the Savings Bank department of the Post Office. Then Mr. Curtenty drew from his breast-pocket a yellowish bank-book, which showed that twenty pounds stood to his credit, and he carefully put the withdrawal form within the book and replaced the book in his pocket.

Surely you are not surprised! A prudent man must have something up his sleeve for the last emergencies. Mr. Curtenty had maintained that twenty pounds in reserve throughout a year of privation and humiliation. He had lied about it for a year and more than a year. No matter how terrible a plight you may be in, it is always possible to conceive yourself in a still worse plight. That twenty pounds was Mr. Curtenty's bulwark against the imaginable worse—the fear of which had plagued him for forty years. It was the last defence and resource of his independence.

"Where ye been?" asked his waking wife, as he re-entered their home.

"Getting a breath of air," said Mr. Curtenty.

II

IN THE EVENING, about half-past seven, Mrs. Curtenty was lying in bed (for warmth) and Mr. Curtenty was sitting on one of the two chairs, all in the dark, when Mr. Curtenty, after a little shuffling of his legs and scrunching of the chair legs on the bare boards, suddenly rose and felt his way to the door, where his cap and muffler hung on a hook. The pair had had two lean meals and one snack; all the fish was eaten, but not quite all the bread; some tea remained for breakfast. Mr. Curtenty had been abroad once, in the afternoon, and during that period he had cashed the warrant for two shillings. Whether or not his wife had gone out in the same interval he did not know. They had scarcely spoken to each other, not from unfriendliness, but from habit. Not a word had been said about the morrow, or Mr. Curtenty's intentions regarding the morrow. Mrs. Curtenty had not dared to challenge him on the great matter. Indeed, he could not safely be challenged.

Mrs. Curtenty thought to herself now, as she sometimes remarked to her daughter: "Things'll work themselves out if you leave 'em alone."

This was her philosophy in face of Mr. Curtenty's terrible estranging dignity and independence. All she said was, as Mr. Curtenty fumbled on the cheek of the door: "Where ye going?"

And all he replied was: "A breath of air."

He left without looking at the companion of his life. Even if he had looked at her he could not have seen her in the darkness. Still, he might have lit the last inch of candle for a few seconds and looked at her, for the moment was one of farewell after a companionship of thirty years. But his sentimental emotions had been numbed, frozen by misfortune, by spiritual pride, by privation, by secretiveness, by hidden anger against fate, and by self-righteousness. So he just went. He knew that his young wife would fall asleep and stay asleep.

It was a raw night in Woodisun Lane, and a muddy.

He had not meant to visit the Free Reference Library in the Wedgwood Institution, but as a measure of precaution he decided to do so. He was at home in that warm refuge of the unemployed, the Wedgwood Institution. The horrid, stuffy, damp smell of the Reference Library delighted his nose. After the usual formalities he obtained Quain's *Dictionary of Medicine*, and, taking the thick volume to a desk, he turned over its pages with the deliberate majesty of a vicar searching in the Bible for the lesson appointed to be read.

His brain was absolutely clear. He was not out of his mind, nor out of any part of his mind. In no circumstances would he migrate to his son-in-law's. His wife might go; she indeed would go; and she would be happy there, or at least contented. The twenty pounds (less two shillings) which he had guarded for an ultimate contingency would be useless to him, because too soon exhausted. He might of course fend for himself, all alone, for a time on the twenty pounds; but if he did so his family would know for sure that he had had a secret hoard after all, and he could not bear that revelation; it would too seriously humiliate him. Moreover, when the twenty pounds was gone—what then? Merely the same crucial, unanswerable problem as now! No! He had had enough, and there could be but one answer to the question: To be or not to be?

Quain was perfectly explicit: "The soluble cyanides, more especially the cyanide of potassium, largely used by photographers and by electroplaters, are common articles of commerce, and produce the same deadly results as the acid itself. The fatal dose of prussic acid is the equivalent of less than one grain of the anhydrous acid."

Nothing could be simpler to the understanding. He had read it before, but he wished to refresh his memory and so avoid the possibility of blunder. He refrained from proceeding to read about the effect of the poison; he had read that also before; it was rather disturbing, sensational.

He closed the stately tome and grandly handed it back across the counter to the pert young thing in a jersey who had dominion there. None could have guessed, as he calmly descended the broad steps of the Institution, that he was solemnly marked out and divided that night from every other soul in the town.

He made his way to Critchlow's in St. Luke's Square. Critchlow's was the oldest chemist in Bursley. He knew Critchlow slightly—a sardonic and antique being who would as lief as not sell poison to a customer who he guessed meant to drink it. Not that there was any trouble about buying poisons in those distant days at the end of the nineteenth century. You could pick a phial of tablets out of a mahogany case and pay for it and walk off with, for instance, as much sulphonal as would finish a whole family—and no question asked and no eyebrow lifted. And if perchance Critchlow should ask a question about 'Scheele's Acid', the trade name of the anhydrous prussic, Mr. Curtenty (who had never heard of sulphonal) could easily refer to electro-plating; for he had once had a temporary job on a small electro-plating works in Knype; hence his knowledge of the matter.

Critchlow's, however, was closed. Monstrous that the shop should be closed on that night of all nights! Holl's clock across the Square showed six minutes to eight, and Critchlow's had no right to be closed until eight. But Critchlow's was closed. The old fellow was allowing himself to become a bit capricious in his latter years.

Mr. Curtenty had purposely driven the transaction as late as convenient, for he desired a deserted, nocturnal town for his mortal work; but he now saw the possibility of having cut the thing too fine. Still, there was Salter's, in the Market Place—all on the way to the empty playground, beyond the Town Hall, which he had selected for his end. He walked to the top of the Square, and turned to the right where the Market Place was. He had an idea that Salter's kept open till nine o'clock. Salter's was open, and he entered the shop, which happened to be empty, behind the counter as well as in front of it.

Salter's was the new chemistry in Bursley. Salter, a daring and optimistic fellow from Birmingham, had taken over the ramshackle old shop from the dying hand of the historic chemist who, for more than fifty years, had sold drugs and given advice to the old-fashioned élite of the ramshackle old town. Salter had provided a new ideal for the ramshackle old town. The interior of the shop had been expensively refurnished from floor to high ceiling. It shone; it glittered; it was orderly; it was the cleanest thing in Bursley; it had an antiseptic, tonic odour; its clock was accurate; it offered chairs, mirrors, and a weighing-machine for the use of customers. It displayed more tooth-brushes than a quarter of a century earlier had been employed in the whole of Bursley. Mr. Curtenty was not impressed. He had the native's distaste for and suspicion of all that was 'showy' and that was not ramshackle.

A fine young gentleman, Mr. Salter himself (no apron), appeared from the dark backward of the establishment, glided along the length of the counter, and became a note of interrogation to Mr. Curtenty, whose tongue—very surprisingly—clave to his palate and whose throat grew parched.

"I want some Scheele's Acid."

Mr. Salter stared at Mr. Curtenty, and Mr. Curtenty, invigorated and challenged by the stare, returned it.

"Photographic work?"

Mr. Curtenty nodded. "Aye!"

"How much?"

"Dun' know. Smallish bottle."

"Half a pint?"

"Aye! That'll do."

"I'll get you to sign the poison book."

"Aye!"

Mr. Salter moved about behind the counter, and in a startlingly brief space of time was slapping a salmon-tinted poison label on a corked bottle. (Never within Mr. Curtenty's experience had seconds passed so quickly.) The next instant he had screwed the bottle into a bit of wrapping-paper, and he was in the act of handing it to Mr. Curtenty when a great lady entered the shop and Mr. Salter turned to her with eager and yet dignified deference, excusing himself negligently to Mr. Curtenty.

But Mr. Curtenty held the bottle. He held it victoriously; and it was no longer a bottle in a bit of paper—it was a sacred phial, magic, omnipotent, more powerful than man and than God. It held the key to the riddle of the future, and the short answer to the arguments of the past. It gave Mr. Curtenty a sense of absolutism, of independence, of dignity, of conquest over earth, such as he had never had. It rendered Mr. Curtenty heroic, magnificent. Already he was leaving earth. He had no interest in earth; he was sick of it, disgusted with it. He yearned bitterly to be quit of it. He had little or no fear, for fear presumes imagination, and he had little or no imagination. He forgot the teachings of religion and the wrath of God, or, if he remembered them, remembered them only to despise them. He was the supreme egotist. He thought of nobody but himself. He was absorbed in himself. Some faint vision of an inquest flickered transiently through his brain. He sniggered at it and it vanished. He was triumphant. He was a hero, a conqueror, a poet. He was God.

"One-and-twopence, please," murmured Mr. Salter, between two respectful sentences addressed to the lady.

"*One-and-twopence!*" cried Mr. Curtenty, dropping the florin which he was holding suspended in mid-pocket. "*One-and-twopence!* Why! It hadn't ought to be more than tenpence-halfpenny!"

"I'm afraid it's one-and-two," said Mr. Salter, calmly.

"Not *me!*" Mr. Curtenty growled with finality, and, dropping the bottle on to the round indiarubber mat intended to receive coins, he walked with fury and grandeur out of the shop, not caring for forty Salters nor forty great ladies.

He muttered things to himself. Did Salter suppose that *he* was going to help to pay for all the fal-lals and gim-crackery of his new shop? Not him! They called him a miser and a skinflint. They might. But fair was fair, and impudence was impudence. Impudence, that was what it was! Impudence! Let Mr. Salter charge his one-and-twopence to them as had quarterly bills and wouldn't pay cash. But not to *him!* He knew to a certainty that Fresson, the 'cash chemist' in Hanbridge, the great price cutter, would sell him half a pint of Scheele's Acid for tenpence, if not ninepence-halfpenny. And to Fresson's he would go. Fresson's did not close until ten o'clock. Fresson was the friend of the poor and a hard-working man who toiled early and late ... Impudence! Impudence! ...

People passing in the Market Place heard and saw Mr. Curtenty muttering and chuntering to himself. He noticed with resentment that he was observed, and walked off in the direction of Hanbridge. His resolution to carry out his plan was as firm as ever—for nothing could shake it—but he was equally determined not to be done in the eye.

III

WOODISUN LANE is one of the ways from Bursley to Hanbridge. Indeed, from Bursley Market Place it is the shortest and the oldest way, but by far the worst way, by reason both of its gradients and its foul surface. However, Mr. Curtenty took it, in order, by a glance at the window of his home, to see whether Mrs. Curtenty was wastefully burning the last inch of the candle. She was not; the window gave no sign of light. Strange to say, Mrs. Curtenty's thriftiness disappointed him, because he wanted another grievance, he wanted dozens of grievances, to gather into his breast as St. Sebastian gathered arrows.

He had to be content with the one great grievance against Mr. Salter —Mr. Salter, who by his rapacity was forcing a determined and desperate man to walk unnecessarily over to Hanbridge on a dank night. Soon, by dint of reflection and savage concentration, the grievance swelled till it filled his whole mind and heart and soul.

Nearly at the top of the hill, at Bleakridge, Woodisun Lane debouches into the main thoroughfare, Trafalgar Road. Somewhat farther on is the football ground, where Bursley had never yet defeated Knype, and then there is a corner upon which had stood for centuries a small earthenware manufactory—one small manufactory succeeding another there from Plantagenet times onwards. Young Eddie Colclough had recently razed a small manufactory to the ground and was just finishing the erection of a new one of an experimental type wherein various modern dodges of economic organisation were to be tested.

As he passed the building Mr. Curtenty's watchman's-nose sniffed the air, in the manner of a tiger sniffing distant blood. Mr. Curtenty became a nose and nothing but a nose; and his grievance and his purpose were equally forgotten. It might be said that Mr. Curtenty had no trade, but that he had a profession was richly demonstrated in that sniffing moment. He sniffed the night-watchman's arch-foe—smoke, indicating fire.

He looked at the façade, whose upper windows were still unglazed, and could see no curling wisp of smoke. But he had faith in his nose. Though the gates of the large central archway had not yet been put in place, the archway was stoutly boarded, and Mr. Curtenty could not get through it. He ran along and climbed a rough fence at the side of the manufactory, and so reached the back, which was less securely protected than the front from marauders. The next instant he was in the strewn quadrangle, or 'yard' as it is called. And his nose was justified, for he saw smoke meandering furtively, ominously, from a first-floor window. And his eyes detected a faint glow within.

Mr. Curtenty was gloriously alive. The price of Scheele's Acid was nothing to him. He was professionally inspired. He was happy in the midst of calamity and conflagration. He knew the first thing to do and the second thing to do, and did not hesitate a moment. In a quarter of a minute he was in Trafalgar Road again. A policeman, a policeman to take charge! But there was no policeman. In the Five Towns, so different from other localities, when you are engaged in the practice of virtue and philanthropy there never is a policeman within a mile; it is only when you happen to be delinquent that policemen spring magically out of the earth. There was nobody except three giggling and shrieking girls, arms mutually entwined round necks, swinging along the oozy pavement. Mr. Curtenty ignored them. But at the corner of the tiny Square, in front of Bleakridge's yellow church, burned a red lamp. Dr. Ackerington's, of course! Mr. Curtenty, forgetting dignity, and yet somehow preserving it, ran to the house and violently rang the bell. He rang it three times with increasing violence.

The door opened.

78

"'Ere! You're in a 'urry," said a stern, fat, middle-aged maid in cap and apron, as soon as she had satisfied herself that Mr. Curtenty did not belong to the ruling class.

"'Ave ye got th' telephone here?" Mr. Curtenty demanded stiffly.

"And if we have! You can't use it."

"Who wants for to use it? You tell your master or missus as Colclough's new pot-banks afire, and they mun telephone for th' fire brigade." And as the wench, startled and impressed and stricken, did not immediately move, he added: "And look slippy!" Then he ran off.

Within the quadrangle of the works once more he descried in the darkness what looked like a mound of sand. He put his hand into it. It was a mound of sand. Seizing one of several buckets which the builder's men had left, he filled it with sand and searched for and found stairs and gingerly mounted them in the black darkness, and guided by his triumphant nose he passed through a corridor and into a large suffocating room, which room was illuminated by the fire.

Planks of wood were just beginning to crackle. With the sand he smothered their ardour. But there was not enough sand. He descended again, with empty bucket, bungled the stairs, fell, hurt his ankle, swore, limped, got more sand, ascended. After three such ascents he had extinguished the fire and was in darkness. But he had seen enough to decide the origin of the fire. The usual thing! Workmen's negligence. They had been bivouacking in the room, they had made a fire in the grateless hearth—one of your sprawling fires—and they had not put it out on leaving. A few embers had reached a plank leaning at a broad angle against the mantelpiece, had patiently attacked the root of the plank—a slow business, but in the end successful; the plank, deprived of its base, had fallen sideways on to a heap of other planks. And so on. Had not the entire place sweated with damp it might have been a heap of ruins at the moment when Mr. Salter's rapacity had driven Mr. Curtenty in the direction of Hanbridge.

Mr. Curtenty, his occupation gone, limped through other corridors and rooms until he saw the light of Trafalgar Road street-lamps through an unglazed window. He looked out, himself unseen. A crowd, small but increasing, was gazing stolidly up at the façade of the works. It could perceive nothing of interest; it had no impulse to do anything; it merely gazed, in the faint hope of witnessing some terrific catastrophe. No policeman! No fire-engine! A tramcar roared by, unheeding. Mr. Curtenty continued to look out, proud, patient, invisible, scornful of the crowd. He was triumphant—nearly as triumphant as he had been fifty minutes earlier when he held the sacred phial in his hand. What a world! What destiny!

The expectant crowd in the mire was in due course rewarded by the exciting arrival, from Hanbridge way, of a motor-car full of people—Eddie Colclough, a young newly-married wife, and friends. Dr. Ackerington being out, Mrs. Ackerington had telephoned not only to the fire brigade, but to Eddie, who lived at Cauldron, between Hanbridge and Oldcastle. Mr. and Mrs. Eddie were entertaining at dinner two gentlemen and a lady, and, all being young and adventurous, they had instantly decided to leave dinner and come in a body to the scene of the announced conflagration.

Mr. Curtenty, seeing them and guessing that Mr. Colclough must be among them, went downstairs with pain in his ankle. Eddie, followed by Mrs. Eddie and the others, was in the quadrangle almost before him.

"Where's the fire?" Mr. Colclough demanded fiercely, in bewilderment; he was intensely relieved to see no evidence of a fire, but also—rather illogically—annoyed to see no evidence of a fire.

"It ain't anywhere. I've put it out," answered Mr. Curtenty, coldly, challengingly.

"And who the devil are you, anyway?" cried Mr. Colclough, who was of an aggressive and hasty disposition.

"Mr. Curtenty's my name," said Mr. Curtenty, "and if you'll come upstairs I'll shownd ye a thing or two." His tone gave pause to Mr. Colclough, and at the same time allayed Mr. Colclough's rising suspicion of some hanky-panky in the rumour of the fire.

"Strike a match," ordered Mr. Colclough at the dark stairs, feeling vainly in his pockets.

"I dunna smoke," said Mr. Curtenty, grimly.

However, one of the other gentlemen had one of the new-fangled electric torches. The six of them stood in the scene of the conflagration and heard Mr. Curtenty's description of the great episode: how he was passing, how his nose gave the alarm, how he sent for the fire brigade, how he used the sand, how he sprained his ankle, and how all's well that ends well; the whole recital being supported by charred timber and the heavy odour of wood-smoke.

The ray of the electric torch lighted Mr. Curtenty's smoke-grimed face. The rest of them—the fashionable aristocracy, including two young and beautiful women—were in shadow. Mr. Curtenty's tale was faultless; it extorted admiration, a little unwilling perhaps at first from Eddie Colclough, but spontaneous enough from the others, and especially from the women.

"Well, here's something for you," said Mr. Colclough, and handed Mr. Curtenty a sovereign.

"Thank ye."

"You must be used to fires," said Mrs. Colclough, smiling warmly.

Mr. Curtenty majestically offered some of his personal history.

"And who are you working for now?" asked Mr. Colclough.

"I'm playing (out of work)," said Mr. Curtenty.

Mr. Colclough paused. "What did you say your name was?"

"Mr. Curtenty."

"Well, look here, Curtenty," said Mr. Colclough, and paused again, as though hesitating in his mind.

Mr. Curtenty did not repine at the rough, careless omission of the 'Mr.'; experience had been teaching him.

"Look here, Curtenty. There's no watchman here yet. D'you want a job?"

Mr. Curtenty was engaged on the spot.

Suddenly he hurried from the room. The others followed him. The electric torch lighted him from behind. His ears had been copying the excellent example of his nose. He reached one of the front unglazed windows and put his head through a square. A fire engine had arrived with an enormous fluster and bluster and glint of brass helmets. A fine effort on the part of the Bursley Fire Brigade—forty minutes!

Mr. Curtenty bawled angrily, disdainfully, to the brigade: "It's out! Get away wi' yer sprinklin' mashane! It's out! I'm a-telling on ye!"

Then he turned and faced the torch.

"You perfect *duck!*" exclaimed young Mrs. Colclough, and carried away by gratitude for a great deed, and by her youthful sentimentalism and the general influence of a honeymoon and the comicality of Mr. Curtenty's dirty tweed cap—in all her beauty and all her finery she put her ringed hands on the shoulders of the old man and kissed his sooty plain face.

IV

IN DUCK SQUARE (which is really only a bit of Duck Bank and not a square at all) there is an establishment (not to be confused with the Boro' Dining Rooms two doors off) which stays open till a late hour nightly, brilliantly lit amid the surrounding gloom, and which exudes from its interior an odour so appetizing and powerful that it has been known to interfere with the Wednesday evening prayer meeting in the Wesleyan chapel a hundred yards away on the opposite side of Trafalgar Road.

Mr. Curtenty entered this establishment and, pulling a florin from his pocket, bought two plenteous portions of the finest fried fish. He then bought a candle, though candles were not in her line of business, from the white-clad proprietress, who gave him a few matches into the bargain. Then he went across to the fast-closing Dragon Hotel and in the nick of time bought a bottle of beer. Having unlocked the door of the cottage in Woodisun Lane with his own key, he took off his boots at the bottom of the stairs, struck a light, and proceeded upwards, heavily encumbered, into his one-roomed home.

Young Mrs. Curtenty was fast asleep; the blaze of the candle did not awaken her. He examined her face with a new interest. His heart was loudly beating (but that, of course, was the effect of the stairs—what else could it be?). He was vaguely aware, too, of a non-fleshy throbbing, a quaking, a half-pleasant, half-frightening general disturbance in his mind or his soul or somewhere. He could not quite surely identify the phenomenon. It might have been some imperfect realization of the dread fact that but for the accident of a fire he would at that moment have been elsewhere, or nowhere at all and nothing at all. On the other hand, it might be due to alarm at his own wild and reckless expenditure in the fried fish shop and the Dragon Hotel.

It was the heavenly odour of the fried fish that first caused his wife to dream a delicious dream and then woke her. As her senses gradually brought her back into the sphere of reality, she opened her ingenuous eyes and saw Mr. Curtenty bending over her, candle in hand. The memory of Mrs. Colclough's kiss was now the chief thing in Mr. Curtenty's mind. It somehow thrilled him, and it somehow took thirty years off Mrs. Curtenty's age.

"Rally thysen up, wench," said Mr. Curtenty in a tone so startlingly new and attractive to Mrs. Curtenty that she could not move.

He wanted to bend down and embrace her, but was prevented by an unconquerable complex that held him fast and told him not to be ridiculous.

"Rally thysen up," he repeated, "and put th' blanket round thy shoulders."

"Jimmy," said she, hopefully, "then us'll go to Harriet's at Longshaw to-morrow?"

"Not me!"

"I shall," said she, sadly. "They'll make me. Ay, lad, I'm going, I am!" She sighed.

"Thee isna," he almost shouted. "I've gotten a job. Rally up and set this 'ere fish on a platter."

She raised herself on her elbows and kissed him; *she* had no forbidding complex. The kiss was what he wanted. This kiss was the second in one hour, and the second in perhaps six months or more. And the lips were as cool and fresh as Mrs. Colclough's. And the kiss had a quality mysteriously surpassing that of Mrs. Colclough's. Mr. Curtenty felt himself obliged for form's sake to show impatience at the salute.

"'Ere," he grunted. "Thou'rt shaking candle grease all o'er th' bed."

Nevertheless, he himself adjusted the blanket round his wife's exposed arms and neck.

ANTHONY BERKELEY

1894–1971

"It is no business of the reader to find out what sort of person the author is." This remark, attributed to Anthony Berkeley Cox, reflected his passion for anonymity. It was as "Anthony Berkeley" and "Francis Iles" that he became both a distinguished critic of detective fiction and one of its leading exponents, setting the trend for the modern crime novel.

The Avenging Chance

ROGER SHERINGHAM was inclined to think afterwards that the Poisoned Chocolates Case, as the papers called it, was perhaps the most perfectly planned murder he had ever encountered. The motive was so obvious, when you knew where to look for it—but you didn't know; the method was so significant, when you had grasped its real essentials—but you didn't grasp them; the traces were so thinly covered, when you had realized what was covering them—but you didn't realize. But for a piece of the merest bad luck, which the murderer could not possibly have foreseen, the crime must have been added to the classical list of great mysteries.

This is the gist of the case, as Chief Inspector Moresby told it one evening to Roger in the latter's rooms in the Albany a week or so after it happened.

ON FRIDAY MORNING, the fifteenth of November, at half-past ten in the morning, in accordance with his invariable custom, Sir William Anstruther walked into his club in Piccadilly, the very exclusive Rainbow Club, and asked for his letters. The porter handed him three and a small parcel. Sir William walked to the fire-place in the big lounge hall to open them.

A few minutes later another member entered the club, a Mr. Graham

83

Beresford. There were a letter and a couple of circulars for him, and he also strolled over to the fire-place, nodding to Sir William, but not speaking to him. The two men only knew each other very slightly, and had probably never exchanged more than a dozen words in all.

Having glanced through his letters, Sir William opened the parcel and, after a moment, snorted with disgust. Beresford looked at him, and with a grunt Sir William thrust out a letter which had been enclosed in the parcel. Concealing a smile (Sir William's ways were a matter of some amusement to his fellow-members), Beresford read the letter. It was from a big firm of chocolate manufacturers, Mason & Sons, and set forth that they were putting on the market a new brand of liqueur-chocolates designed especially to appeal to men; would Sir William do them the honour of accepting the enclosed two-pound box and letting the firm have his candid opinion on them?

"Do they think I'm a blank chorus-girl?" fumed Sir William. "Write 'em testimonials about their blank chocolates, indeed! Blank 'em! I'll complain to the blank committee. That sort of blank thing can't blank well be allowed here."

"Well, it's an ill wind so far as I'm concerned," Beresford soothed him. "It's reminded me of something. My wife and I had a box at the Imperial last night. I bet her a box of chocolates to a hundred cigarettes that she wouldn't spot the villain by the end of the second act. She won. I must remember to get them. Have you seen it—*The Creaking Skull?* Not a bad show."

Sir William had not seen it, and said so with force.

"Want a box of chocolates, did you say?" he added, more mildly. "Well, take this blank one. I don't want it."

For a moment Beresford demurred politely and then, most unfortunately for himself, accepted. The money so saved meant nothing to him for he was a wealthy man; but trouble was always worth saving.

By an extraordinary lucky chance neither the outer wrapper of the box nor its covering letter were thrown into the fire, and this was the more fortunate in that both men had tossed the envelopes of their letters into the flames. Sir William did, indeed, make a bundle of the wrapper, letter, and string, but he handed it over to Beresford, and the latter simply dropped it inside the fender. This bundle the porter subsequently extracted and, being a man of orderly habits, put it tidily away in the waste-paper basket, whence it was retrieved later by the police.

Of the three unconscious protagonists in the impending tragedy, Sir William was without doubt the most remarkable. Still a year or two under fifty, he looked, with his flaming red face and thick-set figure, a typical country squire of the old school, and both his manners and his language were in accordance with tradition. His habits, especially as regards women, were also in accordance with tradition—the tradition of the bold, bad baronet which he undoubtedly was.

In comparison with him, Beresford was rather an ordinary man, a tall, dark, not unhandsome fellow of two-and-thirty, quiet and reserved. His father had left him a rich man, but idleness did not appeal to him, and he had a finger in a good many business pies.

Money attracts money, Graham Beresford had inherited it, he made it, and, inevitably, he had married it, too. The daughter of a late ship-owner in Liverpool, with not far off half a million in her own right. But the money was incidental, for he needed her and would have married her just as inevitably (said his friends) if she had not had a farthing. A tall, rather serious-minded, highly cultured girl, not so young that her character had not had time to form (she was twenty-five when Beresford married her, three years ago), she was the ideal wife for him. A bit of a Puritan perhaps in some ways, but Beresford, whose wild oats, though duly sown, had been a sparse crop, was ready enough to be a Puritan himself by that time if she was. To make no bones about it, the Beres-fords succeeded in achieving that eighth wonder of the modern world, a happy marriage. And into the middle of it there dropped with irre-trievable tragedy, the box of chocolates.

Beresford gave them to her after lunch as they sat over their coffee, with some jesting remark about paying his honourable debts, and she opened the box at once. The top layer, she noticed, seemed to consist only of kirsch and maraschino. Beresford, who did not believe in spoiling good coffee, refused when she offered him the box, and his wife ate the first one alone. As she did so she exclaimed in surprise that the filling seemed exceedingly strong and positively burnt her mouth.

Beresford explained that they were samples of a new brand and then, made curious by what his wife had said, took one too. A burning taste, not intolerable but much too strong to be pleasant, followed the release of the liquid, and the almond flavouring seemed quite excessive.

"By Jove," he said, "they are strong. They must be filled with neat alcohol."

"Oh, they wouldn't do that, surely," said his wife, taking another. "But they are very strong. I think I rather like them, though."

Beresford ate another, and disliked it still more. "I don't," he said with decision. "They make my tongue feel quite numb. I shouldn't eat any more of them if I were you, I think there's something wrong with them."

"Well, they're only an experiment, I suppose," she said. "But they do burn. I'm not sure whether I like them or not."

A few minutes later Beresford went out to keep a business appoint-ment in the City. He left her still trying to make up her mind whether she liked them, and still eating them to decide. Beresford remembered that scrap of conversation afterwards very vividly, because it was the last time he saw his wife alive.

That was roughly half-past two. At a quarter to four Beresford arrived at his club from the City in a taxi, in a state of collapse. He was helped into the building by the driver and the porter, and both described him subsequently as pale to the point of ghastliness, with staring eyes and livid lips, and his skin damp and clammy. His mind seemed unaffected, however, and when they had got him up the steps he was able to walk, with the porter's help, into the lounge.

The porter, thoroughly alarmed, wanted to send for a doctor at once, but Beresford, who was the last man in the world to make a fuss, refused to let him, saying that it must be indigestion and he would be all right in a few minutes. To Sir William Anstruther, however, who was in the lounge at the time, he added after the porter had gone:

"Yes, and I believe it was those infernal chocolates you gave me, now I come to think of it. I thought there was something funny about them at the time. I'd better go and find out if my wife——" He broke off abruptly. His body, which had been leaning back limply in his chair, suddenly heaved rigidly upright; his jaws locked together, the livid lips drawn back in a horrible grin, and his hands clenched on the arms of his chair. At the same time Sir William became aware of an unmistakable smell of bitter almonds.

Thoroughly alarmed, believing indeed that the man was dying under his eyes, Sir William raised a shout for the porter and a doctor. The other occupants of the lounge hurried up, and between them they got the convulsed body of the unconscious man into a more comfortable position. Before the doctor could arrive a telephone message was received at the club from an agitated butler asking if Mr. Beresford was there, and if so would he come home at once as Mrs. Beresford had been taken seriously ill. As a matter of fact she was already dead.

Beresford did not die. He had taken less of the poison than his wife, who after his departure must have eaten at least three more of the chocolates, so that its action was less rapid and the doctor had time to save him. As a matter of fact it turned out afterwards that he had not had a fatal dose. By about eight o'clock that night he was conscious; the next day he was practically convalescent.

As for the unfortunate Mrs. Beresford, the doctor had arrived too late to save her, and she passed away very rapidly in a deep coma.

The police had taken the matter in hand as soon as Mrs. Beresford's death was reported to them and the fact of poison established, and it was only a very short time before things had become narrowed down to the chocolates as the active agent.

Sir William was interrogated, the letter and wrapper were recovered from the waste-paper basket, and, even before the sick man was out of danger, a detective inspector was asking for an interview with the managing director of Mason & Sons. Scotland Yard moves quickly.

It was the police theory at this stage, based on what Sir William and the two doctors had been able to tell them, that by an act of criminal carelessness on the part of one of Mason's employees, an excessive amount of oil of bitter almonds had been included in the filling mixture of the chocolates, for that was what the doctors had decided must be the poisoning ingredient. However, the managing director quashed this idea at once: oil of bitter almonds, he asserted, was never used by Mason's.

He had more interesting news still. Having read with undisguised astonishment the covering letter, he at once declared that it was a forgery. No such letter, no such samples had been sent out by the firm at all; a new variety of liqueur-chocolates had never even been mooted. The fatal chocolates were their ordinary brand.

Unwrapping and examining one more closely, he called the inspector's attention to a mark on the underside, which he suggested was the remains of a small hole drilled in the case, through which the liquid could have been extracted and the fatal filling inserted, the hole afterwards being stopped up with softened chocolate, a perfectly simple operation.

He examined it under a magnifying-glass and the inspector agreed. It was now clear to him that somebody had been trying deliberately to murder Sir William Anstruther.

Scotland Yard doubled its activities. The chocolates were sent for analysis, Sir William was interviewed again, and so was the now conscious Beresford. From the latter the doctor insisted that the news of his wife's death must be kept till the next day, as in his weakened condition the shock might be fatal, so that nothing very helpful was obtained from him.

Nor could Sir William throw any light on the mystery or produce a single person who might have any grounds for trying to kill him. He was living apart from his wife, who was the principal beneficiary in his will, but she was in the South of France, as the French police subsequently confirmed. His estate in Worcestershire, heavily mortgaged, was entailed and went to a nephew; but as the rent he got for it barely covered the interest on the mortgage, and the nephew was considerably better off than Sir William himself, there was no motive there. The police were at a dead end.

The analysis brought one or two interesting facts to light. Not oil of bitter almonds but nitrobenzine, a kindred substance, chiefly used in the manufacture of aniline dyes, was the somewhat surprising poison employed. Each chocolate in the upper layer contained exactly six minims of it, in a mixture of kirsch and maraschino. The chocolates in the other layers were harmless.

As to the other clues, they seemed equally useless. The sheet of Mason's notepaper was identified by Merton's, the printers, as of their work, but there was nothing to show how it had got into the murderer's possession. All that could be said was that, the edges being distinctly yellowed, it must be an old piece. The machine on which the letter had been typed, of course, could not be traced. From the wrapper, a piece of ordinary brown paper with Sir William's address hand-printed on it in large capitals, there was nothing to be learnt at all beyond that the parcel had been posted at the office in Southampton Street between the hours of 8.30 and 9.30 on the previous evening.

Only one thing was quite clear. Whoever had coveted Sir William's life had no intention of paying for it with his or her own.

"AND NOW YOU know as much as we do, Mr. Sheringham," concluded Chief Inspector Moresby, "and if you can say who sent those chocolates to Sir William, you'll know a good deal more."

Roger nodded thoughtfully.

"It's a brute of a case. I met a man only yesterday who was at school with Beresford. He didn't know him well because Beresford was on the modern side and my friend was a classical bird, but they were in the same house. He says Beresford's absolutely knocked over by his wife's death. I wish you could find out who sent those chocolates, Moresby."

"So do I, Mr. Sheringham," said Moresby gloomily.

"It might have been any one in the whole world," Roger mused. "What about feminine jealousy, for instance? Sir William's private life doesn't seem to be immaculate. I dare say there's a good deal of off with the old light-o'-love and on with the new."

"Why, that's just what I've been looking into, Mr. Sheringham, sir," retorted Chief Inspector Moresby reproachfully. "That was the first thing that came to me. Because if anything does stand out about this business it is that it's a woman's crime. Nobody but a woman would send poisoned chocolates to a man. Another man would send a poisoned sample of whisky, or something like that."

"That's a very sound point, Moresby," Roger meditated. "Very sound indeed. And Sir William couldn't help you?"

"Couldn't," said Moresby, not without a trace of resentment, "or wouldn't. I was inclined to believe at first that he might have his suspicions and was shielding some woman. But I don't think so now."

"Humph!" Roger did not seem quite so sure. "It's reminiscent, this case, isn't it? Didn't some lunatic once send poisoned chocolates to the Commissioner of Police himself? A good crime always gets imitated, as you know."

Moresby brightened.

"It's funny you should say that, Mr. Sheringham, because that's the very conclusion I've come to. I've tested every other theory, and so far as I know there's not a soul with an interest in Sir William's death, whether from motives of gain, revenge, or what you like, whom I haven't had to rule quite out of it. In fact, I've pretty well made up my mind that the person who sent these chocolates was some irresponsible lunatic of a woman, a social or religious fanatic who's probably never even seen him. And if that's the case," Moresby sighed, "a fat chance I have of ever laying hands on her."

"Unless Chance steps in, as it so often does," said Roger brightly, "and helps you. A tremendous lot of cases get solved by a stroke of sheer luck, don't they? *Chance the Avenger.* It would make an excellent film-title. But there's a lot of truth in it. If I were superstitious, which I'm not, I should say it wasn't chance at all, but Providence avenging the victim."

"Well, Mr. Sheringham," said Moresby, who was not superstitious either, "to tell the truth, I don't mind what it is, so long as it lets me get my hands on the right person."

If Moresby had paid his visit to Roger Sheringham with any hope of tapping that gentleman's brains, he went away disappointed.

To tell the truth, Roger was inclined to agree with the chief inspector's conclusion, that the attempt on the life of Sir William Anstruther and the actual murder of the unfortunate Mrs. Beresford must be the work of some unknown criminal lunatic. For this reason, although he thought about it a good deal during the next few days, he made no attempt to take the case in hand. It was the sort of affair necessitating endless inquiries that a private person would have neither the time nor the authority to carry out, which can be handled only by the official police. Roger's interest in it was purely academic.

It was hazard, a chance encounter nearly a week later, which translated this interest from the academic into the personal.

Roger was in Bond Street, about to go through the distressing ordeal of buying a new hat. Along the pavement he suddenly saw bearing down on him Mrs. Verreker-le-Flemming. Mrs. Verreker-le-Flemming was small, exquisite, rich, and a widow, and she sat at Roger's feet whenever he gave her the opportunity. But she talked. She talked, in fact, and talked and talked. And Roger, who rather liked talking himself, could not bear it. He tried to dart across the road, but there was no opening in the traffic stream. He was cornered.

89

Mrs. Verreker-le-Flemming fastened on him gladly.

"Oh, Mr. Sheringham! *Just* the person I wanted to see. Mr. Sheringham, *do* tell me. In confidence. *Are* you taking up this dreadful business of poor Joan Beresford's death?"

Roger, the frozen and imbecile grin of civilized intercourse on his face, tried to get a word in; without result.

"I was horrified when I heard of it—simply horrified. You see, Joan and I were such very close friends. Quite intimate. And the awful thing, the truly *terrible* thing is that Joan brought the whole business on herself. Isn't that *appalling*?"

Roger no longer wanted to escape.

"What did you say?" he managed to insert incredulously.

"I suppose it's what they call tragic irony," Mrs. Verreker-le-Flemming chattered on. "Certainly it was tragic enough, and I've never heard anything so terribly ironical. You know about that bet she made with her husband, of course, so that he had to get her a box of chocolates, and if he hadn't Sir William would never have given him the poisoned ones and he'd have eaten them and died himself and good riddance? Well, Mr. Sheringham——" Mrs. Verreker-le-Flemming lowered her voice to a conspirator's whisper and glanced about her in the approved manner. "I've never told anybody else this, but I'm telling you because I know you'll appreciate it. *Joan wasn't playing fair.*"

"How do you mean?" Roger asked, bewildered.

Mrs. Verreker-le-Flemming was artlessly pleased with her sensation.

"Why, she'd seen the play before. We went together, the very first week it was on. She *knew* who the villain was all the time."

"By Jove!" Roger was as impressed as Mrs. Verreker-le-Flemming could have wished. "Chance the Avenger! We're none of us immune from it."

"Poetic justice, you mean?" twittered Mrs. Verreker-le-Flemming, to whom these remarks had been somewhat obscure. "Yes, but Joan Beresford of all people! That's the extraordinary thing. I should never have thought Joan *would* do a thing like that. She was such a *nice* girl. A little close with money, of course, considering how well off they are, but that isn't anything. Of course it was only fun, and pulling her husband's leg, but I always used to think Joan was such a *serious* girl, Mr. Sheringham. I mean, ordinary people don't talk about honour and truth, and playing the game, and all those things one takes for granted. But Joan did. She was always saying that this wasn't honourable, or that wouldn't be playing the game. Well, she paid herself for not playing the game, poor girl, didn't she? Still, it all goes to show the truth of the old saying, doesn't it?"

"What old saying?" said Roger, hypnotized by this flow.

"Why, that still waters run deep. Joan must have been deep, I'm afraid." Mrs. Verreker-le-Flemming sighed. It was evidently a social error to be deep. "I mean, she certainly took me in. She can't have been quite so honourable and truthful as she was always pretending, can she? And I can't help wondering whether a girl who'd deceived her husband in a little thing like that might not—oh, well, I don't want to say anything against poor Joan now she's dead, poor darling, but she can't have been *quite* such a plaster saint after all, can she? I mean," said Mrs. Verreker-le-Flemming, in hasty extenuation of these suggestions, "I do think psychology is so very interesting, don't you, Mr. Sheringham?"

"Sometimes, very," Roger agreed gravely. "But you mentioned Sir William Anstruther just now. Do you know him, too?"

"I used to," Mrs. Verreker-le-Flemming replied, without particular interest. "Horrible man! Always running after some woman or other. And when he's tired of her, just drops her—biff!—like that. At least," added Mrs. Verreker-le-Flemming somewhat hastily, "so I've heard."

"And what happens if she refuses to be dropped?"

"Oh dear, I'm sure I don't know. I suppose you've heard the latest?" Mrs. Verreker-le-Flemming hurried on, perhaps a trifle more pink than the delicate aids to nature on her cheeks would have warranted.

"He's taken up with that Bryce woman now. You know, the wife of the oil man, or petrol, or whatever he made his money in. It began about three weeks ago. You'd have thought that dreadful business of being responsible, in a way, for poor Joan Beresford's death would have sobered him up a little, wouldn't you? But not a bit of it; he——"

Roger was following another line of thought.

"What a pity you weren't at the Imperial with the Beresfords that evening. She'd never have made that bet if you had been." Roger looked extremely innocent. "You weren't, I suppose?"

"I?" queried Mrs. Verreker-le-Flemming in surprise, "Good gracious, no. I was at the new revue at the Pavilion. Lady Gavelstroke had a box and asked me to join her party."

"Oh, yes. Good show, isn't it? I thought that sketch *The Sempiternal Triangle* very clever. Didn't you?"

"*The Sempiternal Triangle?*" wavered Mrs. Verreker-le-Flemming.

"Yes, in the first half."

"Oh! Then I didn't see it. I got there disgracefully late, I'm afraid. But then," said Mrs. Verreker-le-Flemming with pathos, "I always do seem to be late for simply everything."

Roger kept the rest of the conversation resolutely upon theatres. But before he left her he had ascertained that she had photographs of both Mrs. Beresford and Sir William Anstruther and had obtained permission to borrow them some time. As soon as she was out of view he hailed a taxi and gave Mrs. Verreker-le-Flemming's address. He thought it better to take advantage of her permission at a time when he would not have to pay for it a second time over.

The parlour-maid seemed to think there was nothing odd in his mission, and took him up to the drawing-room at once. A corner of the room was devoted to the silver-framed photographs of Mrs. Verreker-le-Flemming's friends, and there were many of them. Roger examined them with interest, and finally took away with him not two photographs but six, those of Sir William, Mrs. Beresford, Beresford, two strange males who appeared to belong to the Sir William period, and, lastly a likeness of Mrs. Verreker-le-Flemming herself. Roger liked confusing his trail.

For the rest of the day he was very busy.

His activities would have no doubt seemed to Mrs. Verreker-le-Flemming not merely baffling but pointless. He paid a visit to a public library, for instance, and consulted a work of reference, after which he took a taxi and drove to the offices of the Anglo-Eastern Perfumery Company, where he inquired for a certain Mr. Joseph Lea Hardwick and seemed much put out on hearing that no such gentleman was known to the firm and was certainly not employed in any of their branches. Many questions had to be put about the firm and its branches before he consented to abandon the quest.

After that he drove to Messrs. Weall & Wilson, the well-known institution which protects the trade interests of individuals and advises its subscribers regarding investments. Here he entered his name as a subscriber, and explaining that he had a large sum of money to invest, filled in one of the special inquiry-forms which are headed Strictly Confidential.

Then he went to the Rainbow Club, in Piccadilly.

Introducing himself to the porter without a blush as connected with Scotland Yard, he asked the man a number of questions, more or less trivial, concerning the tragedy. "Sir William, I understand," he said finally, as if by the way, "did not dine here the evening before?"

There it appeared that Roger was wrong. Sir William had dined in the club, as he did about three times a week.

"But I quite understood he wasn't here that evening?" Roger said plaintively.

The porter was emphatic. He remembered quite well. So did a waiter, whom the porter summoned to corroborate him. Sir William had dined, rather late, and had not left the dining-room till about nine o'clock. He spent the evening there, too, the waiter knew, or at least some of it, for he himself had taken him a whisky-and-soda in the lounge not less than half an hour later.

Roger retired.

He retired to Merton's in a taxi.

It seemed that he wanted some new notepaper printed, of a very special kind, and to the young woman behind the counter he specified at great length and in wearisome detail exactly what he did want. The young woman handed him the books of specimen pieces and asked him to see if there was any style there which would suit him. Roger glanced through them, remarking garrulously to the young woman that he had been recommended to Merton's by a very dear friend, whose photograph he happened to have on him at that moment. Wasn't that a curious coincidence? The young woman agreed that it was.

"About a fortnight ago, I think, my friend was in here last," said Roger, producing the photograph. "Recognize this?"

The young woman took the photograph, without apparent interest.

"Oh, yes. I remember. About some notepaper, too, wasn't it? So that's your friend. Well, it's a small world. Now this is a line we're selling a good deal of just now."

Roger went back to his rooms to dine. Afterwards, feeling restless, he wandered out of the Albany and turned up Piccadilly. He wandered round the Circus, thinking hard, and paused for a moment out of habit to inspect the photographs of the new revue hung outside the Pavilion. The next thing he realized was that he had got as far as Jermyn Street and was standing outside the Imperial Theatre. Glancing at the advertisements of *The Creaking Skull*, he saw that it began at half-past eight. Glancing at his watch, he saw that the time was twenty-nine minutes past that hour. He had an evening to get through somehow. He went inside.

The next morning, very early for Roger, he called on Moresby at Scotland Yard.

"Moresby," he said without preamble, "I want you to do something for me. Can you find me a taximan who took a fare from Piccadilly Circus or its neighbourhood at about ten past nine on the evening before the Beresford crime, to the Strand somewhere near the bottom of Southampton Street, and another who took a fare back between those points. I'm not sure about the first. Or one taxi might have been used for the double journey, but I doubt that. Anyhow, try to find out for me, will you?"

"What are you up to now, Mr. Sheringham?" Moresby asked suspiciously.

"Breaking down an interesting alibi," replied Roger serenely. "By the way, I know who sent those chocolates to Sir William. I'm just building up a nice structure of evidence for you. Ring up my rooms when you've got those taximen."

He strolled out, leaving Moresby positively gaping after him.

The rest of the day he spent apparently trying to buy a second-hand typewriter. He was very particular that it should be a Hamilton No. 4. When the shop-people tried to induce him to consider other makes he refused to look at them, saying that he had had the Hamilton No. 4 so strongly recommended to him by a friend, who had bought one about three weeks ago. Perhaps it was at this very shop? No? They hadn't sold a Hamilton No. 4 for the last three months? How odd!

But at one shop they had sold a Hamilton No. 4 within the last month, and that was odder still.

At half-past four Roger got back to his rooms to await the telephone message from Moresby. At half-past five it came.

"There are fourteen taxi-drivers here, littering up my office," said Moresby offensively. "What do you want me to do with 'em?"

"Keep them till I come, Chief Inspector," returned Roger with dignity.

The interview with the fourteen was brief enough, however. To each man in turn Roger showed a photograph, holding it so that Moresby could not see it, and asked if he could recognize his fare. The ninth man did so, without hesitation.

At a nod from Roger, Moresby dismissed them, then sat at his table and tried to look official. Roger seated himself on the table, looking most unofficial, and swung his legs. As he did so, a photograph fell unnoticed out of his pocket and fluttered, face downwards, under the table. Moresby eyed it but did not pick it up.

"And now, Mr. Sheringham, sir," he said, "perhaps you'll tell me what you've been doing?"

"Certainly, Moresby," said Roger blandly. "Your work for you. I really have solved the thing, you know. Here's your evidence." He took from his note-case an old letter and handed it to the Chief Inspector. "Was that typed on the same machine as the forged letter from Mason's, or was it not?"

Moresby studied it for a moment, then drew the forged letter from a drawer of his table and compared the two minutely.

"Mr. Sheringham," he said soberly, "where did you get hold of this?"

"In a second-hand typewriter shop in St. Martin's Lane. The machine was sold to an unknown customer about a month ago. They identified the customer from that same photograph. As it happened, this machine had been used for a time in the office after it was repaired, to see that it was O.K., and I easily got hold of that specimen of its work."

"And where is the machine now?"

"Oh, at the bottom of the Thames, I expect," Roger smiled. "I tell you, this criminal takes no unnecessary chances. But that doesn't matter. There's your evidence."

"Humph! It's all right so far as it goes," conceded Moresby. "But what about Mason's paper?"

"That," said Roger calmly, "was extracted from Merton's book of sample notepapers, as I'd guessed from the very yellowed edges might be the case. I can prove contact of the criminal with the book, and there is a page which will certainly turn out to have been filled by that piece of paper."

"That's fine," Moresby said more heartily.

"As for that taximan, the criminal had an alibi. You've heard it broken down. Between ten past nine and twenty-five past, in fact during the time when the parcel must have been posted, the murderer took a hurried journey to that neighbourhood, going probably by bus or underground, but returning as I expected, by taxi, because time would be getting short."

"And the murderer, Mr. Sheringham?"

"The person whose photograph is in my pocket," Roger said unkindly. "By the way, do you remember what I was saying the other day about Chance the Avenger, my excellent film-title? Well, it's worked again. By a chance meeting in Bond Street with a silly woman I was put, by the merest accident, in possession of a piece of information which showed me then and there who had sent those chocolates addressed to Sir William. There were other possibilities, of course, and I tested them, but then and there on the pavement I saw the whole thing, from first to last."

"Who was the murderer, then, Mr. Sheringham?" repeated Moresby.

"It was so beautifully planned," Roger went on dreamily. "We never grasped for one moment that we were making the fundamental mistake that the murderer all along intended us to make."

"And what was that," asked Moresby.

"Why, that the plan had miscarried. That the wrong person had been killed. That was just the beauty of it. The plan had *not* miscarried. It had been brilliantly successful. The wrong person was *not* killed. Very much the right person was."

Moresby gaped.

"Why, how on earth do you make that out, sir?"

"Mrs. Beresford was the objective all the time. That's why the plot was so ingenious. Everything was anticipated. It was perfectly natural that Sir William should hand the chocolates over to Beresford. It was foreseen that we should look for the criminal among Sir William's associates and not the dead woman's. It was probably even foreseen that the crime would be considered the work of a woman!"

Moresby, unable to wait any longer, snatched up the photograph.

"Good heavens! But Mr. Sheringham, you don't mean to tell me that . . . Sir William himself!"

"He wanted to get rid of Mrs. Beresford," Roger continued. "He had liked her well enough at the beginning, no doubt, though it was her money he was after all the time.

"But the real trouble was that she was too close with her money. He wanted it, or some of it, pretty badly; and she wouldn't part. There's no doubt about the motive. I made a list of the firms he's interested in and got a report on them. They're all rocky, every one. He'd got through all his own money, and he had to get more.

"As for the nitrobenzine which puzzled us so much, that was simple enough. I looked it up and found that beside the uses you told me, it's used largely in perfumery. And he's got a perfumery business. The Anglo-Eastern Perfumery Company. That's how he'd know about it being poisonous, of course. But I shouldn't think he got his supply from there. He'd be cleverer than that. He probably made the stuff himself. And schoolboys know how to treat benzol with nitric acid to get nitrobenzine."

"But," stammered Moresby, "but Sir William . . . He was at Eton."

"Sir William?" said Roger sharply. "Who's talking about Sir William? I told you the photograph of the murderer was in my pocket." He whipped out the photograph in question and confronted the astounded chief inspector with it. "Beresford, man! Beresford's the murderer of his own wife.

"Beresford, who still had hankerings after a gay life," he went on more mildly, "didn't want his wife but did want her money. He contrived this plot, providing as he thought against every contingency that could possibly arise. He established a mild alibi, if suspicion ever should arise, by taking his wife to the Imperial, and slipped out of the theatre at the first interval. (I sat through the first act of the dreadful thing myself last night to see when the interval came.) Then he hurried down to the Strand, posted his parcel, and took a taxi back. He had ten minutes, but nobody would notice if he got back to the box a minute late.

"And the rest simply followed. He knew Sir William came to the club every morning at ten-thirty, as regularly as clockwork; he knew that for a psychological certainty he could get the chocolates handed over to him if he hinted for them; he knew that the police would go chasing after all sorts of false trails starting from Sir William. And as for the wrapper and the forged letter he carefully didn't destroy them because they were calculated not only to divert suspicion but actually to point away from him to some anonymous lunatic."

"Well, it's very smart of you, Mr. Sheringham," Moresby said, with a little sigh, but quite ungrudgingly. "Very smart indeed. What was it the lady told you that showed you the whole thing in a flash?"

"Why, it wasn't so much what she actually told me as what I heard between her words, so to speak. What she told me was that Mrs. Beresford knew the answer to that bet; what I deduced was that, being the sort of person she was, it was quite incredible that she should have made a bet to which she knew the answer. *Ergo*, she didn't. *Ergo*, there never was such a bet. *Ergo*, Beresford was lying. *Ergo*, Beresford wanted to get hold of those chocolates for some reason other than he stated. After all, we only had Beresford's word for the bet, hadn't we?

"Of course he wouldn't have left her that afternoon till he'd seen her take, or somehow made her take, at least six of the chocolates, more than a lethal dose. That's why the stuff was in the meticulous six-minim doses. And so that he could take a couple himself, of course. A clever stroke, that."

Moresby rose to his feet.

"Well, Mr. Sheringham, I'm much obliged to you sir. And now I shall have to get busy myself." He scratched his head. "Chance the Avenger, eh? Well, I can tell one pretty big thing Beresford left to Chance the Avenger, Mr. Sheringham. Suppose Sir William hadn't handed over the chocolates after all? Supposing he'd kept 'em, to give to one of his own ladies?"

Roger positively snorted. He felt a personal pride in Beresford by this time.

"Really, Moresby! It wouldn't have had any serious results if Sir William had. Do give my man credit for being what he is. You don't imagine he sent the poisoned ones to Sir William, do you? Of course not! He'd send harmless ones, and exchange them for the others on his way home. Dash it all, he wouldn't go right out of his way to present opportunities to Chance.

"If," added Roger, "Chance really is the right word."

ALGERNON BLACKWOOD

1869–1951

In spite of a chequered career in a wide range of
worldly activities—farmer, prospector, hotel keeper, artist's model,
manager of a dried-milk business—his preoccupation with life's
spiritual aspects remained untarnished. His writing has a rare
beauty as fantastic as the incidents he describes.

Running Wolf

THE MAN WHO enjoys an adventure outside the
general experience of the race, and imparts it to
others, must not be surprised if he is taken for either
a liar or a fool, as Malcolm Hyde, hotel clerk on a
holiday, discovered in due course. Nor is 'enjoy'
the right word to use in describing his emotions;
the word he chose was probably 'survive'.

When he first set eyes on Medicine Lake he was
struck by its still, sparkling beauty, lying there in
the vast Canadian backwoods; next, by its extreme
loneliness; and, lastly—a good deal later, this—by
its combination of beauty, loneliness, and singular
atmosphere, due to the fact that it was the scene of
his adventure.

"It's fairly stiff with big fish," said Morton of
the Montreal Sporting Club. "Spend your holiday
there—up Mattawa way, some fifteen miles west of Stony Creek.
You'll have it all to yourself except for an old Indian who's got a shack
there. Camp on the east side—if you'll take a tip from me." He then
talked for half an hour about the wonderful sport; yet he was not
otherwise very communicative, and did not suffer questions gladly,
Hyde noticed. Nor had he stayed there very long himself. If it was such
a paradise as Morton, its discoverer and the most experienced rod in the
province, claimed, why had he himself spent only three days there?

"Ran short of grub," was the explanation offered; but to another friend he had mentioned briefly, "flies," and to a third, so Hyde learned later, he gave the excuse that his half-breed "took sick," necessitating a quick return to civilisation.

Hyde, however, cared little for the explanations; his interest in these came later. 'Stiff with fish' was the phrase he liked. He took the Canadian Pacific train to Mattawa, laid in his outfit at Stony Creek, and set off thence for the fifteen-mile canoe trip without a care in the world.

Travelling light, the portages did not trouble him: the water was swift and easy, the rapids negotiable; everything came his way, as the saying is. Occasionally he saw fish making for the deeper pools, and was sorely tempted to stop; but he resisted. He pushed on between the immense world of forests that stretched for hundreds of miles, known to deer, bear, moose, and wolf, but strange to any echo of human tread, a deserted and primeval wilderness. The autumn day was calm, the water sang and sparkled, the blue sky hung cloudless over all, ablaze with light. Toward evening he passed an old beaver-dam, rounded a little point, and had his first sight of Medicine Lake. He lifted his dripping paddle; the canoe shot with silent glide into calm water. He gave an exclamation of delight, for the loveliness caught his breath away. Though primarily a sportsman, he was not insensible to beauty. The lake formed a crescent, perhaps four miles long, its width between a mile and half a mile. The slanting gold of sunset flooded it. No wind stirred its crystal surface. Here it had lain since the Redskin's god first made it; here it would lie until he dried it up again. Towering spruce and hemlock trooped to its very edge, majestic cedars leaned down as if to drink, crimson sumachs shone in fiery patches, and maples gleamed orange and red beyond belief. The air was like wine, with the silence of a dream.

It was here the Red men formerly 'made medicine', with all the wild ritual and tribal ceremony of an ancient day. But it was of Morton, rather than of Indians, that Hyde thought. If this lonely, hidden paradise was really stiff with big fish, he owed a lot to Morton for the information. Peace invaded him, but the excitement of the hunter lay below.

He looked about him with quick, practised eye for a camping-place before the sun sank below the forests and the half-lights came. The Indian's shack, lying in full sunshine on the eastern shore, he found at once; but the trees lay too thick about it for comfort, nor did he wish to be so close to its inhabitant. Upon the opposite side, however, an ideal clearing offered. This lay already in shadow, the huge forest darkening it toward evening; but the open space attracted. He paddled over quickly and examined it. The ground was hard and dry, he found, and a little brook ran tinkling down one side of it into the lake. This outfall, too, would be a good fishing spot. Also it was sheltered. A few low willows marked the mouth.

An experienced camper soon makes up his mind. It was a perfect site, and some charred logs, with traces of former fires, proved that he was not the first to think so. Hyde was delighted. Then, suddenly, disappointment came to tinge his pleasure. His kit was landed, and preparations for putting up the tent were begun, when he recalled a detail that excitement had so far kept in the background of his mind— Morton's advice. But not Morton's only, for the storekeeper at Stony Creek had reinforced it. The big fellow with straggling moustache and stooping shoulders, dressed in shirt and trousers, had handed him out a final sentence with the bacon, flour, condensed milk, and sugar. He had repeated Morton's half-forgotten words:

"Put yer tent on the east shore. I should," he had said at parting.

He remembered Morton, too, apparently. "A shortish fellow, brown as an Indian and fairly smelling of the woods. Travelling with Jake, the half-breed." That assuredly was Morton. "Didn't stay long, now, did he?" he added in a reflective tone.

"Going Windy Lake way, are yer? Or Ten Mile Water, maybe?" he had first inquired of Hyde.

"Medicine Lake."

"Is that so?" the man said, as though he doubted it for some obscure reason. He pulled at his ragged moustache a moment. "Is that so, now?" he repeated. And the final words followed him downstream after a considerable pause—the advice about the best shore on which to put his tent. All this now suddenly flashed back upon Hyde's mind with a tinge of disappointment and annoyance, for when two experienced men agreed, their opinion was not to be lightly disregarded. He wished he had asked the storekeeper for more details. He looked about him, he reflected, he hesitated. His ideal camping-ground lay certainly on the forbidden shore. What in the world, he wondered, could be the objection to it?

But the light was fading; he must decide quickly one way or the other. After staring at his unpacked dunnage and the tent, already half erected, he made up his mind with a muttered expression that consigned both Morton and the storekeeper to less pleasant places. "They must have had *some* reason," he growled to himself; "fellows like that usually know what they're talking about. I guess I'd better shift over to the other side —for to-night, at any rate."

He glanced across the water before actually reloading. No smoke rose from the Indian's shack. He had seen no sign of a canoe. The man, he decided, was away. Reluctantly, then, he left the good camping-ground and paddled across the lake, and half an hour later his tent was up, firewood collected, and two small trout were already caught for supper. But the bigger fish, he knew, lay waiting for him on the other side by the little outfall, and he fell asleep at length on his bed of balsam boughs, annoyed and disappointed, yet wondering how a mere sentence could have persuaded him so easily against his own better judgment. He slept like the dead; the sun was well up before he stirred.

But his morning mood was a very different one. The brilliant light, the peace, the intoxicating air, all this was too exhilarating for the mind to harbour foolish fancies, and he marvelled that he could have been so weak the night before. No hesitation lay in him anywhere. He struck camp immediately after breakfast, paddled back across the strip of shining water, and quickly settled in upon the forbidden shore, as he now called it, with a contemptuous grin. And the more he saw of the spot, the better he liked it. There was plenty of wood, running water to drink, an open space about the tent, and there were no flies. The fishing, moreover, was magnificent. Morton's description was fully justified, and 'stiff with big fish' for once was not an exaggeration.

The useless hours of the early afternoon he passed dozing in the sun, or wandering through the underbrush beyond the camp. He found no sign of anything unusual. He bathed in a cool, deep pool; he revelled in the lonely little paradise. Lonely it certainly was, but the loneliness was part of its charm; the stillness, the peace, the isolation of this beautiful backwoods lake delighted him. The silence was divine. He was entirely satisfied.

After a brew of tea, he strolled toward evening along the shore, looking for the first sign of a rising fish. A faint ripple on the water, with the lengthening shadows, made good conditions. *Plop* followed *plop*, as the big fellows rose, snatched at their food, and vanished into the depths. He hurried back. Ten minutes later he had taken his rods and was gliding cautiously in the canoe through the quiet water.

So good was the sport, indeed, and so quickly did the big trout pile up in the bottom of the canoe that, despite the growing lateness, he found it hard to tear himself away. "One more," he said, "and then I really will go." He landed that 'one more', and was in the act of taking it off the hook, when the deep silence of the evening was curiously disturbed. He became abruptly aware that someone watched him. A pair of eyes, it seemed, were fixed upon him from some point in the surrounding shadows.

Thus, at least, he interpreted the odd disturbance in his happy mood; for thus he felt it. The feeling stole over him without the slightest warning. He was not alone. The slippery big trout dropped from his fingers. He sat motionless, and stared about him.

Nothing stirred; the ripple on the lake had died away; there was no wind; the forest lay a single purple mass of shadow; the yellow sky, fast fading, threw reflections that troubled the eye and made distances

101

uncertain. But there was no sound, no movement; he saw no figure anywhere. Yet he knew that someone watched him, and a wave of quite unreasoning terror gripped him. The nose of the canoe was against the bank. In a moment, and instinctively, he shoved it off and paddled into deeper water. The watcher, it came to him also instinctively, was quite close to him upon that bank. But where? And who? Was it the Indian?

Here, in deeper water, and some twenty yards from the shore, he paused and strained both sight and hearing to find some possible clue. He felt half ashamed, now that the first strange feeling passed a little. But the certainty remained. Absurd as it was, he felt positive that someone watched him with concentrated and intent regard. Every fibre in his being told him so; and though he could discover no figure, no new outline on the shore, he could even have sworn in which clump of willow bushes the hidden person crouched and stared. His attention seemed drawn to that particular clump.

The water dripped slowly from his paddle, now lying across the thwarts. There was no other sound. The canvas of his tent gleamed dimly. A star or two were out. He waited. Nothing happened.

Then, as suddenly as it had come, the feeling passed, and he knew that the person who had been watching him intently had gone. It was as if a current had been turned off; the normal world flowed back; the landscape emptied as if someone had left a room. The disagreeable feeling left him at the same time, so that he instantly turned the canoe in to the shore again, landed, and, paddle in hand, went over to examine the clump of willows he had singled out as the place of concealment. There was no one there, of course, nor any trace of recent human occupancy. No leaves, no branches stirred, nor was a single twig displaced; his keen and practised sight detected no sign of tracks upon the ground. Yet for all that, he felt positive that a little time ago someone had crouched among these very leaves and watched him. He remained absolutely convinced of it. The watcher, whether Indian, hunter, stray lumberman, or wandering half-breed, had now withdrawn, a search was useless, and dusk was falling. He returned to his little camp, more disturbed perhaps than he cared to acknowledge. He cooked his supper, hung up his catch on a string, so that no prowling animal could get at it during the night, and prepared to make himself comfortable until bedtime. Unconsciously, he built a bigger fire than usual, and found himself peering over his pipe into the deep shadows beyond the firelight, straining his ears to catch the slightest sound. He remained generally on the alert in a way that was new to him.

A man under such conditions and in such a place need not know discomfort until the sense of loneliness strikes him as too vivid a reality. Loneliness in a backwoods camp brings charm; pleasure, and a happy sense of calm until, and unless, it comes too near. It should remain an ingredient only among other conditions; it should not be directly, vividly noticed. Once it has crept within short range, however, it may easily cross the narrow line between comfort and discomfort, and darkness is an undesirable time for the transition. A curious dread may easily follow—the dread lest the loneliness suddenly be disturbed, and the solitary human feel himself open to attack.

For Hyde, now, this transition had been already accomplished; the too intimate sense of his loneliness had shifted abruptly into the worse condition of no longer being quite alone. It was an awkward moment, and the hotel clerk realized his position exactly. He did not quite like it. He sat there, with his back to the blazing logs, a very visible object in the light, while all about him the darkness of the forest lay like an impenetrable wall. He could not see a foot beyond the small circle of his campfire; the silence about him was like the silence of the dead. No leaf rustled, no wave lapped; he himself sat motionless as a log.

Then again he became suddenly aware that the person who watched him had returned, and that same intent and concentrated gaze as before was fixed upon him where he lay. There was no warning; he heard no stealthy tread or snapping of dry twigs, yet the owner of those steady eyes was very close to him, probably not a dozen feet away. This sense of proximity was overwhelming.

It is unquestionable that a shiver ran down his spine. This time, moreover, he felt positive that the man crouched just beyond the firelight, the distance he himself could see being nicely calculated, and straight in front of him. For some minutes he sat without stirring a single muscle, yet with each muscle ready and alert, straining his eyes in vain to pierce the darkness, but only succeeding in dazzling his sight with the reflected light. Then, as he shifted his position slowly, cautiously, to obtain another angle of vision, his heart gave two big thumps against his ribs and the hair seemed to rise on his scalp with the sense of cold that shot horribly up his spine. In the darkness facing him he saw two small and greenish circles that were certainly a pair of eyes, yet not the eyes of Indian, hunter, or of any human being. It was a pair of animal eyes that stared so fixedly at him out of the night. And this certainty had an immediate and natural effect upon him.

For, at the menace of those eyes, the fears of millions of long dead hunters since the dawn of time woke in him. Hotel clerk though he was, heredity surged through him in an automatic wave of instinct. His hand groped for a weapon. His fingers fell on the iron head of his small camp axe, and at once he was himself again. Confidence returned; the vague, superstitious dread was gone. This was a bear or wolf that smelt his catch and came to steal it. With beings of that sort he knew instinctively

how to deal, yet admitting, by this very instinct, that his original dread
had been of quite another kind.

"I'll damned quick find out what it is," he exclaimed aloud, and
snatching a burning brand from the fire, he hurled it with good aim
straight at the eyes of the beast before him.

The bit of pitch-pine fell in a shower of sparks that lit the dry grass
this side of the animal, flared up a moment, then died quickly down
again. But in that instant of bright illumination he saw clearly what his
unwelcome visitor was. A big timber wolf sat on its hind quarters,
staring steadily at him through the firelight. He saw its legs and shoulders,
he saw its hair, he saw also the big hemlock trunks lit up behind it, and
the willow scrub on each side. It formed a vivid, clear-cut picture shown
in clear detail by the momentary blaze. To his amazement, however, the
wolf did not turn and bolt away from the burning log, but withdrew a
few yards only, and sat there again on its haunches, staring, staring as
before. Heavens, how it stared! He shoo-ed it, but without effect; it did
not budge. He did not waste another good log on it, for his fear was
dissipated now; a timber wolf was a timber wolf, and it might sit there
as long as it pleased, provided it did not try to steal his catch. No alarm
was in him any more. He knew that wolves were harmless in the summer
and autumn, and even when 'packed' in the winter, they would attack
a man only when suffering desperate hunger. So he lay and watched the
beast, threw bits of stick in its direction, even talked to it, wondering
only that it never moved. "You can stay there for ever, if you like," he
remarked to it aloud, "for you cannot get at my fish, and the rest of the
grub I shall take into the tent with me!"

The creature blinked its bright green eyes, but made no move.

Why, then, if his fear was gone, did he think of certain things as he
rolled himself in the Hudson Bay blankets before going to sleep? The
immobility of the animal was strange, its refusal to turn and bolt was still
stranger. Never before had he known a wild creature that was not afraid
of fire. Why did it sit and watch him, as with purpose in its dreadful
eyes? How had he felt its presence earlier and instantly? A timber wolf,
especially a solitary timber wolf, was a timid thing, yet this one feared
neither man nor fire. Now, as he lay there wrapped in his blankets inside
the cosy tent, it sat outside beneath the stars, beside the fading embers,
the wind chilly in its fur, the ground cooling beneath its planted paws,
watching him, steadily watching him, perhaps until the dawn.

It was unusual, it was strange. Having neither imagination nor
tradition, he called upon no store of racial visions. Matter-of-fact, a
hotel clerk on a fishing holiday, he lay there in his blankets, merely
wondering and puzzled. A timber wolf was a timber wolf and nothing
more. Yet this timber wolf—the idea haunted him—was different. In a

word, the deeper part of his original uneasiness remained. He tossed about, he shivered sometimes in his broken sleep; he did not go out to see, but he woke early and unrefreshed.

Again, with the sunshine and the morning wind, however, the incident of the night before was forgotten, almost unreal. His hunting zeal was uppermost. The tea and fish were delicious, his pipe had never tasted so good, the glory of this lonely lake amid primeval forests went to his head a little; he was a hunter before the Lord, and nothing else. He tried the edge of the lake, and in the excitement of playing a big fish, knew suddenly that *it*, the wolf, was there. He paused with the rod, exactly as if struck. He looked about him, he looked in a definite direction. The brilliant sunshine made every smallest detail clear and sharp—boulders of granite, burned stems, crimson sumach, pebbles along the shore in neat, separate detail—without revealing where the watcher hid. Then, his sight wandering farther inshore among the tangled undergrowth, he suddenly picked up the familiar, half-expected outline. The wolf was lying behind a granite boulder, so that only the head, the muzzle, and the eyes were visible. It merged in its background. Had he not known it was a wolf, he could never have separated it from the landscape. The eyes shone in the sunlight.

There it lay. He looked straight at it. Their eyes, in fact, actually met full and square. "Great Scott!" he exclaimed aloud, "why, it's like looking at a human being!" From that moment, unwittingly, he established a singular personal relation with the beast. And what followed confirmed this undesirable impression, for the animal rose instantly and came down in leisurely fashion to the shore, where it stood looking back at him. It stood and stared into his eyes like some great wild dog, so that he was aware of a new and almost incredible sensation—that it courted recognition. "Well! well!" he exclaimed again, relieving his feelings by addressing it aloud, "if this doesn't beat everything I ever saw! What d'you want, anyway?"

He examined it now more carefully. He had never seen a wolf so big before; it was a tremendous beast, a nasty customer to tackle, he reflected, if it ever came to that. It stood there absolutely fearless and full of confidence. In the clear sunlight he took in every detail of it—a huge, shaggy, lean-flanked timber wolf, its wicked eyes staring straight into his own, almost with a kind of purpose in them. He saw its great jaws, its teeth, and its tongue, hung out, dropping saliva a little. And yet the idea of its savagery, its fierceness, was very little in him.

He was amazed and puzzled beyond belief. He wished the Indian would come back. He did not understand this strange behaviour in an animal. Its eyes, the odd expression in them, gave him a queer, unusual, difficult feeling. Had his nerves gone wrong? he almost wondered.

105

The beast stood on the shore and looked at him. He wished for the first time that he had brought a rifle. With a resounding smack he brought his paddle down flat upon the water, using all his strength, till the echoes rang as from a pistol-shot that was audible from one end of the lake to the other. The wolf never stirred. He shouted, but the beast remained unmoved. He blinked his eyes, speaking as to a dog, a domestic animal, a creature accustomed to human ways. It blinked its eyes in return.

At length, increasing his distance from the shore, he continued fishing, and the excitement of the marvellous sport held his attention—his surface attention, at any rate. At times he almost forgot the attendant beast; yet whenever he looked up, he saw it there. And worse; when he slowly paddled home again, he observed it trotting along the shore as though to keep him company. Crossing a little bay, he spurted, hoping to reach the other point before his undesired and undesirable attendant. Instantly the brute broke into that rapid, tireless lope that, except on ice, can run down anything on four legs in the woods. When he reached the distant point, the wolf was waiting for him. He raised his paddle from the water, pausing a moment for reflection; for this very close attention—there were dusk and night yet to come—he certainly did not relish. His camp was near; he had to land; he felt uncomfortable even in the sunshine of broad day, when, to his keen relief, about half a mile from the tent, he saw the creature suddenly stop and sit down in the open. He waited a moment, then paddled on. It did not follow. There was no attempt to move; it merely sat and watched him. After a few hundred yards, he looked back. It was still sitting where he had left it. And the absurd, yet significant, feeling came to him that the beast divined his thought, his anxiety, his dread, and was now showing him, as well as it could, that it entertained no hostile feeling and did not meditate attack.

He turned the canoe toward the shore; he landed; he cooked his supper in the dusk; the animal made no sign. Not far away it certainly lay and watched, but it did not advance. And to Hyde, observant now in a new way, came one sharp, vivid reminder of the strange atmosphere into which his commonplace personality had strayed: he suddenly recalled that his relations with the beast, already established, had progressed distinctly a stage further. This startled him, yet without the accompanying alarm he must certainly have felt twenty-four hours before. He had an understanding with the wolf. He was aware of friendly thoughts toward it. He even went so far as to set out a few big fish on the spot where he had first seen it sitting the previous night. "If he comes," he thought, "he is welcome to them. I've got plenty, anyway." He thought of it now as 'he'.

Yet the wolf made no appearance until he was in the act of entering his tent a good deal later. It was close on ten o'clock, whereas nine was his hour, and late at that, for turning in. He had, therefore, unconsciously been waiting for him. Then, as he was closing the flap, he saw the eyes close to where he had placed the fish. He waited, hiding himself, and expecting to hear sounds of munching jaws; but all was silence. Only the eyes glowed steadily out of the background of pitch darkness. He closed the flap. He had no slightest fear. In ten minutes he was sound asleep.

He could not have slept very long, for when he woke up he could see the shine of a faint red light through the canvas, and the fire had not died down completely. He rose and cautiously peeped out. The air was very cold; he saw his breath. But he also saw the wolf, for it had come in, and was sitting by the dying embers, not two yards away from where he crouched behind the flap. And this time, at these very close quarters, there was something in the attitude of the big wild thing that caught his attention with a vivid thrill of startled surprise and a sudden shock of cold that held him spellbound. He stared, unable to believe his eyes; for the wolf's attitude conveyed to him something familiar that at first he was unable to explain. Its pose reached him in the terms of another thing with which he was entirely at home. What was it? Did his senses betray him? Was he still asleep and dreaming? Then, suddenly, with a start of uncanny recognition, he knew. Its attitude was that of a dog. Having found the clue, his mind then made an awful leap. For it was, after all, no dog in appearance aped, but something nearer to himself, and more familiar still. Good heavens! It sat there with the pose, the attitude, the gesture in repose of something almost human. And then, with a second shock of biting wonder, it came to him like a revelation. The wolf sat beside that camp-fire as a man might sit.

Before he could weigh his extraordinary discovery, before he could examine it in detail or with care, the animal, sitting in this ghastly fashion, seemed to feel his eyes fixed on it. It slowly turned and looked him in the face, and for the first time Hyde felt a full-blooded, super-stitious fear flood through his entire being. He seemed transfixed with that nameless terror that is said to attack human beings who suddenly face the dead, finding themselves bereft of speech and movement. This moment of paralysis certainly occurred. Its passing, however, was as singular as its advent. For almost at once he was aware of something beyond and above this mockery of human attitude and pose, something that ran along unaccustomed nerves and reached his feeling, even perhaps his heart. The revulsion was extraordinary, its result still more extraordinary and unexpected. Yet the fact remains. He was aware of another thing that had the effect of stilling his terror as soon as it was born. He was aware of appeal, silent, half expressed, yet vastly pathetic.

He saw in the savage eyes a beseeching, even a yearning, expression that changed his mood as by magic from dread to natural sympathy. The great grey brute, symbol of cruel ferocity, sat there beside his dying fire and appealed for help. This gulf betwixt animal and human seemed in that instant bridged. It was, of course, incredible. Hyde, sleep still possibly clinging to his inner being with the shades and half shapes of dream yet about his soul acknowledged, how he knew not, the amazing fact. He found himself nodding to the brute in half consent, and instantly, without more ado, the lean grey shape rose like a wraith and trotted off swiftly, but with stealthy tread, into the background of the night.

When Hyde woke in the morning his first impression was that he must have dreamed the entire incident. His practical nature asserted itself. There was a bite in the fresh autumn air; the bright sun allowed no half lights anywhere; he felt brisk in mind and body. Reviewing what had happened, he came to the conclusion that it was utterly vain to speculate; no possible explanation of the animal's behaviour occurred to him; he was dealing with something entirely outside his experience. His fear, however, had completely left him. The odd sense of friendliness remained. The beast had a definite purpose, and he himself was included in that purpose. His sympathy held good.

But with the sympathy there was also an intense curiosity. "If it shows itself again," he told himself, "I'll go up close and find out what it wants." The fish laid out the night before had not been touched.

It must have been a full hour after breakfast when he next saw the brute; it was standing on the edge of the clearing, looking at him in the way now become familiar. Hyde immediately picked up his axe and advanced toward it boldly, keeping his eyes fixed straight upon its own. There was nervousness in him, but kept well under; nothing betrayed it; step by step he drew nearer until some ten yards separated them. The wolf had not stirred a muscle as yet. Its jaws hung open, its eyes observed him intently; it allowed him to approach without a sign of what its mood might be. Then, with these ten yards between them it turned abruptly and moved slowly off, looking back first over one shoulder and then over the other, exactly as a dog might do, to see if he was following.

A singular journey it was they then made together, animal and man. The trees surrounded them at once, for they left the lake behind them, entering the tangled bush beyond. The beast, Hyde noticed, obviously picked the easiest track for him to follow; for obstacles that meant nothing to the four-legged expert, yet were difficult for a man, were carefully avoided with an almost uncanny skill, while yet the general direction was accurately kept. Occasionally there were windfalls to be surmounted; but though the wolf bounded over these with ease, it was always waiting for the man on the other side after he had laboriously climbed over. Deeper and deeper into the heart of the lonely forest they penetrated in this singular fashion, cutting across the arc of the lake's crescent, it seemed to Hyde; for after two miles or so, he recognized the big rocky bluff that overhung the water at its northern end. This outstanding bluff he had seen from his camp, one side of it falling sheer into the water; it was probably the spot, he imagined, where the Indians held their medicine-making ceremonies, for it stood out in isolated fashion, and its top formed a private plateau not easy of access. And it was here, close to a big spruce at the foot of the bluff upon the forest side, that the wolf stopped suddenly and for the first time since its appearance gave audible expression to its feelings. It sat down on its haunches, lifted its muzzle with open jaws, and gave vent to a subdued and long-drawn howl that was more like the wail of a dog than the fierce barking cry associated with a wolf.

By this time Hyde had lost not only fear, but caution too; nor, oddly enough, did this warning howl revive a sign of unwelcome emotion in him. In that curious sound he detected the same message that the eyes conveyed—appeal for help. He paused, nevertheless, a little startled, and while the wolf sat waiting for him, he looked about him quickly. There was young timber here; it had once been a small clearing, evidently. Axe and fire had done their work, but there was evidence to an experienced eye that it was Indians and not white men who had once been busy here. Some part of the medicine ritual, doubtless, took place in the little clearing, thought the man, as he advanced again toward his patient leader. The end of their queer journey, he felt, was close at hand.

He had not taken two steps before the animal got up and moved very slowly in the direction of some low bushes that formed a clump just beyond. It entered these, first looking back to make sure that its companion watched. The bushes hid it: a moment later it emerged again. Twice it performed this pantomime, each time, as it reappeared, standing still and staring at the man with as distinct an expression of appeal in the eyes as an animal may compass, probably. Its excitement, meanwhile, certainly increased, and this excitement was, with equal certainty, communicated to the man. Hyde made up his mind quickly. Gripping his axe tightly, and ready to use it at the first hint of malice, he moved slowly nearer to the bushes, wondering with something of a tremor what would happen.

If he expected to be startled, his expectation was at once fulfilled; but it was the behaviour of the beast that made him jump. It positively frisked about him like a happy dog. It frisked for joy. Its excitement was intense, yet from its open mouth no sound was audible. With a sudden leap, then, it bounded past him into the clump of bushes, against whose

109

very edge he stood, and began scraping vigorously at the ground. Hyde stood and stared, amazement and interest now banishing all his nervousness, even when the beast, in its violent scraping, actually touched his body with its own. He had, perhaps, the feeling that he was in a dream, one of those fantastic dreams in which things may happen without involving an adequate surprise; for otherwise the manner of scraping and scratching at the ground must have seemed an impossible phenomenon. No wolf, no dog certainly, used its paws in the way those paws were working. Hyde had the odd, distressing sensation that it was hands, not paws, he watched. And yet, somehow, the natural, adequate surprise he should have felt was absent. The strange action seemed not entirely unnatural. In his heart some deep hidden spring of sympathy and pity stirred instead. He was aware of pathos.

The wolf stopped in its task and looked up into his face. Hyde acted without hesitation then. Afterwards he was wholly at a loss to explain his own conduct. It seemed he knew what to do, divined what was asked, expected of him. Between his mind and the dumb desire yearning through the savage animal there was intelligent and intelligible communication. He cut a stake and sharpened it, for the stones would blunt his axe-edge. He entered the clump of bushes to complete the digging his four-legged companion had begun. And while he worked, though he did not forget the close proximity of the wolf, he paid no attention to it; often his back was turned as he stooped over the laborious clearing away of the hard earth; no uneasiness or sense of danger was in him any more. The wolf sat outside the clump and watched the operations. Its concentrated attention, its patience, its intense eagerness, the gentleness and docility of the grey, fierce, and probably hungry brute, its obvious pleasure and satisfaction, too, at having won the human to its mysterious purpose—these were colours in the strange picture that Hyde thought of later when dealing with the human herd in his hotel again. At the moment he was aware chiefly of pathos and affection. The whole business was, of course, not to be believed, but that discovery came later, too, when telling it to others.

The digging continued for fully half an hour before his labour was rewarded by the discovery of a small whitish object. He picked it up and examined it—the finger-bone of a man. Other discoveries then followed quickly and in quantity. The *cache* was laid bare. He collected nearly the complete skeleton. The skull, however, he found last, and might not have found at all but for the guidance of his strangely alert companion. It lay some few yards away from the central hole now dug, and the wolf stood nuzzling the ground with its nose before Hyde understood that he was meant to dig exactly in that spot for it. Between the beast's very paws his stake struck hard upon it. He scraped the earth from the bone and examined it carefully. It was perfect, save for the fact that some wild animal had gnawed it, the teeth-marks being still plainly visible. Close beside it lay the rusty iron head of a tomahawk. This and the smallness of the bones confirmed him in his judgment that it was the skeleton not of a white man, but of an Indian.

During the excitement of the discovery of the bones one by one, and finally of the skull, but, more especially, during the period of intense interest while Hyde was examining them, he had paid little, if any, attention to the wolf. He was aware that it sat and watched him, never moving its keen eyes for a single moment from the actual operations, but of sign or movement it made none at all. He knew that it was pleased and satisfied, he knew also that he had now fulfilled its purpose in a great measure. The further intuition that now came to him, derived, he felt positive, from his companion's dumb desire, was perhaps the cream of the entire experience to him. Gathering the bones together in his coat, he carried them, together with the tomahawk, to the foot of the big spruce where the animal had first stopped. His leg actually touched the creature's muzzle as he passed. It turned its head to watch, but did not follow, nor did it move a muscle while he prepared the platform of boughs upon which he then laid the poor worn bones of an Indian who had been killed, doubtless, in sudden attack or ambush, and to whose remains had been denied the last grace of proper tribal burial. He wrapped the bones in bark; he laid the tomahawk beside the skull; he lit the circular fire round the pyre, and the blue smoke rose upward into the clear bright sunshine of the Canadian autumn morning till it was lost among the mighty trees far overhead.

In the moment before actually lighting the little fire he had turned to note what his companion did. It sat five yards away, he saw, gazing intently, and one of its front paws was raised a little from the ground. It made no sign of any kind. He finished the work, becoming so absorbed in it that he had eyes for nothing but the tending and guarding of his careful ceremonial fire. It was only when the platform of boughs collapsed, laying their charred burden gently on the fragrant earth among the soft wood ashes, that he turned again, as though to show the wolf what he had done, and seek, perhaps, some look of satisfaction in its curiously expressive eyes. But the place he searched was empty. The wolf had gone.

He did not see it again; it gave no sign of its presence anywhere; he was not watched. He fished as before, wandered through the bush about his camp, sat smoking round his fire after dark, and slept peacefully in his cosy little tent. He was not disturbed. No howl was ever audible in the distant forest, no twig snapped beneath a stealthy tread, he saw no eyes. The wolf that behaved like a man had gone for ever.

111

It was the day before he left that Hyde, noticing smoke rising from the shack across the lake, paddled over to exchange a word or two with the Indian, who had evidently now returned. The Redskin came down to meet him as he landed, but it was soon plain that he spoke very little English. He emitted the familiar grunts at first; then bit by bit Hyde stirred his limited vocabulary into action. The net result, however, was slight enough, though it was certainly direct.

"You camp there?" the man asked, pointing to the other side.

"Yes."

"Wolf come?"

"Yes."

"You see wolf?"

"Yes."

The Indian stared at him fixedly, a keen, wondering look upon his coppery, creased face. "You 'fraid wolf?" he asked after a moment's pause.

"No," replied Hyde, truthfully. He knew it was useless to ask questions of his own, though he was eager for information. The other would have told him nothing. It was sheer luck that the man had touched on the subject at all, and Hyde realized that his own best role was merely to answer, but to ask no questions.

Then, suddenly, the Indian became comparatively voluble. There was awe in his voice and manner. "Him no wolf. Him big medicine wolf. Him spirit wolf." Whereupon he drank the tea the other had brewed for him, closed his lips tightly, and said no more. His outline was discernible on the shore, rigid and motionless, an hour later, when Hyde's canoe turned the corner of the lake three miles away, and he landed to make the portages up the first rapid of his homeward stream.

It was Morton who, after some persuasion, supplied further details of what he called the legend. Some hundred years before, the tribe that lived in the territory beyond the lake began their annual medicine-making ceremonies on the big rocky bluff at the northern end; but no medicine could be made. The spirits, declared the chief medicine man, would not answer. They were offended. An investigation followed. It was discovered that a young brave had recently killed a wolf, a thing strictly forbidden, since the wolf was the totem animal of the tribe. To make matters worse, the name of the guilty man was Running Wolf. The offence being unpardonable, the man was cursed and driven from the tribe: "Go out. Wander alone among the woods, and if we see you we slay you. Your bones shall be scattered in the forest, and your spirit shall not enter the Happy Hunting Grounds till one of another race shall find and bury them."

"Which meant," explained Morton laconically, his only comment on the story, "probably for ever."

112

ELIZABETH BOWEN

1899–1973

She was a tall, humorous woman, of great personal distinction,
and for fully fifty years a successful, versatile and respected writer.
During World War II she worked in London with the Ministry
of Information, and has uniquely captured in her stories
the haunted emptiness of the beleaguered city.

The Demon Lover

TOWARDS THE END of her day in London Mrs.
Drover went round to her shut-up house to look
for several things she wanted to take away. Some
belonged to herself, some to her family, who were
by now used to their country life. It was late
August; it had been a steamy, showery day: at the
moment the trees down the pavement glittered in
an escape of humid yellow afternoon sun. Against
the next batch of clouds, already piling up ink-
dark, broken chimneys and parapets stood out. In
her once familiar street, as in any unused channel,
an unfamiliar queerness had silted up; a cat wove
itself in and out of railings, but no human eye
watched Mrs. Drover's return. Shifting some parcels under her arm, she
slowly forced round her latchkey in an unwilling lock, then gave the
door, which had warped, a push with her knee. Dead air came out to
meet her as she went in.

The staircase window having been boarded up, no light came down
into the hall. But one door, she could just see, stood ajar, so she went
quickly through into the room and unshuttered the big window in there.
Now the prosaic woman, looking about her, was more perplexed than
she knew by everything that she saw, by traces of her long former habit
of life—the yellow smoke-stain up the white marble mantelpiece, the
ring left by a vase on the top of the escritoire; the bruise in the wallpaper
where, on the door being thrown open widely, the china handle had

113

always hit the wall. The piano, having gone away to be stored, had left what looked like claw-marks on its part of the parquet. Though not much dust had seeped in, each object wore a film of another kind; and, the only ventilation being the chimney, the whole drawing-room smelled of the cold hearth. Mrs. Drover put down her parcels on the escritoire and left the room to proceed upstairs; the things she wanted were in a bedroom chest.

She had been anxious to see how the house was—the part-time caretaker she shared with some neighbours was away this week on his holiday, known to be not yet back. At the best of times he did not look in often, and she was never sure that she trusted him. There were some cracks in the structure, left by the last bombing, on which she was anxious to keep an eye. Not that one could do anything.

A shaft of refracted daylight now lay across the hall. She stopped dead and stared at the hall table—on this lay a letter addressed to her.

She thought first—then the caretaker *must* be back. All the same, who, seeing the house shuttered, would have dropped a letter in at the box? It was not a circular, it was not a bill. And the post office redirected, to the address in the country, everything for her that came through the post. The caretaker (even if he *were* back) did not know she was due in London today—her call here had been planned to be a surprise—so his negligence in the manner of this letter, leaving it to wait in the dusk and the dust, annoyed her. Annoyed, she picked up the letter, which bore no stamp. But it cannot be important, or they would know . . . She took the letter rapidly upstairs with her, without a stop to look at the writing till she reached what had been her bedroom, where she let in light. The room looked over the garden and other gardens: the sun had gone in; as the clouds sharpened and lowered, the trees and rank lawns seemed already to smoke with dark. Her reluctance to look again at the letter came from the fact that she felt intruded upon—and by someone contemptuous of her ways. However, in the tenseness preceding the fall of rain she read it: it was a few lines.

Dear Kathleen:

You will not have forgotten that today is our anniversary, and the day we said. The years have gone by at once slowly and fast. In view of the fact that nothing has changed, I shall rely upon you to keep your promise. I was sorry to see you leave London, but was satisfied that you would be back in time. You may expect me, therefore, at the hour arranged. Until then . . .   K.

Mrs. Drover looked for the date: it was today's. She dropped the letter on to the bed-springs, then picked it up to see the writing again—her lips, beneath the remains of lipstick, beginning to go white. She felt so much the change in her own face that she went to the mirror, polished a clear patch in it and looked at once urgently and stealthily in. She was confronted by a woman of forty-four, with eyes starting out under a hat-brim that had been rather carelessly pulled down. She had not put on any more powder since she left the shop where she ate her solitary tea. The pearls her husband had given her on their marriage hung loose round her now rather thinner throat, slipping in the V of the pink wool jumper her sister knitted last autumn as they sat round the fire. Mrs. Drover's most normal expression was one of controlled worry, but of assent. Since the birth of the third of her little boys, attended by a quite serious illness, she had had an intermittent muscular flicker to the left of her mouth, but in spite of this she could always sustain a manner that was at once energetic and calm.

Turning from her own face as precipitately as she had gone to meet it, she went to the chest where the things were, unlocked it, threw up the lid and knelt to search. But as rain began to come crashing down she could not keep from looking over her shoulder at the stripped bed on which the letter lay. Behind the blanket of rain the clock of the church that still stood struck six—with rapidly heightening apprehension she counted each of the slow strokes. "The hour arranged . . . My God," she said, "*what* hour? How should I . . .? After twenty-five years . . ."

THE YOUNG GIRL talking to the soldier in the garden had not ever completely seen his face. It was dark; they were saying good-bye under a tree. Now and then—for it felt, from not seeing him at this intense moment, as though she had never seen him at all—she verified his presence for these few moments longer by putting out a hand, which he each time pressed, without very much kindness, and painfully, on to one of the breast buttons of his uniform. That cut of the button on the palm of her hand was, principally, what she was to carry away. This was so near the end of a leave from France that she could only wish him already gone. It was August 1916. Being not kissed, being drawn away from and looked at intimidated Kathleen till she imagined spectral glitters in the place of his eyes. Turning away and looking back up the lawn she saw, through branches of trees, the drawing-room window alight: she caught a breath for the moment when she could go running back there into the safe arms of her mother and sister, and cry: "What shall I do, what shall I do? He has gone."

Hearing her catch her breath, her fiancé said, without feeling: "Cold?"

"You're going away such a long way."

"Not so far as you think."

"I don't understand?"

115

"You don't have to," he said. "You will. You know what we said."

"But that was—suppose you—I mean, suppose."

"I shall be with you," he said, "sooner or later. You won't forget that. You need do nothing but wait."

Only a little more than a minute later she was free to run up the silent lawn. Looking in through the window at her mother and sister, who did not for the moment perceive her, she already felt that unnatural promise drive down between her and the rest of all human kind. No other way of having given herself could have made her feel so apart, lost and foresworn. She could not have plighted a more sinister troth.

Kathleen behaved well when, some months later, her fiancé was reported missing, presumed killed. Her family not only supported her but were able to praise her courage without stint because they could not regret, as a husband for her, the man they knew almost nothing about. They hoped she would, in a year or two, console herself—and had it been only a question of consolation things might have gone much straighter ahead. But her trouble, behind just a little grief, was a complete dislocation from everything. She did not reject other lovers, for these failed to appear: for years she failed to attract men—and with the approach of her thirties she became natural enough to share her family's anxiousness on this score. She began to put herself out, to wonder; and at thirty-two she was very greatly relieved to find herself being courted by William Drover. She married him, and the two of them settled down in this quiet, arboreal part of Kensington: in this house the years piled up, her children were born and they all lived till they were driven out by the bombs of the next war. Her movements as Mrs. Drover were circumscribed, and she dismissed any idea that they were still watched.

As things were—dead or living the letter-writer sent her only a threat. Unable, for some minutes, to go on kneeling with her back exposed to the empty room, Mrs. Drover rose from the chest to sit on an upright chair whose back was firmly against the wall. The desuetude of her former bedroom, her married London home's air of being a cracked cup from which memory, with its reassuring power, had either evaporated or leaked away, made a crisis—and at just this crisis the letter-writer had, knowledgeably, struck. The hollowness of the house this evening cancelled years on years of voices, habits and steps. Through the shut windows she only heard rain fall on the roofs around. To rally herself, she said she was in a mood—and, for two or three seconds shutting her eyes, told herself that she had imagined the letter. But she opened them—there it lay on the bed.

On the supernatural side of the letter's entrance she was not permitting her mind to dwell. Who, in London, knew she meant to call at the house today? Evidently, however, this had been known. The caretaker, *had* he come back, had had no cause to expect her: he would have taken the letter in his pocket, to forward it, at his own time, through the post. There was no other sign that the caretaker had been in—but, if not? Letters dropped in at doors of deserted houses do not fly or walk to tables in halls. They do not sit on the dust of empty tables with the air of certainty that they will be found. There is needed some human hand—but nobody but the caretaker had a key. Under circumstances she did not care to consider, a house can be entered without a key. It was possible that she was not alone now. She might be being waited for, downstairs. Waited for—until when? Until 'the hour arranged'. At least that was not six o'clock: six has struck.

She rose from the chair and went over and locked the door.

The thing was, to get out. To fly? No, not that: she had to catch her train. As a woman whose utter dependability was the keystone of her family life she was not willing to return to the country, to her husband, her little boys and her sister, without the objects she had come up to fetch. Resuming work at the chest she set about making up a number of parcels in a rapid, fumbling-decisive way. These, with her shopping parcels, would be too much to carry; these meant a taxi—at the thought of the taxi her heart went up and her normal breathing resumed. I will ring up the taxi now; the taxi cannot come too soon: I shall hear the taxi out there running its engine, till I walk calmly down to it through the hall. I'll ring up—But no: the telephone is cut off . . . She tugged at a knot she had tied wrong.

The idea of flight . . . He was never kind to me, not really. I don't remember him kind at all. Mother said he never considered me. He was set on me, that was what it was—not love. Not love, not meaning a person well. What did he do, to make me promise like that? I can't remember—but she found that she could.

She remembered with such dreadful acuteness that the twenty-five years since then dissolved like smoke and she instinctively looked for the weal left by the button on the palm of her hand. She remembered not only all that he said and did but the complete suspension of *her* existence during that August week. I was not myself—they all told me so at the time. She remembered—but with one white burning blank as where acid has dropped on a photograph: *under no conditions* could she remember his face.

So, wherever he may be waiting, I shall not know him. You have no time to run from a face you do not expect.

The thing was to get to the taxi before any clock struck what could be the hour. She would slip down the street and round the side of the square to where the square gave on the main road. She would return in the taxi, safe, to her own door, and bring the solid driver into the house

117

with her to pick up the parcels from room to room. The idea of the taxi driver made her decisive, bold: she unlocked her door, went to the top of the staircase and listened down.

She heard nothing—but while she was hearing nothing the *passé* air of the staircase was disturbed by a draught that travelled up to her face. It emanated from the basement: down there a door or window was being opened by someone who chose this moment to leave the house.

The rain had stopped; the pavements steamily shone as Mrs. Drover let herself out by inches from her own front door into the empty street. The unoccupied houses opposite continued to meet her look with their damaged stare. Making towards the thoroughfare and the taxi, she tried not to keep looking behind. Indeed, the silence was so intense—one of those creeks of London silence exaggerated this summer by the damage of war—that no tread could have gained on hers unheard. Where her street debouched on the square where people went on living, she grew conscious of, and checked, her unnatural pace. Across the open end of the square two buses impassively passed each other: women, a perambulator, cyclists, a man wheeling a barrow signalized, once again, the ordinary flow of life. At the square's most populous corner should be— and was—the short taxi rank. This evening, only one taxi—but this, although it presented its blank rump, appeared already to be alertly waiting for her. Indeed, without looking round the driver started his engine as she panted up from behind and put her hand on the door. As she did so, the clock struck seven. The taxi faced the main road: to make the trip back to her house it would have to turn—she had settled back on the seat and the taxi *had* turned before she, surprised by its knowing movement, recollected that she had not 'said where'. She leaned forward to scratch at the glass panel that divided the driver's head from her own.

The driver braked to what was almost a stop, turned round and slid the glass panel back: the jolt of this flung Mrs. Drover forward till her face was almost into the glass. Through the aperture driver and passenger, not six inches between them, remained for an eternity eye to eye. Mrs. Drover's mouth hung open for some seconds before she could issue her first scream. After that she continued to scream freely and to beat with her gloved hands on the glass all round as the taxi, accelerating without mercy, made off with her into the hinterland of deserted streets.

G. K. CHESTERTON

1874–1936

As journalist, essayist, poet and novelist, this great and
lovable eccentric, with his irrepressible zest for life, entertained and
stimulated a vast and devoted public, never ceasing to attack
"the blasphemy of pessimism". In 1922 he was received into the
Roman Catholic Church by his friend Father O'Connor,
the original of Father Brown, his reverend detective.

The Hammer of God

THE LITTLE VILLAGE of Bohun Beacon
was perched on a hill so steep that the tall
spire of its church seemed only like the peak
of a small mountain. At the foot of the church
stood a smithy, generally red with fires and
always littered with hammers and scraps
of iron; opposite to this, over a rude cross of
cobbled paths, was 'The Blue Boar', the only
inn of the place. It was upon this crossway,
in the lifting of a leaden and silver daybreak,
that two brothers met in the street and
spoke; though one was beginning the day
and the other finishing it. The Rev. and
Hon. Wilfred Bohun was very devout, and
was making his way to some austere exercises of prayer or contemplation at dawn. Colonel the Hon. Norman Bohun, his elder brother,
was by no means devout, and was sitting in evening dress on the
bench outside 'The Blue Boar', drinking what the philosophic observer was free to regard either as his last glass on Tuesday or his
first on Wednesday. The colonel was not particular.

The Bohuns were one of the very few aristocratic families really dating
from the Middle Ages, and their pennon had actually seen Palestine.
But it is a great mistake to suppose that such houses stand high in
chivalric tradition. Few except the poor preserve traditions. Aristocrats
live not in traditions but in fashions. The Bohuns had been Mohocks

119

under Queen Anne and Mashers under Queen Victoria. But like more than one of the really ancient houses, they had rotted in the last two centuries into mere drunkards and dandy degenerates, till there had even come a whisper of insanity. Certainly there was something hardly human about the colonel's wolfish pursuit of pleasure, and his chronic resolution not to go home till morning had a touch of the hideous clarity of insomnia. He was a tall, fine animal, elderly, but with hair still startlingly yellow. He would have looked merely blond and leonine, but his blue eyes were sunk so deep in his face that they looked black. They were a little too close together. He had very long yellow moustaches; on each side of them a fold or furrow from nostril to jaw, so that a sneer seemed cut into his face. Over his evening clothes he wore a curious pale yellow coat that looked more like a very light dressing-gown than an overcoat, and on the back of his head was stuck an extraordinary broad-brimmed hat of a bright green colour, evidently some oriental curiosity caught up at random. He was proud of appearing in such incongruous attires—proud of the fact that he always made them look congruous.

His brother the curate had also the yellow hair and the elegance, but he was buttoned up to the chin in black, and his face was clean-shaven, cultivated, and a little nervous. He seemed to live for nothing but his religion; but there were some who said (notably the blacksmith, who was a Presbyterian) that it was a love of Gothic architecture rather than of God, and that his haunting of the church like a ghost was only another and purer turn of the almost morbid thirst for beauty which sent his brother raging after women and wine. This charge was doubtful, while the man's practical piety was indubitable. Indeed, the charge was mostly an ignorant misunderstanding of the love of solitude and secret prayer, and was founded on his being often found kneeling, not before the altar, but in peculiar places, in the crypts or gallery, or even in the belfry. He was at the moment about to enter the church through the yard of the smithy, but stopped and frowned a little as he saw his brother's cavernous eyes staring in the same direction. On the hypothesis that the colonel was interested in the church he did not waste any speculations. There only remained the blacksmith's shop, and though the blacksmith was a Puritan and none of his people, Wilfred Bohun had heard some scandals about a beautiful and rather celebrated wife. He flung a suspicious look across the shed, and the colonel stood up laughing to speak to him.

"Good morning, Wilfred," he said. "Like a good landlord I am watching sleeplessly over my people. I am going to call on the black-smith."

Wilfred looked at the ground, and said: "The blacksmith is out. He is over at Greenford."

"I know," answered the other with silent laughter; "that is why I am calling on him."

"Norman," said the cleric, with his eye on a pebble in the road, "are you ever afraid of thunderbolts?"

"What do you mean?" asked the colonel. "Is your hobby meteorology?"

"I mean," said Wilfred, without looking up, "do you ever think that God might strike you in the street?"

"I beg your pardon," said the colonel; "I see your hobby is folk-lore."

"I know your hobby is blasphemy," retorted the religious man, stung in the one live place of his nature. "But if you do not fear God, you have good reason to fear man."

The elder raised his eyebrows politely. "Fear man?" he said.

"Barnes the blacksmith is the biggest and strongest man for forty miles round," said the clergyman sternly. "I know you are no coward or weakling, but he could throw you over the wall."

This struck home, being true, and the lowering line by mouth and nostril darkened and deepened. For a moment he stood with the heavy sneer on his face. But in an instant Colonel Bohun had recovered his own cruel good humour and laughed, showing two dog-like front teeth under his yellow moustache. "In that case, my dear Wilfred," he said quite carelessly, "it was wise for the last of the Bohuns to come out partially in armour."

And he took off the queer round hat covered with green, showing that it was lined within with steel. Wilfred recognised it indeed as a light Japanese or Chinese helmet torn down from a trophy that hung in the old family hall. "It was the first hat to hand," explained his brother airily; "always the nearest hat—and the nearest woman."

"The blacksmith is away at Greenford," said Wilfred quietly; "the time of his return is unsettled."

And with that he turned and went into the church with bowed head, crossing himself like one who wishes to be quit of an unclean spirit. He was anxious to forget such grossness in the cool twilight of his tall Gothic cloisters; but on that morning it was fated that his still round of religious exercises should be everywhere arrested by small shocks. As he entered the church, hitherto always empty at that hour, a kneeling figure rose hastily to its feet and came towards the full daylight of the doorway. When the curate saw it he stood still with surprise. For the early worshipper was none other than the village idiot, a nephew of the blacksmith, one who neither would nor could care for the church or for anything else. He was always called 'Mad Joe', and seemed to have no other name; he was a dark, strong, slouching lad, with a heavy white face, dark straight hair, and a mouth always open. As he passed the priest, his moon-calf countenance gave no hint of what he had been doing or thinking of. He had never been known to pray before. What sort of prayers was he saying now? Extraordinary prayers surely.

Wilfred Bohun stood rooted to the spot long enough to see the idiot go out into the sunshine, and even to see his dissolute brother hail him with a sort of avuncular jocularity. The last thing he saw was the colonel throwing pennies at the open mouth of Joe, with the serious appearance of trying to hit it.

This ugly sunlight picture of the stupidity and cruelty of the earth sent the ascetic finally to his prayers for purification and new thoughts. He went up to a pew in the gallery, which brought him under a coloured window which he loved and always quieted his spirit; a blue window with an angel carrying lilies. There he began to think less about the half-wit, with his livid face and mouth like a fish. He began to think less of his evil brother, pacing like a lean lion in his terrible hunger. He sank deeper and deeper into those cold and sweet colours of silver blossoms and sapphire sky.

In this place half an hour afterwards he was found by Gibbs, the village cobbler, who had been sent for him in some haste. He got to his feet with promptitude, for he knew that no small matter would have brought Gibbs into such a place at all. The cobbler was, as in many villages, an atheist, and his appearance in church was a shade more extraordinary than Mad Joe's. It was a morning of theological enigmas.

"What is it?" asked Wilfred Bohun rather stiffly, but putting out a trembling hand for his hat.

The atheist spoke in a tone that, coming from him, was quite startlingly respectful, and even, as it were, huskily sympathetic.

"You must excuse me, sir," he said in a hoarse whisper, "but we didn't think it right not to let you know at once. I'm afraid a rather dreadful thing has happened, sir. I'm afraid your brother—"

Wilfred clenched his frail hands. "What devilry has he done now?" he cried in involuntary passion.

"Why, sir," said the cobbler, coughing, "I'm afraid he's done nothing, and won't do anything. I'm afraid he's done for. You had really better come down, sir."

The curate followed the cobbler down a short winding stair, which brought them out at an entrance rather higher than the street. Bohun saw the tragedy in one glance, flat underneath him like a plan. In the yard of the smithy were standing five or six men mostly in black, one in an inspector's uniform. They included the doctor, the Presbyterian minister, and the priest from the Roman Catholic chapel, to which the blacksmith's wife belonged. The latter was speaking to her, indeed, very rapidly, in an undertone, as she, a magnificent woman with red-gold hair, was sobbing blindly on a bench. Between these two groups, and just clear of the main heap of hammers, lay a man in evening dress, spread-eagled and flat on his face. From the height above Wilfred could have sworn to every item of his costume and appearance, down to the Bohun rings upon his fingers; but the skull was only a hideous splash, like a star of blackness and blood.

Wilfred Bohun gave but one glance, and ran down the steps into the yard. The doctor, who was the family physician, saluted him, but he scarcely took any notice. He could only stammer out: "My brother is dead. What does it mean? What is this horrible mystery?" There was an unhappy silence; and then the cobbler, the most outspoken man present, answered: "Plenty of horror, sir," he said, "but not much mystery."

"What do you mean?" asked Wilfred, with a white face.

"It's plain enough," answered Gibbs. "There is only one man for forty miles round that could have struck such a blow as that, and he's the man that had most reason to."

"We must not prejudge anything," put in the doctor, a tall, black-bearded man, rather nervously; "but it is competent for me to corroborate what Mr. Gibbs says about the nature of the blow, sir; it is an incredible blow. Mr. Gibbs says that only one man in this district could have done it. I should have said myself that nobody could have done it."

A shudder of superstition went through the slight figure of the curate. "I can hardly understand," he said.

"Mr. Bohun," said the doctor in a low voice, "metaphors literally fail me. It is inadequate to say that the skull was smashed to bits like an egg-shell. Fragments of bone were driven into the body and the ground like bullets into a mud wall. It was the hand of a giant."

He was silent a moment, looking grimly through his glasses; then he added: "The thing has one advantage—that it clears most people of suspicion at one stroke. If you or I or any normally made man in the country were accused of this crime, we should be acquitted as an infant would be acquitted of stealing the Nelson Column."

"That's what I say," repeated the cobbler obstinately; "there's only one man that could have done it, and he's the man that would have done it. Where's Simeon Barnes, the blacksmith?"

"He's over at Greenford," faltered the curate.

"More likely over in France," muttered the cobbler.

"No; he is in neither of those places," said a small and colourless voice, which came from the little Roman priest who had joined the group. "As a matter of fact, he is coming up the road at this moment."

The little priest was not an interesting man to look at, having stubbly brown hair and a round and stolid face. But if he had been as splendid as Apollo no one would have looked at him at that moment. Everyone turned round and peered at the pathway which wound across the plain below, along which was indeed walking, at his own huge stride and with a hammer on his shoulder, Simeon the smith. He was a bony and gigantic man, with deep, dark, sinister eyes and a dark chin beard. He was walking and talking quietly with two other men; and though he was never specially cheerful, he seemed quite at his ease.

"My God!" cried the atheistic cobbler, "and there's the hammer he did it with."

"No," said the inspector, a sensible-looking man with a sandy moustache, speaking for the first time. "There's the hammer he did it with over there by the church wall. We have left it and the body exactly as they are."

All glanced round, and the short priest went across and looked down in silence at the tool where it lay. It was one of the smallest and the lightest of the hammers, and would not have caught the eye among the rest; but on the iron edge of it were blood and yellow hair.

After a silence the short priest spoke without looking up, and there was a new note in his dull voice. "Mr. Gibbs was hardly right," he said, "in saying that there is no mystery. There is at least the mystery of why so big a man should attempt so big a blow with so little a hammer."

"Oh, never mind that," cried Gibbs, in a fever. "What are we to do with Simeon Barnes?"

"Leave him alone," said the priest quietly. "He is coming here of himself. I know those two men with him. They are very good fellows from Greenford, and they have come over about the Presbyterian chapel."

Even as he spoke the tall smith swung round the corner of the church, and strode into his own yard. Then he stood there quite still, and the hammer fell from his hand. The inspector, who had preserved impenetrable propriety, immediately went up to him.

"I won't ask you, Mr. Barnes," he said, "whether you know anything about what has happened here. You are not bound to say. I hope you don't know, and that you will be able to prove it. But I must go through the form of arresting you in the King's name for the murder of Colonel Norman Bohun."

"You are not bound to say anything," said the cobbler in officious excitement. "They've got to prove everything. They haven't proved yet that it is Colonel Bohun, with the head all smashed up like that."

"That won't wash," said the doctor aside to the priest. "That's out of the detective stories. I was the colonel's medical man, and I knew his body better than he did. He had very fine hands, but quite peculiar ones. The second and third fingers were the same in length. Oh, that's the colonel right enough."

As he glanced at the brained corpse upon the ground the iron eyes of the motionless blacksmith followed them, and rested there also.

"Is Colonel Bohun dead?" said the smith quite calmly. "Then he's damned."

"Don't say anything! Oh, don't say anything," cried the atheist cobbler, dancing about in an ecstasy of admiration of the English legal system. For no man is such a legalist as the good Secularist.

The blacksmith turned on him over his shoulder the august face of a fanatic.

"It's well for you infidels to dodge like foxes because the world's law favours you," he said; "but God guards His own in His pocket, as you shall see this day."

Then he pointed to the colonel and said: "When did this dog die in his sins?"

"Moderate your language," said the doctor.

"Moderate the Bible's language, and I'll moderate mine. When did he die?"

"I saw him alive at six o'clock this morning," stammered Wilfred Bohun.

"God is good," said the smith. "Mr. Inspector, I have not the slightest objection to being arrested. It is you who may object to arresting me. I don't mind leaving the court without a stain on my character. You do mind, perhaps, leaving the court with a bad set-back in your career."

The solid inspector for the first time looked at the blacksmith with a lively eye; as did everybody else, except the short, strange priest, who was still looking down at the little hammer that had dealt the dreadful blow.

"There are two men standing outside this shop," went on the blacksmith with ponderous lucidity, "good tradesmen in Greenford whom you all know, who will swear that they saw me from before midnight till daybreak and long after in the committee-room of our Revival Mission, which sits all night, we save souls so fast. In Greenford itself twenty people could swear to me for all that time. If I were a heathen, Mr. Inspector, I would let you walk on to your downfall. But as a Christian man I feel bound to give you your chance, and ask you whether you will hear my alibi now or in court."

The inspector seemed for the first time disturbed, and said, "Of course I should be glad to clear you altogether now."

The smith walked out of his yard with the same long and easy stride, and returned to his two friends from Greenford, who were indeed friends of nearly everyone present. Each of them said a few words which no one ever thought of disbelieving. When they had spoken, the innocence of Simeon stood up as solid as the great church above them.

One of those silences struck the group which are more strange and insufferable than any speech. Madly, in order to make conversation, the curate said to the Catholic priest:

"You seem very much interested in that hammer, Father Brown."

"Yes, I am," said Father Brown; "why is it such a small hammer?"

The doctor swung round on him.

"By George, that's true," he cried; "who would use a little hammer with ten larger hammers lying about?"

Then he lowered his voice in the curate's ear and said: "Only the kind of person that can't lift a large hammer. It is not a question of force or courage between the sexes. It's a question of lifting power in the shoulders. A bold woman could commit ten murders with a light hammer and never turn a hair. She could not kill a beetle with a heavy one."

Wilfred Bohun was staring at him with a sort of hypnotised horror, while Father Brown listened with his head a little on one side, really interested and attentive. The doctor went on with more hissing emphasis:

"Why do these idiots always assume that the only person who hates the wife's lover is the wife's husband? Nine times out of ten the person who most hates the wife's lover is the wife. Who knows what insolence or treachery he had shown her—look there?"

He made a momentary gesture towards the red-haired woman on the bench. She had lifted her head at last and the tears were drying on her splendid face. But the eyes were fixed on the corpse with an electric glare that had in it something of idiocy.

The Rev. Wilfred Bohun made a limp gesture as if waving away all desire to know; but Father Brown, dusting off his sleeve some ashes blown from the furnace, spoke in his indifferent way.

"You are like so many doctors," he said; "your mental science is really suggestive. It is your physical science that is utterly impossible. I agreed that the woman wants to kill the co-respondent much more than the petitioner does. And I agree that a woman will always pick up a small hammer instead of a big one. But the difficulty is one of physical impossibility. No woman ever born could have smashed a man's skull out flat like that." Then he added reflectively, after a pause: "These people haven't grasped the whole of it. The man was actually wearing an iron helmet, and the blow scattered it like broken glass. Look at that woman. Look at her arms."

Silence held them all up again, and then the doctor said rather sulkily: "Well, I may be wrong; there are objections to everything. But I stick to the main point. No man but an idiot would pick up that little hammer if he could use a big hammer."

With that the lean and quivering hands of Wilfred Bohun went up to his head and seemed to clutch his scanty yellow hair. After an instant they dropped, and he cried: "That was the word I wanted; you have said the word."

Then he continued, mastering his discomposure: "The words you said were, 'No man but an idiot would pick up the small hammer'."

"Yes," said the doctor. "Well?"

"Well," said the curate, "no man but an idiot did." The rest stared at him with eyes arrested and riveted, and he went on in a febrile and feminine agitation.

"I am a priest," he cried unsteadily, "and a priest should be no shedder of blood. I—I mean that he should bring no one to the gallows. And I thank God that I see the criminal clearly now—because he is a criminal who cannot be brought to the gallows."

"You will not denounce him?" enquired the doctor.

"He would not be hanged if I did denounce him," answered Wilfred with a wild but curiously happy smile. "When I went into the church this morning I found a madman praying there—that poor Joe, who has been wrong all his life. God knows what he prayed; but with such strange folk it is not incredible to suppose that their prayers are all upside down. Very likely a lunatic would pray before killing a man. When I last saw poor Joe he was with my brother. My brother was mocking him."

"By Jove!" cried the doctor, "this is talking at last. But how do you explain—"

The Rev. Wilfred was almost trembling with the excitement of his own glimpse of the truth. "Don't you see; don't you see," he cried feverishly; "that is the only theory that covers both the queer things, that answers both the riddles. The two riddles are the little hammer and the big blow. The smith might have struck the big blow, but would not have chosen the little hammer. His wife would have chosen the little hammer, but she could not have struck the big blow. But the madman might have done both. As for the little hammer—why, he was mad and might have picked up anything. And for the big blow, have you never heard, doctor, that a maniac in his paroxysm may have the strength of ten men?"

The doctor drew a deep breath and then said, "By golly, I believe you've got it."

Father Brown had fixed his eyes on the speaker so long and steadily as to prove that his large grey, ox-like eyes were not quite so insignificant as the rest of his face. When silence had fallen he said with marked respect: "Mr. Bohun, yours is the only theory yet propounded which holds water every way and is essentially unassailable. I think, therefore,

127

that you deserve to be told, on my positive knowledge, that it is not the true one." And with that the old little man walked away and stared again at the hammer.

"That fellow seems to know more than he ought to," whispered the doctor peevishly to Wilfred. "Those popish priests are deucedly sly."

"No, no," said Bohun, with a sort of wild fatigue. "It was the lunatic. It was the lunatic."

The group of the two clerics and the doctor had fallen away from the more official group containing the inspector and the man he had arrested. Now, however, that their own party had broken up, they heard voices from the others. The priest looked up quietly and then looked down again as he heard the blacksmith say in a loud voice:

"I hope I've convinced you, Mr. Inspector. I'm a strong man, as you say, but I couldn't have flung my hammer bang here from Greenford. My hammer hasn't any wings that it should come flying half a mile over hedges and fields."

The inspector laughed amicably and said: "No, I think you can be considered out of it, though it's one of the rummiest coincidences I ever saw. I can only ask you to give us all the assistance you can in finding a man as big and strong as yourself. By George! you might be useful, if only to hold him! I suppose you yourself have no guess at the man?"

"I may have a guess," said the pale smith, "but it is not at a man." Then, seeing the scared eyes turn towards his wife on the bench, he put his huge hand on her shoulder and said: "Nor a woman either."

"What do you mean?" asked the inspector jocularly. "You don't think cows use hammers, do you?"

"I think no thing of flesh held that hammer," said the blacksmith in a stifled voice; "mortally speaking, I think the man died alone."

Wilfred made a sudden forward movement and peered at him with burning eyes.

"Do you mean to say, Barnes," came the sharp voice of the cobbler, "that the hammer jumped up of itself and knocked the man down?"

"Oh, you gentlemen may stare and snigger," cried Simeon; "you clergymen who tell us on Sunday in what a stillness the Lord smote Sennacherib. I believe that One who walks invisible in every house defended the honour of mine, and laid the defiler dead before the door of it. I believe the force in that blow was just the force there is in earthquakes, and no force less."

Wilfred said, with a voice utterly undescribable: "I told Norman myself to beware of the thunderbolt."

"That agent is outside my jurisdiction," said the inspector with a slight smile.

128

"You are not outside His," answered the smith; "see you to it," and, turning his broad back, he went into the house.

The shaken Wilfred was led away by Father Brown, who had an easy and friendly way with him. "Let us get out of this horrid place, Mr. Bohun," he said. "May I look inside your church? I hear it's one of the oldest in England. We take some interest, you know," he added with a comical grimace, "in old English churches."

Wilfred Bohun did not smile, for humour was never his strong point. But he nodded rather eagerly, being only too ready to explain the Gothic splendours to someone more likely to be sympathetic than the Presbyterian blacksmith or the atheist cobbler.

"By all means," he said; "let us go in at this side." And he led the way into the high side entrance at the top of the flight of steps. Father Brown was mounting the first step to follow him when he felt a hand on his shoulder, and turned to behold the dark, thin figure of the doctor, his face darker yet with suspicion.

"Sir," said the physician harshly, "you appear to know some secrets in this black business. May I ask if you are going to keep them to yourself?"

"Why, doctor," answered the priest, smiling quite pleasantly, "there is one very good reason why a man of my trade should keep things to himself when he is not sure of them, and that is that it is so constantly his duty to keep them to himself when he is sure of them. But if you think I have been discourteously reticent with you or anyone, I will go to the extreme limit of my custom. I will give you two very large hints."

"Well, sir?" said the doctor gloomily.

"First," said Father Brown quietly, "the thing is quite in your own province. It is a matter of physical science. The blacksmith is mistaken, not perhaps in saying that the blow was divine, but certainly in saying that it came by a miracle. It was no miracle, doctor, except in so far as a man is himself a miracle, with his strange and wicked and yet half-heroic heart. The force that smashed that skull was a force well known to scientists—one of the most frequently debated of the laws of nature."

The doctor, who was looking at him with frowning intentness, only said: "And the other hint!"

"The other hint is this," said the priest. "Do you remember the blacksmith, though he believes in miracles, talking scornfully of the impossible fairy tale that his hammer had wings and flew half a mile across country?"

"Yes," said the doctor, "I remember that."

"Well," added Father Brown, with a broad smile, "that fairy tale was the nearest thing to the real truth that has been said to-day." And with that he turned his back and stumped up the steps after the curate.

The Reverend Wilfred, who had been waiting for him, pale and impatient, as if this little delay were the last straw for his nerves, led him immediately to his favourite corner of the church, that part of the gallery closest to the carved roof and lit by the wonderful window with the angel. The little Latin priest explored and admired everything exhaustively, talking cheerfully but in a low voice all the time. When in the course of his investigation he found the side exit and the winding stair down which Wilfred had rushed to find his brother dead, Father Brown ran not down but up, with the agility of a monkey, and his clear voice came from an outer platform above.

"Come up here, Mr. Bohun," he called. "The air will do you good."

Bohun followed him, and came out on a kind of stone gallery or balcony outside the building, from which one could see the illimitable plain in which their small hill stood, wooded away to the purple horizon and dotted with villages and farms. Clear and square, but quite small beneath them, was the blacksmith's yard, where the inspector still stood taking notes and the corpse still lay like a smashed fly.

"Might be the map of the world, mightn't it?" said Father Brown.

"Yes," said Bohun very gravely, and nodded his head.

Immediately beneath and about them the lines of the Gothic building plunged outwards into the void with a sickening swiftness akin to suicide. There is that element of Titan energy in the architecture of the Middle Ages that, from whatever aspect it be seen, it always seems to be rushing away, like the strong back of some maddened horse. This church was hewn out of ancient and silent stone, bearded with old fungoids and stained with the nests of birds. And yet, when they saw it from below, it sprang like a fountain at the stars; and when they saw it, as now, from above, it poured like a cataract into a voiceless pit. For these two men on the tower were left alone with the most terrible aspect of the Gothic; the monstrous foreshortening and disproportion, the dizzy perspectives, the glimpses of great things small and small things great; a topsy-turvydom of stone in the mid-air. Details of stone, enormous by their proximity, were relieved against a pattern of fields and farms, pygmy in their distance. A carved bird or beast at a corner seemed like some vast walking or flying dragon wasting the pastures and villages below. The whole atmosphere was dizzy and dangerous, as if men were upheld in air amid the gyrating wings of colossal genii; and the whole of that old church, as tall and rich as a cathedral, seemed to sit upon the sunlit country like a cloud-burst.

"I think there is something rather dangerous about standing on these high places even to pray," said Father Brown. "Heights were made to be looked at, not to be looked from."

"Do you mean that one may fall over?" asked Wilfred.

"I mean that one's soul may fall if one's body doesn't," said the other priest.

"I scarcely understand you," remarked Bohun indistinctly.

"Look at that blacksmith, for instance," went on Father Brown calmly; "a good man, but not a Christian—hard, imperious, unforgiving. Well, his Scotch religion was made up by men who prayed on hills and high crags, and learnt to look down on the world more than to look up at heaven. Humility is the mother of giants. One sees great things from the valley; only small things from the peak."

"But he—he didn't do it," said Bohun tremulously.

"No," said the other in an odd voice; "we know he didn't do it."

After a moment he resumed, looking tranquilly out over the plain with his pale grey eyes. "I knew a man," he said, "who began by worshipping with others before the altar, but who grew fond of high and lonely places to pray from, corners or niches in the belfry or the spire. And once in one of those dizzy places, where the whole world seemed to turn under him like a wheel, his brain turned also, and he fancied he was God. So that though he was a good man, he committed a great crime."

Wilfred's face was turned away, but his bony hands turned blue and white as they tightened on the parapet of stone.

"He thought it was given to *him* to judge the world and strike down the sinner. He would never have had such a thought if he had been kneeling with other men upon a floor. But he saw all men walking about like insects. He saw one especially strutting just below him, insolent and evident by the bright green hat—a poisonous insect."

Rooks cawed round the corners of the belfry; but there was no other sound till Father Brown went on.

"This also tempted him, that he had in his hand one of the most awful engines of nature; I mean gravitation, that mad and quickening rush by which all earth's creatures fly back to her heart when released. See, the inspector is strutting just below us in the smithy. If I were to toss a pebble over this parapet it would be something like a bullet by the time it struck him. If I were to drop a hammer—even a small hammer—"

Wilfred Bohun threw one leg over the parapet, and Father Brown had him in a minute by the collar.

"Not by that door," he said quite gently; "that door leads to hell."

Bohun staggered back against the wall, and stared at him with frightful eyes.

"How do you know all this?" he cried. "Are you a devil?"

"I am a man," answered Father Brown gravely; "and therefore have all devils in my heart. Listen to me," he said after a short pause.

131

"I know what you did—at least, I can guess the great part of it. When you left your brother you were racked with no unrighteous rage to the extent even that you snatched up a small hammer, half inclined to kill him with his foulness on his mouth. Recoiling, you thrust it under your buttoned coat instead, and rushed into the church. You pray wildly in many places, under the angel window, upon the platform above, and on a higher platform still, from which you could see the colonel's Eastern hat like the back of a green beetle crawling about. Then something snapped in your soul, and you let God's thunderbolt fall."

Wilfred put a weak hand to his head, and asked in a low voice: "How did you know that his hat looked like a green beetle?"

"Oh, that," said the other with the shadow of a smile, "that was common sense. But hear me further. I say I know all this; but no one else shall know it. The next step is for you; I shall take no more steps; I will seal this with the seal of confession. If you ask me why, there are many reasons, and only one that concerns you. I leave things to you because you have not yet gone very far wrong, as assassins go. You did not help to fix the crime on the smith when it was easy; or on his wife, when that was easy. You tried to fix it on the imbecile because you knew that he could not suffer. That was one of the gleams that it is my business to find in assassins. And now come down into the village, and go your own way as free as the wind; for I have said my last word."

They went down the winding stairs in utter silence, and came out into the sunlight by the smithy. Wilfred Bohun carefully unlatched the wooden gate of the yard, and going up to the inspector, said: "I wish to give myself up; I have killed my brother."

WILLIAM WILKIE COLLINS

1824–1889

Best known for *The Moonstone* and *The Woman in White*,
he was a gay, sociable man, mildly Bohemian. It was entirely
from his avid reading of the popular press—and his own
lively imagination—that he derived the sinister backgrounds
to his exciting and sensational stories.

The Traveller's Story of a Terribly Strange Bed

SHORTLY AFTER my education at college was finished, I happened to be staying at Paris with an English friend. We were both young men then, and lived, I am afraid, rather a wild life, in the delightful city of our sojourn. One night we were idling about the neighbourhood of the Palais Royal, doubtful to what amusement we should next betake ourselves. My friend proposed a visit to Frascati's; but his suggestion was not to my taste. I knew Frascati's, as the French saying is, by heart; had lost and won plenty of five-franc pieces there, merely for amusement's sake, until it was amusement no longer, and was thoroughly tired, in fact, of all the ghastly respectabilities of such a social anomaly as a respectable gambling-house. "For Heaven's sake," said I to my friend, "let us go somewhere where we can see a little genuine, blackguard, poverty-stricken gaming, with no false gingerbread glitter thrown over it at all. Let us get away from fashionable Frascati's to a house where they don't mind letting in a man with a ragged coat, or a man with no coat, ragged or otherwise."—"Very well," said my friend, "we needn't go out of the

Palais Royal to find the sort of company you want. Here's the place just before us; as blackguard a place, by all report, as you could possibly wish to see." In another minute we arrived at the door, and entered the house, the back of which you have drawn in your sketch.*

When we got upstairs, and left our hats and sticks with the door-keeper, we were admitted into the chief gambling-room. We did not find many people assembled there. But, few as the men were who looked up at us on our entrance, they were all types—lamentably true types—of their respective classes.

We had come to see blackguards; but these men were something worse. There is a comic side, more or less appreciable, in all black-guardism—here there was nothing but tragedy—mute, weird tragedy. The quiet in the room was horrible. The thin, haggard, long-haired young man, whose sunken eyes fiercely watched the turning up of the cards, never spoke; the flabby, fat-faced, pimply player, who pricked his piece of pasteboard perseveringly, to register how often black won, and how often red—never spoke; the dirty, wrinkled old man, with the vulture eyes and the darned greatcoat, who had lost his last *sou*, and still looked on desperately, after he could play no longer—never spoke. Even the voice of the croupier sounded as if it were strangely dulled and thickened in the atmosphere of the room. I had entered the place to laugh, but the spectacle before me was something to weep over. I soon found it necessary to take refuge in excitement from the depression of spirits which was fast stealing on me. Unfortunately I sought the nearest excitement, by going to the table, and beginning to play. Still more unfortunately, as the event will show, I won—won prodigiously; won incredibly; won at such a rate, that the regular players at the table crowded round me; and staring at my stakes with hungry, superstitious eyes, whispered to one another that the English stranger was going to break the bank.

The game was *Rouge et Noir*. I had played at it in every city in Europe, without, however, the care or the wish to study the Theory of Chances—that philosopher's stone of all gamblers! And a gambler, in the strict sense of the word, I had never been. I was heartwhole from the corroding passion for play. My gaming was a mere idle amusement. I never resorted to it by necessity, because I never knew what it was to want money. I never practised it so incessantly as to lose more than I could afford, or to gain more than I could coolly pocket without being thrown off my balance by my good luck. In short, I had hitherto frequented gambling-tables—just as I frequented ballrooms and opera-houses—because they amused me, and because I had nothing better to

*The story is supposed to be narrated by its chief actor, to the artist who is painting his portrait.

do with my leisure hours. But on this occasion it was very different—now, for the first time in my life, I felt what the passion for play really was. My success first bewildered, and then, in the most literal meaning of the word, intoxicated me. Incredible as it may appear, it is nevertheless true, that I only lost when I attempted to estimate chances, and played according to previous calculation. If I left everything to luck, and staked without any care or consideration, I was sure to win—to win in the face of every recognized probability in favour of the bank. At first, some of the men present ventured their money safely enough on my colour; but I speedily increased my stakes to sums which they dared not risk. One after another they left off playing, and breathlessly looked on at my game.

Still, time after time, I staked higher and higher, and still won. The excitement in the room rose to fever pitch. The silence was interrupted by a deep-muttered chorus of oaths and exclamations in different languages, every time the gold was shovelled across to my side of the table—even the imperturbable croupier dashed his rake on the floor in a (French) fury of astonishment at my success. But one man present preserved his self-possession; and that man was my friend. He came to my side, and whispering in English, begged me to leave the place, satisfied with what I had already gained. I must do him the justice to say that he repeated his warnings and entreaties several times, and only left me and went away, after I had rejected his advice (I was to all intents and purposes gambling-drunk) in terms which rendered it impossible for him to address me again that night.

Shortly after he had gone, a hoarse voice behind me cried: "Permit me, my dear sir!—permit me to restore to their proper place two Napoleons which you have dropped. Wonderful luck, sir! I pledge you my word of honour, as an old soldier, in the course of my long experience in this sort of thing, I never saw such luck as yours!—never! Go on, sir—*Sacré mille bombes!* Go on boldly, and break the bank!"

I turned round and saw, nodding and smiling at me with inveterate civility, a tall man, dressed in a frogged and braided surtout.

If I had been in my senses, I should have considered him, personally, as being rather a suspicious specimen of an old soldier. He had goggling blood-shot eyes, mangy mustachios, and a broken nose. His voice betrayed a barrack-room intonation of the worst order, and he had the dirtiest pair of hands I ever saw—even in France. These little personal peculiarities exercised, however, no repelling influence on me. In the mad excitement, the reckless triumph of that moment, I was ready to 'fraternize' with anybody who encouraged me in my game. I accepted the old soldier's offered pinch of snuff; clapped him on the back, and swore he was the honestest fellow in the world—the most glorious relic of the Grand Army that I had ever met with. "Go on!" cried my military friend, snapping his fingers in ecstasy,—"Go on, and win! Break the Bank—*Mille tonnerres!* my gallant English comrade, break the bank!"

And I *did* go on—went on at such a rate, that in another quarter of an hour the croupier called out: "Gentlemen! the bank has discontinued for to-night." All the notes, and all the gold in that 'bank', now lay in a heap under my hands; the whole floating capital of the gambling-house was waiting to pour into my pockets!

"Tie up the money in your pocket-handkerchief, my worthy sir," said the old soldier, as I wildly plunged my hands into my heap of gold. "Tie it up, as we used to tie up a bit of dinner in the Grand Army; your winnings are too heavy for any breeches pockets that ever were sewed. There! that's it!—shovel them in, notes and all! *Crediê!* what luck!— Stop! another Napoleon on the floor! *Ah! sacré petit polisson de Napoléon!* have I found thee at last? Now then, sir—two tight double knots each way with your honourable permission, and the money's safe. Feel it! feel it, fortunate sir! hard and round as a cannon ball—*Ah, bah!* if they had only fired such cannon balls at us at Austerlitz—*nom d'une pipe!* if they only had! And now, as an ancient grenadier, as an ex-brave of the French army, what remains for me to do? I ask what? Simply this: to entreat my valued English friend to drink a bottle of champagne with me, and toast the goddess Fortune in foaming goblets before we part!"

Excellent ex-brave! Convivial ancient grenadier! Champagne by all means! An English cheer for an old soldier! Hurrah! hurrah! Another English cheer for the goddess Fortune! Hurrah! hurrah! hurrah!

"Bravo! the Englishman; the amiable, gracious Englishman, in whose veins circulates the vivacious blood of France! Another glass? *Ah, bah!* —the bottle is empty! Never mind! *Vive le vin!* I, the old soldier, order another bottle, and half-a-pound of *bonbons* with it!"

"No, no, ex-brave; never—ancient grenadier! *Your* bottle last time; *my* bottle this. Behold it! Toast away! The French Army!—the great Napoleon!—the present company! the croupier! the honest croupier's wife and daughters—if he has any! the Ladies generally! Everybody in the world!" By the time the second bottle of champagne was emptied, I felt as if I had been drinking liquid fire—my brain seemed all a-flame. No excess in wine had ever had this effect on me before in my life. Was it the result of a stimulant acting upon my system when I was in a highly excited state? Was my stomach in a particularly disordered condition? Or was the champagne amazingly strong?

"Ex-brave of the French Army!" cried I, in a mad state of exhilaration, "*I* am on fire! how are *you?* You have set me on fire! Do you hear, my hero of Austerlitz? Let us have a third bottle of champagne to put the flame out!"

The old soldier wagged his head, rolled his goggle eyes, until I expected to see them slip out of their sockets; placed his dirty forefinger by the side of his broken nose; solemnly ejaculated "Coffee!" and immediately ran off into an inner room.

The word pronounced by the eccentric veteran seemed to have a magical effect on the rest of the company present. With one accord they all rose to depart. Probably they had expected to profit by my intoxication; but finding that my new friend was benevolently bent on preventing me from getting dead drunk, had now abandoned all hope of thriving pleasantly on my winnings. Whatever their motive might be, at any rate they went away in a body. When the old soldier returned, and sat down again opposite to me at the table, we had the room to ourselves. I could see the croupier, in a sort of vestibule which opened out of it, eating his supper in solitude. The silence was now deeper than ever.

A sudden change, too, had come over the 'ex-brave'. He assumed a portentously solemn look; and when he spoke to me again, his speech was ornamented by no oaths, enforced by no finger-snapping, enlivened by no apostrophes or exclamations.

"Listen, my dear sir," said he, in mysteriously confidential tones— "listen to an old soldier's advice. I have been to the mistress of the house (a very charming woman, with a genius for cookery!) to impress on her the necessity of making us some particularly strong and good coffee. You must drink this coffee in order to get rid of your little amiable exaltation of spirits before you think of going home—you *must*, my good and gracious friend! With all that money to take home to-night, it is a sacred duty to yourself to have your wits about you. You are known to be a winner to an enormous extent by several gentlemen present to-night, who, in a certain point of view, are very worthy and excellent fellows, but they are mortal men, my dear sir, and they have their amiable weaknesses! Need I say more? Ah, no, no! you understand me! Now, this is what you must do—send for a cabriolet when you feel quite well again—draw up all the windows when you get into it—and tell the driver to take you home only through the large and well-lighted thoroughfares. Do this; and you and your money will be safe. Do this; and to-morrow you will thank an old soldier for giving you a word of honest advice."

Just as the ex-brave ended his oration in very lachrymose tones, the coffee came in, ready poured out in two cups. My attentive friend handed me one of the cups with a bow. I was parched with thirst, and drank if off at a draught. Almost instantly afterwards, I was seized with a fit of giddiness, and felt more completely intoxicated than ever. The room whirled round and round furiously; the old soldier seemed to be regularly bobbing up and down before me like the piston of a steam-engine. I was half deafened by a violent singing in my ears; a feeling of utter bewilderment, helplessness, idiocy, overcame me. I rose from my chair, holding on by the table to keep my balance; and stammered out, that I felt dreadfully unwell—so unwell that I did not know how I was to get home.

"My dear friend," answered the old soldier—and even his voice seemed to be bobbing up and down as he spoke—"my dear friend, it would be madness to go home in *your* state; you would be sure to lose your money; you might be robbed and murdered with the greatest ease. *I* am going to sleep here; do *you* sleep here, too—they make up capital beds in this house—take one; sleep off the effects of the wine, and go home safely with your winnings to-morrow—to-morrow, in broad daylight."

I had but two ideas left:—one, that I must never let go hold of my handkerchief full of money; the other, that I must lie down somewhere immediately, and fall off into a comfortable sleep. So I agreed to the proposal about the bed, and took the offered arm of the old soldier, carrying my money with my disengaged hand. Preceded by the croupier, we passed along some passages and up a flight of stairs into the bedroom which I was to occupy. The ex-brave shook me warmly by the hand, proposed that we should breakfast together, and then, followed by the croupier, left me for the night.

I ran to the wash-hand stand; drank some of the water in my jug; poured the rest out, and plunged my face into it; then sat down in a chair and tried to compose myself. I soon felt better. The change for my lungs, from the fetid atmosphere of the gambling-room to the cool air of the apartment I now occupied; the almost equally refreshing change for my eyes, from the glaring gas-lights of the 'Salon' to the dim, quiet flicker of one bedroom candle, aided wonderfully the restorative effects of cold water. The giddiness left me, and I began to feel a little like a reasonable being again. My first thought was of the risk of sleeping all night in a gambling-house; my second, of the still greater risk of trying to get out after the house was closed, and of going home alone at night, through the streets of Paris, with a large sum of money about me. I had slept in worse places than this on my travels; so I determined to lock, bolt, and barricade my door, and take my chance till the next morning.

Accordingly, I secured myself against all intrusion; looked under the bed, and into the cupboard; tried the fastening of the window; and then, satisfied that I had taken every proper precaution, pulled off my upper clothing, put my light, which was a dim one, on the hearth among a feathery litter of wood ashes, and got into bed, with the handkerchief full of money under my pillow. I soon felt not only that I could not go to sleep, but that I could not even close my eyes. I was wide awake, and in a high fever. Every nerve in my body trembled—every one of my senses seemed to be preternaturally sharpened. I tossed and rolled, and tried every kind of position, and perseveringly sought out the cold corners of the bed, and all to no purpose. Now, I thrust my arms over the clothes; now, I poked them under the clothes; now, I violently shot my legs straight out down to the bottom of the bed; now, I convulsively coiled them up as near my chin as they would go; now, I shook out my crumpled pillow, changed it to the cool side, patted it flat, and lay down quietly on my back; now, I fiercely doubled it in two, set it up on end, thrust it against the board of the bed, and tried a sitting posture. Every effort was in vain; I groaned with vexation, as I felt that I was in for a sleepless night.

What could I do? I had no book to read. And yet, unless I found out some method of diverting my mind, I felt certain that I was in the condition to imagine all sorts of horrors; to rack my brain with forebodings of every possible and impossible danger; in short, to pass the night in suffering all conceivable varieties of nervous terror.

I raised myself on my elbow, and looked about the room—which was brightened by a lovely moonlight pouring straight through the window— to see if it contained any pictures or ornaments that I could at all clearly distinguish. While my eyes wandered from wall to wall, a remembrance of Le Maistre's delightful little book, *Voyage autôur de ma Chambre*, occurred to me. I resolved to imitate the French author, and find occupation and amusement enough to relieve the tedium of my wakefulness, by making a mental inventory of every article of furniture I could see, and by following up to their sources the multitude of associations which even a chair, a table, or a wash-hand stand may be made to call forth.

In the nervous unsettled state of my mind at that moment, I found it much easier to make my inventory than to make my reflections, and thereupon soon gave up all hope of thinking in Le Maistre's fanciful track—or, indeed, of thinking at all. I looked about the room at the different articles of furniture, and did nothing more.

There was, first, the bed I was lying in; a four-post bed, of all things in the world to meet with in Paris!—yes, a thorough clumsy British four-poster, with the regular top lined with chintz—the regular fringed valance all round—the regular stifling unwholesome curtains, which I remembered having mechanically drawn back against the posts without particularly noticing the bed when I first got into the room. Then there was the marble-topped wash-hand stand, from which the water I had spilt, in my hurry to pour it out, was still dripping, slowly and more slowly, on to the brick floor. Then two small chairs, with my coat, waistcoat, and trousers flung on them. Then a large elbow-chair covered with dirty-white dimity, with my cravat and shirt-collar thrown over the back. Then a chest of drawers with two of the brass handles off, and a tawdry, broken china inkstand placed on it by way of ornament for the top. Then the dressing-table, adorned by a very small looking-glass, and a very large pincushion. Then the window—an unusually large window. Then a dark old picture, which the feeble candle dimly showed me. It was the picture of a fellow in a high Spanish hat, crowned with a plume of towering feathers. A swarthy sinister ruffian, looking upward, shading his eyes with his hand, and looking intently upward—it might be at some tall gallows at which he was going to be hanged. At any rate, he had the appearance of thoroughly deserving it.

This picture put a kind of constraint upon me to look upward too—at the top of the bed. It was a gloomy and not an interesting object, and I looked back at the picture. I counted the feathers in the man's hat—they stood out in relief—three white, two green. I observed the crown of his hat, which was of a conical shape, according to the fashion supposed to have been favoured by Guido Fawkes. I wondered what he was looking up at. It couldn't be at the stars; such a desperado was neither astrologer nor astronomer. It must be at the high gallows, and he was going to be hanged presently. Would the executioner come into possession of his conical-crowned hat and plume of feathers? I counted the feathers again—three white, two green.

While I still lingered over this very improving and intellectual employment, my thoughts insensibly began to wander. The moonlight shining into the room reminded me of a certain moonlight night in England—the night after a picnic party in a Welsh valley. Every incident of the drive homeward, through lovely scenery, which the moonlight made lovelier than ever, came back to my remembrance, though I had never given the picnic a thought for years; though, if I had *tried* to recollect it, I could certainly have recalled little or nothing of that scene long past. Of all the wonderful faculties that help to tell us we are immortal, which speaks the sublime truth more eloquently than memory? Here was I, in a strange house of the most suspicious character, in a situation of uncertainty, and even of peril, which might seem to make the cool exercise of my recollection almost out of the question; nevertheless, remembering, quite involuntarily, places, people, conversations, minute circumstances of every kind, which I had thought forgotten for ever; which I could not possibly have recalled at will, even under the most favourable auspices. And what cause had produced in a moment the whole of this strange, complicated, mysterious effect? Nothing but some rays of moonlight shining in at my bedroom window.

I was still thinking of the picnic—of our merriment on the drive home—of the sentimental young lady who *would* quote *Childe Harold* because it was moonlight. I was absorbed by these past scenes and past amusements, when, in an instant, the thread on which my memories hung snapped asunder; my attention immediately came back to present things more vividly than ever, and I found myself, I neither knew why nor wherefore, looking hard at the picture again.

Looking for what?

Good God! the man had pulled his hat down on his brows!—No! the hat itself was gone! Where was the conical crown? Where the feathers—three white, two green? Not there? In place of the hat and feathers, what dusky object was it that now hid his forehead, his eyes, his shading hand? Was the bed moving?

I turned on my back and looked up. Was I mad? drunk? dreaming? giddy again? or was the top of the bed really moving down—sinking slowly, regularly, silently, horribly, right down throughout the whole of its length and breadth—right down upon me, as I lay underneath?

My blood seemed to stand still. A deadly paralysing coldness stole all over me, as I turned my head round on the pillow, and determined to test whether the bed-top was really moving or not, by keeping my eye on the man in the picture.

The next look in that direction was enough. The dull, black, frowsy outline of the valance above me was within an inch of being parallel with his waist. I still looked breathlessly. And steadily, and slowly—very slowly—I saw the figure, and the line of frame below the figure, vanish, as the valance moved down before it.

I am, constitutionally, anything but timid. I have been on more than one occasion in peril of my life, and have not lost my self-possession for an instant; but when the conviction first settled on my mind that the bed-top was really moving, was steadily and continuously sinking down upon me, I looked up shuddering, helpless, panic-stricken, beneath the hideous machinery for murder, which was advancing closer and closer to suffocate me where I lay.

I looked up, motionless, speechless, breathless. The candle, fully spent, went out; but the moonlight still brightened the room. Down and down, without pausing and without sounding, came the bed-top, and still my panic-terror seemed to bind me faster and faster to the mattress on which I lay—down and down it sank, till the dusty odour from the lining of the canopy came stealing into my nostrils.

At the final moment the instinct of self-preservation startled me out of my trance, and I moved at last. There was just room for me to roll myself sideways off the bed. As I dropped noiselessly to the floor, the edge of the murderous canopy touched me on the shoulder.

141

Without stopping to draw my breath, without wiping the cold sweat from my face, I rose instantly on my knees to watch the bed-top. I was literally spell-bound by it. If I had heard footsteps behind me, I could not have turned round; if a means of escape had been miraculously provided for me, I could not have moved to take advantage of it. The whole life in me was, at that moment, concentrated in my eyes.

It descended—the whole canopy, with the fringe round it, came down —down—close down; so close that there was not room now to squeeze my finger between the bed-top and the bed. I felt at the sides, and discovered that what had appeared to me from beneath to be the ordinary light canopy of a four-post bed, was in reality a thick, broad mattress, the substance of which was concealed by the valance and its fringe. I looked up and saw the four posts rising hideously bare. In the middle of the bed-top was a huge wooden screw that had evidently worked it down through a hole in the ceiling, just as ordinary presses are worked down on the substance selected for compression. The frightful apparatus moved without making the faintest noise. There had been no creaking as it came down; there was now not the faintest sound from the room above. Amid a dead and awful silence I beheld before me—in the nineteenth century, and in the civilized capital of France— such a machine for secret murder by suffocation as might have existed in the worst days of the Inquisition, in the lonely inns among the Hartz Mountains, in the mysterious tribunals of Westphalia! Still, as I looked on it, I could not move, I could hardly breathe, but I began to recover the power of thinking, and in a moment I discovered the murderous conspiracy framed against me in all its horror.

My cup of coffee had been drugged, and drugged too strongly. I had been saved from being smothered by having taken an overdose of some narcotic. How I had chafed and fretted at the fever-fit which had preserved my life by keeping me awake! How recklessly I had confided myself to the two wretches who had led me into this room, determined, for the sake of my winnings, to kill me in my sleep by the surest and most horrible contrivance for secretly accomplishing my destruction! How many men, winners like me, had slept, as I had proposed to sleep, in that bed, and had never been seen or heard of more! I shuddered at the bare idea of it.

But, ere long, all thought was again suspended by the sight of the murderous canopy moving once more. After it had remained on the bed—as nearly as I could guess—about ten minutes, it began to move up again. The villains who worked it from above evidently believed that their purpose was now accomplished. Slowly and silently, as it had descended, that horrible bed-top rose towards its former place. When it reached the upper extremities of the four posts, it reached the ceiling too. Neither hole nor screw could be seen; the bed became in appearance an ordinary bed again—the canopy an ordinary canopy—even to the most suspicious eyes.

Now, for the first time, I was able to move—to rise from my knees—to dress myself in my upper clothing—and to consider of how I should escape. If I betrayed, by the smallest noise, that the attempt to suffocate me had failed, I was certain to be murdered. Had I made any noise already? I listened intently, looking towards the door.

No! no footsteps in the passage outside—no sound of a tread, light or heavy, in the room above—absolute silence everywhere. Besides locking and bolting my door, I had moved an old wooden chest against it, which I had found under the bed. To remove this chest (my blood ran cold as I thought of what its contents *might* be!) without making some disturbance was impossible; and, moreover, to think of escaping through the house, now barred up for the night, was sheer insanity. Only one chance was left me—the window. I stole to it on tiptoe.

My bedroom was on the first floor, above an *entresol*, and looked into the back street, which you have sketched in your view. I raised my hand to open the window, knowing that on that action hung, by the merest hair's-breadth, my chance of safety. They keep vigilant watch in a House of Murder. If any part of the frame cracked, if the hinge creaked, I was a lost man! It must have occupied me at least five minutes, reckoning by time—five *hours*, reckoning by suspense—to open that window. I succeeded in doing it silently—in doing it with all the dexterity of a housebreaker—and then looked down into the street. To leap the distance beneath me would be almost certain destruction! Next, I looked round at the sides of the house. Down the left side ran the thick water-pipe which you have drawn—it passed close by the outer edge of the window. The moment I saw the pipe, I knew I was saved. My breath came and went freely for the first time since I had seen the canopy of the bed moving down upon me!

To some men the means of escape which I had discovered might have seemed difficult and dangerous enough—to *me* the prospect of slipping down the pipe into the street did not suggest even a thought of peril. I had always been accustomed, by the practice of gymnastics, to keep up my schoolboy powers as a daring and expert climber; and knew that my head, hands, and feet would serve me faithfully in any hazards of ascent or descent. I had already got one leg over the window-sill, when I remembered the handkerchief filled with money under my pillow. I could well have afforded to leave it behind me, but I was revengefully determined that the miscreants of the gambling-house should miss their plunder as well as their victim. So I went back to the bed and tied the heavy handkerchief at my back by my cravat.

143

Just as I had made it tight and fixed it in a comfortable place, I thought I heard a sound of breathing outside the door. The chill feeling of horror ran through me again as I listened. No! dead silence still in the passage—I had only heard the night-air blowing softly into the room. The next moment I was on the window-sill—and the next I had a firm grip on the water-pipe with my hands and knees.

I slid down into the street easily and quietly, as I thought I should, and immediately set off at the top of my speed to a branch 'Prefecture' of Police, which I knew was situated in the immediate neighbourhood. A 'Sub-prefect', and several picked men among his subordinates, happened to be up, maturing, I believe, some scheme for discovering the perpetrator of a mysterious murder which all Paris was talking of just then. When I began my story, in a breathless hurry and in very bad French, I could see that the Sub-prefect suspected me of being a drunken Englishman who had robbed somebody; but he soon altered his opinion as I went on, and before I had anything like concluded, he shoved all the papers before him into a drawer, put on his hat, supplied me with another (for I was bare-headed), ordered a file of soldiers, desired his expert followers to get ready all sorts of tools for breaking open doors and ripping up brick-flooring, and took my arm, in the most friendly and familiar manner possible, to lead me with him out of the house. I will venture to say, that when the Sub-prefect was a little boy, and was taken for the first time to the play, he was not half as much pleased as he was now at the job in prospect for him at the gambling-house!

Away we went through the streets, the Sub-prefect cross-examining and congratulating me in the same breath as we marched at the head of our formidable *posse comitatus*. Sentinels were placed at the back and front of the house the moment we got to it; a tremendous battery of knocks was directed against the door; a light appeared at a window; I was told to conceal myself behind the police—then came more knocks, and a cry of "Open in the name of the law!" At that terrible summons bolts and locks gave way before an invisible hand, and the moment after the Sub-prefect was in the passage, confronting a waiter half-dressed and ghastly pale. This was the short dialogue which immediately took place:—

"We want to see the Englishman who is sleeping in this house?"

"He went away hours ago."

"He did no such thing. His friend went away; *he* remained. Show us to his bedroom!"

"I swear to you, Monsieur le Sous-préfet, he is not here! he——"

"I swear to you, Monsieur le Garçon, he is. He slept here—he didn't find your bed comfortable—he came to us to complain of it—here he is

144

among my men—and here am I ready to look for a flea or two in his bedstead. Renaudin!" (calling to one of the subordinates, and pointing to the waiter) "collar that man, and tie his hands behind him. Now, then, gentlemen, let us walk upstairs!"

Every man and woman in the house was secured—the 'Old Soldier' the first. Then I identified the bed in which I had slept, and then we went into the room above.

No object that was at all extraordinary appeared in any part of it. The Sub-prefect looked round the place, commanded everybody to be silent, stamped twice on the floor, called for a candle, looked attentively at the spot he had stamped on, and ordered the flooring there to be carefully taken up. This was done in no time. Lights were produced, and we saw a deep rafted cavity between the floor of this room and the ceiling of the room beneath. Through this cavity there ran perpendicularly a sort of case of iron thickly greased; and inside the case appeared the screw, which communicated with the bed-top below. Extra lengths of screw, freshly oiled; levers covered with felt; all the complete upper works of a heavy press—constructed with infernal ingenuity so as to join the fixtures below, and when taken to pieces again to go into the smallest possible compass—were next discovered and pulled out on the floor. After some little difficulty the Sub-prefect succeeded in putting the machinery together, and, leaving his men to work it, descended with me to the bedroom. The smothering canopy was then lowered, but not noiselessly as I had seen it lowered. When I mentioned this to the Sub-prefect, his answer, simple as it was, had a terrible significance. "My men," said he, "are working down the bed-top for the first time— the men whose money you won were in better practice."

We left the house in the sole possession of two police agents—every one of the inmates being removed to prison on the spot. The Sub-prefect, after taking down my *procès-verbal* in his office, returned with me to my hotel to get my passport. "Do you think," I asked, as I gave it to him, "that any men have really been smothered in that bed, as they tried to smother *me*?"

"I have seen dozens of drowned men laid out at the Morgue," answered the Sub-prefect, "in whose pocket-books were found letters, stating that they had committed suicide in the Seine, because they had lost everything at the gaming-table. Do I know how many of those men entered the same gambling-house that *you* entered? won as *you* won? took that bed as *you* took it? slept in it? were smothered in it? and were privately thrown into the river, with a letter of explanation written by the murderers and placed in their pocket-books? No man can say how many or how few have suffered the fate from which you have escaped. The people of the gambling-house kept their bedstead machinery a secret from *us*—even from the police! The dead kept the rest of the secret for them. Good night, or rather good morning, Monsieur Faulkner! Be at my office again at nine o'clock—in the meantime, *au revoir!*"

The rest of my story is soon told. I was examined and re-examined; the gambling-house was strictly searched all through from top to bottom; the prisoners were separately interrogated; and two of the less guilty among them made a confession. *I* discovered that the Old Soldier was the master of the gambling-house—*justice* discovered that he had been drummed out of the army as a vagabond years ago; that he had been guilty of all sorts of villainies since; that he was in possession of stolen property, which the owners identified; and that he, the croupier, another accomplice, and the woman who had made my cup of coffee, were all in the secret of the bedstead. There appeared some reason to doubt whether the inferior persons attached to the house knew anything of the suffocating machinery; and they received the benefit of that doubt, by being treated simply as thieves and vagabonds. As for the Old Soldier and his two head-myrmidons, they went to the galleys; the woman who had drugged my coffee was imprisoned for I forget how many years; the regular attendants at the gambling-house were considered 'suspicious', and placed under 'surveillance'; and I became, for one whole week (which is a long time), the head lion' in Parisian society. My adventure was dramatized by three illustrious playmakers, but never saw theatrical daylight; for the censorship forbade the introduction on the stage of a correct copy of the gambling-house bedstead.

One good result was produced by my adventure, which any censorship must have approved:—it cured me of ever again trying *Rouge et Noir* as an amusement. The sight of a green cloth, with packs of cards and heaps of money on it, will henceforth be for ever associated in my mind with the sight of a bed-canopy descending to suffocate me in the silence and darkness of the night.

JOSEPH CONRAD

1857–1924

A Ukrainian seaman of Polish extraction who became an enormously
successful English author, Conrad was a man whose life story reads like
an episode from one of his own books. But, though he wrote
vividly of adventure in many countries, it is undoubtedly
for his sea stories that he is most renowned.

The Brute

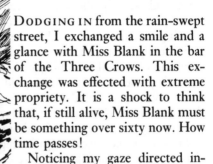

DODGING IN from the rain-swept
street, I exchanged a smile and a
glance with Miss Blank in the bar
of the Three Crows. This exchange was effected with extreme
propriety. It is a shock to think
that, if still alive, Miss Blank must
be something over sixty now. How
time passes!

Noticing my gaze directed in-
quiringly at the partition of glass and varnished wood, Miss Blank was
good enough to say, encouragingly: "Only Mr. Jermyn and Mr. Stonor
in the parlour with another gentleman I've never seen before."

I moved towards the parlour door. A voice discoursing on the other
side (it was but a matchboard partition), rose so loudly that the concluding words became quite plain in all their atrocity.

"That fellow Wilmot fairly dashed her brains out, and a good job,
too!"

This inhuman sentiment, since there was nothing profane or improper
in it, failed to do as much as to check the slight yawn Miss Blank was
achieving behind her hand. And she remained gazing fixedly at the
window-panes, which streamed with rain.

As I opened the parlour door the same voice went on in the same
cruel strain: "I was glad when I heard she got the knock from somebody
at last. Sorry enough for poor Wilmot, though. That man and I used

147

to be chums at one time. Of course that was the end of him. A clear case if there ever was one. No way out of it. None at all."

The voice belonged to the gentleman Miss Blank had never seen before. He straddled his long legs on the hearthrug. Jermyn, leaning forward, held his pocket-handkerchief spread out before the grate. He looked back dismally over his shoulder, and as I slipped behind one of the little wooden tables, I nodded to him. On the other side of the fire, imposingly calm and large, sat Mr. Stonor, jammed tight into a capacious Windsor armchair. There was nothing small about him but his short, white side-whiskers. Yards and yards of extra superfine blue cloth (made up into an overcoat) reposed on a chair by his side. And he must just have brought some liner from sea, because another chair was smothered under his black waterproof, ample as a pall, and made of three-fold oiled silk, double-stitched throughout. A man's hand-bag of the usual size looked like a child's toy on the floor near his feet.

I did not nod to him. He was too big to be nodded to in that parlour. He was a senior Trinity pilot and condescended to take his turn in the cutter only during the summer months. He had been many times in charge of royal yachts in and out of Port Victoria. Besides, it's no use nodding to a monument. And he was like one. He didn't speak, he didn't budge. He just sat there, holding his handsome old head up, immovable, and almost bigger than life. It was extremely fine. Mr. Stonor's presence reduced poor old Jermyn to a mere shabby wisp of a man, and made the talkative stranger in tweeds on the hearthrug look absurdly boyish. The latter must have been a few years over thirty, and was certainly not the sort of individual that gets abashed at the sound of his own voice, because gathering me in, as it were, by a friendly glance, he kept it going without a check.

"I was glad of it," he repeated, emphatically. "You may be surprised at it, but then you haven't gone through the experience I've had of her. I can tell you, it was something to remember. Of course, I got off scot free myself—as you can see. She did her best to break up my pluck for me tho'. She jolly near drove as fine a fellow as ever lived into a mad-house. What do you say to that—eh?"

Not an eyelid twitched in Mr. Stonor's enormous face. Monumental! The speaker looked straight into my eyes.

"It used to make me sick to think of her going about the world murdering people."

Jermyn approached the handkerchief a little nearer to the grate and groaned. It was simply a habit he had.

"I've seen her once," he declared, with mournful indifference. "She had a house——"

The stranger in tweeds turned to stare down at him, surprised.

148

"She had three houses," he corrected, authoritatively. But Jermyn was not to be contradicted.

"She had a house, I say," he repeated, with dismal obstinacy. "A great, big, ugly, white thing. You could see it from miles away—sticking up."

"So you could," assented the other readily. "It was old Colchester's notion, though he was always threatening to give her up. He couldn't stand her racket any more, he declared; it was too much of a good thing for him; he would wash his hands of her, if he never got hold of another —and so on. I daresay he would have chucked her, only—it may surprise you—his missus wouldn't hear of it. Funny, eh? But with women, you never know how they will take a thing, and Mrs. Colchester, with her moustaches and big eyebrows, set up for being as strong-minded as they make them. She used to walk about in a brown silk dress, with a great gold cable flopping about her bosom. You should have heard her snapping out: 'Rubbish!' or 'Stuff and nonsense!' I dare-say she knew when she was well off. They had no children, and had never set up a home anywhere. When in England she just made shift to hang out anyhow in some cheap hotel or boarding-house. I daresay she liked to get back to the comforts she was used to. She knew very well she couldn't gain by any change. And, moreover, Colchester, though a first-rate man, was not what you may call in his first youth, and, perhaps, she may have thought that he wouldn't be able to get hold of another (as he used to say) so easily. Anyhow, for one reason or another, it was 'Rubbish' and 'Stuff and nonsense' for the good lady. I overheard once young Mr. Apse himself say to her confidentially: 'I assure you, Mrs. Colchester, I am beginning to feel unhappy about the name she's getting for herself.' 'Oh,' says she, with her deep little hoarse laugh, 'if one took notice of all the silly talk,' and she showed Apse all her ugly false teeth at once. 'It would take more than that to make me lose my confidence in her, I assure you,' says she."

At this point, without any change of facial expression, Mr. Stonor emitted a short, sardonic laugh. It was very impressive, but I didn't see the fun. I looked from one to another. The stranger on the hearthrug had an ugly smile.

"And Mr. Apse shook both Mrs. Colchester's hands, he was so pleased to hear a good word said for their favourite. All these Apses, young and old you know, were perfectly infatuated with that abominable, dangerous——"

"I beg your pardon," I interrupted, for he seemed to be addressing himself exclusively to me; "but who on earth are you talking about?"

"I am talking of the Apse family," he answered courteously.

I nearly let out a damn at this. But just then the respected Miss Blank

149

put her head in, and said that the cab was at the door, if Mr. Stonor wanted to catch the eleven-three up.

At once the senior pilot arose in his mighty bulk and began to struggle into his coat, with awe-inspiring upheavals. The stranger and I hurried impulsively to his assistance, and directly we laid our hands on him he became perfectly quiescent. We had to raise our arms very high, and to make efforts. It was like caparisoning a docile elephant. With a "Thanks, gentlemen," he dived under and squeezed himself through the door in a great hurry.

We smiled at each other in a friendly way.

"I wonder how he manages to hoist himself up a ship's side-ladder," said the man in tweeds; and poor Jermyn, who was a mere North Sea pilot, without official status or recognition of any sort, pilot only by courtesy, groaned.

"He makes eight hundred a year."

"Are you a sailor?" I asked the stranger, who had gone back to his position on the rug.

"I used to be till a couple of years ago, when I got married," answered this communicative individual. "I even went to sea first in that very ship we were speaking of when you came in."

"What ship?" I asked, puzzled. "I never heard you mention a ship."

"I've just told you her name, my dear sir," he replied. "The *Apse Family*. Surely you've heard of the great firm of Apse & Sons, ship-owners. They had a pretty big fleet. There was the *Lucy Apse*, and the *Harold Apse*, and *Anne, John, Malcolm, Clara, Juliet*, and so on—no end of *Apses*. Every brother, sister, aunt, cousin, wife—and grandmother, too, for all I know—of the firm had a ship named after them. Good, solid, old-fashioned craft they were, too, built to carry and to last. None of your new-fangled, labour-saving appliances in them, but plenty of men and plenty of good salt beef and hard tack put aboard—and off you go to fight your way out and home again."

The miserable Jermyn made a sound of approval, which sounded like a groan of pain. Those were the ships for him. He pointed out in doleful tones that you couldn't say to labour-saving appliances: "Jump lively now, my hearties." No labour-saving appliance would go aloft on a dirty night with the sands under your lee.

"No," assented the stranger, with a wink at me. "The Apses didn't believe in them either, apparently. They treated their people well—as people don't get treated nowadays, and they were awfully proud of their ships. Nothing ever happened to them. This last one, the *Apse Family*, was to be like the others, only she was to be still stronger, still safer, still more roomy and comfortable. I believe they meant her to last for ever. They had her built composite—iron, teak-wood, and green heart, and her scantling was something fabulous. If ever an order was given for a ship in a spirit of pride this one was. Everything of the best. The commodore captain of the employ was to command her, and they planned the accommodation for him like a house on shore under a big, tall poop that went nearly to the mainmast. No wonder Mrs. Colchester wouldn't let the old man give her up. Why, it was the best home she ever had in all her married days. She had a nerve, that woman.

"The fuss that was made while that ship was building! Let's have this a little stronger, and that a little heavier; and hadn't that other thing better be changed for something a little thicker. The builders entered into the spirit of the game, and there she was, growing into the clumsiest, heaviest ship of her size right before all their eyes, without anybody becoming aware of it somehow. She was to be 2,000 tons register, or a little over; no less on any account. But see what happens. When they came to measure her she turned out 1,999 tons and a fraction. General consternation! And they say old Mr. Apse was so annoyed when they told him that he took to his bed and died. The old gentleman had retired from the firm twenty-five years before, and was ninety-six years old if a day, so his death wasn't, perhaps, so surprising. Still Mr. Lucian Apse was convinced that his father would have lived to a hundred. So we may put him at the head of the list. Next comes the poor devil of a shipwright that brute caught and squashed as she went off the ways. They called it the launch of a ship, but I've heard people say that, from the wailing and yelling and scrambling out of the way, it was more like letting a devil loose upon the river. She snapped all her checks like pack-thread, and went for the tugs in attendance like a fury. Before anybody could see what she was up to she sent one of them to the bottom, and laid up another for three months' repairs. One of her cables parted, and then, suddenly—you couldn't tell why—she let herself be brought up with the other as quiet as a lamb.

"That's how she was. You could never be sure what she would be up to next. There are ships difficult to handle, but generally you can depend on them behaving rationally. With *that* ship, whatever you did with her you never knew how it would end. She was a wicked beast. Or, perhaps, she was only just insane."

He uttered this supposition in so earnest a tone that I could not refrain from smiling. He left off biting his lower lip to apostrophize me.

"Eh! Why not? Why couldn't there be something in her build, in her lines corresponding to—— What's madness? Only something just a tiny bit wrong in the make of your brain. Why shouldn't there be a mad ship—I mean mad in a ship-like way, so that under no circumstances could you be sure she would do what any other sensible ship would naturally do for you. There are ships that steer wildly, and ships that

151

can't be quite trusted always to stay; others want careful watching when running in a gale; and, again, there may be a ship that will make heavy weather of it in every little blow. But then you expect her to be always so. You take it as part of her character, as a ship, just as you take account of a man's peculiarities of temper when you deal with him. But with her you couldn't. She was unaccountable. If she wasn't mad, then she was the most evil-minded, underhand, savage brute that ever went afloat. I've seen her run in a heavy gale beautifully for two days, and on the third broach to twice in the same afternoon. The first time she flung the helmsman clean over the wheel, but as she didn't quite manage to kill him she had another try about three hours afterwards. She swamped herself fore and aft, burst all the canvas we had set, scared all hands into a panic, and even frightened Mrs. Colchester down there in those beautiful stern cabins that she was so proud of. When we mustered the crew there was one man missing. Swept overboard, of course, without being either seen or heard, poor devil! and I only wonder more of us didn't go.

"Always something like that. Always. I heard an old mate tell Captain Colchester once that it had come to this with him, that he was afraid to open his mouth to give any sort of order. She was as much of a terror in harbour as at sea. You could never be certain what would hold her. On the slightest provocation she would start snapping ropes, cables, wire hawsers, like carrots. She was heavy, clumsy, unhandy—but that does not quite explain that power for mischief she had. You know, somehow, when I think of her I can't help remembering what we hear of incurable lunatics breaking loose now and then."

He looked at me inquisitively. But, of course, I couldn't admit that a ship could be mad.

"In the ports where she was known," he went on, "they dreaded the sight of her. She thought nothing of knocking away twenty feet or so of solid stone facing off a quay or wiping off the end of a wooden wharf. She must have lost miles of chain and hundreds of tons of anchors in her time. When she fell aboard some poor unoffending ship it was the very devil of a job to haul her off again. And she never got hurt herself —just a few scratches or so, perhaps. They had wanted to have her strong. And so she was. Strong enough to ram Polar ice with. And as she began so she went on. From the day she was launched she never let a year pass without murdering somebody. I think the owners got very worried about it. But they were a stiff-necked generation all these Apses; they wouldn't admit there could be anything wrong with the *Apse Family*. They wouldn't even change her name. 'Stuff and nonsense,' as Mrs. Colchester used to say. They ought at least to have shut her up for life in some dry dock or other, away up the river, and never let her smell salt water again. I assure you, my dear sir, that she invariably did kill someone every voyage she made. It was perfectly well-known. She got a name for it, far and wide."

I expressed my surprise that a ship with such a deadly reputation could ever get a crew.

"Then, you don't know what sailors are, my dear sir. Let me just show you by an instance. One day in dock at home, while loafing on the forecastle head, I noticed two respectable salts come along, one a middle-aged, competent, steady man, evidently, the other a smart, youngish chap. They read the name on the bows and stopped to look at her. Says the elder man: '*Apse Family*. That's the sanguinary female dog' (I'm putting it in that way) 'of a ship, Jack, that kills a man every voyage. I wouldn't sign in her—not for Joe, I wouldn't.' And the other says: 'If she were mine, I'd have her towed on the mud and set on fire, blamme if I wouldn't.' Then the first man chimes in: 'Much do they care! Men are cheap, God knows.' The younger one spat in the water alongside. 'They won't have me—not for double wages.'

"They hung about for some time and then walked up the dock. Half an hour later I saw them both on our deck looking about for the mate, and apparently very anxious to be taken on. And they were."

"How do you account for this?" I asked.

"What would you say?" he retorted. "Recklessness! The vanity of boasting in the evening to all their chums: 'We've just shipped in that there *Apse Family*. Blow her. She ain't going to scare us.' Sheer sailor-like perversity! A sort of curiosity. Well—a little of all that, no doubt. I put the question to them in the course of the voyage. The answer of the elderly chap was:

"'A man can die but once.' The younger assured me in a mocking tone that he wanted to see 'how she would do it this time.' But I tell you what; there was a sort of fascination about the brute."

Jermyn, who seemed to have seen every ship in the world, broke in sulkily: "I saw her once out of this very window towing up the river; a great black ugly thing, going along like a big hearse."

"Something sinister about her looks, wasn't there?" said the man in tweeds, looking down at old Jermyn with a friendly eye. "I always had a sort of horror of her. She gave me a beastly shock when I was no more than fourteen, the very first day—nay, hour—I joined her. Father came up to see me off, and was to go down to Gravesend with us. I was his second boy to go to sea. My big brother was already an officer then. We got on board about eleven in the morning, and found the ship ready to drop out of the basin, stern first. She had not moved three times her own length when, at a little pluck the tug gave her to enter the dock gates, she made one of her rampaging starts, and put such a weight on the check rope—a new six-inch hawser—that forward there they had no chance to ease it round in time, and it parted. I saw the broken end fly up high in the air, and the next moment that brute brought her quarter against the pier-head with a jar that staggered everybody about her decks. She didn't hurt herself. Not she! But one of the boys the mate had sent aloft on the mizzen to do something, came down on the poop-deck—thump—right in front of me. He was not much older than myself. We had been grinning at each other only a few minutes before. He must have been handling himself carelessly, not expecting to get such a jerk. I heard his startled cry—Oh!—in a high treble as he felt himself going, and looked up in time to see him go limp all over as he fell. Ough! Poor father was remarkably white about the gills when we shook hands in Gravesend. 'Are you all right?' he says, looking hard at me. 'Yes, father.' 'Quite sure?' 'Yes, father.' 'Well, then good-bye, my boy.' He told me afterwards that for half a word he would have carried me off home with him there and then. I am the baby of the family—you know," added the man in tweeds, stroking his moustache with an ingenuous smile.

I acknowledged this interesting communication by a sympathetic murmur. He waved his hand carelessly.

"This might have utterly spoiled a chap's nerve for going aloft, you know—utterly. He fell within two feet of me, cracking his head on a mooring-bitt. Never moved. Stone dead. Nice looking little fellow, he was. I had just been thinking we would be great chums. However, that wasn't yet the worst that brute of a ship could do. I served in her three years of my time, and then I got transferred to the *Lucy Apse*, for a year. The sailmaker we had in the *Apse Family* turned up there, too, and I remember him saying to me one evening, after we had been a week at sea: 'Isn't she a meek little ship?' No wonder we thought the *Lucy Apse* a dear, meek, little ship after getting clear of that big, rampaging savage brute. It was like heaven. Her officers seemed to me the restfullest lot of men on earth. To me who had known no ship but the *Apse Family*, the *Lucy* was like a sort of magic craft that did what you wanted her to do of her own accord. One evening we got caught aback pretty sharply from right ahead. In about ten minutes we had her full again, sheets aft, tacks down, decks cleared, and the officer of the watch leaning against the weather rail peacefully. It seemed simply marvellous to me. The other would have stuck for half an hour in irons, rolling her decks full of water, knocking the men about—spars cracking, braces snapping, yards taking charge, and a confounded scare going on aft because of her beastly rudder, which she had a way of flapping about fit to raise your hair on end. I couldn't get over my wonder for days.

"Well, I finished my last year of apprenticeship in that jolly little ship—she wasn't so little either, but after that other heavy devil she seemed but a plaything to handle. I finished my time and passed; and then just as I was thinking of having three weeks of real good time on shore I got at breakfast a letter asking me the earliest day I could be ready to join the *Apse Family* as third mate. I gave my plate a shove that shot it into the middle of the table; dad looked up over his paper; mother raised her hands in astonishment, and I went out bare-headed into our bit of garden, where I walked round and round for an hour.

"When I came in again mother was out of the dining-room, and dad had shifted berth into his big armchair. The letter was lying on the mantelpiece.

"'It's very creditable to you to get the offer, and very kind of them to make it,' he said. 'And I see also that Charles has been appointed chief mate of that ship for one voyage.'

"There was, overleaf, a P.S. to that effect in Mr. Apse's own hand-writing, which I had overlooked. Charley was my big brother.

"'I don't like very much to have two of my boys together in one ship,' father goes on, in his deliberate, solemn way. 'And I may tell you that I would not mind writing Mr. Apse a letter to that effect.'

"Dear old dad! He was a wonderful father. What would you have done? The mere notion of going back (and as an officer, too), to be worried and bothered, and kept on the jump night and day by that brute, made me feel sick. But she wasn't a ship you could afford to fight shy of. Besides, the most genuine excuse could not be given without mortally offending Apse & Sons. The firm, and I believe the whole family down to the old unmarried aunts in Lancashire, had grown desperately touchy about that accursed ship's character. This was the case for answering 'Ready now' from your very death-bed if you wished to die in their good graces. And that's precisely what I did answer—by wire, to have it over and done with at once.

"The prospect of being shipmates with my big brother cheered me up considerably, though it made me a bit anxious, too. Ever since I remember myself as a little chap he had been very good to me, and I looked upon him as the finest fellow in the world. And so he was. No better officer ever walked the deck of a merchant ship. And that's a fact. He was a fine, strong, upstanding, sun-tanned, young fellow, with his brown hair curling a little, and an eye like a hawk. He was just splendid. We hadn't seen each other for many years, and even this time, though he had been in England three weeks already, he hadn't showed up at home yet, but had spent his spare time in Surrey somewhere making up to Maggie Colchester, old Captain Colchester's niece. Her father, a great friend of dad's, was in the sugar-broking business, and Charley made a sort of second home of their house. I wondered what my big brother would think of me. There was a sort of sternness about Charley's face which never left it, not even when he was larking in his rather wild fashion.

"He received me with a great shout of laughter. He seemed to think my joining as an officer the greatest joke in the world. There was a difference of ten years between us, and I suppose he remembered me best in pinafores. I was a kid of four when he first went to sea. It surprised me to find how boisterous he could be.

"'Now we shall see what you are made of,' he cried. And he held me off by the shoulders, and punched my ribs, and hustled me into his berth. 'Sit down, Ned. I am glad of the chance of having you with me. I'll put the finishing touch to you, my young officer, providing you're worth the trouble. And, first of all, get it well into your head that we are not going to let this brute kill anybody this voyage. We'll stop her racket.'

"I perceived he was in dead earnest about it. He talked grimly of the ship, and how we must be careful and never allow this ugly beast to catch us napping with any of her damned tricks.

"He gave me a regular lecture on special seamanship for the use of the *Apse Family;* then changing his tone, he began to talk at large, rattling off the wildest, funniest nonsense, till my sides ached with laughing. I could see very well he was a bit above himself with high spirits. It couldn't be because of my coming. Not to that extent. But, of course, I wouldn't have dreamt of asking what was the matter. I had a proper respect for my big brother, I can tell you. But it was all made plain enough a day or two afterwards, when I heard that Miss Maggie Colchester was coming for the voyage. Uncle was giving her a sea-trip for the benefit of her health.

"I don't know what could have been wrong with her health. She had a beautiful colour, and a deuce of a lot of fair hair. She didn't care a rap for wind, or rain, or spray, or sun, or green seas, or anything. She was a blue-eyed, jolly girl of the very best sort, but the way she cheeked my big brother used to frighten me. I always expected it to end in an awful row. However, nothing decisive happened till after we had been in Sydney for a week. One day, in the men's dinner hour, Charley sticks his head into my cabin. I was stretched out on my back on the settee, smoking in peace. 'Come ashore with me, Ned,' he says, in his curt way.

"I jumped up, of course, and away after him down the gangway and up George Street. He strode along like a giant, and I at his elbow, panting. It was confoundedly hot. 'Where on earth are you rushing me to, Charley?' I made bold to ask.

"'Here,' he says.

"'Here' was a jeweller's shop. I couldn't imagine what he could want

156

there. It seemed a sort of mad freak. He thrusts under my nose three rings, which looked very tiny on his big, brown palm, growling out—

"'For Maggie! Which?'

"I got a kind of scare at this. I couldn't make a sound, but I pointed at the one that sparkled white and blue. He put it in his waistcoat pocket, paid for it·with a lot of sovereigns, and bolted out. When we got on board I was quite out of breath. 'Shake hands, old chap,' I gasped out. He gave me a thump on the back. 'Give what orders you like to the boatswain when the hands turn-to,' says he; 'I am off duty this afternoon.'

"Then he vanished from the deck for a while, but presently he came out of the cabin with Maggie, and these two went over the gangway publicly, before all hands, going for a walk together on that awful, blazing hot day, with clouds of dust flying about. They came back after a few hours looking very staid, but didn't seem to have the slightest idea where they had been. Anyway, that's the answer they both made to Mrs. Colchester's question at tea-time.

"And didn't she turn on Charley, with her voice like an old night cabman's. 'Rubbish. Don't know where you've been! Stuff and nonsense. You've walked the girl off her legs. Don't do it again.'

"It's surprising how meek Charley could be with that old woman. Only on one occasion he whispered to me, 'I'm jolly glad she isn't Maggie's aunt, except by marriage. That's no sort of relationship.' But I think he let Maggie have too much of her own way. She was hopping all over that ship in her yachting skirt and a red tam o' shanter like a bright bird on a dead black tree. The old salts used to grin to themselves when they saw her coming along, and offered to teach her knots .or splices. I believe she liked the men, for Charley's sake, I suppose.

"As you may imagine, the fiendish propensities of that cursed ship were never spoken of on board. Not in the cabin, at any rate. Only once on the homeward passage Charley said incautiously, something about bringing all her crew home this time. Captain Colchester began to look uncomfortable at once, and that silly, hard-bitten old woman flew out at Charley as though he had said something indecent. I was quite confounded myself; as to Maggie, she sat completely mystified, opening her blue eyes very wide. Of course, before she was a day older she wormed it all out of me. She was a very difficult person to lie to. 'How awful,' she said, quite solemn. 'So many poor fellows. I am glad the voyage is nearly over. I won't have a moment's peace about Charley now.'

"I assured her Charley was all right. It took more than that ship knew to get over a seaman like Charley. And she agreed with me.

"Next day we got the tug off Dungeness; and when the tow-rope was fast Charley rubbed his hands and said to me in an undertone—

157

" 'We've baffled her, Ned.'

" 'Looks like it,' I said, with a grin at him. It was beautiful weather, and the sea as smooth as a millpond. We went up the river without a shadow of trouble except once, when off Hole Haven, the brute took a sudden sheer and nearly had a barge anchored just clear of the fairway. But I was aft, looking after the steering, and she did not catch me napping that time. Charley came up on the poop, looking very concerned. 'Close shave,' says he.

" 'Never mind, Charley,' I answered cheerily. 'You've tamed her.'

"We were to tow right up to the dock. The river pilot boarded us below Gravesend, and the first words I heard him say were: 'You may just as well take your port anchor inboard at once, Mr. Mate.'

"This had been done when I went forward. I saw Maggie on the forecastle head enjoying the bustle and I begged her to go aft, but she took no notice of me, of course. Then Charley, who was very busy with the head gear, caught sight of her and shouted in his biggest voice: 'Get off the forecastle head, Maggie. You're in the way here.' For all answer she made a funny face at him, and I saw poor Charley turn away, hiding a smile. She was flushed with the excitement of getting home again, and her blue eyes seemed to snap electric sparks as she looked at the river. A collier brig had gone round just ahead of us, and our tug had to stop her engines in a hurry to avoid running into her.

"In a moment, as is usually the case, all the shipping in the reach seemed to get into a hopeless tangle. A schooner and a ketch got up a small collision all to themselves right in the middle of the river. It was exciting to watch, and, meantime, our tug remained stopped. Any other ship than that brute could have been coaxed to keep straight for a couple of minutes—but not she! Her head fell off at once, and she began to drift down, taking her tug along with her. I noticed a cluster of coasters at anchor within a quarter of a mile of us, and I thought I had better speak to the pilot. 'If you let her get amongst that lot,' I said, quietly, 'she will grind some of them to bits before we get her out again.'

" 'Don't I know her!' cries he, stamping his foot in a perfect fury. And he out with his whistle to make that bothered tug get the ship's head up again as quick as possible. He blew like mad, waving his arm to port, and presently we could see that the tug's engines had been set going ahead. Her paddles churned the water, but it was as if she had been trying to tow a rock—she couldn't get an inch out of that ship. Again the pilot blew his whistle, and waved his arm to port. We could see the tug's paddles turning faster and faster away, broad on our bow.

"For a moment tug and ship hung motionless in a crowd of moving shipping, and then the terrific strain that evil, stony-hearted brute would always put on everything, tore the towing-chock clean out. The tow-rope surged over, snapping the iron stanchions of the head-rail one after another as if they had been sticks of sealing-wax. It was only then I noticed that in order to have a better view over our heads, Maggie had stepped upon the port anchor as it lay flat on the forecastle deck.

"It had been lowered properly into its hardwood beds, but there had been no time to take a turn with it. Anyway, it was quite secure as it was, for going into dock; but I could see directly that the tow-rope would sweep under the fluke in another second. My heart flew up right into my throat, but not before I had time to yell out: 'Jump clear of that anchor!' But I hadn't time to shriek out her name. I don't suppose she heard me at all. The first touch of the hawser against the fluke threw her down; she was up on her feet again quick as lightning, but she was up on the wrong side. I heard a horrid, scraping sound, and then that anchor, tipping over, rose up like something alive; its great, rough iron arm caught Maggie round the waist, seemed to clasp her close with a dreadful hug, and flung itself with her over and down in a terrible clang of iron, followed by heavy ringing blows that shook the ship from stem to stern—because the ring stopper held!"

"How horrible!" I exclaimed.

"I used to dream for years afterwards of anchors catching hold of girls," said the man in tweeds, a little wildly. He shuddered. "With a most pitiful howl Charley was over after her almost on the instant. But, Lord! he didn't see as much as a gleam of her red tam o' shanter in the water. Nothing! nothing whatever! In a moment there were half-a-dozen boats around us, and he got pulled into one. I, with the boatswain and the carpenter, let go the other anchor in a hurry and brought the ship up somehow. The pilot had gone silly. He walked up and down the forecastle head wringing his hands and muttering to himself: 'Killing women, now! Killing women, now!' Not another word could you get out of him.

"Dusk fell, then a night black as pitch; and peering upon the river I heard a low, mournful hail, 'Ship, ahoy!' Two Gravesend watermen came alongside. They had a lantern in their wherry, and looked up the ship's side, holding on to the ladder without a word. I saw in the patch of light a lot of loose, fair hair down there." He shuddered again. "After the tide turned poor Maggie's body had floated clear of one of them big mooring buoys," he explained. "I crept aft, feeling half-dead, and managed to send a rocket up—to let the other searchers know, on the river. And then I slunk away forward like a cur, and spent the night sitting on the heel of the bowsprit so as to be as far as possible out of Charley's way."

"Poor fellow!" I murmured.

"Yes. Poor fellow," he repeated, musingly. "That brute wouldn't let him—not even him—cheat her of her prey. But he made her fast in dock next morning. He did. We hadn't exchanged a word—not a single look for that matter. I didn't want to look at him. When the last rope was fast he put his hands to his head and stood gazing down at his feet as if trying to remember something. The men waited on the main deck for the words that end the voyage. Perhaps that is what he was trying to remember. I spoke for him. 'That'll do, men.'

"I never saw a crew leave a ship so quietly. They sneaked over the rail one after another, taking care not to bang their sea chests too heavily. They looked our way, but not one had the stomach to come up and offer to shake hands with the mate as is usual.

"I followed him all over the empty ship to and fro, here and there, with no living soul about but the two of us, because the old ship-keeper had locked himself up in the galley—both doors. Suddenly poor Charley mutters, in a crazy voice: 'I'm done here,' and strides down the gangway with me at his heels, up the dock, out at the gate, on towards Tower Hill. He used to take rooms with a decent old landlady in America Square, to be near his work.

"All at once he stops short, turns round, and comes back straight at me. 'Ned,' says he, 'I am going home.' I had the good luck to sight a four-wheeler and got him in just in time. His legs were beginning to give way. In our hall he fell down on a chair, and I'll never forget father's and mother's amazed, perfectly still faces as they stood over him. They couldn't understand what had happened to him till I blubbered out 'Maggie got drowned, yesterday, in the river.'

"Mother let out a little cry. Father looks from him to me, and from me to him, as if comparing our faces—for, upon my soul, Charley did not resemble himself at all. Nobody moved; and the poor fellow raises his big brown hands slowly to his throat, and with one single tug rips everything open—collar, shirt, waistcoat—a perfect wreck and ruin of a man. Father and I got him upstairs somehow, and mother pretty nearly killed herself nursing him through a brain fever."

The man in tweeds nodded at me significantly. "Ah! there was nothing that could be done with that brute. She had a devil in her."

"Where's your brother?" I asked, expecting to hear he was dead. But he was commanding a smart steamer on the China coast, and never came home now.

Jermyn fetched a heavy sigh, and the handkerchief being now sufficiently dry, put it up tenderly to his red and lamentable nose.

"She was a ravening beast," the man in tweeds started again. "Old Colchester put his foot down and resigned. And would you believe it? Apse & Sons wrote to ask whether he wouldn't reconsider his decision!

Anything to save the good name of the *Apse Family!* Old Colchester went to the office then and said that he would take charge again but only to sail her out into the North Sea and scuttle her there. He was nearly off his chump. He used to be darkish iron-grey, but his hair went snow-white in a fortnight. And Mr. Lucian Apse (they had known each other as young men) pretended not to notice it. Eh? Here's infatuation if you like! Here's pride for you!

"They jumped at the first man they could get to take her, for fear of the scandal of the *Apse Family* not being able to find a skipper. He was a festive soul, I believe, but he stuck to her grim and hard. Wilmot was his second mate. A harum-scarum fellow, and pretending to a great scorn for all the girls. The fact is he was really timid. But let only one of them do as much as lift her little finger in encouragement, and there was nothing that could hold the beggar. As apprentice, once, he deserted abroad after a petticoat, and would have gone to the dogs then, if his skipper hadn't taken the trouble to find him and lug him by the ears out of some house of perdition or other.

"It was said that one of the firm had been heard once to express a hope that this brute of a ship would get lost soon. I can hardly credit the tale, unless it might have been Mr. Alfred Apse, whom the family didn't think much of. They had him in the office, but he was considered a bad egg altogether, always flying off to race meetings and coming home drunk. You would have thought that a ship so full of deadly tricks would run herself ashore some day out of sheer cussedness. But not she! She was going to last for ever. She had a nose to keep off the bottom."

Jermyn made a grunt of approval.

"A ship after a pilot's own heart, eh?" jeered the man in tweeds.

"Well, Wilmot managed it. He was the man for it, but even he, perhaps, couldn't have done the trick without the green-eyed governess, or nurse, or whatever she was to the children of Mr. and Mrs. Pamphilius.

"Those people were passengers in her from Port Adelaide to the Cape. Well, the ship went out and anchored outside for the day. The skipper—hospitable soul—had a lot of guests from town to a farewell lunch—as usual with him. It was five in the evening before the last shore boat left the side, and the weather looked ugly and dark in the gulf. There was no reason for him to get under way. However, as he had told everybody he was going that day, he imagined it was proper to do so anyhow. But as he had no mind after all these festivities to tackle the straits in the dark, with a scant wind, he gave orders to keep the ship under lower topsails and foresail as close as she would lie, dodging along the land till the morning. Then he sought his virtuous couch. The mate was on deck, having his face washed very clean with hard rain squalls. Wilmot relieved him at midnight.

"The *Apse Family* had, as you observed, a house on her poop . . ."

"A big, ugly white thing, sticking up," Jermyn murmured, sadly, at the fire.

"That's it: a companion for the cabin stairs and a sort of chart-room combined. The rain drove in gusts on the sleepy Wilmot. The ship was then surging slowly to the southward, close hauled, with the coast within three miles or so to windward. There was nothing to look out for in that part of the gulf, and Wilmot went round to dodge the squalls under the lee of that chart-room, whose door on that side was open. The night was black, like a barrel of coal-tar. And then he heard a woman's voice whispering to him.

"That confounded green-eyed girl of the Pamphilius people had put the kids to bed a long time ago, of course, but it seems couldn't get to sleep herself. She heard eight bells struck, and the chief mate come below to turn in. She waited a bit, then got into her dressing-gown and stole across the empty saloon and up the stairs into the chart-room. She sat down on the settee near the open door to cool herself, I daresay.

"I suppose when she whispered to Wilmot it was as if somebody had struck a match in the fellow's brain. I don't know how it was they had got so very thick. I fancy he had met her ashore a few times before. I couldn't make it out, because, when telling the story, Wilmot would break off to swear something awful at every second word. We had met on the quay in Sydney, and he had an apron of sacking up to his chin, a big whip in his hand. A wagon-driver. Glad to do anything not to starve. That's what he had come down to.

"However, there he was, with his head inside the door, on the girl's shoulder as likely as not—officer of the watch! The helmsman, on giving his evidence afterwards, said that he shouted several times that the binnacle lamp had gone out. It didn't matter to him, because his orders were to 'sail her close'. 'I thought it funny,' he said, 'that the ship should keep on falling off in squalls, but I luffed her up every time as close as I was able. It was so dark I couldn't see my hand before my face, and the rain came in bucketsful on my head.'

"The truth was that at every squall the wind hauled aft a little, till gradually the ship came to be heading straight for the coast, without a single soul in her being aware of it. Wilmot himself confessed that he had not been near the standard compass for an hour. He might well have confessed! The first thing he knew was the man on the look-out shouting blue murder forward there. He tore his neck free, he says, and yelled back at him: 'What do you say?'

"'I think I hear breakers ahead, sir,' howled the man, and came rushing aft with the rest of the watch, in the 'awfullest blinding deluge that ever fell from the sky', Wilmot says. For a second or so he was so scared and bewildered that he could not remember on which side of the gulf the ship was. He wasn't a good officer, but he was a seaman all the same. He pulled himself together in a second, and the right orders sprang to his lips without thinking. They were to hard up with the helm and shiver the main and mizzen-topsails.

"It seems that the sails actually fluttered. He couldn't see them, but he heard them rattling and banging above his head. 'No use! She was too slow in going off,' he went on, his dirty face twitching, and the damn'd carter's whip shaking in his hand. 'She seemed to stick fast.' And then the flutter of the canvas above his head ceased. At this critical moment the wind hauled aft again with a gust, filling the sails and sending the ship with a great way upon the rocks on her lee bow. She had overreached herself in her last little game. Her time had come—the hour, the man, the black night, the treacherous gust of wind—the right woman to put an end to her. The brute deserved nothing better. Strange are the instruments of Providence. There's a sort of poetical justice——"

The man in tweeds looked hard at me.

"The first ledge she went over stripped the false keel off her. Rip! The skipper, rushing out of his berth, found a crazy woman, in a red flannel dressing-gown, flying round and round the cuddy, screeching like a cockatoo.

"The next bump knocked her clean under the cabin table. It also started the stern-post and carried away the rudder, and then that brute ran up a shelving, rocky shore, tearing her bottom out, till she stopped short, and the foremast dropped over the bows like a gangway."

"Anybody lost?" I asked.

"No one, unless that fellow, Wilmot," answered the gentleman unknown to Miss Blank, looking round for his cap. "And his case was worse than drowning for a man. Everybody got ashore all right. Gale didn't come on till next day, dead from the West, and broke up that brute in a surprisingly short time. It was as though she had been rotten at heart." . . . He changed his tone, "Rain left off. I must get my bike and rush home to dinner. I live in Herne Bay—came out for a spin this morning."

He nodded at me in a friendly way, and went out with a swagger.

"Do you know who he is, Jermyn?" I asked.

The North Sea pilot shook his head, dismally. "Fancy losing a ship in that silly fashion! Oh, dear! oh dear!" he groaned in lugubrious tones, spreading his damp handkerchief again like a curtain before the glowing grate.

On going out I exchanged a glance and a smile (strictly proper) with the respectable Miss Blank, barmaid of the Three Crows.

A.E. COPPARD

1878–1957

In his own affectionate words, "the son of George the tailor
and Emily Alma the housemaid," he left school at the age
of nine, ran errands, sold paraffin, read voraciously. Soon
he was writing: first verses, then short stories, quickly to
become famous, in which he described with moving tenderness
the lives of the simple people he knew and loved.

The Higgler

ON A COLD April afternoon a
higgler was driving across Shag
Moor in a two-wheeled cart.

H. WITLOW
Dealer in Poultry
DINNOP

was painted on the hood; the horse
was of mean appearance but notorious ancestry. A high upland
common was this moor, two miles from end to end, and full of furze and
bracken. There were no trees and not a house, nothing but a line of
telegraph poles following the road, sweeping with rigidity from north to
south; nailed upon one of them a small scarlet notice to stonethrowers
was prominent as a wound. On so high and wide a region as Shag Moor
the wind always blew, or if it did not quite blow there was a cool activity
in the air. The furze was always green and growing, and, taking no
account of seasons, often golden. Here in summer solitude lounged and
snoozed; at other times, as now, it shivered and looked sinister.

Higglers in general are ugly and shrewd, old and hard, crafty and
callous, but Harvey Witlow, though shrewd, was not ugly; he was hard
but not old, crafty but not at all unkind. If you had eggs to sell he would
buy them, by the score he would, or by the long hundred. Other odds
and ends he would buy or do, paying good bright silver, bartering a bag
of apples, carrying your little pig to market, or fetching a tree from the

164

nurseries. But the season was backward, eggs were scarce, trade was bad—by crumps, it was indeed!—and as he crossed the moor Harvey could not help discussing the situation with himself. "If things don't change, and change for the better, and change soon, I can't last and I can't endure it; I'll be damned and done, and I'll have to sell," he said, prodding the animal with the butt of his whip, "this cob. And," he said, as if in afterthought, prodding the footboard, "this cart, and go back to the land. And I'll have lost my fifty pounds. Well, that's what war does for you. It does it for you, sir," he announced sharply to the vacant moor, "and it does it for me. Fifty pounds! I was better off in the war. I was better off working for farmers—much. But it's no good chattering about it, it's the trick of life; when you get so far, then you can go and order your funeral. Get along, Dodger!"

The horse responded briskly for a few moments.

"I tell ye," said Harvey adjuring the ambient air, "you can go and order your funeral. Get along, Dodger!"

Again Dodger got along.

"Then there's Sophy, what about Sophy and me?"

He was not engaged to Sophy Daws, not exactly, but he was keeping company with her. He was not pledged or affianced, he was just keeping company with her. But Sophy, as he knew, not only desired a marriage with Mr. Witlow, she expected it, and expected it soon. So did her parents, her friends, and everybody in the village, including the postman who didn't live in it but wished he did, and the parson who did live in it but wished he didn't.

"Well, that's damned and done, fair damned and done now, unless things take a turn, and soon, so it's no good chattering about it."

And just then and there things did take a turn. He had never been across the moor before; he was prospecting for trade. At the end of Shag Moor he saw standing back on the common, fifty yards from the road, a neat square house set in a little farm. Twenty acres, perhaps. The house was girded by some white palings; beside it was a snug orchard in a hedge covered with blackthorn bloom. It was very green and pleasant in front of the house. The turf was cleared and closely cropped, some ewes were grazing and under the blackthorn, out of the wind, lay half a dozen lambs, but what chiefly moved the imagination of Harvey Witlow was a field on the far side of the house. It had a small rickyard with a few small stacks in it; everything here seemed on the small scale, but snug, very snug; and in that field and yard were hundreds of fowls, hundreds, of good breed, and mostly white. Leaving his horse to sniff the greensward, the higgler entered a white wicket gateway and passed to the back of the house, noting as he did so a yellow wagon inscribed

ELIZABETH SADGROVE. PRATTLE CORNER.

At the kitchen door he was confronted by a tall gaunt woman of middle age with a teapot in her hands.

"Afternoon, ma'am. Have you anything to sell?" began Harvey Witlow, tilting his hat with a confident affable air. The tall woman was cleanly dressed, a superior person; her hair was grey. She gazed at him.

"It's cold," he continued. She looked at him as uncomprehendingly as a mouse might look at a gravestone.

"I'll buy any mottal thing, ma'am. Except trouble; I'm full up wi' that already. Eggs? Fowls?"

"I've not seen you before," commented Mrs. Sadgrove a little bleakly, in a deep husky voice.

"No, 'tis the first time as ever I drove in this part. To tell you the truth, ma'am, I'm new to the business. Six months. I was in the war a year ago. Now I'm trying to knock up a connection. Difficult work. Things are very quiet." Mrs. Sadgrove silently removed the lid of the teapot, inspected the interior of the pot with an intent glance, and then replaced the lid as if she had seen a black beetle there.

"Ah, well," sighed the higgler. "You've a neat little farm here, ma'am."

"It's quiet enough," said she.

"Sure it is, ma'am. Very lonely."

"And it's difficult work too." Mrs. Sadgrove almost smiled.

"Sure it is, ma'am; but you does it well, I can see. Oh, you've some nice little ricks of corn, eh! I does well enough at the dealing now and again, but it's teasy work and mostly I don't earn enough to keep my horse in shoe leather."

"I've a few eggs, perhaps," said she.

"I could do with a score or two, ma'am, if you could let me have 'em."

"You'll have to come all my way if I do."

"Name your own price, ma'am, if you don't mind trading with me."

"Mind! Your money's as good as my own, isn't it?"

"It must be, ma'am. That's meaning no disrespects to you," the young higgler assured her hastily, and was thereupon invited to enter the kitchen.

A stone floor with two or three mats; open hearth with burning logs; a big dresser painted brown, carrying a row of white cups on brass hooks and shelves of plates overlapping each other like the scales of fish. A dark settle half hid a flight of stairs with a small gate at the top. Under the window a black sofa, deeply indented, invited you a little repellingly, and in the middle of the room stood a large table, exquisitely scrubbed, with one end of it laid for tea. Evidently a living-room as well as kitchen. A girl, making toast at the fire, turned as the higgler entered. Beautiful she was: red hair, a complexion like the inside of a nut, blue eyes, and the hands of a lady. He saw it all at once, jacket of bright green wool, black dress, grey stockings and shoes, and forgot his errand, her mother, his fifty pounds, Sophy—momentarily he forgot everything. The girl stared strangely at him. He was tall, clean-shaven, with a loop of black hair curling handsomely over one side of his brow. "Good afternoon," said Harvey Witlow, as softly as if he had entered a church.

"Some eggs, Mary," Mrs. Sadgrove explained. The girl laid down her toasting-fork. She was less tall than her mother, whom she resembled only enough for the relationship to be noted. Silently she crossed the kitchen and opened a door that led into a dairy. Two pans of milk were creaming on a bench there and on the flags were two great baskets filled with eggs.

"How many are there?" asked Mrs. Sadgrove, and the girl replied: "Fifteen score, I think."

"Take the lot, higgler?"

"Yes, ma'am," he cried eagerly, and ran out to his cart and fetched a number of trays. In them he packed the eggs as the girl handed them to him from the baskets. Mrs. Sadgrove left them together. For a time the higgler was silent.

"No," at length he murmured, "I've never been this road before."

There was no reply from Mary. Sometimes their fingers touched, and often, as they bent over the eggs, her bright hair almost brushed his face.

"It is a loneish spot," he ventured again.

"Yes," said Mary Sadgrove.

When the eggs were all transferred her mother came in again.

"Would you buy a few pullets, higgler?"

"Any number, ma'am," he declared quickly. Any number; by crumps, the tide was turning! He followed the mother into the yard, and there again she left him, waiting. He mused about the girl and wondered about the trade. If they offered him ten thousand chickens, he'd buy them, somehow, he would! She had stopped in the kitchen. Just in there she was, just behind him, a few feet away. Over the low wall of the yard a fat black pony was strolling in a field of bright greensward. In the yard, watching him, was a young gander, and on a stone staddle beside it lay a dead thrush on its back, its legs stiff in the air. The girl stayed in the kitchen; she was moving about, though, he could hear her; perhaps she was spying at him through the window. Twenty million eggs he would buy if Mrs. Sadgrove had got them. She was gone a long time. It was very quiet. The gander began to comb its white breast with its beak. Its three-toed feet were a most tender pink, shaped like wide diamonds, and at each of the three forward points there was a toe like a small blanched nut. It lifted one foot, folding the webs, and hid it under its wing and sank into a resigned meditation on one leg. It had a blue eye that was meek—it had two, but you could only see one at a time—a meek

167

blue eye, set in a pink rim that gave it a dissolute air, and its beak had raw red nostrils as if it suffered from the damp. Altogether a beautiful bird. And in some absurd way it resembled Mrs. Sadgrove.

"Would you sell that young gollan, ma'am?" Harvey inquired when the mother returned.

Yes, she would sell him, and she also sold him two dozen pullets. Harvey packed the fowls in a crate.

"Come on," he cried cuddling the squawking gander in his arms, "you needn't be afraid of me, I never kills anything afore Saturdays."

He roped it by its leg to a hook inside his cart. Then he took out his bag of money, paid Mrs. Sadgrove her dues, said "Good day, ma'am, good day," and drove off without seeing another sign or stitch of that fine young girl.

"Get along, Dodger, get along wi' you." They went bowling along for nearly an hour, and then he could see the landmark on Dan'el Green's Hill, a windmill that never turned though it looked a fine competent piece of architecture, just beyond Dinnop.

Soon he reached his cottage and was chaffing his mother, a hearty buxom dame, who stayed at home and higgled with any chance callers. At this business she was perhaps more enlightened than her son. It was almost a misfortune to get into her clutches.

"How much you give for this?" he cried, eyeing with humorous contempt an object in a coop that was neither flesh nor rude red herring.

"Oh crumps," he declared, when she told him, "I am damned and done!"

"Go on with you, that's a good bird, I tell you, with a full heart, as will lay in a month."

"I doubt it's a hen at all," he protested. "Oh, what a ravenous beak! Damned and done I am."

Mrs. Witlow's voice began indignantly to rise.

"Oh, well," mused her son, "it's thrifty perhaps. It ain't quite right, but it's not so wrong as to make a fuss about, especially as I be pretty sharp set. And if it's hens you want," he continued triumphantly, dropping the crate of huddled fowls before her, "there's hens for you; and a gander! There's a gander for you, if it's a gander you want."

Leaving them all in his cottage yard he went and stalled the horse and cart at the inn, for he had no stable of his own. After supper he told his mother about the Sadgroves of Prattle Corner. "Prettiest girl you ever seen, but the shyest mottal alive. Hair like a squirrel, lovely."

"An't you got to go over and see Sophy tonight?" inquired his mother, lighting the lamp.

"Oh lord, if I an't clean forgot that! Well, I'm tired, shan't go tonight. See her tomorrow."

MRS. SADGROVE had been a widow for ten years—and she was glad of it. Prattle Corner was her property, she owned it and farmed it with the aid of a little old man· and a large lad. The older this old man grew, and the less wages he received (for Elizabeth Sadgrove was reputed a 'grinder'), the more ardently he worked; the older the lad grew the less he laboured and the more he swore. She was thriving. She was worth money was Mrs. Sadgrove. Ah! And her daughter Mary, it was clear, had received an education fit for a lord's lady; she had been at a seminary for gentlefolk's females until she was seventeen. Well, whether or no, a clock must run as you time it; but it wronged her for the work of a farm, it spoiled her, it completely deranged her for the work of a farm; and this was a pity and foolish, because some day the farm was coming to her as didn't know hay from a bull's foot.

All this, and more, the young higgler quickly learned, and plenty more he soon divined. Business began to flourish with him now; his despair was gone, he was established, he could look forward, to whatever it was he wanted to look forward, with equanimity and such pleasurable anticipation as the chances and charges of life might engender. Every week, and twice a week, he would call at the farm, and though these occasions had their superior business inducements they often borrowed a less formal tone and intention.

"Take a cup of tea, higgler?" Mrs. Sadgrove would abruptly invite him; and he would drink tea and discourse with her for half an hour on barndoor ornithology, on harness, and markets, the treatment of swine, the wear and tear of gear. Mary, always present, was always silent, seldom uttering a word to the higgler; yet a certain grace emanated from her to him, an interest, a light, a favour, circumscribed indeed by some modesty, shyness, some inhibition, that neither of them had the wit or the opportunity to overcome.

One evening he pulled up at the white palings of Prattle Corner. It was a calm evening in May, the sun was on its downgoing, chaffinches and wrens sung ceaselessly. Mary in the orchard was heavily veiled; he could see her over the hedge, holding a brush in her gloved hands, and a bee skep. A swarm was clustered like a great gnarl on the limb of an apple tree. Bloom was thickly covering the twigs. She made several timid attempts to brush the bees into the skep, but they resented this.

"They knows if you be afraid of 'em," bawled· Harvey; "I better come and give you a hand."

When he took the skep and brush from her she stood like one helpless, released by fate from a task ill-understood and gracelessly waived. But he liked her shyness, her almost uncouth immobility.

"Never mind about that," said Harvey, as she unfastened her veil, scattering the white petals that had collected upon it; "when they kicks they hurts, but I've been stung so often that I'm 'nocolated against 'em. They knows if you be afraid of 'em."

Wearing neither veil nor gloves he went confidently to the tree, and collected the swarm without mishap.

"Don't want to show no fear of them," said Harvey. "Nor of anything else, come to that," he added with a guffaw, "nor anybody."

At that she blushed and thanked him very softly, and she did look straight and clearly at him.

Never anything beyond a blush and a thank you. When, in the kitchen or the parlour, Mrs. Sadgrove sometimes left them alone together Harvey would try a lot of talk, blarneying talk or sensible talk, or talk about events in the world that was neither the one nor the other. No good. The girl's responses were ever brief and confused. Why was this? Again and again he asked himself that question. Was there anything the matter with her? Nothing that you could see; she was a bright and beautiful being. And it was not contempt, either, for despite her fright, her voicelessness, her timid eyes, he divined her friendly feeling for himself; and he would discourse to his own mother about her and her mother:

"They are well-up people, you know, well off, plenty of money and nothing to do with it. The farm's their own, freehold. A whole row of cottages she's got, too, in Smoorton Comfrey, so I heard; good cottages, well let. She's worth a few thousands, I warrant. Mary's beautiful. I took a fancy to that girl the first moment I see her. But she's very highly cultivated—and, of course, there's Sophy."

To this enigmatic statement Mrs. Witlow offered no response; but mothers are inscrutable beings to their sons, always.

Once he bought some trees of cherries from Mrs. Sadgrove, and went on a July morning to pick the fruit. Under the trees Mary was walking slowly to and fro, twirling a clapper to scare away the birds. He stood watching her from the gateway. Among the bejewelled trees she passed, turning the rattle with a listless air, as if beating time to a sad music that only she could hear. The man knew that he was deeply fond of her. He passed into the orchard, bade her good morning, and, lifting his ladder into one of the trees nearest the hedge, began to pluck cherries. Mary moved slimly in her white frock up and down a shady avenue in the orchard waving the clapper. The brightness of sun and sky was almost harsh; there was a little wind that feebly lifted the despondent leaves. He had doffed his coat; his shirt was white and clean. The lock of dark hair drooped over one side of his forehead; his face was brown and pleasant, his bare arms brown and powerful. From his high perch among the leaves Witlow watched for the girl to draw near to him in her perambulation. Knavish birds would scatter at her approach, only to drop again into the trees she had passed. His soul had an immensity of longing for her, but she never spoke a word to him. She would come from the shade of the little avenue, through the dumb trees that could only bend to greet her, into the sunlight whose dazzle gilded her own triumphant bloom. Fine! Fine! And always as she passed his mind refused to register a single thought he could offer her, or else his tongue would refuse to utter it. But his glance never left her face until she had passed out of sight again, and then he would lean against the ladder in the tree, staring down at the ground, seeing nothing or less than nothing, except a field mouse climbing to the top of a coventry bush in the hedge below him, nipping off one thick leaf and descending with the leaf in its mouth. Sometimes Mary rested at the other end of the avenue; the clapper would be silent and she would not appear for—oh, hours! She never rested near the trees Witlow was denuding. The mouse went on ascending and descending, and Witlow filled his basket, and shifted his stand, and wondered.

At noon he got down and sat on the hedge bank to eat a snack of lunch. Mary had gone indoors for hers, and he was alone for awhile. Capriciously enough, his thoughts dwelt upon Sophy Daws. Sophy was a fine girl, too; not such a lady as Mary Sadgrove—oh lord, no! her father was a gamekeeper!—but she was jolly and ample. She had been a little captious lately, said he was neglecting her. That wasn't true; hadn't he been busy? Besides, he wasn't bound to her in any sort of way, and of course he couldn't afford any marriage yet awhile. Sophy hadn't got any money, never had any. What she did with her wages— she was a parlourmaid—was a teaser! Harvey grunted a little, and said "Well!" And that is all he said, and all he thought, about Sophy Daws, then, for he could hear Mary's clapper begin again in a corner of the orchard.

He went back to his work. There at the foot of the tree were the baskets full of cherries, and those yet to be filled.

"Phew, but that's hot!" commented the man, "I'm as dry as a rattle."

A few cherries had spilled from one basket and lay on the ground. The little furry mouse had found them and was industriously nibbling at one. The higgler nonchalantly stamped his foot upon it, and kept it so for a moment or two. Then he looked at the dead mouse. A tangle of entrails had gushed from its whiskered muzzle.

He resumed his work and the clapper rattled on throughout the afternoon, for there were other cherry trees that other buyers would come to strip in a day or two. At four o'clock he was finished. Never a word had he spoken with Mary, or she with him. When he went over to the house to pay Mrs. Sadgrove Mary stopped in the orchard scaring the birds.

"Take a cup of tea, Mr. Witlow," said Mrs. Sadgrove; and then she surprisingly added, "Where's Mary?"

"Still a-frightening the birds, and pretty well tired of that, I should think, ma'am."

The mother had poured out three cups of tea.

"Shall I go and call her in?" he asked, rising.

"You might," said she.

In the orchard the clappering had ceased. He walked all round, and in among the trees, but saw no sign of Mary; nor on the common, nor in the yard. But when he went back to the house Mary was there already, chatting at the table with her mother. She did not greet him, though she ceased talking to her mother as he sat down. After drinking his tea he went off briskly to load the baskets into the cart. As he climbed up to drive off Mrs. Sadgrove came out and stood beside the horse.

"You're off now?" said she.

"Yes, ma'am; all loaded, and thank you."

She glanced vaguely along the road he had to travel. The afternoon was as clear as wine, the greensward itself dazzled him; lonely Shag Moor stretched away, humped with sweet yellow furze and pilastered with its telegraph poles. No life there, no life at all. Harvey sat on his driving board, musingly brushing the flank of his horse with the trailing whip.

"Ever round this way on Sundays?" inquired the woman, peering up at him.

"Well, not in a manner of speaking, I'm not, ma'am," he answered her.

The widow laid her hand on the horse's back, patting vaguely. The horse pricked up its ears, as if it were listening.

"If you are, at all, ever, you must look in and have a bit of dinner with us."

"I will, ma'am, I will."

"Next Sunday?" she went on.

"I will, ma'am, yes, I will," he repeated, "and thank you."

"One o'clock?" The widow smiled up at him.

"At one o'clock, ma'am; next Sunday; I will, and thank you," he said.

She stood away from the horse and waved her hand. The first tangible thought that floated mutely out of the higgler's mind as he drove away was: "I'm damned if I ain't a-going it, Sophy!"

He told his mother of Mrs. Sadgrove's invitation with an air of curbed triumph. "Come round—she says. Yes—I says—I 'ull. That's right—she says—so do."

III

ON THE SUNDAY morn he dressed himself gallantly. It was again a sweet unclouded day. The church bell at Dinnop had begun to ring. From his window, as he fastened his most ornate tie, Harvey could observe his neighbour's two small children in the next garden, a boy and girl clad for church-going and each carrying a clerical book. The tiny boy placed his sister in front of a hen-roost and, opening his book, began to pace to and fro before her, shrilly intoning: "Jesus is the shepherd, ring the bell. Oh lord, ring the bell, am I a good boy? Amen. Oh lord, ring the bell." The little girl bowed her head piously over her book. The lad then picked up from the ground a dish which had contained the dog's food, and presented it momentarily before the lilac bush, the rabbit in a hutch, the axe fixed in a chopping block, and then before his sister. Without lifting her peering gaze from her book she meekly dropped two pebbles in the plate, and the boy passed on, lightly moaning, to the clothes-line post and a cock scooping in some dust.

"Ah, the little impets!" cried Harvey Witlow. "Here, Toby! Here, Margaret!" He took two pennies from his pocket and lobbed them from the window to the astonished children. As they stooped to pick up the coins Harvey heard the hoarse voice of neighbour Nathan, their father, bawl from his kitchen: "Come on in, and shut that bloody door, d'y'ear!"

Harnessing his moody horse to the gig Harvey was soon bowling away to Shag Moor, and as he drove along he sang loudly. He had a pink rose in his buttonhole. Mrs. Sadgrove received him almost affably, and though Mary was more shy than ever before, Harvey had determined to make an impression. During the dinner he fired off his bucolic jokes, and pleasant tattle of a more respectful and sober nature; but after dinner Mary sat like Patience, not upon a monument, but as if upon a rocking-horse, shy and fearful, and her mother made no effort to inspire her as the higgler did, unsuccessful though he was. They went to the pens to look at the pigs, and as they leaned against the low walls and poked the maudlin inhabitants, Harvey began, "Reminds me, when I was in the war . . ."

"Were you in the war?" interrupted Mrs. Sadgrove.

"Oh, yes, I was in that war, ah, and there was a pig. . . . Danger? Oh lord, bless me, it was a bit dangerous, but you never knew where it was or what it 'ud be at next; it was like the sword of Damockels. There was a bullet once come 'ithin a foot of my head, and it went through a board an inch thick, slap through that board." Both women gazed at him apprehendingly. "Why, I might 'a been killed, you know," said Harvey, cocking his eye musingly at the weather-vane on the barn. "We was in billets at St. Gratien, and one day a chasseur came up—a French

173

yoossar, you know—and he began talking to our sergeant. That was Hubert Luxter, the butcher: died a month or two ago of measles. But this yoossar couldn't speak English at all, and none of us chaps could make sense of him. I never could understand that lingo somehow, never; and though there was half a dozen of us chaps there, none of us were man enough for it neither. 'Nil compree,' we says, 'non compos.' I told him straight, 'You ought to learn English,' I said, 'it's much easier than your kind of bally chatter.' So he kept shaping up as if he was holding a rifle, and then he'd say 'Fusee—bang!' and then he'd say 'cushion'—kept on saying 'cushion'. Then he gets a bit of chalk and draws on the wall something that looks like a horrible dog, and says 'cushion' again."

"Pig," interjected Mary Sadgrove softly.

"Yes, yes!" ejaculated Harvey, "so 'twas! Do you know any French lingo?"

"Oh, yes," declared her mother, "Mary knows it very well."

"Ah," sighed the higgler, "I don't, although I been to France. And I couldn't do it now, not for luck nor love. You learnt it, I suppose. Well, this yoossar wants to borrow my rifle, but of course I can't lend him. So he taps on this horrible pig he'd drawn, and then he taps on his own head, and rolls his eyes about dreadful! 'Mad?' I says. And that was it, that was it. He'd got a pig on his little farm there what had gone mad, and he wanted us to come and shoot it; he was on leave and he hadn't got any ammunition. So Hubert Luxter he says, 'Come on, some of you,' and we all goes with the yoossar and shot the pig for him. Ah, that was a pig! And when it died it jumped a somersault just like a rabbit. It had got the mange, and was mad as anything I ever see in my life; it was full of madness. Couldn't hit him at all at first, and it kicked up bobs-a-dying. 'Ready, present, fire!' Hubert Luxter says, and bang goes the six of us, and every time we missed him he spotted us and we had to run for our lives."

As Harvey looked up he caught a glance of the girl fixed on him. She dropped her gaze at once and, turning away, walked off to the house.

"Come and take a look at the meadow," said Mrs. Sadgrove to him, and they went into the soft smooth meadow where the black pony was grazing. Very bright and green it was, and very blue the sky. He sniffed at the pink rose in his buttonhole, and determined that come what might he would give it to Mary if he could get a nice quiet chance to offer it. And just then, while he and Mrs. Sadgrove were strolling alone in the soft smooth meadow, quite alone, she suddenly, startlingly, asked him: "Are you courting anybody?"

"Beg pardon, ma'am?" he exclaimed.

"You haven't got a sweetheart, have you?" she asked, most deliberately. Harvey grinned sheepishly: "Ha, ha, ha," and then he said, "no."

"I want to see my daughter married," the widow went on significantly.

"Miss Mary!" he cried.

"Yes," said she; and something in the higgler's veins began to pound rapidly. His breast might have been a revolving cage and his heart a demon squirrel. "I can't live for ever," said Mrs. Sadgrove, almost with levity, "in fact, not for long, and so I'd like to see her settled soon with some decent understanding young man, one that could carry on here, and not make a mess of things."

"But, but," stuttered the understanding young man, "I'm no scholar, and she's a lady. I'm a poor chap, rough, and no scholar, ma'am. But mind you . . ."

"That doesn't matter at all," the widow interrupted, "not as things are. You want a scholar for learning, but for the land . . ."

"Ah, that's right, Mrs. Sadgrove, but . . ."

"I want to see her settled. This farm, you know, with the stock and things are worth nigh upon three thousand pounds."

"You want a farmer for farming, that's true, Mrs. Sadgrove, but when you come to marriage, well, with her learning and French and all that . . ."

"A sensible woman will take a man rather than a box of tricks any day of the week," the widow retorted. "Education may be a fine thing, but it often costs a lot of foolish money."

"It do, it do. You want to see her settled?"

"I want to see her settled and secure. When she is twenty-five she comes into five hundred pounds of her own right."

The distracted higgler hummed and haa-ed in his bewilderment as if he had just been offered the purchase of a dubious duck. "How old is she, ma'am?" he at last huskily inquired.

"Two-and-twenty nearly. She's a good healthy girl, for I've never spent a pound on a doctor for her, and very quiet she is, and very sensible; but she's got a strong will of her own, though you might not think it or believe it."

"She's a fine creature, Mrs. Sadgrove, and I'm very fond of her. I don't mind owning up to that, very fond of her I am."

"Well, think it over, take your time, and see what you think. There's no hurry, I hope, please God."

"I shan't want much time," he declared with a laugh, "but I doubt I'm the fair right sort for her."

"Oh, fair days, fair doings!" said she inscrutably, "I'm not a long liver, I'm afraid."

"God forbid, ma'am!" His ejaculation was intoned with deep gravity.

"No, I'm not a long-living woman." She surveyed him with her calm eyes, and he returned her gaze. Hers was a long sallow face, with heavy

175

lips. Sometimes she would stretch her features (as if to keep them from petrifying) in an elastic grin, and display her dazzling teeth; the lips would curl thickly, no longer crimson, but blue. He wondered if there were any sign of a doom registered upon her gaunt face. She might die, and die soon. "You couldn't do better than think it over, then, eh?" she had a queer frown as she regarded him.

"I couldn't do worse than not, Mrs. Sadgrove," he said gaily.

They left it at that. He had no reason for hurrying away, and he couldn't have explained his desire to do so, but he hurried away. Driving along past the end of the moor, and peering back at the lonely farm where they dwelled amid the thick furze snoozing in the heat, he remembered that he had not asked if Mary was willing to marry him! Perhaps the widow took her agreement for granted. That would be good fortune, for otherwise how the devil was he to get round a girl who had never spoken half a dozen words to him! And never would! She was a lady, a girl of fortune, knew her French; but there it was, the girl's own mother was asking him to wed her. Strange, very strange! He dimly feared something, but he did not know what it was he feared. He had still got the pink rose in his buttonhole.

IV

AT FIRST his mother was incredulous; when he told her of the astonishing proposal she declared he was a joker; but she was soon as convinced of his sincerity as she was amazed at his hesitation. And even vexed: "Was there anything the matter with this Mary?"

"No, no, no! She's quiet, very quiet indeed, I tell you, but a fine young woman, and a beautiful young woman. Oh, she's all right, right as rain, right as a trivet, right as ninepence. But there's a catch in it somewhere, I fear. I can't see through it yet, but I shall afore long, or I'd have the girl, like a shot I would. 'Tain't the girl, mother, it's the money, if you understand me."

"Well, I don't understand you, certainly I don't. What about Sophy?"

"Oh lord!" He scratched his head ruefully.

"You wouldn't think of giving this the go-by for Sophy, Harvey, would you? A girl as you ain't even engaged to, Harvey, would you?"

"We don't want to chatter about that," declared her son. "I got to think it over, and it's going to tie my wool, I can tell you, for there's a bit of craft somewhere, I'll take my oath. If there ain't, there ought to be!" Over the alluring project his decision wavered for days, until his mother became mortified at his inexplicable vacillation.

"I tell you," he cried, "I can't make tops or bottoms of it all. I like the girl well enough, but I like Sophy, too, and it's no good beating about the bush. I like Sophy, she's the girl I love, but Mary's a fine creature, and money like that wants looking at before you throw it away, love or no love. Three thousand pounds! I'd be a made man."

And as if in sheer spite to his mother; as if a bushel of money lay on the doorstep for him to kick over whenever the fancy seized him; in short (as Mrs. Witlow very clearly intimated) as if in contempt of Providence he began to pursue Sophy Daws with a new fervour, and walked with that young girl more than he was accustomed to, more than ever before; in fact, as his mother bemoaned, more than he had need to. It was unreasonable, it was a shame, a foolishness; it wasn't decent and it wasn't safe.

On his weekly visits to the farm his mind still wavered. Mrs. Sadgrove let him alone; she was very good, she did not pester him with questions and entreaties. There was Mary with her white dress and her red hair and her silence; a girl with a great fortune, walking about the yard, or sitting in the room, and casting not a glance upon him. Not that he would have known it if she did, for now he was just as shy of her. Mrs. Sadgrove often left them alone, but when they were alone he could not dish up a word for the pretty maid; he was dumb as a statue. If either she or her mother had lifted so much as a finger then there would have been an end to his hesitations or suspicions, for in Mary's presence the fine glory of the girl seized him incontinently; he was again full of a longing to press her lips, to lay down his doubts, to touch her bosom—though he could not think she would ever allow that! Not an atom of doubt about *her* ever visited him; she was unaware of her mother's queer project. Rather, if she became aware he was sure it would be the end of him. Too beautiful she was, too learned, and too rich. Decidedly it was his native cunning, and no want of love, that inhibited him. Folks with property did not often come along and bid you help yourself. Not very often! And throw in a grand bright girl, just for good measure as you might say. Not very often!

For weeks the higgler made his customary calls, and each time the outcome was the same; no more, no less. "Some dodge," he mused, "something the girl don't know and the mother does." Were they going bankrupt, or were they mortgaged up to the neck, or was there anything the matter with the girl, or was it just the mother wanted to get hold of him? He knew his own value if he didn't know his own mind, and his value couldn't match that girl any more than his mind could. So what *did* they want him for? Whatever it was Harvey Witlow was ready for it whenever he was in Mary's presence, but once away from her his own craftiness asserted itself: it was a snare, they were trying to make a mock of him!

But nothing could prevent his own mother mocking him, and her treatment of Sophy was so unbearable that if the heart of that dusky beauty had not been proof against all impediments, Harvey might have had to whistle for her favour. But whenever he was with Sophy he had only one heart, undivided and true, and certain as time itself.

"I love Sophy best. It's true enough I love Mary, too, but I love Sophy better. I know it; Sophy's the girl I must wed. It might not be so if I weren't all dashed and doddered about the money; I don't know. But I do know that Mary's innocent of all this craftiness; it's her mother trying to mogue me into it."

Later he would be wishing he could only forget Sophy and do it. Without the hindrance of conscience he could do it, catch or no catch.

He went on calling at the farm, with nothing said or settled, until October. Then Harvey made up his mind, and without a word to the Sadgroves he went and married Sophy Daws and gave up calling at the farm altogether. This gave him some feeling of dishonesty, some qualm, and a vague unhappiness; likewise he feared the cold hostility of Mrs. Sadgrove. She would be terribly vexed. As for Mary, he was nothing to her, poor girl; it was a shame. The last time he drove that way he did not call at the farm. Autumn was advancing, and the apples were down, the bracken dying, the furze out of bloom, and the farm on the moor looked more and more lonely, and most cold, though it lodged a flame-haired silent woman, fit for a nobleman, whom they wanted to mate with a common higgler. Crafty, you know, too crafty!

V

THE MARRIAGE was a gay little occasion, but they did not go away for a honeymoon. Sophy's grandmother from a distant village, Cassandra Fundy, who had a deafness and a speckled skin, brought her third husband, Amos, whom the family had never seen before. Not a very wise man, indeed he was a common man, stooping like a decayed tree, he was so old. But he shaved every day and his hairless skull was yellow. Cassandra, who was yellow too, had long since turned into a fool; she did not shave, though she ought to have done. She was like to die soon, but everybody said old Amos would live to be a hundred; it was expected of him, and he, too, was determined. The guests declared that a storm was threatening, but Amos Fundy denied it and scorned it.

"Thunder p'raps, but 'twill clear; 'tis only de pride o' der morning."

"Don't you be a fool," remarked his wife enigmatically, "you'll die soon enough."

"You must behold der moon," continued the octogenarian; "de closer it is to der wheel, de closer der rain; de furder away it is, de furder der rain."

"You could pour that man's brains into a thimble," declared Cassandra of her spouse, "and they wouldn't fill it—he's deaf."

Fundy was right; the day did clear. The marriage was made and the guests returned with the man and his bride to their home. But Fundy was also wrong, for storm came soon after and rain set in. The guests stayed on for tea, and then, as it was no better, they feasted and stayed till night. And Harvey began to think they never would go, but of course they couldn't and so there they were. Sophy was looking wonderful in white stockings and shiny shoes and a red frock with a tiny white apron. A big girl she seemed, with her shaken dark hair and flushed face. Grandmother Fundy spoke seriously, but not secretly to her.

"I've had my fourteen touch of children," said Grandmother Fundy. "Yes, they were flung on the mercy of God—poor little devils. I've followed most of 'em to the churchyard. You go slow, Sophia."

"Yes, granny."

"Why," continued Cassandra, embracing the whole company, as it were, with her disclosure, "my mother had me by some gentleman!"

The announcement aroused no response except sympathetic, and perhaps encouraging, nods from the women. "She had me by some gentleman—she ought to ha' had a twal' month, she did!"

"Wasn't she ever married?" Sophy inquired of her grandmother.

"Married? Yes, course she was," replied the old dame, "of course. But marriage ain't everything. Twice she was, but not to he, she wasn't."

"Not to the gentleman?"

"No! Oh, no! He'd got money—bushels! Marriage ain't much, not with these gentry."

"Ho, ho, that's a tidy come-up!" laughed Harvey.

"Who was that gentleman?" Sophia's interest was deeply engaged. But Cassandra Fundy was silent, pondering like a china image. Her gaze was towards the mantelpiece, where there were four lamps—but only one usable—and two clocks—but only one going—and a coloured greeting card a foot long with large letters KEEP SMILING adorned with lithographic honeysuckle.

"She's hard of hearing," interpolated grandfather Amos, "very hard, gets worse. She've a horn at home, big as that . . ." His eyes roved the room for an object of comparison, and he seized upon the fire shovel that lay in the fender. "Big as that shovel. Crown silver it is, and solid, a beautiful horn, but"—he brandished the shovel before them—"her won't use 'en."

"Granny, who was that gentleman?" shouted Sophy. "Did you know him?"

"No! no!" declared the indignant dame. "I dunno ever his name, nor I don't want to. He took hisself off to Ameriky, and now he's in the land

179

of heaven. I never seen him. If I had, I'd a given it to him properly;
oh, my dear, not blay-guarding him, you know, but just plain language!
Where's your seven commandments?"

At last the rain abated. Peeping into the dark garden you could see
the fugitive moonlight hung in a million raindrops in the black twigs of
all sorts of bushes and trees, while along the cantle of the porch a line
of raindrops hung, even and regular, as if they were nailheads made of
glass. So all the guests departed, in one long staggering, struggling,
giggling and guffawing body, into the village street. The bride and her
man stood in the porch, watching and waving hands. Sophy was
momentarily grieving: what a lot of trouble and fuss when you announced that henceforward you were going to sleep with a man because
you loved him true! She had said goodbye to her grandmother Cassandra, to her father and her little sister. She had hung on her mother's
breast, sighing an almost intolerable farewell to innocence—never
treasured until it is gone, and thenceforward a pretty sorrow cherished
more deeply than wider joys.

Into Harvey's mind, as they stood there at last alone, momentarily
stole an image of a bright-haired girl, lovely, silent, sad, whom he felt
he had deeply wronged. And he was sorry. He had escaped the snare,
but if there had been no snare he might this night have been sleeping
with a different bride. And it would have been just as well. Sophy looked
but a girl with her blown hair and wet face. She was wiping her tears
on the tiny apron. But she had the breasts of a woman and decoying
eyes. "Sophy, Sophy!" breathed Harvey, wooing her in the darkness.

"It blows and it rains, and it rains and it blows," chattered the
crumpled bride, "and I'm all so bescambled I can't tell wet from windy."

"Come, my love," whispered the bridegroom, "come in, to home."

VI

FOUR OR FIVE months later the higgler's affairs had again taken a rude
turn. Marriage, alas, was not all it might be; his wife and his mother
quarrelled unendingly. Sometimes he sided with one and sometimes
with the other. He could not yet afford to install his mother in a separate
cottage, and therefore even Sophy had to admit that her mother-in-law
had a right to be living there with them, the home being hers. Harvey
hadn't bought much of it; and though he was welcome to it all now, and
it would be exclusively his as soon as she died, still, it was her furniture,
and you couldn't drive any woman (even your mother) off her own
property. Sophy, who wanted a home of her own, was vexed and moody,
and antagonistic to her man. Business, too, had gone down sadly of late.
He had thrown up the Shag Moor round months ago; he could not

bring himself to go there again, and he had not been able to square up the loss by any substantial new connections. On top of it all his horse died. It stumbled on a hill one day and fell, and it couldn't get up, or it wouldn't—at any rate, it didn't. Harvey thrashed it and coaxed it, then he cursed it and kicked it; after that he sent for a veterinary man, and the veterinary man ordered it to be shot. And it was shot. A great blow to Harvey Witlow was that. He had no money to buy another horse; money was tight with him, very tight; and so he had to hire at fabulous cost a decrepit nag that ate like a good one. It ate—well, it would have astonished you to see what that creature disposed of, with hay the price it was, and corn gone up to heaven nearly. In fact Harvey found that he couldn't stand the racket much longer, and as he could not possibly buy another it looked very much as if he was in queer street once more, unless he could borrow the money from some friendly person. Of course there were plenty of friendly persons, but they had no money, just as there were many persons who had the money but were not what you might call friendly; and so the higgler began to reiterate twenty times a day, and forty times a day, that he was entirely and absolutely damned and done. Things were thus very bad with him, they were at their worst —for he had a wife to keep now, as well as a mother, and a horse that ate like Satan, and worked like a gnat—when it suddenly came into his mind that Mrs. Sadgrove was reputed to have a lot of money, and had no call to be unfriendly to him. He had his grave doubts about the size of her purse, but there could be no harm in trying so long as you approached her in a right reasonable manner.

For a week or two he held off from this appeal, but the grim spectre of destitution gave him no rest, and so, near the close of a wild March day he took his desperate courage and his cart and the decrepit nag to Shag Moor. Wild it was, though dry, and the wind against them, a vast turmoil of icy air strident and baffling. The nag threw up its head and declined to trot. Evening was but an hour away, the fury of the wind did not retard it, nor the clouds hasten it. Low down the sun was quitting the wrack of storm, exposing a jolly orb of magnifying fire that shone flush under eaves and through the casements of cottages, casting a pattern of lattice and tossing boughs upon the interior walls, lovelier than dreamed-of pictures. The heads of mothers and old dames were also imaged there, recognizable in their black shadows; and little children held up their hands between window and wall to make five-fingered shapes upon the golden screen. To drive on the moor then was to drive into blasts more dire. Darkness began to fall, and bitter cold it was. No birds to be seen, neither beast nor man; empty of everything it was except sound and a marvel of dying light, and Harvey Witlow of Dinnop with a sour old nag driving from end to end of it. At Prattle Corner

181

dusk was already abroad: there was just one shaft of light that broached a sharp-angled stack in the rickyard, an ark of darkness, along whose top the gads and wooden pins and tilted straws were miraculously fringed in the last glare. Hitching his nag to the palings he knocked at the door, and knew in the gloom that it was Mary who opened it and stood peering forth at him. "Good evening," he said, touching his hat.

"Oh!" the girl uttered a cry, "Higgler! What do you come for?" It was the longest sentence she had ever spoken to him; a sad frightened voice.

"I thought," he began, "I'd call—and see Mrs. Sadgrove. I wondered . . ."

"Mother's dead," said the girl. She drew the door farther back, as if inviting him, and he entered. The door was shut behind him, and they were alone in darkness, together. The girl was deeply grieving. Trembling, he asked the question: "What is it you tell me, Mary?"

"Mother's dead," repeated the girl, "all day, all day, all day." They were close to each other, but he could not see her. All round the house the wind roved lamentingly, shuddering at doors and windows. "She died in the night. The doctor was to have come, but he has not come all day," Mary whispered, "all day, all day. I don't understand; I have waited for him, and he has not come. She died, she was dead in her bed this morning, and I've been alone all day, all day, and I don't know what is to be done."

"I'll go for the doctor," he said hastily, but she took him by the hand and drew him into the kitchen. There was no candle lit; a fire was burning there, richly glowing embers, that laid a gaunt shadow of the table across a corner of the ceiling. Every dish on the dresser gleamed, the stone floor was rosy, and each smooth curve on the dark settle was shining like ice. Without invitation he sat down.

"No," said the girl, in a tremulous voice, "you must help me." She lit a candle: her face was white as the moon, her lips were sharply red, and her eyes were wild. "Come," she said, and he followed her behind the settle and up the stairs to a room where there was a disordered bed, and what might be a body lying under the quilt. The higgler stood still staring at the form under the quilt. The girl, too, was still and staring. Wind dashed upon the ivy at the window and hallooed like a grieving multitude. A crumpled gown hid the body's head, but thrust from under it, almost as if to greet him, was her naked lean arm, the palm of the hand lying uppermost. At the foot of the bed was a large washing bowl, with sponge and towels.

"You've been laying her out! Yourself!" exclaimed Witlow. The pale girl set down the candle on a chest of drawers. "Help me now," she said, and moving to the bed she lifted the crumpled gown from off the face of the dead woman, at the same time smoothing the quilt closely up to the body's chin. "I cannot put the gown on, because of her arm, it has gone stiff." She shuddered, and stood holding the gown as if offering it to the man. He lifted that dead naked arm and tried to place it down at the body's side, but it resisted and he let go his hold. The arm swung back to its former outstretched position, as if it still lived and resented that pressure. The girl retreated from the bed with a timorous cry. "Get me a bandage," he said, "or something we can tear up."

She gave him some pieces of linen.

"I'll finish this for you," he brusquely whispered, "you get along downstairs and take a swig of brandy. Got any brandy?"

She did not move. He put his arm around her and gently urged her to the door. "Brandy," he repeated, "and light your candles."

He watched her go heavily down the stairs before he shut the door. Returning to the bed he lifted the quilt. The dead body was naked and smelt of soap. Dropping the quilt he lifted the outstretched arm again, like cold wax to the touch and unpliant as a sturdy sapling, and tried once more to bend it to the body's side. As he did so the bedroom door blew open with a crash. It was only a draught of the wind, and a loose latch—Mary had opened a door downstairs, perhaps—but it awed him, as if some invisible looker were there resenting his presence. He went and closed the door, the latch had a loose hasp, and tiptoeing nervously back he seized the dreadful arm with a sudden brutal energy, and bent it by thrusting his knee violently into the hollow of the elbow. Hurriedly he slipped the gown over the head and inserted the arm in the sleeve. A strange impulse of modesty stayed him for a moment: should he call the girl and let her complete the robing of the naked body under the quilt? That preposterous pause seemed to add a new anger to the wind, and again the door sprang open. He delayed no longer, but letting it remain open, he uncovered the dead woman. As he lifted the chill body the long outstretched arm moved and tilted like the boom of a sail, but crushing it to its side he bound the limb fast with the strips of linen. So Mrs. Sadgrove was made ready for her coffin. Drawing the quilt back to her neck, with a gush of relief he glanced about the room. It was a very ordinary bedroom: bed, washstand, chest of drawers, chair, and two pictures—one of deeply religious import, and the other a little pink print, in a gilded frame, of a bouncing nude nymph recumbent upon a cloud. It was queer: a lot of people, people whom you wouldn't think it of, had that sort of picture in their bedrooms.

Mary was now coming up the stairs again, with a glass half full of liquid. She brought it to him.

"No, you drink it," he urged, and Mary sipped the brandy.

"I've finished—I've finished," he said as he watched her, "she's quite comfortable now." The girl looked her silent thanks at him, again holding out the glass. "No, sup it yourself," he said; but as she stood in the dim light, regarding him with her strange gaze, and still offering the drink, he took it from her, drained it at a gulp and put the glass upon the chest, beside the candle. "She's quite comfortable now. I'm very grieved, Mary," he said with awkward kindness, "about all this trouble that's come on you."

She was motionless as a wax image, as if she had died in her steps, her hand still extended as when he took the glass from it. So piercing was her gaze that his own drifted from her face and took in again the objects in the room: the washstand, the candle on the chest, the little pink picture. The wind beat upon the ivy outside the window as if a monstrous whip were lashing its slaves.

"You must notify the registrar," he began again, "but you must see the doctor first."

"I've waited for him all day," Mary whispered, "all day. The nurse will come again soon. She went home to rest in the night." She turned towards the bed. "She has only been ill a week."

"Yes?" he lamely said. "Dear me, it is sudden."

"I must see the doctor," she continued.

"I'll drive you over to him in my gig." He was eager to do that.

"I don't know," said Mary slowly.

"Yes, I'll do that, soon's you're ready. Mary," he fumbled with his speech, "I'm not wanting to pry into your affairs, or any thing as don't concern me, but how are you going to get along now? Have you got any relations?"

"No," the girl shook her head, "no."

"That's bad. What was you thinking of doing? How has she left you—things were in a baddish way, weren't they?"

"Oh, no," Mary looked up quickly. "She has left me very well off. I shall go on with the farm; there's the old man and the boy—they've gone to a wedding today; I shall go on with it. She was so thoughtful for me, and I would not care to leave all this, I love it."

"But you can't do it by yourself, alone?"

"No. I'm to get a man to superintend, a working bailiff," she said.

"Oh!" And again they were silent. The girl went to the bed and lifted the covering. She saw the bound arm and then drew the quilt tenderly over the dead face. Witlow picked up his hat and found himself staring again at the pink picture. Mary took the candle preparatory to descending the stairs. Suddenly the higgler turned to her and ventured: "Did you know as she once asked me to marry you?" he blurted.

Her eyes turned from him, but he guessed—he could feel that she *had* known.

"I've often wondered why," he murmured, "why she wanted that."

"She didn't," said the girl.

That gave pause to the man; he felt stupid at once, and roved his fingers in a silly way along the roughened nap of his hat.

"Well, she asked me to," he bluntly protested.

"She knew," Mary's voice was no louder than a sigh, "that you were courting another girl, the one you married."

"But, but," stuttered the honest higgler, "if she knew that why did she want for me to marry you?"

"She didn't," said Mary again; and again, in the pause, he did silly things to his hat. How shy this girl was, how lovely in her modesty and grief!

"I can't make tops or bottoms of it," he said; "but she asked me, as sure as God's my maker."

"I know. It was me, I wanted it."

"You!" he cried, "you wanted to marry me!"

The girl bowed her head, lovely in her grief and modesty, "She was against it, but I made her ask you."

"And I hadn't an idea that you cast a thought on me," he murmured. "I feared it was a sort of trick she was playing on me. I didn't understand, I had no idea that you knew about it even. And so I didn't ever ask you."

"Oh, why not, why not? I was fond of you then," whispered she. "Mother tried to persuade me against it, but I was fond of you—then."

He was in a queer distress and confusion: "Oh, if you'd only tipped me a word, or given me a sort of look," he sighed. "Oh, Mary!"

She said no more, but went downstairs. He followed her and immediately fetched the lamps from his gig. As he lit the candles: "How strange," Mary said, "that you should come back just as I most needed help. I am very grateful."

"Mary, I'll drive you to the doctor's now." She shook her head; she was smiling. "Then I'll stay till the nurse comes."

"No, you must go. Go at once."

He picked up the two lamps, and turning at the door said, "I'll come again tomorrow." Then the wind rushed into the room: "Goodbye," she cried, shutting the door quickly behind him. He drove away into deep darkness, the wind howling, his thoughts strange and bitter. He had thrown away a love, a love that was dumb and hid itself. By God, he had thrown away a fortune, too! And he had forgotten all about his real errand until now, forgotten all about the loan! Well, let it go; give it up. He would give up higgling; he would take on some other job; a bailiff, a working bailiff, that was the job that would suit him, a working bailiff. Of course there was Sophy; but still—Sophy!

185

ROALD DAHL

1916–1990

"Violence accompanied by wit and humour is loved."
This master of the macabre (who was born in Wales of Norwegian
parents but who lived in England for many years) was
speaking of his highly successful children's books. Equally
well, he might have been referring to his bizarre and
world-famous short stories.

Parson's Pleasure

MR. BOGGIS was driving the car slowly, leaning back comfortably in the seat with one elbow resting on the sill of the open window. How beautiful the countryside, he thought; how pleasant to see a sign or two of summer once again. The primroses especially. And the hawthorn. The hawthorn was exploding white and pink and red along the hedges and the primroses were growing underneath in little clumps, and it was beautiful.

He took one hand off the wheel and lit himself a cigarette. The best thing now, he told himself, would be to make for the top of Brill Hill. He could see it about half a mile ahead. And that must be the village of Brill, that cluster of cottages among the trees right on the very summit. Excellent. Not many of his Sunday sections had a nice elevation like that to work from.

He drove up the hill and stopped the car just short of the summit on the outskirts of the village. Then he got out and looked around. Down below, the countryside was spread out before him like a huge green carpet. He could see for miles. It was perfect. He took a pad and pencil from his pocket, leaned against the back of the car, and allowed his practised eye to travel slowly over the landscape.

He could see one medium farmhouse over on the right, back in the fields, with a track leading to it from the road. There was another larger one beyond it. There was a house surrounded by tall elms that looked as though it might be a Queen Anne, and there were two likely farms away over on the left. Five places in all. That was about the lot in this direction.

Mr. Boggis drew a rough sketch on his pad showing the position of each so that he'd be able to find them easily when he was down below, then he got back into the car and drove up through the village to the other side of the hill. From there he spotted six more possibles—five farms and one big white Georgian house. He studied the Georgian house through his binoculars. It had a clean prosperous look, and the garden was well ordered. That was a pity. He ruled it out immediately. There was no point in calling on the prosperous.

In this square then, in this section, there were ten possibles in all. Ten was a nice number, Mr. Boggis told himself. Just the right amount for a leisurely afternoon's work. What time was it now? Eleven o'clock. He would have liked a pint of beer in the pub before he started, but on Sundays they didn't open until twelve. Very well, he would have it later. He glanced at the notes on his pad. He decided to take the Queen Anne first, the house with the elms. It had looked nicely dilapidated through the binoculars. The people there could probably do with some money. He was always lucky with Queen Annes, anyway. Mr. Boggis climbed back into the car, released the handbrake, and began cruising slowly down the hill without the engine.

Apart from the fact that he was at this moment disguised in the uniform of a clergyman, there was nothing very sinister about Mr. Cyril Boggis. By trade he was a dealer in antique furniture, with his own shop and showroom in the King's Road, Chelsea. His premises were not large, and generally he didn't do a great deal of business, but because he always bought cheap, very very cheap, and sold very very dear, he managed to make quite a tidy little income every year. He was a talented salesman, and when buying or selling a piece he could slide smoothly into whichever mood suited the client best. He could become grave and charming for the aged, obsequious for the rich, sober for the godly, masterful for the weak, mischievous for the widow, arch and saucy for the spinster. He was well aware of his gift, using it shamelessly on every possible occasion; and often, at the end of an unusually good performance, it was as much as he could do to prevent himself from turning aside and taking a bow or two as the thundering applause of the audience went rolling through the theatre.

In spite of this rather clownish quality of his, Mr. Boggis was not a fool. In fact, it was said of him by some that he probably knew as much about French, English, and Italian furniture as anyone else in

187

London. He also had surprisingly good taste, and he was quick to recognize and reject an ungraceful design, however genuine the article might be. His real love, naturally, was for the work of the great eighteenth-century English designers, Ince, Mayhew, Chippendale, Robert Adam, Manwaring, Inigo Jones, Hepplewhite, Kent, Johnson, George Smith, Lock, Sheraton, and the rest of them, but even with these he occasionally drew the line. He refused, for example, to allow a single piece from Chippendale's Chinese or Gothic period to come into his showroom, and the same was true of some of the heavier Italian designs of Robert Adam.

During the past few years, Mr. Boggis had achieved considerable fame among his friends in the trade by his ability to produce unusual and often quite rare items with astonishing regularity. Apparently the man had a source of supply that was almost inexhaustible, a sort of private warehouse, and it seemed that all he had to do was to drive out to it once a week and help himself. Whenever they asked him where he got the stuff, he would smile knowingly and wink and murmur something about a little secret.

The idea behind Mr. Boggis's little secret was a simple one, and it had come to him as a result of something that had happened on a certain Sunday afternoon nearly nine years before, while he was driving in the country. He had gone out in the morning to visit his old mother, who lived in Sevenoaks, and on the way back the fanbelt on his car had broken, causing the engine to overheat and the water to boil away. He had got out of the car and walked to the nearest house, a smallish farm building about fifty yards off the road, and had asked the woman who answered the door if he could please have a jug of water.

While he was waiting for her to fetch it, he happened to glance in through the door to the living room, and there, not five yards from where he was standing, he spotted something that made him so excited the sweat began to come out all over the top of his head. It was a large oak armchair of a type that he had only seen once before in his life. Each arm, as well as the panel at the back, was supported by a row of eight beautifully turned spindles. The back panel itself was decorated by an inlay of the most delicate floral design, and the head of a duck was carved to lie along half the length of either arm. Good God, he thought. This thing is late fifteenth century!

He poked his head in further through the door, and there, by heavens, was another of them on the other side of the fireplace!

He couldn't be sure, but two chairs like that must be worth at least a thousand pounds up in London. And oh, what beauties they were!

When the woman returned, Mr. Boggis introduced himself and straight away asked if she would like to sell her chairs.

Dear me, she said. But why on earth should she want to sell her chairs?

No reason at all, except that he might be willing to give her a pretty nice price.

And how much would he give? They were definitely not for sale, but just out of curiosity, just for fun, you know, how much would he give?

Thirty-five pounds.

How much?

Thirty-five pounds.

Dear me, thirty-five pounds. Well, well, that was very interesting. She'd always thought they were valuable. They were very old. They were very comfortable too. She couldn't possibly do without them, not possibly. No, they were not for sale but thank you very much all the same.

They weren't really so very old, Mr. Boggis told her, and they wouldn't be at all easy to sell, but it just happened that he had a client who rather liked that sort of thing. Maybe he could go up another two pounds—call it thirty-seven. How about that?

They bargained for half an hour, and of course in the end Mr. Boggis got the chairs and agreed to pay her something less than a twentieth of their value.

That evening, driving back to London in his old station-wagon with the two fabulous chairs tucked away snugly in the back, Mr. Boggis had suddenly been struck by what seemed to him to be a most remarkable idea.

Look here, he said. If there is good stuff in one farmhouse, then why not in others? Why shouldn't he search for it? Why shouldn't he comb the countryside? He could do it on Sundays. In that way, it wouldn't interfere with his work at all. He never knew what to do with his Sundays.

So Mr. Boggis bought maps, large scale maps of all the counties around London, and with a fine pen he divided each of them up into a series of squares. Each of these squares covered an actual area of five miles by five, which was about as much territory, he estimated, as he could cope with on a single Sunday, were he to comb it thoroughly. He didn't want the towns and the villages. It was the comparatively isolated places, the large farmhouses and the rather dilapidated country mansions, that he was looking for; and in this way, if he did one square each Sunday, fifty-two squares a year, he would gradually cover every farm and every country house in the home counties.

But obviously there was a bit more to it than that. Country folk are a suspicious lot. So are the impoverished rich. You can't go about ringing their bells and expecting them to show you around their houses just for the asking, because they won't do it. That way you would never get beyond the front door. How then was he to gain admittance? Perhaps it would be best if he didn't let them know he was a dealer at all. He could be the telephone man, the plumber, the gas inspector. He could even be a clergyman . . .

From this point on, the whole scheme began to take on a more practical aspect. Mr. Boggis ordered a large quantity of superior cards on which the following legend was engraved:

THE REVEREND

CYRIL WINNINGTON BOGGIS

President of the Society   *In association with*
for the Preservation of   *The Victoria and*
Rare Furniture   *Albert Museum*

From now on, every Sunday, he was going to be a nice old parson spending his holiday travelling around on a labour of love for the 'Society', compiling an inventory of the treasures that lay hidden in the country homes of England. And who in the world was going to kick him out when they heard that one?

Nobody.

And then, once he was inside, if he happened to spot something he really wanted, well—he knew a hundred different ways of dealing with that.

Rather to Mr. Boggis's surprise, the scheme worked. In fact, the friendliness with which he was received in one house after another through the countryside was, in the beginning, quite embarrassing, even to him. A slice of cold pie, a glass of port, a cup of tea, a basket of plums, even a full sit-down Sunday dinner with the family, such things were constantly being pressed upon him. Sooner or later, of course, there had been some bad moments and a number of unpleasant incidents, but then nine years is more than four hundred Sundays, and that adds up to a great quantity of houses visited. All in all, it had been an interesting, exciting, and lucrative business.

And now it was another Sunday and Mr. Boggis was operating in the county of Buckinghamshire, in one of the most northerly squares on his map, about ten miles from Oxford, and as he drove down the hill and headed for his first house, the dilapidated Queen Anne, he began to get the feeling that this was going to be one of his lucky days.

He parked the car about a hundred yards from the gates and got out to walk the rest of the way. He never liked people to see his car until after a deal was completed. A dear old clergyman and a large station-wagon somehow never seemed quite right together. Also the short walk gave him time to examine the property closely from the outside and to assume the mood most likely to be suitable for the occasion.

Mr. Boggis strode briskly up the drive. He was a small fat-legged man with a belly. The face was round and rosy, quite perfect for the part, and the two large brown eyes that bulged out at you from this rosy face gave an impression of gentle imbecility. He was dressed in a black suit with the usual parson's dog-collar round his neck, and on his head a soft black hat. He carried an old oak walking-stick which lent him, in his opinion, a rather rustic easy-going air.

He approached the front door and rang the bell. He heard the sound of footsteps in the hall and the door opened and suddenly there stood before him, or rather above him, a gigantic woman dressed in riding-breeches. Even through the smoke of her cigarette he could smell the powerful odour of stables and horse manure that clung about her.

"Yes?" she asked, looking at him suspiciously. "What is it you want?"

Mr. Boggis, who half expected her to whinny any moment, raised his hat, made a little bow, and handed her his card. "I do apologize for bothering you," he said, and then he waited, watching her face as she read the message.

"I don't understand," she said, handing back the card. "What is it you want?"

Mr. Boggis explained about the Society for the Preservation of Rare Furniture.

"This wouldn't by any chance be something to do with the Socialist Party?" she asked, staring at him fiercely from under a pair of pale bushy brows.

From then on, it was easy. A Tory in riding-breeches, male or female, was always a sitting duck for Mr. Boggis. He spent two minutes delivering an impassioned eulogy on the extreme Right Wing of the Conservative Party, then two more denouncing the Socialists. As a clincher, he made particular reference to the Bill that the Socialists had once introduced for the abolition of bloodsports in the country, and went on to inform his listener that his idea of heaven—"though you better not tell the bishop, my dear"—was a place where one could hunt the fox, the stag, and the hare with large packs of tireless hounds from morn till night every day of the week, including Sundays.

Watching her as he spoke, he could see the magic beginning to do its work. The woman was grinning now, showing Mr. Boggis a set of enormous, slightly yellow teeth.

"Madam," he cried, "I beg of you, *please* don't get me started on Socialism." At that point, she let out a great guffaw of laughter, raised an enormous red hand, and slapped him so hard on the shoulder that he nearly went over.

191

"Come in!" she shouted. "I don't know what the hell you want, but come on in!"

Unfortunately, and rather surprisingly, there was nothing of any value in the whole house, and Mr. Boggis, who never wasted time on barren territory, soon made his excuses and took his leave. The whole visit had taken less than fifteen minutes, and that, he told himself as he climbed back into his car and started off for the next place, was exactly as it should be.

From now on, it was all farmhouses, and the nearest was about half a mile up the road. It was a large half-timbered brick building of considerable age, and there was a magnificent pear tree still in blossom covering almost the whole of the south wall.

Mr. Boggis knocked on the door. He waited, but no one came. He knocked again, but still there was no answer, so he wandered around the back to look for the farmer among the cowsheds. There was no one there either.

He guessed that they must all still be in church, so he began peering in the windows to see if he could spot anything interesting. There was nothing in the dining room. Nothing in the library either. He tried the next window, the living room, and there, right under his nose, in the little alcove that the window made, he saw a beautiful thing, a semi-circular card-table in mahogany, richly veneered, and in the style of Hepplewhite, built around 1780.

"Ah-ha," he said aloud, pressing his face against glass. "Well done, Boggis."

But that was not all. There was a chair there as well, a single chair, and if he were not mistaken it was of an even finer quality than the table. Another Hepplewhite, wasn't it? And oh, what a beauty! The lattices on the back were finely carved with the honeysuckle, the husk, and the paterae, the caning on the seat was original, the legs were very gracefully turned and the two back ones had that peculiar outward splay that meant so much. It was an exquisite chair. "Before this day is done," Mr. Boggis said softly, "I shall have the pleasure of sitting down upon that lovely seat." He never bought a chair without doing this. It was a favourite test of his, and it was always an intriguing sight to see him lowering himself delicately into the seat, waiting for the 'give', expertly gauging the precise but infinitesimal degree of shrinkage that the years had caused in the mortice and dovetail joints.

But there was no hurry, he told himself. He would return here later. He had the whole afternoon before him.

The next farm was situated some way back in the fields, and in order to keep his car out of sight, Mr. Boggis had to leave it on the road and walk about six hundred yards along a straight track that led directly into the back yard of the farmhouse. This place, he noticed as he approached, was a good deal smaller than the last, and he didn't hold out much hope for it. It looked rambling and dirty, and some of the sheds were clearly in bad repair.

There were three men standing in a close group in a corner of the yard, and one of them had two large black greyhounds with him, on leashes. When the men caught sight of Mr. Boggis walking forward in his black suit and parson's collar, they stopped talking and seemed suddenly to stiffen and freeze, becoming absolutely still, motionless, three faces turned towards him, watching him suspiciously as he approached.

The oldest of the three was a stumpy man with a wide frog mouth and small shifty eyes, and although Mr. Boggis didn't know it, his name was Rummins and he was the owner of the farm.

The tall youth beside him, who appeared to have something wrong with one eye, was Bert, the son of Rummins.

The shortish flat-faced man with a narrow corrugated brow and immensely broad shoulders was Claud. Claud had dropped in on Rummins in the hope of getting a piece of pork or ham out of him from the pig that had been killed the day before. Claud knew about the killing—the noise of it had carried far across the fields—and he also knew that a man should have a government permit to do that sort of thing, and that Rummins didn't have one.

"Good afternoon," Mr. Boggis said. "Isn't it a lovely day?"

None of the three men moved. At that moment they were all thinking precisely the same thing—that somehow or other this clergyman, who was certainly not the local fellow, had been sent to poke his nose into their business and to report what he found to the government.

"What beautiful dogs," Mr. Boggis said. "I must say I've never been greyhound-racing myself, but they tell me it's a fascinating sport."

Again the silence, and Mr. Boggis glanced quickly from Rummins to Bert, then to Claud, then back again to Rummins, and he noticed that each of them had the same peculiar expression on his face, something between a jeer and a challenge, with a contemptuous curl to the mouth and a sneer around the nose.

"Might I enquire if you are the owner?" Mr. Boggis asked, undaunted, addressing himself to Rummins.

"What is it you want?"

"I do apologize for troubling you, especially on a Sunday."

Mr. Boggis offered his card and Rummins took it and held it up close to his face. The other two didn't move, but their eyes swivelled over to one side, trying to see.

"And what exactly might you be wanting?" Rummins asked.

For the second time that morning, Mr. Boggis explained at some length the aims and ideals of the Society for the Preservation of Rare Furniture.

"We don't have any," Rummins told him when it was over. "You're wasting your time."

"Now, just a minute, sir," Mr. Boggis said, raising a finger. "The last man who said that to me was an old farmer down in Sussex, and when he finally let me into his house, d'you know what I found? A dirty-looking old chair in the corner of the kitchen, and it turned out to be worth *four hundred pounds!* I showed him how to sell it, and he bought himself a new tractor with the money."

"What on earth are you talking about?" Claud said. "There ain't no chair in the world worth four hundred pound."

"Excuse me," Mr. Boggis answered primly, "but there are plenty of chairs in England worth more than twice that figure. And you know where they are? They're tucked away in the farms and cottages all over the country, with the owners using them as steps and ladders and standing on them with hobnailed boots to reach a pot of jam out of the top cupboard or to hang a picture. This is the truth I'm telling you, my friends."

Rummins shifted uneasily on his feet. "You mean to say all you want to do is go inside and stand there in the middle of the room and look around?"

"Exactly," Mr. Boggis said. He was at last beginning to sense what the trouble might be. "I don't want to pry into your cupboards or into your larder. I just want to look at the furniture to see if you happen to have any treasures here, and then I can write about them in our Society magazine."

"You know what I think?" Rummins said, fixing him with his small wicked eyes. "I think you're after buying the stuff yourself. Why else would you be going to all this trouble?"

"Oh, dear me. I only wish I had the money. Of course, if I saw something that I took a great fancy to, and it wasn't beyond my means, I might be tempted to make an offer. But alas, that rarely happens."

"Well," Rummins said, "I don't suppose there's any harm in your taking a look around if that's all you want." He led the way across the yard to the back door of the farmhouse, and Mr. Boggis followed him; so did the son, Bert, and Claud with his two dogs. They went through the kitchen, where the only furniture was a cheap deal table with a dead chicken lying on it, and they emerged into a fairly large, exceedingly filthy living room.

And there it was! Mr. Boggis saw it at once, and he stopped dead in his tracks and gave a little shrill gasp of shock. Then he stood there for five, ten, fifteen seconds at least, staring like an idiot, unable to believe, not daring to believe what he saw before him. It *couldn't* be true, not possibly! But the longer he stared, the more true it began to seem. After all, there it was standing against the wall right in front of him, as real and as solid as the house itself. And who in the world could possibly make a mistake about a thing like that? Admittedly it was painted white, but that made not the slightest difference. Some idiot had done that. The paint could easily be stripped off. But good God! Just look at it! And in a place like this!

At this point, Mr. Boggis became aware of the three men, Rummins, Bert, and Claud, standing together in a group over by the fireplace, watching him intently. They had seen him stop and gasp and stare, and they must have seen his face turning red, or maybe it was white, but in any event they had seen enough to spoil the whole goddamn business if he didn't do something about it quick. In a flash, Mr. Boggis clapped one hand over his heart, staggered to the nearest chair, and collapsed into it, breathing heavily.

"What's the matter with you?" Claud asked.

"It's nothing," he gasped. "I'll be all right in a minute. Please— a glass of water. It's my heart."

Bert fetched him the water, handed it to him, and stayed close beside him, staring down at him with a fatuous leer on his face.

"I thought maybe you were looking at something," Rummins said. The wide frog-mouth widened a fraction further into a crafty grin, showing the stubs of several broken teeth.

"No, no," Mr. Boggis said. "Oh dear me, no. It's just my heart. I'm so sorry. It happens every now and then. But it goes away quite quickly. I'll be all right in a couple of minutes."

He *must* have time to think, he told himself. More important still, he must have time to compose himself thoroughly before he said another word. Take it gently, Boggis. And whatever you do, keep calm. These people may be ignorant, but they are not stupid. They are suspicious and wary and sly. And if it is really true—no it *can't* be, it *can't* be true . . .

He was holding one hand up over his eyes in a gesture of pain, and now, very carefully, secretly, he made a little crack between two of the fingers and peeked through.

Sure enough, the thing was still there, and on this occasion he took a good long look at it. Yes—he had been right the first time! There wasn't the slightest doubt about it! It was really unbelievable!

What he saw was a piece of furniture that any expert would have given almost anything to acquire. To a layman, it might not have appeared particularly impressive, especially when covered over as it was with

195

dirty white paint, but to Mr. Boggis it was a dealer's dream. He knew, as does every other dealer in Europe and America, that among the most celebrated and coveted examples of eighteenth-century English furniture in existence are the three famous pieces known as 'The Chippendale Commodes'. He knew their history backwards—that the first was 'discovered' in 1920, in a house at Moreton-in-Marsh, and was sold at Sotheby's the same year; that the other two turned up in the same auction rooms a year later, both coming out of Raynham Hall, Norfolk. They all fetched enormous prices. He couldn't quite remember the exact figure for the first one, or even the second, but he knew for certain that the last one to be sold had fetched thirty-nine hundred guineas. And that was in 1921! Today the same piece would surely be worth ten thousand pounds. Some man, Mr. Boggis couldn't remember his name, had made a study of these commodes fairly recently and had proved that all three must have come from the same workshop, for the veneers were all from the same log, and the same set of templates had been used in the construction of each. No invoices had been found for any of them, but all the experts were agreed that these three commodes could have been executed only by Thomas Chippendale himself, with his own hands, at the most exalted period in his career.

And here, Mr. Boggis kept telling himself as he peered cautiously through the crack in his fingers, here was the fourth Chippendale Commode! And *he* had found it! He would be rich! He would also be famous! Each of the other three was known throughout the furniture world by a special name—The Chastleton Commode, The First Raynham Commode, The Second Raynham Commode. This one would go down in history as The Boggis Commode! Just imagine the faces of the boys up there in London when they got a look at it tomorrow morning! And the luscious offers coming in from the big fellows over in the West End—Frank Partridge, Mallett, Jetley, and the rest of them! There would be a picture of it in *The Times*, and it would say, 'The very fine Chippendale Commode which was recently discovered by Mr. Cyril Boggis, a London dealer . . .' Dear God, what a stir he was going to make!

This one here, Mr. Boggis thought, was almost exactly similar to the Second Raynham Commode. (All three, the Chastleton and the two Raynhams, differed from one another in a number of small ways.) It was a most impressive handsome affair, built in the French rococo style of Chippendale's Directoire period, a kind of large fat chest-of-drawers set upon four carved and fluted legs that raised it about a foot from the ground. There were six drawers in all, two long ones in the middle and two shorter ones on either side. The serpentine front was magnificently ornamented along the top and sides and bottom, and also vertically

196

between each set of drawers, with intricate carvings of festoons and scrolls and clusters. The brass handles, although partly obscured by white paint, appeared to be superb. It was, of course, a rather 'heavy' piece, but the design had been executed with such elegance and grace that the heaviness was in no way offensive.

"How're you feeling now?" Mr. Boggis heard someone saying.

"Thank you, thank you, I'm much better already. It passes quickly. My doctor says it's nothing to worry about really so long as I rest for a few minutes whenever it happens. Ah yes," he said, raising himself slowly to his feet. "That's better. I'm all right now."

A trifle unsteadily, he began to move around the room examining the furniture, one piece at a time, commenting upon it briefly. He could see at once that apart from the commode it was a very poor lot.

"Nice oak table," he said. "But I'm afraid it's not old enough to be of any interest. Good comfortable chairs, but quite modern, yes, quite modern. Now this cupboard, well, it's rather attractive, but again, not valuable. This chest-of-drawers"—he walked casually past the Chippendale Commode and gave it a little contemptuous flip with his fingers—"worth a few pounds, I dare say, but no more. A rather crude reproduction, I'm afraid. Probably made in Victorian times. Did you paint it white?"

"Yes," Rummins said. "Bert did it."

"A very wise move. It's considerably less offensive in white."

"That's a strong piece of furniture," Rummins said. "Some nice carving on it too."

"Machine-carved," Mr. Boggis answered superbly, bending down to examine the exquisite craftsmanship. "You can tell it a mile off. But still, I suppose it's quite pretty in its way. It has its points."

He began to saunter off, then he checked himself and turned slowly back again. He placed the tip of one finger against the point of his chin, laid his head over to one side, and frowned as though deep in thought.

"You know what?" he said, looking at the commode, speaking so casually that his voice kept trailing off. "I've just remembered . . . I've been wanting a set of legs something like that for a long time. I've got a rather curious table in my own little home, one of those low things that people put in front of the sofa, sort of a coffee-table, and last Michaelmas, when I moved house, the foolish movers damaged the legs in the most shocking way. I'm very fond of that table. I always keep my big Bible on it, and all my sermon notes."

He paused, stroking his chin with the finger.

"Now I was just thinking. These legs on your chest-of-drawers might be very suitable. Yes, they might indeed. They could easily be cut off and fixed on to my table."

He looked around and saw the three men standing absolutely still, watching him suspiciously, three pairs of eyes, all different but equally mistrusting, small pig-eyes for Rummins, large slow eyes for Claud, and two odd eyes for Bert, one of them very queer and boiled and misty pale, with a little black dot in the centre, like a fish eye on a plate.

Mr. Boggis smiled and shook his head. "Come, come, what on earth am I saying? I'm talking as though I owned the piece myself. I do apologize."

"What you mean to say is you'd like to buy it," Rummins said.

"Well . . ." Mr. Boggis glanced back at the commode, frowning. "I'm not sure. I might . . . and then again . . . on second thoughts . . . no . . . I think it might be a bit too much trouble. It's not worth it. I'd better leave it."

"How much were you thinking of offering?" Rummins asked.

"Not much, I'm afraid. You see, this is not a genuine antique. It's merely a reproduction."

"I'm not so sure about that," Rummins told him. "It's been in *here* over twenty years, and before that it was up at the Manor House. I bought it there myself at auction when the old Squire died. You can't tell me that thing's new."

"It's not exactly new, but it's certainly not more than about sixty years old."

"It's more than that," Rummins said. "Bert, where's that bit of paper you once found at the back of one of them drawers? That old bill."

The boy looked vacantly at his father.

Mr. Boggis opened his mouth, then quickly shut it again without uttering a sound. He was beginning literally to shake with excitement, and to calm himself he walked over to the window and stared out at a plump brown hen pecking around for stray grains of corn in the yard.

"It was in the back of that drawer underneath all them rabbit-snares," Rummins was saying. "Go on and fetch it out and show it to the parson."

When Bert went forward to the commode, Mr. Boggis turned round again. He couldn't stand not watching him. He saw him pull out one of the big middle drawers, and he noticed the beautiful way in which the drawer slid open. He saw Bert's hand dipping inside and rummaging around among a lot of wires and strings.

"You mean this?" Bert lifted out a piece of folded yellowing paper and carried it over to the father, who unfolded it and held it up close to his face.

"You can't tell me this writing ain't bloody old," Rummins said, and he held the paper out to Mr. Boggis, whose whole arm was shaking as he took it. It was brittle and it crackled slightly between his fingers. The writing was in a long sloping copperplate hand:

Edward Montagu, Esq.   **Dr.**

To Thos. Chippendale

A large mahogany Commode Table of exceeding fine wood, very rich carvd, set upon fluted legs, two very neat shapd long drawers in the middle part and two ditto on each side, with rich chasd Brass Handles and Ornaments, the whole completely finished in the most exquisite taste............£87

Mr. Boggis was holding on to himself tight and fighting to suppress the excitement that was spinning round inside him and making him dizzy. Oh God, it was wonderful! With the invoice, the value had climbed even higher. What in heaven's name would it fetch now? Twelve thousand pounds? Fourteen? Maybe fifteen or even twenty? Who knows?

Oh, boy!

He tossed the paper contemptuously on to the table and said quietly, "It's exactly what I told you, a Victorian reproduction. This is simply the invoice that the seller—the man who made it and passed it off as an antique—gave to his client. I've seen lots of them. You'll notice that he doesn't say he made it himself. That would give the game away."

"Say what you like," Rummins announced, "but that's an old piece of paper."

"Of course it is, my dear friend. It's Victorian, late Victorian. About eighteen ninety. Sixty or seventy years old. I've seen hundreds of them. That was a time when masses of cabinet-makers did nothing else but apply themselves to faking the fine furniture of the century before."

"Listen, Parson," Rummins said, pointing at him with a thick dirty finger, "I'm not saying as how you may not know a fair bit about this furniture business, but what I *am* saying is this: How on earth can you be so mighty sure it's a fake when you haven't even seen what it looks like underneath all that paint?"

"Come here," Mr. Boggis said. "Come over here and I'll show you." He stood beside the commode and waited for them to gather round. "Now, anyone got a knife?"

Claud produced a horn-handled pocket knife, and Mr. Boggis took it and opened the smallest blade. Then, working with apparent casualness but actually with extreme care, he began chipping off the white paint from a small area on the top of the commode. The paint flaked away cleanly from the old hard varnish underneath, and when he had cleared away about three square inches, he stepped back and said, "Now, take a look at that!"

It was beautiful—a warm little patch of mahogany, glowing like a topaz, rich and dark with the true colour of its two hundred years.

"What's wrong with it?" Rummins asked.

"It's processed! Anyone can see that!"

"How can you see it, Mister? You tell us."

"Well, I must say that's a trifle difficult to explain. It's chiefly a matter of experience. My experience tells me that without the slightest doubt this wood has been processed with lime. That's what they use for mahogany, to give it that dark aged colour. For oak, they use potash salts, and for walnut it's nitric acid, but for mahogany it's always lime."

The three men moved a little closer to peer at the wood. There was a slight stirring of interest among them now. It was always intriguing to hear about some new form of crookery or deception.

"Look closely at the grain. You see that touch of orange in among the dark red-brown. That's the sign of lime."

They leaned forward, their noses close to the wood, first Rummins, then Claud, then Bert.

"And then there's the patina," Mr. Boggins continued.

"The what?"

He explained to them the meaning of this word as applied to furniture.

"My dear friends, you've no idea the trouble these rascals will go to to imitate the hard beautiful bronze-like appearance of genuine patina. It's terrible, really terrible, and it makes me quite sick to speak of it!" He was spitting each word sharply off the tip of the tongue and making a sour mouth to show his extreme distaste. The men waited, hoping for more secrets.

"The time and trouble that some mortals will go to in order to deceive the innocent!" Mr. Boggis cried. "It's perfectly disgusting! D'you know what they did here, my friends? I can recognize it clearly. I can almost *see* them doing it, the long, complicated ritual of rubbing the wood with linseed oil, coating it over with french polish that has been cunningly coloured, brushing it down with pumice-stone and oil, bees-waxing it with a wax that contains dirt and dust, and finally giving it the heat treatment to crack the polish so that it looks like two-hundred-year-old varnish! It really upsets me to contemplate such knavery!"

The three men continued to gaze at the little patch of dark wood.

"Feel it!" Mr. Boggis ordered. "Put your fingers on it! There, how does it feel, warm or cold?"

"Feels cold," Rummins said.

"Exactly, my friend! It happens to be a fact that faked patina is always cold to the touch. Real patina has a curiously warm feel to it."

"This feels normal," Rummins said, ready to argue.

"No, sir, it's cold. But of course it takes an experienced and sensitive finger-tip to pass a positive judgement. You couldn't really be expected to judge this any more than I could be expected to judge the quality of your barley. Everything in life, my dear sir, is experience."

200

The men were staring at this queer moon-faced clergyman with the bulging eyes, not quite so suspiciously now because he did seem to know a bit about his subject. But they were still a long way from trusting him.

Mr. Boggis bent down and pointed to one of the metal drawer-handles on the commode. "This is another place where the fakers go to work," he said. "Old brass normally has a colour and character all of its own. Did you know that?"

They stared at him, hoping for still more secrets.

"But the trouble is that they've become exceedingly skilled at matching it. In fact it's almost impossible to tell the difference between 'genuine old' and 'faked old'. I don't mind admitting that it has me guessing. So there's not really any point in our scraping the paint off these handles. We wouldn't be any the wiser."

"How can you possibly make new brass look like old?" Claud said. "Brass doesn't rust, you know."

"You are quite right, my friend. But these scoundrels have their own secret methods."

"Such as what?" Claud asked. Any information of this nature was valuable, in his opinion. One never knew when it might come in handy.

"All they have to do," Mr. Boggis said, "is to place these handles overnight in a box of mahogany shavings saturated in sal ammoniac. The sal ammoniac turns the metal green, but if you rub off the green, you will find underneath it a fine soft silvery-warm lustre, a lustre identical to that which comes with very old brass. Oh, it is so bestial, the things they do! With iron they have another trick."

"What do they do with iron?" Claud asked, fascinated.

"Iron's easy," Mr. Boggis said. "Iron locks and plates and hinges are simply buried in common salt and they come out all rusted and pitted in no time."

"All right," Rummins said. "So you admit you can't tell about the handles. For all you know, they may be hundreds and hundreds of years old. Correct?"

"Ah," Mr. Boggis whispered, fixing Rummins with two big bulging brown eyes. "That's where you're wrong. Watch this."

From his jacket pocket, he took out a small screwdriver. At the same time, although none of them saw him do it, he also took out a little brass screw which he kept well hidden in the palm of his hand. Then he selected one of the screws in the commode—there were four to each handle—and began carefully scraping all traces of white paint from its head. When he had done this, he started slowly to unscrew it.

"If this is a genuine old brass screw from the eighteenth century," he was saying, "the spiral will be slightly uneven and you'll be able to

201

see quite easily that it has been hand-cut with a file. But if this brass-work is faked from more recent times, Victorian or later, then obviously the screw will be of the same period. It will be a mass-produced, machine-made article. Anyone can recognize a machine-made screw. Well, we shall see."

It was not difficult, as he put his hands over the old screw and drew it out, for Mr. Boggis to substitute the new one hidden in his palm. This was another little trick of his, and through the years it had proved a most rewarding one. The pockets of his clergyman's jacket were always stocked with a quantity of cheap brass screws of various sizes.

"There you are," he said, handing the modern screw to Rummins. "Take a look at that. Notice the exact evenness of the spiral? See it? Of course you do. It's just a cheap common little screw that you yourself could buy today in any ironmonger's in the country."

The screw was handed round from the one to the other, each examin-ing it carefully. Even Rummins was impressed now.

Mr. Boggis put the screwdriver back in his pocket together with the fine hand-cut screw that he'd taken from the commode, and then he turned and walked slowly past the three men towards the door.

"My dear friends," he said, pausing at the entrance to the kitchen, "it was so good of you to let me peep inside your little home—so kind. I do hope I haven't been a terrible old bore."

Rummins glanced up from examining the screw. "You didn't tell us what you were going to offer," he said.

"Ah," Mr. Boggis said. "That's quite right. I didn't, did I? Well, to tell you the honest truth, I think it's all a bit too much trouble. I think I'll leave it."

"How much would you give?"

"You mean that you really wish to part with it?"

"I didn't say I wished to part with it. I asked you how much."

Mr. Boggis looked across at the commode, and he laid his head first to one side, then to the other, and he frowned, and pushed out his lips, and shrugged his shoulders, and gave a little scornful wave of the hand as though to say the thing was hardly worth thinking about really, was it?

"Shall we say . . . ten pounds. I think that would be fair."

"Ten pounds!" Rummins cried. "Don't be so ridiculous, Parson, *please!*"

"It's worth more'n that for firewood!" Claud said, disgusted.

"Look here at the bill!" Rummins went on, stabbing that precious document so fiercely with his dirty fore-finger that Mr. Boggis became alarmed. "It tells you exactly what it cost! Eighty-seven pounds! And that's when it was new. Now it's antique it's worth double!"

"If you'll pardon me, no, sir, it's not. It's a second-hand reproduction. But I'll tell you what, my friend—I'm being rather reckless, I can't help it—I'll go up as high as fifteen pounds. How's that?"

"Make it fifty," Rummins said.

A delicious little quiver like needles ran all the way down the back of Mr. Boggis's legs and then under the soles of his feet. He had it now. It was his. No question about that. But the habit of buying cheap, as cheap as it was humanly possible to buy, acquired by years of necessity and practice, was too strong in him now to permit him to give in so easily. "My dear man," he whispered softly, "I only *want* the legs. Possibly I could find some use for the drawers later on, but the rest of it, the carcass itself, as your friend so rightly said, it's firewood, that's all."

"Make it thirty-five," Rummins said.

"I *couldn't* sir, I *couldn't!* It's not worth it. And I simply mustn't allow myself to haggle like this about a price. It's all wrong. I'll make you one final offer, and then I must go. Twenty pounds."

"I'll take it," Rummins snapped. "It's yours."

"Oh dear," Mr. Boggis said, clasping his hands. "There I go again. I should never have started this in the first place."

"You can't back out now, Parson. A deal's a deal."

"Yes, yes, I know."

"How're you going to take it?"

"Well, let me see. Perhaps if I were to drive my car up into the yard, you gentlemen would be kind enough to help me load it?"

"In a car? This thing'll never go in a car! You'll need a truck for this!"

"I don't think so. Anyway, we'll see. My car's on the road. I'll be back in a jiffy. We'll manage it somehow, I'm sure."

Mr. Boggis walked out into the yard and through the gate and then down the long track that led across the field towards the road. He found himself giggling quite uncontrollably, and there was a feeling inside him as though hundreds and hundreds of tiny bubbles were rising up from his stomach and bursting merrily in the top of his head, like sparkling-water. All the buttercups in the field were suddenly turning into golden sovereigns, glistening in the sunlight. The ground was littered with them, and he swung off the track on to the grass so that he could walk among them and tread on them and hear the little metallic tinkle they made as he kicked them around with his toes. He was finding it difficult to stop himself from breaking into a run. But clergymen never run; they walk slowly. Walk slowly, Boggis. Keep calm, Boggis. There's no hurry now. The commode is yours! Yours for twenty pounds, and it's worth fifteen or twenty thousand! The Boggis Commode! In ten minutes it'll be loaded into your car—it'll go in easily—

and you'll be driving back to London and singing all the way! Mr. Boggis driving the Boggis Commode home in the Boggis car. Historic occasion. What *wouldn't* a newspaperman give to get a picture of that! Should he arrange it? Perhaps he should. Wait and see. Oh, glorious day! Oh, lovely sunny summer day! Oh, glory be!

Back in the farmhouse, Rummins was saying, "Fancy that old bastard giving twenty pound for a load of junk like this."

"You did very nicely, Mr. Rummins," Claud told him. "You think he'll pay you?"

"We don't put it in the car till he do."

"And what if it won't go in the car?" Claud asked. "You know what I think, Mr. Rummins? You want my honest opinion? I think the bloody thing's too big to go in the car. And then what happens? Then he's going to say to hell with it and just drive off without it and you'll never see him again. Nor the money either. He didn't seem all that keen on having it, you know."

Rummins paused to consider this new and rather alarming prospect.

"How can a thing like that possibly go in a car?" Claud went on relentlessly. "A parson never has a big car anyway. You ever seen a parson with a big car, Mr. Rummins?"

"Can't say I have."

"Exactly! And now listen to me. I've got an idea. He told us, didn't he, that it was only the legs he was wanting. Right? So all we've got to do is to cut 'em off quick right here on the spot before he comes back, then it'll be sure to go in the car. All we're doing is saving him the trouble of cutting them off himself when he gets home. How about it, Mr. Rummins?" Claud's flat bovine face glimmered with a mawkish pride.

"It's not such a bad idea at that," Rummins said, looking at the commode. "In fact it's a bloody good idea. Come on then, we'll have to hurry. You and Bert carry it out into the yard. I'll get the saw. Take the drawers out first."

Within a couple of minutes, Claud and Bert had carried the commode outside and had laid it upside down in the yard amidst the chicken droppings and cow dung and mud. In the distance, halfway across the field, they could see a small black figure striding along the path towards the road. They paused to watch. There was something rather comical about the way in which this figure was conducting itself. Every now and again it would break into a trot, then it did a kind of hop skip and jump, and once it seemed as though the sound of a cheerful song came rippling faintly to them from across the meadow.

"I reckon he's balmy," Claud said, and Bert grinned darkly, rolling his misty eye slowly round in its socket.

Rummins came waddling over from the shed, squat and froglike, carrying a long saw. Claud took the saw away from him and went to work:

"Cut 'em close," Rummins said. "Don't forget he's going to use 'em on another table."

The mahogany was hard and very dry, and as Claud worked, a fine red dust sprayed out from the edge of the saw and fell softly to the ground. One by one, the legs came off, and when they were all severed, Bert stooped down and arranged them carefully in a row.

Claud stepped back to survey the results of his labour. There was a longish pause.

"Just let me ask you one question, Mr. Rummins," he said slowly. "Even now, could *you* put that enormous thing into the back of a car?"

"Not unless it was a van."

"Correct!" Claud cried. "And parsons don't have vans, you know. All they've got usually is piddling little Morris Eights or Austin Sevens."

"The legs is all he wants," Rummins said. "If the rest of it won't go in, then he can leave it. He can't complain. He's got the legs."

"Now you know better'n that, Mr. Rummins," Claud said patiently. "You know damn well he's going to start knocking the price if he don't get every single bit of this into the car. A parson's just as cunning as the rest of 'em when it comes to money, don't you make any mistake about that. Especially this old boy. So why don't we give him his firewood now and be done with it. Where d'you keep the axe?"

"I reckon that's fair enough," Rummins said. "Bert, go fetch the axe."

Bert went into the shed and fetched a tall woodcutter's axe and gave it to Claud. Claud spat on the palms of his hands and rubbed them together. Then, with a long-armed high-swinging action, he began fiercely attacking the legless carcass of the commode.

It was hard work, and it took several minutes before he had the whole thing more or less smashed to pieces.

"I'll tell you one thing," he said, straightening up, wiping his brow. "That was a bloody good carpenter put this job together and I don't care what the parson says."

"We're just in time!" Rummins called out. "Here he comes!"

LEN DEIGHTON

b. 1929

Nations make wars. Men fight them. The reasons why
are seldom as obvious as they might seem. In his best-selling
spy novels Deighton has frequently exposed the irony of these reasons.
In his short stories also he writes with a sharp appreciation
of war's illogicalities.

Winter's Morning

MAJOR RICHARD WINTER
was a tall man with hard
black eyes, a large nose and
close-cropped hair. He hated
getting out of bed, especially
when assigned to dawn
patrols on a cold morning. As he always said—and by now the whole
Officers' Mess could chant it in unison—"If there must be dawn patrols
in winter, let there be no Winter in the dawn patrols."

Winter believed that if they stopped flying them, the enemy
would also stop. In 1914, the front-line soldiers of both armies had
decided to live and let live for a few weeks. So now, during the coldest
weather, some squadrons had allowed the dawn patrol to become a
token couple of scouts hurrying over the frosty wire of no-man's-land
after breakfast. The warm spirit of humanity that Christmas 1914
conjured had given way to the cold reality of self-preservation. Those
wiser squadrons kept the major offensive patrol until last light, when
the sun was mellow and the air less turbulent. At St. Antoine Farm
airfield, however, dawn patrol was still a gruelling obligation that none
could escape.

"Oatmeal, toast, eggs and sausage, sir." Like everyone else in the
Mess tent—except Winter—the waiter spoke in a soft whisper that
befitted the small hours. Winter preferred his normal booming voice.

"Just coffee," he said. "But hot, really hot."

"Very good, Major Winter, sir."

206

The wind blew with enough force to make the canvas flap and roar, as though at any moment the whole tent would blow away. From outside they heard the sound of tent pegs being hammered more firmly into the hard chalky soil.

A young Lieutenant sitting opposite offered his cigarette case, but Winter waved it aside in favour of a dented tin from which he took cheap dark tobacco and a paper to fashion a misshapen cigarette. The young officer did not light one of his own in the hope that he would be invited to share in this ritual. But Winter lit up, blew the noxious smoke across the table, coughed twice and pushed the tin back into his pocket.

Each time someone entered through the flap there was a clatter of canvas and ropes and a gust of cold air, but Winter looked in vain for a triangle of grey sky. The only light came from six acetylene lamps that were placed along the breakfast table. The pump of one of them was faulty; its light was dull and it left a smell of mould on the air. The other lamps hissed loudly and their eerie greenish light shone upon the Mess silver, folded linen and empty plates. The table had been set the previous night for the regular squadron breakfast at 8 a.m., and the Mess servants were anxious that these three early-duty pilots shouldn't disarrange it too much.

Everyone stiffened as they heard the clang of the engine cylinder and con. rod that hung outside for use as a gas warning. Winter laughed when Ginger, the tallest pilot on the squadron, emerged from the darkness rubbing his head and scowling in pain. Ginger walked over to the ancient piano and pulled back the edge of the tarpaulin that protected it from damp. He played a silly melody with one finger.

"Hot coffee, sir." The waiter emphasized the word 'hot', and the liquid spluttered as it poured over the metal spout. Winter clamped his cold hands round the pot like a drowning man clinging to flotsam. He twisted his head to see Ginger's watch. Six twenty-five. What a time to be having breakfast: it was still night.

Winter yawned and wrapped his ankle-length fur coat round his legs. New pilots thought that his fur overcoat had earned him his nickname of 'the Bear', but that had come months before the coat.

The others kept a few seats between themselves and Winter. They spoke only when he addressed them, and then answered only in brief formalities.

"You flying with me, Lieutenant?"

The young ex-cavalry officer looked around the table. Ginger was munching his bread and jam, and gave no sign of having heard.

"Yes, sir," said the young man.

"How many hours?"

207

Always the same question. Everyone here was graded solely by flying time, though few cared whether the hours had been spent stunting, fighting or just hiding in the clouds. "Twenty-eight and a half, solo, sir."

"Twenty-eight *and a half*," nodded Winter. "Twenty-eight *and a half! Solo!* Did you hear that, Lieutenant?" The question was addressed to Ginger, who was paying unusually close attention to the sugar bowl. Winter turned back to the new young pilot. "You'd better watch yourself."

Winter divided new pilots into assets and liabilities at either side of seventy hours. Assets sometimes became true friends and close comrades. Assets might even be told your misgivings. The demise of assets could spread grief through the whole Mess. This boy would be dead within a month, Winter decided. He looked at him: handsome, in the pallid, aristocratic manner of such youngsters. His tender skin was chapped by the rain and there were cold sores on his lip. His blond hair was too long for Winter's taste, and his eyebrows girlish. This boy's kit had never known a quartermaster's shelf. It had come from an expensive tailor: a cavalry tunic fashionably nipped at the waist, tight trousers and boots as supple as velvet. The ensemble was supplemented by accessories from the big department stores. His cigarette case was the sort that, it was advertised, could stop a bullet.

The young man returned Richard Winter's close examination with interest. So this rude fellow, so proud of his chauffeur's fur coat, was the famous Bear Winter who had twenty-nine enemy aircraft to his credit. He was a blotchy-faced devil, with bloodshot eyes and a fierce twitching eyebrow that he sometimes rubbed self-consciously, as if he knew that it undid his carefully contrived aplomb. The youngster wondered whether he would end up looking like this: dirty shirt, long finger-nails, unshaven jaw and a cauliflower-knobbly head, shaved razor-close to avoid lice. Except for his quick eyes and occasional wry smile Winter looked like the archetypal Prussian *schweinhund*.

Major Richard Winter had been flying in action for nearly two years without a leave. He was a natural pilot who'd flown every type of plane the makers could provide, and some enemy planes too. He could dismantle and assemble an engine as well as any squadron fitter, and as a precaution against jams he personally supervised the loading of every bullet he would use. Why must he be so rude to young pilots who hero-worshipped him, and would follow him to hell itself? And yet that too was part of the legend.

The young officer swallowed. "May I ask, sir, where you bought your magnificent fur coat?"

Winter gulped the rest of his coffee and got to his feet as he heard the first of the scout's engines start. "Came off a mug I shot down in

September," he bellowed. "It's from a fashionable shop, I'm told. Never travelled much myself, except here to France." Winter poked his fingers through four holes in the front. Did the boy go a shade paler, or had he imagined it in the glare of the gas lights? "Don't let some smart bastard get your overcoat, sonny."

"No, sir," said the boy. Behind him Ginger grinned. The Bear was behaving true to form. Ginger dug his knife into a tin of butter he'd scrounged from the kitchen and then offered it to the cavalry officer. The boy sniffed the tin doubtfully. It smelled rancid but he scraped a little on to his bread and swamped it with jam to hide the taste.

"This your first patrol?" asked Ginger.

"No, sir. Yesterday one of the chaps took me as far as Cambrai to see the lie of the land. Before that I did a few hours around the aerodrome here. These scouts are new to me."

"Did you see anything at Cambrai yesterday?"

"Anti-aircraft gunfire."

Winter interrupted. "Let's see if we can't do better than that for you today, sonny." He leaned close to the boy and asked in his most winning voice, "Think you could down a couple before lunch?"

The boy didn't answer. Winter winked at Ginger and buttoned his fur coat. The other motors had started, so Winter shouted, "That's it, sonny. Don't try to be a hero. Don't try to be an ace in the first week you're out here. Just keep under my stinking armpit. Just keep close. Close, you understand? Bloody damn close." Winter flicked his cigarette end on to the canvas floor of the tent and put his heel on it. He coughed and growled, "Hurry up," although he could see that the others were waiting for him.

From the far side of the wind-swept tarmac, Major Winter's Sergeant Fitter saw a flash of greenish light as the Mess tent flap opened and the duty pilots emerged. Winter came towards him out of the darkness, walking slowly because of his thick woollen underwear and thigh-length fleece boots. His hands were tucked into his sleeves for warmth, and his head was sunk into the high collar that stood up around his ears like a cowl. Exactly like a monk, thought the Sergeant, not for the first time. Perhaps Winter cultivated this resemblance. He'd outlived all the pilots who had been here when he arrived, to become as high in rank as scout pilots ever became. Yet his moody introspective manner and his offhand attitude to high and low had prevented him from becoming the commanding officer. So Winter remained a taciturn misanthrope, without any close companions, except for Ginger who had the same skills of survival and responded equally coldly to overtures of friendship from younger pilots.

The Sergeant Fitter—Pops—had been here even longer than the

Bear. He'd always looked after his aeroplane, right from his first patrol when Winter was the same sort of noisy friendly fool as the kid doing his first patrol this morning. Aeroplanes, he should have said: the Bear had written off seven of them. Pops spat as the fumes from the engine collected in his lungs. It was a bad business, watching these kids vanish one by one. Last year it had been considered lucky to touch Pop's bald head before take-off. For twelve months the fitter had refused leave, knowing that the pilots were truly anxious about their joke. But Pop's bald head had proved as fallible as all the other talismans. One after another the faces had been replaced by similar faces until they were all the same pink-faced smiling boy.

Pops spat again, then cut the motor and climbed out of the cockpit. The other planes were also silent. From the main road came the noise of an army convoy hurrying to get to its destination before daylight made it vulnerable to attack. Any moment now artillery observers would be climbing into the balloons that enabled them to see far across no-man's-land.

"Good morning, Major."

"Morning, Pops."

"The old firm, eh, sir?"

"Yes, you, me and Ginger," said Winter, laughing in a way that he'd not done in the Mess tent. "Sometimes I think we are fighting this war all on our own, Pops."

"We are," chuckled Pops. This was the way the Bear used to laugh. "The rest of them are just part-timers, sir."

"I'm afraid they are, Pops," said Winter. He climbed stiffly into the cramped cockpit and pulled the fur coat round him. There was hardly enough room to move his elbows and the tiny seat creaked under his weight. The instruments were simple: compass, altimeter, speedometer and rev counter. The workmanship was crude and the finish was hasty, like a toy car put together by a bungling father. "Switches off," said Pops. Winter looked at the brass switches and then pressed them as if not sure of his vision. "Switches off," he said.

"Fuel on," said Pops.

"Fuel on."

"Suck in."

"Suck in."

Pops cuddled the polished wooden prop blade to his ear. It was cold against his face. He walked it round to prime the cylinders. That was the thing Pops liked about Winter: when he said off, you knew it was off. Pops waited while Winter pulled on his close-fitting flying helmet; its fur trimmed a tonsure of leather that had faded to the colour of flesh.

"Contact."

"Contact."

Pops stretched high into the dark night and brought the blade down with a graceful sweep of his hands. Like brass and percussion responding to a conductor, the engine began its performance with a blinding sheet of yellow flame and a drum roll. Winter throttled back, slowing the drum and changing the shape and colour of the flame to a gaseous feather of blue that danced around the exhaust pipes and made his face swell and contract as the shadows exploded and died. Winter held a blue flickering hand above his head. He felt the wheels lurch forward as the chocks were removed and he dabbed at the rudder bar so that he could see around the aircraft's nose. There was no brake or pitch adjustment and Winter let her gather speed while keeping the tail skid tight down upon the ground.

They took off in vic threes, bumping across frozen ruts in the balding field with only the glare of the exhausts to light their going. It was easy for Winter; as formation leader he relied on the others to watch his engine and formate on him accordingly. At full screaming throttle they climbed over the trees at the south end of the airfield. A gusty crosswind hit them. Winter banked a wing-tip dangerously close to the tree tops rather than slew into the boy's line of flight. Ginger did the same to avoid his Major. The boy, unused to these heavy operational machines with high-compression engines, found his aircraft almost wrenched from his grasp. He yawed across the trees, a hundred yards from the others, before he put her nose up to regain his position in formation. Close, he must keep close. Winter spared him only a brief glance over the shoulder between searching the sombre sky for the miniscule dots of other aeroplanes. For by now the black lid of night had tilted and an orange wedge prised open the eastern horizon. Winter led the way to the front lines, the others tight against his tailplane.

The first light of the sun revealed a land covered by a grey eiderdown of mist, except where a loose thread of river matched the silver of the sky. Over the front line they turned south. Winter glanced eastwards, where the undersides of some low clouds were leaking dribbles of gold paint on to the earth. As the world awakened stoves were lit and villages were marked by dirty smoke that trailed southwards.

Major Winter noted the north wind and glanced back to see Ginger's aeroplane catch the first light of the sun as it bent far enough over the horizon to reach them at fifteen thousand feet above the earth. The propeller blades made a perfect circle of yellow gauze, through which reflections from the polished-metal cowling winked and wavered as the aeroplanes rose and sank gently on the clear morning air.

Here, on the Arras section of the front, the German and French lines could be clearly seen as careless scrawls in the livid chalk. Near the River

Scarpe at Feuchy, Winter saw a constant flicker of artillery shells exploding: the morning hate. Pinheads of pink, only just visible through the mist. Counter-battery fire he guessed, from its concentration some way behind the lines.

He pulled his fur collar as high round his face as it could go, then raised his goggles. The icy wind made his eyes water, but not before he had scanned the entire horizon and banked enough to see below him. He pulled the goggles down again. It was more comfortable, but they acted like blinkers. Already ice had formed in the crevices of his eyes and he felt its pinpricks like daggers. His nose was numb and he let go of the stick to massage it.

The cavalry officer—Willy, they called him—was staring anxiously at the other two aeroplanes. He probably thought that the banking search was a wing-rocking signal that the enemy was sighted. They read too many cheap magazines, these kids, but then so had Winter before his first posting out here: 'Ace of the Black Cross', 'Flying Dare-Devils', 'True War Stories'.

Well, now Winter knew true war stories. When old men decided to barter young men for pride and profit, the transaction was called war. It was another Richard Winter who had come to war. An eighteen-year-old child with a scrapbook of cuttings about Blériot and the Wright brothers, a roomful of models which his mother wasn't permitted to dust and thirteen hours of dangerous experiments on contraptions that were bigger, but no more airworthy, than his dusty models. That Richard Winter was long-since dead. Gone was the gangling boy whose only regret about the war was leaving his mongrel dog. Winter smiled as he remembered remonstrating with some pilots who were using fluffy yellow chicks for target practice on the pistol range. That was before he'd seen men burned alive, or, worse, men half-burned alive.

He waved to frightened little Willy who was desperately trying to fly skilfully enough to hold formation on his bad-tempered flight commander. Poor little swine. Two dots almost ahead of them to the south-east. Far below. Ginger had seen them already but the boy wouldn't notice them until they were almost bumping into him. All the new kids were like that. It's not a matter of eyesight, it's a matter of knowledge. Just as a tracker on a safari knows that a wide golden blob in the shadow of a tree at midday is going to be a pride of lions resting after a meal, so in the morning an upright golden blob in the middle of a plain is a cheetah waiting to make a kill. So at five thousand feet, that near the lines, with shellfire visible, they were going to be enemy two-seaters on artillery observation duty. First he must be sure that there wasn't a flight of scouts in ambush above them. He looked at the cumulus and decided that it was too far from the two-seaters to be dangerous. Brownish-black smoke patches appeared around the planes as the anti-aircraft guns went into action.

Winter raised his goggles. Already they had begun to mist up because of the perspiration generated by his excitement. He waggled his wings and began to lose height. He headed east to come round behind them from out of the sun. Ginger loosed off a short burst of fire to be sure his guns were not frozen. Winter and the boy did the same. The altitude had rendered him too deaf to hear it as more than a ticking, as of an anxious pulse.

Winter took another careful look around. Flashes of artillery shells were bursting on the ground just ahead of the enemy planes' track. The ground was still awash with blue gloom, although here and there hillocks and trees were crisply golden in the harsh oblique light of morning. The hedges and buildings threw absurdly long shadows, and a church steeple was bright yellow. Winter now saw that there were four more two-seaters about a mile away. They were beginning to turn.

Winter put down his nose and glanced in his mirror to be sure the others were close behind. The airspeed indicator showed well over a hundred miles an hour and was still rising. The air stream sang across the taut wires with a contented musical note. He held the two aeroplanes steady on his nose, giving the stick and rudder only the lightest of touches as the speed increased their sensitivity.

Five hundred yards: these two still hadn't seen their attackers. The silly bastards were hanging over the side anxious not to get their map references wrong. Four hundred.

The boy saw them much later than Ginger and Winter. He stared in wonder at these foreign aeronauts. At a time when only a handful of madmen had ever tried this truly magical science, and when every flight was a pioneering experiment to discover more about this new world, he hated the idea of killing fellow enthusiasts. He would much rather have exchanged anecdotes and information with them.

Ginger and Winter had no such thoughts. Their minds were delivered to their subconscious. They were checking instruments, cocking guns and judging ever-changing altitudes, range and deflection.

If that stupid kid fires too early . . . damn him, damn him! Oh, well. Ginger and Winter opened fire too. Damn, a real ace gets in close, close, close. They'd both learned that, if nothing else. Stupid boy! The artillery observation leader pulled back on the stick and turned so steeply as almost to collide with the two-seater to his left. He knew what he was doing; he was determined to make himself a maximum-deflection shot. Winter kept his guns going all the way through the turn. The tracer bullets seemed unnaturally bright because his eyes had become accustomed to the morning's gloom. Like glow-worms they were eating the enemy's tailplane. This is what decided a dogfight: vertical turns, tighter and tighter still. Control stick held into the belly, with toes and eyes alert so that the aeroplane doesn't slide an inch out of a turn that glued him to the horizon. It was sheer flying skill. The sun—a watery blob of gold—seemed to drop through his mainplane and on to his engine. Winter could feel the rate of turn by the hardness of his seat. He pulled even harder on the stick to make the tracers crawl along the fuselage. The smell from his guns was acrid and the thin smoke and heat from the blurring breechblocks caused his target to wobble like a jelly. First the observer was hit, then the pilot, throwing up their hands like badly-made marionettes. The two-seater stalled, falling suddenly like a dead leaf. Winter rolled. Two more aeroplanes slid across his sights. He pushed his stick forward to follow the damaged two-seater down. Hearing guns very close to his head, he saw the fabric of his upper plane prodded to tatters by invisible fingers which continued their destruction to the point of breaking a centre section strut and throwing its splinters into his face. His reflexes took over and he went into a vertical turn tighter than any two-seater could manage. Aeroplanes were everywhere. Bright-green and blue wings and black crosses passed across his sights, along with roundels and dark-green fabric. One of them caught the light of the sun and its wings flashed with brilliant blue. All the time Winter kept half an eye upon his rear-view mirror. A two-seater nosed down towards his tail, but Winter avoided him effortlessly. Ginger came under him, thumping his machine-guns with one of the hammers which they all kept in their cockpits. He was red-faced with exertion as he tried to clear the stoppage by force. At this height every movement was exhausting. Ginger wiped his face with the back of his gauntlet and his goggles came unclipped and blew away in the air stream.

Winter had glimpsed Ginger for only a fraction of a second but he'd seen enough to tell him the whole story. If it was a split round he'd never unjam it. Trees flashed under him. The combat had brought them lower and lower, as it always did.

The new boy was half a mile away and below him. Winter knew it was his job to look after the kid but he'd not leave Ginger with a jammed gun. A plane rushed past before he had a chance to fire. Winter saw one of the two-seaters behind Ginger. My God, they were tough, these fellows. You'd think they'd be away, with their tails between their legs. Hold on, Ginger, here I come. Dive, climb, roll; a perfect Immelmann turn. The world upside down; above him the dark earth, below him the dawn sky like a rasher of streaky bacon. Hold that. He centred the stick, keeping the enemy's huge mainplane centred in his sight. Fire. The guns shook the whole airframe and made a foul stink. He kicked the rudder and slid down past the enemy's tail with no more than six feet to spare. A white-faced observer was frozen in fear. Up. Up. Up. Winter leaned out of his cockpit to see below him. The new boy is in trouble. One of the two-seaters is pasting him. The poor kid is trying for the cloud bank but that's half a mile away. Never throttle back in combat, you fool. White smoke? Radiator steam? No, worse: vaporizing petrol from a punctured tank or fractured lead. If it touches a hot pipe he'll go up like a torch. You should have kept close, sonny. What did I tell you. What do I always tell them. Winter flick-rolled and turned to cover Ginger's tail.

Woof: a flamer. The boy: will he jump or burn? The whole world was made up of jumpers or burners. There were no parachutes for pilots yet, so either way a man died. The machine was breaking up. Burning pieces of fuel-soaked wreckage fell away. It would be difficult to invent a more efficient bonfire. Take thin strips of timber, nail them into a framework, stretch fabric over it and paint it with highly inflammable dope. Into the middle of this build a metal tank for 30 gallons of high-grade fuel. Move air across it at 50 m.p.h. Winter couldn't decide whether the boy had jumped. A pity, the chaps in the Mess always wanted to know that, even though few could bear to ask.

The dogfight had scattered the aeroplanes in every direction, but Ginger was just below him and a two-seater was approaching from the south. Ginger waved. His gun was working. Winter side-slipped down behind a two-seater and gave it a burst of fire. The gunner was probably dead, for no return fire came and the gun rocked uselessly on its mounting. The pilot turned steeply on full throttle and kept going in an effort to come round in a vertical turn to Winter's rear. But Ginger was waiting for that. They'd been through this many times. Ginger fired as the two-seater was half way through the turn, raking it from engine to tail. The whole aeroplane lurched drunkenly, and then the port mainplane snapped, its main spar eaten through by Ginger's bullets. As it fell, nose-down, the wings folded back along the fuselage like an umbrella being closed. The shapeless mess of broken struts and tangled steel wire fell vertically to earth, weighted by its heavy engine which was still roaring at full throttle. It was so low that it hit the ground within seconds.

Winter throttled back and came round in a gentle turn to see the wreckage: not a movement. It was just a heap of junk in a field. Ginger was circling it, too. From this height the sky was a vast bowl as smooth and shiny as Ming. They both looked round it but the other two-seaters had gone. There were no planes in sight. Winter increased his throttle and came alongside Ginger. He pushed his goggles up. Ginger was laughing. The artillery fire had stopped, or perhaps its explosions were lost in the mist. They turned for home, scampering across the trees and hedges like two schoolboys.

215

Winter and Ginger came over the airfield in echelon. Eight aeroplanes were lined up outside the canvas hangars that lacked only bunting to be a circus. A dozen officers fell over themselves scrambling out of the Mess tent. One of them waved. Winter's machine, painted bright green with wasp-like white bands, was easily recognized. Winter circled the field while Ginger landed. He'd literally lived in this French field for almost a year and knew each tree, ditch and bump. He'd seen it from every possible angle. He remembered praying for a sight of it with a dead motor and a bootful of blood. Also how he'd focused on blurred blades of its cold dewy grass, following a long night unconscious after a squadron booze-up. He'd vomited, excreted, crashed and fornicated on this field. He couldn't imagine being anywhere else.

For the first time in a month the sun shone, but it gave no warmth. As he switched off his engine the petrol fumes made the trees bend and dance on the heavy vapour. Pops hurried across to him but couldn't resist a quick inspection of the tail before saluting.

"Everything in order, Herr Major?"

Winter was still a little deaf but he guessed what the Sergeant was saying. He always said the same thing. "Yes, Sergeant. The strut is damaged but apart from that it probably just needs a few patches."

Winter unclipped his goggles, unwound his scarf and took off his leather helmet. The cordite deposits from his Spandaus had made a black band across his nose and cheeks.

"Another Englishman?" said Pops. He warmed his hands before the big Mercedes engine, which was groaning softly.

"Bristols: one forced down, one destroyed. We lost the new young officer, though." Winter was ashamed that he didn't know the boy's name, but there were so many of them. He knew he was right to remain unfriendly to all of them. Given half a chance new kids would treat him like some sort of divinity, and that made him feel like hell when they went west.

Winter wiped the protective grease from his face. He was calm. Briefly he watched his own unshaking hand with a nod of satisfaction. He knew himself to be a nerveless and relentless killer, and like any professional assassin he took pride in seeing a victim die. Only such men could become aces.

WALTER DE LA MARE

1873–1956

Doubtless his gifts for fantasy enabled him to survive
eighteen years in the offices of an oil company. In 1908, however,
he received a Civil List pension and started to write full-time,
exercising his childlike curiosity, peculiar imagination
and exquisite craftsmanship on poetry and prose alike.

Physic

EMILIA AND WILLIAM had been keeping one another company in the kitchen. Mary, her trusty substantial cook-general was 'out', and would not be knocking at the door until half-past ten. After that there might be another hour to wait. But then Emilia would be alone. Meanwhile, just like man and wife, William and she would soon be having supper together at two corners of the kitchen table, and William would have an egg—with nine bread-and-butter fingers.

This, once fortnightly, now weekly, Wednesday-night feast had become a kind of ritual, a little secret institution. They called it their covey night. Not even Daddie ever shared it with them; and it was astonishing what mature grown-up company William became on these occasions. It was as if, entirely unknown to himself, he had swallowed one of Jack's bean-seeds and had turned inside into a sort of sagacious second-husband. All that Emilia had to do, then, was merely to become again the child she used to be. And that of course needs only a happy heart.

He was a little dark-skinned boy, William—small for his age. A fringe of gilt-edged fair hair thatched a narrow forehead over his small, restless eyes. His sister Sallie—poor gaunt Aunt Sarah, whom she had been called after, having departed this life when less than a month had

217

passed since the gay christening party—little Sallie, after a restless and peevish afternoon and a wailful bath, was asleep now, upstairs, in her crib. You could tell that almost without having to creep out every now and again to listen at the foot of the stairs.

William had been even more lively and hoppity than usual. He and Emilia had been playing Beggar-my-Neighbour, and he had become steadily more excited when with something very like sheer magic, every sly knave in the pack had rapidly abandoned poor Emilia and managed to slide into his hand. And when—after an excited argument as to where the Queen of Hearts had best be hidden—they changed the game, he laughed and laughed till the tears came into his eyes to see her utter confusion at finding herself for the third time an abject Old Maid! And when supper-time came—plates, spoons, forks—he had all but danced from dresser to table, from table to dresser again. They had borrowed Mary's best blue-check kitchen tablecloth; he had said it looked cooler. "Don't you *think* so, Mummie?" And every now and again he had ejaculated crisp shrill remarks and directions at Emilia, who was looking after the cooking in the outer room, a room she had steadfastly refused to call the 'scullery'. Merely because she disliked the word! Though one day in a sudden moment of inspiration she had defended her priggishness by exclaiming, "Well, spell it with a *k* and then see what you think of it!"

It was a little way Emilia had. As tenaciously as she could she always put off until to-morrow even what it was merely difficult to put up with to-day. Never trouble trouble till trouble troubles you, was her motto when driven into a corner. She hated problems, crises, the least shadow of any horror, though they would sometimes peer up at her out of her mind—and from elsewhere—when she wasn't looking, like animals at evening in the darkening hills. But when they actually neared, and had to be faced; well, that was quite another matter.

For some minutes now, busied over her sizzling pan at the gas stove, she hadn't noticed that William's galvanic sprightly conversation piped up from the kitchen had been steadily dwindling, had almost ceased. He had decided to have his supper egg fried, though 'lightly boiled' was the institution. And Emilia had laughed when, after long debate, he had declared that he had chosen it fried because then it was more indigestible. She was dishing it up from the smoke and splutter—a setting sun on a field of snow, and with a most delicate edging of scorch.

When she came back into the kitchen William was standing by the table, gazing across it at the window. He couldn't be looking *out* of the window, for although there was a crevice a few inches wide between the flowered chintz curtains that had been drawn over it and where the blue linen blind had not been pulled down to the very bottom, it was already pitch dark outside. Yet even at this distance she saw that he couldn't also be staring solely at his own reflection.

He stood motionless, his eyes fixed on this dark glassy patch of window, his head well above the table now. He had not even turned at sound of her footsteps. So far as Emilia's birdlike heart was concerned it was as if a jay had screeched in a spinney. But best not to notice too much. Don't put things into people's heads. "There!" she exclaimed, "Well now, you *have* cut the bread and butter thick, Mr. Stoic! *I'm* going to have that scrap of cold fish. Eat this while it's hot, my precious!"

But William had continued to wait.

"I don't think, Mummie," he said, slowly as if he were reciting something he had been learning by heart, "I don't *think* I'll have my egg after all. I don't think I feel very hungry just now."

All his eagerness and excitement seemed to have died down into this solemn and stagnant reverie; and for a child to have the air and appearance of a sorrowful old dwarf is unutterably far away from its deliciously pretending to be a sedate grown-up.

"Not to have it!" cried Emilia. "Why, look, blessing, it's cooked! Look! Lovely. You wouldn't know it wasn't a tiny half of a peach in cream. Let's pretend."

"I couldn't like even that, Mummie," he said, glancing at it, a slight shudder ending in a decisive shake of the head as he hastily looked away again. "I don't think, you know, I want *any* supper."

Emilia's eyes widened. She stood perfectly still a moment, the hot plate in her hand, staring at him. Then she hurriedly put it down on the table, knelt with incredible quickness beside him, and seized his hand.

"That's what it is," she said. "You don't feel very well, William. You don't feel very well? Your hands are hot. Not sick? Not sore throat? Tell Mummie."

"I'm *not* ill," wailed William obstinately. "Just because I don't want the egg! You *can't* like that horrid cold fish, and if I did feel sick, wouldn't I say so? That's only what *you* say." He paused as if the utmost caution and precision were imperative, then added, nodding his head mournfully and sympathetically in time to the whispered words, "I *have* got a teeny tiny headache, but I didn't notice it until just now." His mouth opened in a prodigious yawn, leaving tears in his eyes. "Isn't it funny, Mummie—you can't really see anything out of the window when it's black like that, yet you needn't look at your*self* in the glass. It's just as if . . ."

His eyes came round from examining the window, and fixed themselves on her face.

"That's what it is," said Emilia, raising herself abruptly from the floor. "That's what it is." She kept squeezing the thin, unresponsive

219

fingers of his hand between her own. "You're feverish. And I knew it. *All* the time. Yes—*how* stupid of me." And instantly her voice had changed, all vain self-recriminations gone. "I'll tell you what we'll *do*, William. First, I'll fill a hot-water bottle. Then I'll run up and get the thermometer. And *you* shall be the doctor. That's much the best thing." And she did not even pause for his consent.

"I expect you know, Dr. Wilson," she had begun at once, "it's something that's disagreed with my little boy. I expect so. Oh, yes, I expect so."

William, pale and attentive, was faltering. "Well, yes, Mrs. Hadleigh, p'raps," he said at last, as if his mouth were cram-full of plums. "You *may* be right. And that depends, you know, on what he has been *eating*."

"Yes, yes, I quite understand, doctor. Then would you perhaps wait here just for one moment, while I see if my little boy is ready for you. I think, you know, he might like to wash his hands first and brush his hair. And *pray* keep on your overcoat in case you should feel cold." She took a large dry Turkey towel that was airing on a horse near by, and draped it over William's shoulders. "I won't be a moment," she assured him. "Not a moment."

Yet she paused to glance again at his shawled-in pale face and fever-bright eyes, as if by mere looking she could bore clean through his body; and stooping once more, she pressed her cheek against his, and then his hand to her lips.

"You said," half tearfully chanted the little boy, "that I was the doctor; and now you are kissing me, Mummie!"

"Well, I could often and often kiss lots of doctors," said his mother, and in a flash she was gone, leaving him alone. She raced up the dark staircase as if she were pursued by twenty demons, not even waiting to switch on the light. And when she came to her bedroom it was as if everything in it were doing its utmost to reassure her. The shining of the street lamp was quietly dappling its walls with shadow. The whole room lay oceans deep in silence; the duskily mounded bed, the glass over the chimney-piece, the glass on the dressing-table. They may until that very moment have been conferring together, but now had, as usual, instantly fallen mute, their profound confabulations for the time being over. But she did not pause even so much as to sip of this refreshing stillness. Her finger touched the electric switch, and in an instant the harmless velvety shadows—frail quivering leaf-shadows—the peace, the serenity, had clean evaporated. It was as if the silence had been stricken with leprosy, so instantaneous was the unnatural glare—even in spite of the rose-pink lamp-shades. For now Emilia was staring indeed.

How, she was asking herself, how by any possibility could that striped school tie of her husband's have escaped from its upper drawer on to the bedspread? How by an utter miracle had she failed to see it when she had carried Sallie into the room only an hour or two ago? Ties don't wriggle out of top-drawers across carpets and climb up valances like serpents in the tropics. Husbands miles away cannot charm such things into antics like *these*!

Mary had been out all the afternoon. She herself had been out for most of it with the children, and she could have vowed, taken her oath, *knew*, that *that* couldn't have been there when she had come up to put on her hat. In the instant that followed, before even she could insist on raising her eyes from this queer scrap of 'evidence', her mind suddenly discovered that it was dazed and in the utmost confusion. It was as if, like visitors to a gaudy Soho restaurant, a jostling crowd of thoughts and images, recollections, doubts, memories, clues, forebodings, apprehensions and reiterated stubborn reassurances had thronged noisy and jostling into consciousness—and then were gone again. And at that, at once, as if by instinct and as unforeseeably as a night moth alights on one out of a multitude of flowers, her stricken glance had encountered her husband's note.

At sight of it her heart had leapt in her body, and then cowered down like a thing smitten with palsy. Novels told you of things like these, but surely not just ordinary life! The note had been scribbled on a half-sheet of her own notepaper, and hastily folded into a cocked hat—perhaps the only old-fashioned device she had ever known that husband to be capable of. It seemed that she had learned by heart the message it contained before even she had unfolded the paper and read it. Indeed, it did not matter what it had to say. It hardly even mattered *how* it had said it. So considerately, yet so clumsily, so blastingly. 'She'—that alone was enough. When shells explode why be concerned with fuse or packing? Edward was gone. That was all that mattered. She had been abandoned—she and the children.

So far, so inevitably. You can in vile moments of suspicion, incredulity and terror foresee things like that. Just that he was gone—and for good. But to have come stealing back in the afternoon into a vacant house, merely for a few clothes or a little money, and she out, and Mary out, and the children out—and everything else out; well, that seemed a funny, an unnecessary thing to do!

"I wouldn't have so much minded . . ." she began to mutter to herself, and then realized that her body was minding far too much. A thin acid water had welled into her mouth. Unlike William, she felt sick and dizzy. She had gone stiff and cold and goose-flesh all over. It was as if some fiendish hand were clutching her back hair and dragging the scalp from her forehead taut as the parchment of a drum over her eyes. It was as if she had swallowed unwittingly a dose of some filthy physic.

221

Her knees trembled. Her hands hung down from her arms as though they were useless. And the only thing she could see at this instant was the other woman's face. But it wasn't looking at her; on purpose. It was turned all but three-quarters away—a becoming angle for the long, fair cheekbone, the drooping eyelashes, the lips, the rounded chin of Clara. And then, suddenly, she saw them both together, stooping a little; at a railway station, it seemed; talking close. Or was it that they had just got out of a cab?

Emilia might as well have been dreaming all this, since although these picturings, this misery, this revulsion of jealousy, and the horror of what was to come persisted in a hideous activity somewhere in her mind, she herself had refused for the time being to have anything to do with it. There was something infinitely more important that must be done at once, without a moment's delay. Husbands may go, love *turn*, the future slip into ruin as silently and irretrievably as a house of cards. But children must not be kept waiting; not sick children. She was already clumsily tugging at the tiny middle drawer of the old mirror, one of their first bargains, on the dressing-table, and she caught at the same instant a glimpse of the face reflected in its glass; but so instantaneously that the eye of the image appeared to be darkened and shut, and therefore blind.

What a boon a little methodicalness may be. What a mercy that in this world *things* stay where they are put; do not hide, deceive, play false, forsake and abandon us. Where she always kept it, *there* lay the slim, metal, sharp-edged case of the thermometer. It was as if it had been faithfully awaiting this very reunion—ever since she had seen it last. In the old days, before she was married and had children, even if she had possessed such a thing, she might have looked for it for hours before discovering it. She had despised thermometers. Now, such a search would have resembled insanity.

She hesitated for scarcely the breadth of a sigh at the door, and then with decision switched off the light. Stuffing her husband's scribbled note into her apron pocket, she flew into the next room, put a match to the fire laid in the grate, pushed the hot-water bottle between the sheets of the bed, and hastened downstairs. Her legs, her body, her hand flitting over the banisters, were as light and sure again as if she had never experienced so much as an hour even of mere disappointment in her life. Besides, for some little time now, that body had been habitually told what it had to do. And so long as her orders came promptly and concisely, it could be trusted to continue to act in the same fashion, to be instantly obedient. That was what being a mother taught you to become, and even taught you to try within limits to teach a young child to become—an animated automaton.

'Dr. Wilson' stood where she had left him beside the table and in precisely the same attitude. He had not even troubled to sit down. He had, apparently, not even so much as moved his eyes.

"Now, doctor," said Emilia.

At this, those eyes first settled on her fingers, then quietly shifted to her face.

"You were a long time gone, Mrs. Hadleigh," he remonstrated in a drawling voice, as if his tongue were sticking to the roof of his mouth. "A very long time." He took the thermometer and pushed it gingerly between his lips, shutting them firmly over the thin glass stem. Then his blue and solemn eyes became fixed again, and, without the faintest stir, he continued to watch his mother, while she in turn watched him. When half a minute had gone by, he lifted his eyebrows. She shook her head. In another half-minute he himself took the thermometer out of his mouth, and, holding it between finger and thumb, gravely scrutinized it under the light. "A hundred and forty-seven," he announced solemnly. "H'm." Then he smiled, a half-secret, half-deprecatory smile. "*That's* nothing to worry about, Mrs. Hadleigh. Nothing at all. It looks to me as if all you did was to worry. Put him to bed; I will send him round a bottle of very nice medicine—*very* nice medicine. And . . ." his voice fell a little fainter, "I'll look in again in the morning."

His eyes had become fixed once more, focused, it seemed, on the faraway. "Mummie, I do wish when Mary pulls down the blinds she would do it to the very bottom. I *hate* seeing—seeing myself in the glass."

But Emilia had not really attended to this fretful and unreasonable complaint. She herself was now examining the thermometer. She was frowning, adjusting it, frowning again. Then she had said something—half-muttered, half-whispered—which Dr. Wilson had failed to catch.

"I'd give him," he again began wearily, "some rice pudding and lemonade, and——" But before the rest of his counsel could be uttered she had wrapped him tighter in his bath towel, had stooped down to him back to front so that he could clasp his hands round her neck, pick-a-back; and next moment he was being whisked up the dark staircase to the blue and white nursery. There she slid him gently down beside the fender, took off his shoes, smoothed his fringe, and tenderly kissed him.

"You have very bright eyes, Dr. Wilson. You mustn't let them get too bright—just for my sake."

"Not at all, Mrs. Hadleigh," he parroted, and then suddenly his whole body began to shiver.

"There," she said, "now just begin to take off your clothes, my own precious, while I see to the fire—though *that*, Dr. Wilson, should have been done *first*. Look, the silly paper has just flared up and gone out.

But it won't be a minute. The sticks are as dry as Guy Fawkes' Day. Soon cosy in bed now."

William with unusually stupid fingers was endeavouring to undo his buttons. He was already tired of being the doctor. "Why," he said, "do your teeth chatter, Mummie, when you are very hot? That seems funny. And why do faces come in the window, horrid faces? Is *that* blind right down to the very bottom? Because I would like it to be. Oh dear, my head does ache, Mummie."

It was extraordinary with what cleverness and dexterity Emilia's hands, unlike her son's, were now doing as they were bidden. The fire, coaxed by a little puffing in lieu of bellows, in a wondrous sheet of yellow, like crocuses, was now sweeping up the chimney as if to devour the universe. A loose under-blanket had been thrust into the bed, the hot bottle wrapped up in a fleecy old shawl, the coal scuttle had been filled, a second pair of small pyjamas had been hung over the fender to air, a saucepan of milk had been stood on the stove with its gas turned low—like a circlet of little blue wavering beads; and William himself, half-naked for less than the fraction of a second, had been tucked up in his bed, one of her own tiny embroidered handkerchiefs sprinkled with lavender water for company. There, he had instantly fallen asleep, though spasmodic jerks of foot and hand, and flickering eyelids showed that his small troubles had not wholly been left behind him.

So swiftly and mechanically had her activities followed one upon the other that Emilia had only just realized that she was still unable to make up her mind whether to telephone at once to the doctor or to venture— to dare—to look in on Sallie.

Blind fool! *Blind* fool!—foreseeing plainly every open or half-hidden hint and threat of to-night's event, smelling it, tasting it, hearing it again and again knocking at the door of her mind, she had yet continually deferred the appalling moment when she must meet it face to face, challenge and be done with it, and accept its consequences. The mere image in her mind of her husband's school tie left abandoned on the bed had made the foreboding of looking at Sallie a last and all but insupportable straw. The futility, the cowardice! What needs most daring must be done instantly. There had not been the least need to debate such a question. You can't do twenty-*one* things at once!

Having stolen another prolonged scrutiny of William's pale dream-distorted face and dilating nostrils, she hastened into her own bedroom again, groped for the tiny switch-pull that dangled by the bed-rail, stooped over the cot beside it, and, screening its inmate's face as much as possible from the glare, looked down and in. The small blonde creature, lovelier and even more delicate to the eye than any flower, had kicked off all its bedclothes, the bright lips were ajar, the cheeks flushed

—an exquisite coral red. And the body was breathing almost as fast and shallowly as a cat's. That children under three years old should talk in their sleep, yes; but with so minute a vocabulary! Still, all vocabularies are minute for what they are sometimes needed to express—or to keep silent about. No sickness, no sore throat; but headache, lassitude, pains all over the body, shivering attacks and fever—you just added up the Yes's and subtracted the Noes; and influenza, or worse, was the obvious answer. Should she or should she not wheel the cot into William's room? Sallie might wake, and wake William. Whereas if she remained here and she herself lay down in the night even for so much as an hour—and began to think, she wouldn't be alone, not hopelessly alone. It was the fear of waking either patient that decided the question. She very gently drew blanket and counterpane over Sallie's nakedness, draped a silk handkerchief over the rose-coloured shade, switched on the electric stove in the fireplace, and ran downstairs. There for a few moments, eyes restlessly glancing, she faced the stark dumbness and blindness of the mouthpiece of the telephone.

Dr. Wilson *was* in. Thank Heaven for that. Incredible, that was his voice! There might have been a maternity case—hours and hours. He might have had a horde of dispensary patients. But no, he would be round in a few minutes. Thank Heaven for that. She put back the receiver with a shuddering sigh of gratitude. All that was now needed—superhuman ordeal—was just to wait.

But this Emilia was to be spared. For midway up the staircase, whose treads now seemed at least twice their usual height, she had suddenly paused. Fingers clutching the banister rail, she stood arrested, stock still, icy, constricted. The garden gate had faintly clicked. There could be only one explanation of that—at least on a Wednesday. Edward's few friends and cronies, every one of them, must have discovered long ago that Wednesdays were now *his* 'evenings out'. And she—she hadn't much fancied friends or company recently. It was he himself, then. He had come back. What to do now? A ghastly revulsion took possession of her, a gnawing ache in the pit of her stomach, another kind of nausea, another *kind*, even, of palpitation.

If only she could snatch a few minutes to regain her balance, to prepare herself, to be alone. Consciousness was like the scene of a fair —a dream-fair, all distortion, glare, noise, diablerie and confusion. And before she was even aware of her decision—to make use of a deceit, a blind, a mere best-thing-for-the-time-being—she had found herself in her bedroom again, had somehow with cold and fumbling fingers folded the note into its pretty cocked-hat shape again, and replaced it where she had first set eyes on it, beside the charming little travelling clock, the gift of Aunt Sarah, in the middle of the mantelpiece.

What light remained in the room behind the blinded and curtained windows could not possibly have been detectable outside. That was certain. In an instant she was in William's room once more—listening, her heart beating against her ribs like the menacing thumping of a drum. She had not long to wait. The latch of the front door had faintly squeaked, the lower edge of the door itself had scraped very gently across the coarse mat within, had as softly and furtively shut.

"Is that you, Edward?" she heard herself very gently and insidiously calling over the banisters from the landing. "How lovely! You *are* home early. I didn't expect you for—for hours and hours!"

And now she had met and kissed him, full in the light of the hall-lamp. "Why, what's the matter, darling . . .? You are ill!" She was peering as if out of an enormous fog at the narrow, beloved, pallid countenance, the pale lips, the hunted, haunted, misery-stricken light-brown eyes in those pits of dark entreaty and despair.

"Is it *that's* brought you home?"

He continued to stare at her as if, spectacles lost, he were endeavouring to read a little book in very small print and in an unfamiliar language. His mouth opened, as if to yawn; he began to tremble a little, and said, "Oh, no; nothing much. A headache; I'm tired. Where *were* you?"

"Me?" But her lips remained faintly, mournfully, sympathetically smiling; her dark eyes were as clear and guileless and empty of reflections as pools of water under the windless blue of the sky. "I was in William's room. It's hateful to say it now, Edward—now that you are so tired yourself—but—but I'm rather afraid, poor mite, he's in for another cold—a little chill—and I shouldn't be surprised if Sallie . . . But don't worry about that—because, because there's nothing of course at all yet to worry about. It's you I'm thinking of. You look so dreadfully fagged and—what a welcome . . . There's nothing . . .?"

Her vocabulary had at last begun to get a little obstinate and inadequate, "You don't mean, Edward, there's anything *seriously* wrong? I fancy, you know"—she deliberately laid her hand for an instant on his, "I fancy *you* may be the least little bit feverish yourself—you too. Well . . ." She turned away, flung up a hand as if to flag off a railway train, "I'll get you something hot at once.

"And Edward"—she turned her head over her shoulder, to find him as motionless as she had left him, in almost as stolid and meaningless an attitude as 'Dr. Wilson's' had been in the kitchen, as he stood brooding on the nightmare faces in the darkness of the glass. "There is just one thing, if you could manage it. Just in *case*, would you in a moment or two first wheel Sallie's cot into William's room. I've lit the fire—and I *had* to ask Dr. Wilson to come. I'm so dreadfully stupid and anxious, when—even when there's no reason to be.

The two faces had starkly confronted one another again, but neither could decipher with any absolute certainty the hitherto unrevealed characters now inscribed on them. Each of them was investigating the map of a familiar country, but the cartographer must now have sketched it from an unprecedentedly eccentric angle. The next moment she had turned away, had whisked upstairs and down again, leaving him free, at liberty, to dispose of himself—and of anything else he might be inclined to. In every family life there are surely potential keepsakes that would be far better destroyed; and perhaps a moment *some* time might come. But now . . .

When she returned with her tray and its contents—a steaming tumbler of milk, a few biscuits and a decanter containing a little whisky —she found him standing beside William's bedroom fire. He watched her, as with the utmost care she put down her burden on the little wicker table.

"Millie," he said, "I'm not sure . . . But, well—it was, I suppose, because of William's being ill that you haven't yet been into—into the other room, our bedroom. And so"—he had gulped, as if there was some little danger of producing his very heart for her inspection—"you have not seen *this*?" He was holding towards her the unfolded note, and with trembling fingers she found herself actually pretending to read its scribbled lines again.

Her face had whitened; she had begun to despair of herself, conscious beyond everything else—the tumult in her mind, the ravaging of her heart—that she could hardly endure the mingled miseries, remorse, humiliation in his eyes, in the very tones of his voice, yet listening at the same time to a message of ineffable reassurance. He has not then deceived me again! At last she had contrived to nod, her chin shaking so stupidly for a while that she could scarcely utter a word. "Yes. I *have* read it. I put it back . . . couldn't face it when I heard you. The children —I had to have time. I'm *sorry*, Edward."

" '*Sorry!*' " he echoed.

"I mean—it *was* an awful, well, revelation; but I was stupid; I ought to have seen . . . I did see. But we won't—I *can't* go into that now. You are tired, ill; but you are back . . . for the present."

Her eyes had managed at last to glance at him, and then to break away, and to keep from weeping. And, as if even in his sleep his usual tact and wisdom had not deserted him, William had suddenly flung back his scorching sheet and in a gasping voice was muttering to an unseen listener in some broken, unintelligible lingo that yet ended with a sound resembling the word faces. "There, darling," she answered him, smoothing back his fair fringe from his forehead, "*I* know. They are gone; all gone now; and the blind *is* down—to its very last inch."

She stayed watching him, couldn't look back just yet.

"You see, Millie . . . She"—her husband was trying to explain—"that is, *we* had arranged to meet. It's hopeless to attempt to say anything more just now . . . I waited. She sent . . . She didn't come."

"I see. And so?"

"Millie, Millie. It wasn't, it wasn't *you*. Oh, I can't bear it any longer. . If I had dreamed—the children!" He had flung himself into a pretty round basket chair and sat shuddering, his face hidden in his lean, bloodless hands.

The few minute sounds in the room, the peevish creakings of the chair, William's rapid, snoring breathing, the fluttering of the fire, were interrupted by the noise of brakes and wheels rasping to a standstill in the street below. A brisk yet cautious knocking had followed, awakening an echo, it seemed, in the very hollow of her breast bone.

"Look," she said, "that's where *that* goes. There's no *time* now." The scrap of paper, more swiftly than a vanishing card in a conjuring trick, had been instantly devoured by the voracious flames, had thinned to an exquisitely delicate fluttering ash, and then, as if with a sudden impulse, wafted itself out of sight like a tiny toy balloon into the sooty vacancy of the chimney.

"Listen. Must *you* see the doctor, to-night? Unless it's not—you know—well *bad* 'flu? Wouldn't it be better not? I'll tell him; I could find out; I could say you had gone to bed. Quick, I must go." Every nerve in her body was clamouring for motion, action, something to face, something to do.

He nodded. "And you'll come back?"

"Yes . . . I'll try. Oh, Edward, I'm sorry, sorry. If only there were words to say it. It must have been awful—awful!" She hesitated, gazing at his bent head, the familiar hands . . .

And now the doctor, having deftly packed up Sallie again, burning hot but seemingly resigned to whatever fate might bring, and having carefully wiped his thermometer on the clean huckaback towel Emilia had handed him, was stuffing his stethoscope back into his little brown case. An almost passionate admiration filled her breast at his assured, unhurried movements, and with it a sort of mute, all-reconciling amusement to see how closely, deep within, behind these gestures, and the careful choice of words, he resembled his small and solemn understudy, William.

She was returning earnestly glance for glance, intently observant of every least change of expression in his dark decisive face, of timbre in his voice. Practically every one of the hungered-for, familiar, foreseen, all-satisfying assurances—like a tiny flock of innocent sheep pattering through a gateway—had been uttered and sagaciously nodded to: "It may be just a feverish attack; it might, it *might* be 'flu." "Don't forget, Mrs. Hadleigh, they are down one moment and up the next!" "I'll send round a bottle of medicine to-night, almost at once, and some powders." "I'll look in again first thing in the morning." Then he had paused, little leather case in hand, his eyes fixed on the fire.

Some day, she told herself, she *must* retaliate in kind: "You must understand, Dr. Wilson, that at this hour of the night it would be utterly stupid of you to breathe the word *pneumonia*, which takes weeks and weeks and weeks; may easily be fatal; and one has just to wait for the crisis!" Or, "Don't be mistaken, Dr. Wilson, even if you were at death's door yourself I shouldn't hesitate to ring you up if their temperatures go over 103"—that kind of thing.

"You know, Mrs. Hadleigh," he was beginning again, "it just beats me why you mothers—quite rational, sensible, almost cynically practical creatures some of you, simply wear yourselves out with worry and anxiety when there's scarcely a shred of justification for it. Quite uselessly. Getting thin and haggard, wasting away, losing all that precious youth and beauty. I say I often *think* these things—wish I could express them. You simply refuse to heed *the* lesson in life: that really great Englishman's, Mr. Asquith's—'Wait and See'. *Condensing*, don't you see, and not squandering all energy, impulse and reserves. 'Never trouble trouble until trouble troubles you.' Isn't *that* good sense? It's what's called an old wives' saying, of course—not a mother's. But I could have saved dozens of precious lives and bodies and all but souls, if only . . . well, literally saved them, I mean, a deuce of a lot of wear and tear."

She was drinking in his words, this delicious lecture, these scoldings; devouring them, as if they were manna dipped in honey, the waters of life. They were a rest and peace beyond expression. A ready help in time of trouble. He shall lead his flock like a shepherd. Yea, though I walk . . . Why all this Bible? Dr. Wilson was not a parson; he was just a doctor. And then another Dr. Wilson had piped up in memory again, " 'You *said* that I was the doctor; and now you are kissing me, Mummie!' . . . 'I could often kiss lots of doctors!' "

"I know, I know," she heard herself meekly assuring him. "I'm utterly stupid about these things. And of course if we were all sensible savages or gipsies there wouldn't be . . . Even—oh, but you can't think what a comfort it is to—to be reassured."

He was eyeing her now more closely, totting up and subtracting Yes's and Noes, it seemed, on his own account, and on hers. It was with difficulty she met the straight clear scrutiny. "Well, there we are," he decided. "Just look what lovely babies you have. Everything a woman could wish for! Gipsies be dashed. There are, I assure you, my dear

Mrs. Hadleigh, spinsters galore in this parish who . . . How's your husband?"

Her dark shining eyes had now at last quivered in their sockets, if only for the fraction of a second.

"It sounds very silly," the words were squeezing out like cooing turtle doves through too narrow an exit, "but *he's* not very well either! It's, it's almost funny, ridiculous—all three at once. Isn't it? He came home rather late from—from the office, and he's gone to bed." It seemed a pity that one's cheeks should flatly refuse not to flame up, when one's eyes were hard as brass. "The fact is, Dr. Wilson, he refused to see you. You know what men are. But could it be, do you think," a little nod towards William's bed had helped her out, "that too?"

"I think," Dr. Wilson had replied drily, a scarcely perceptible forking frown between his eyebrows, "it might very well be that too. But listen, Mrs. Hadleigh. Husbands, of course, are not really of much importance in life—not really. Necessities perhaps; but here to-day and gone to-morrow. *Children* are what the kernel is to the nut; the innermost part of it. And so must be taken great care of. *Therefore*—and this is not advice; this is *orders*: I forbid you to worry; forbid it. I shall throw up the case! If you *must* stay up—you have a maid, a good solid, stolid one too. Wake up her and chance it; she'll love you all the better. And you can share the night between you. Otherwise—unless of course you need me again, and you won't, though I should be *easily* handy—you are not only not to worry (more than you can help) but you are on no account to get up more than twice until the morning to look at your patients— at *our* patients, mind you. It's bad for them, worse for you. When they've had their dose, they'll soon quieten down—unless I'm *wrong*. And—imagine it!—I sometimes am." He was holding out his hand, a look of unadulterated, generous, wholly masculine admiration on his vigilant, assured features.

"By gad!" he said. "All three! But then *you* know *I* know what you can manage when hard pressed. So that's all right." He was plunging downstairs into the night, and Emilia was trying in vain to keep up with him.

"And after the first dose and the powders, Dr. Wilson, I shouldn't, I suppose, wake either of them up to give them any *more* medicine—not until the morning?"

"As a general rule, Mrs. Hadleigh," replied the doctor, carefully putting on his hat and glancing as he did so into the strip of looking-glass on the wall, "it's wiser never to wake *anybody* up, merely to give them physic—and certainly not mere doctor's physic."

CHARLES DICKENS

1812–1870

Unsurpassed as a creative genius, he peopled his famous novels
with brilliantly original characters in all manner of situations.
Indeed, ideas came to him so quickly that often,
as G. K. Chesterton put it, "he wrote short stories
because he had not time to write long ones."

The Poor Relation's Story

 HE WAS VERY reluctant to take precedence of so
many respected members of the family, by beginning
the round of stories they were to relate as they sat in
a goodly circle by the Christmas fire; and he modestly
suggested that it would be more correct if 'John our
esteemed host' (whose health he begged to drink)
would have the kindness to begin. For as to himself,
he said, he was so little used to lead the way that
really—— But as they all cried out here, that he must begin, and agreed
with one voice that he might, could, would, and should begin, he left
off rubbing his hands, and took his legs out from under his arm-chair,
and did begin.

I have no doubt (said the poor relation) that I shall surprise the
assembled members of our family, and particularly John our esteemed
host to whom we are so much indebted for the great hospitality with
which he has this day entertained us, by the confession I am going to
make. But, if you do me the honour to be surprised at anything that falls
from a person so unimportant in the family as I am, I can only say that
I shall be scrupulously accurate in all I relate.

I am not what I am supposed to be. I am quite another thing. Perhaps
before I go further I had better glance at what I *am* supposed to be.

It is supposed, unless I mistake—the assembled members of our
family will correct me if I do, which is very likely (here the poor relation
looked mildly about him for contradiction)—that I am nobody's enemy
but my own. That I never met with any particular success in anything.

231

That I failed in business because I was unbusiness-like and credulous—
in not being prepared for the interested designs of my partner. That I
failed in love because I was ridiculously trustful—in thinking it impossible that Christiana could deceive me. That I failed in my expectations
from my uncle Chill, on account of not being as sharp as he could have
wished in worldly matters. That, through life, I have been rather put
upon and disappointed in a general way. That I am at present a bachelor
of between fifty-nine and sixty years of age, living on a limited income
in the form of a quarterly allowance, to which I see that John our
esteemed host wishes me to make no further allusion.

The supposition as to my present pursuits and habits is to the
following effect.

I live in a lodging in the Clapham Road—a very clean back room, in a
very respectable house—where I am expected not to be at home in the
daytime, unless poorly; and which I usually leave in the morning at
nine o'clock, on pretence of going to business. I take my breakfast—my
roll and butter, and my half-pint of coffee—at the old-established coffee-
shop near Westminster Bridge; and then I go into the City—I don't
know why—and sit in Garraway's Coffee House, and on 'Change, and
walk about, and look into a few offices and counting-houses where some
of my relations or acquaintances are so good as to tolerate me, and where
I stand by the fire if the weather happens to be cold. I get through the
day in this way until five o'clock, and then I dine; at a cost, on the
average, of one and threepence. Having still a little money to spend on
my evening's entertainment, I look into the old-established coffee-shop
as I go home, and take my cup of tea, and perhaps my bit of toast. So,
as the large hand of the clock makes its way round to the morning hour
again, I make my way round to the Clapham Road again, and go to bed
when I get to my lodging—fire being expensive, and being objected to
by the family on account of its giving trouble and making a dirt.

Sometimes one of my relations or acquaintance is so obliging as to
ask me to dinner. These are holiday occasions, and then I generally walk
in the Park. I am a solitary man, and seldom walk with anybody. Not
that I am avoided because I am shabby; for I am not at all shabby,
having always a very good suit of black on (or rather Oxford mixture,
which has the appearance of black and wears much better); but I have
got into a habit of speaking low, and being rather silent, and my spirits
are not high, and I am sensible that I am not an attractive companion.

The only exception to this general rule is the child of my first cousin,
Little Frank. I have a particular affection for that child, and he takes
very kindly to me. He is a diffident boy by nature; and in a crowd he is
soon run over, as I may say, and forgotten. He and I, however, get on
exceedingly well. I have a fancy that the poor child will in time succeed

to my peculiar position in the family. We talk but little; still, we understand each other. We walk about, hand in hand; and without much speaking he knows what I mean, and I know what he means. When he was very little indeed, I used to take him to the windows of the toy-shops, and show him the toys inside. It is surprising how soon he found out that I would have made him a great many presents if I had been in circumstances to do it.

Little Frank and I go and look at the outside of the Monument—he is very fond of the Monument—and at the Bridges, and at all the sights that are free. On two of my birthdays we have dined on *à-la-mode* beef, and gone at half-price to the play, and been deeply interested. I was once walking with him in Lombard Street, which we often visit on account of my having mentioned to him that there are great riches there —he is very fond of Lombard Street—when a gentleman said to me as he passed by, "Sir, your little son has dropped his glove." I assure you, if you will excuse my remarking on so trivial a circumstance, this accidental mention of the child as mine quite touched my heart and brought the foolish tears into my eyes.

When Little Frank is sent to school in the country I shall be very much at a loss what to do with myself, but I have the intention of walking down there once a month and seeing him on a half-holiday. I am told he will then be at play upon the Heath; and if my visits should be objected to, as unsettling the child, I can see him from a distance without his seeing me, and walk back again. His mother comes of a highly genteel family, and rather disapproves, I am aware, of our being too much together. I know that I am not calculated to improve his retiring disposition; but I think he would miss me beyond the feeling of the moment if we were wholly separated.

When I die in the Clapham Road I shall not leave much more in this world than I shall take out of it; but I happen to have a miniature of a bright-faced boy, with a curling head, and an open shirt-frill waving down his bosom (my mother had it taken for me, but I can't believe that it was ever like), which will be worth nothing to sell, and which I shall beg may be given to Frank. I have written my dear boy a little letter with it, in which I have told him that I felt very sorry to part from him, though bound to confess that I knew no reason why I should remain here. I have given him some short advice, the best in my power, to take warning of the consequences of being nobody's enemy but his own; and I have endeavoured to comfort him for what I fear he will consider a bereavement, by pointing out to him that I was only a superfluous something to every one but him; and that having by some means failed to find a place in this great assembly, I am better out of it.

Such (said the poor relation, clearing his throat and beginning to speak a little louder) is the general impression about me. Now, it is a remarkable circumstance, which forms the aim and purpose of my story, that this is all wrong. This is not my life, and these are not my habits. I do not even live in the Clapham Road. Comparatively speaking, I am very seldom there. I reside, mostly, in a—I am almost ashamed to say the word, it sounds so full of pretension—in a Castle. I do not mean that it is an old baronial habitation, but still it is a building always known to every one by the name of a Castle. In it I preserve the particulars of my history; they run thus:

It was when I first took John Spatter (who had been my clerk) into partnership, and when I was still a young man of not more than five-and-twenty, residing in the house of my uncle Chill, from whom I had considerable expectations, that I ventured to propose to Christiana. I had loved Christiana a long time. She was very beautiful, and very winning in all respects. I rather mistrusted her widowed mother, who I feared was of a plotting and mercenary turn of mind; but I thought as well of her as I could, for Christiana's sake. I never had loved any one but Christiana, and she had been all the world, and oh far more than all the world, to me, from our childhood!

Christiana accepted me with her mother's consent, and I was rendered very happy indeed. My life at my uncle Chill's was of a spare dull kind, and my garret chamber was as dull, and bare, and cold as an upper prison room in some stern northern fortress. But, having Christiana's love, I wanted nothing upon earth. I would not have changed my lot with any human being.

Avarice was, unhappily, my uncle Chill's master-vice. Though he was rich, he pinched, and scraped, and clutched, and lived miserably. As Christiana had no fortune, I was for some time a little fearful of confessing our engagement to him; but at length I wrote him a letter, saying how it all truly was. I put it into his hand one night, on going to bed.

As I came downstairs next morning, shivering in the cold December air—colder in my uncle's unwarmed house than in the street, where the winter sun did sometimes shine, and which was at all events enlivened by cheerful faces and voices passing along—I carried a heavy heart towards the long, low breakfast-room in which my uncle sat. It was a large room with a small fire, and there was a great bay window in it which the rain had marked in the night as if with the tears of houseless people. It stared upon a raw yard, with a cracked stone pavement, and some rusted iron railings half uprooted, whence an ugly out-building that had once been a dissecting-room (in the time of the great surgeon who had mortgaged the house to my uncle) stared at it.

We rose so early always that at that time of the year we breakfasted by candle-light. When I went into the room my uncle was so contracted by the cold, and so huddled together in his chair behind the one dim candle, that I did not see him until I was close to the table.

As I held out my hand to him, he caught up his stick (being infirm, he always walked about the house with a stick), and made a blow at me, and said, "You fool!"

"Uncle," I returned, "I didn't expect you to be so angry as this." Nor had I expected it, though he was a hard and angry old man.

"You didn't expect!" said he; "when did you ever expect? When did you ever calculate, or look forward, you contemptible dog?"

"These are hard words, uncle!"

"Hard words? Feathers, to pelt such an idiot as you with," said he. "Here! Betsy Snap! Look at him!"

Betsy Snap was a withered, hard-favoured, yellow old woman—our only domestic—always employed, at this time of the morning, in rubbing my uncle's legs. As my uncle adjured her to look at me, he put his lean grip on the crown of her head, she kneeling beside him, and turned her face towards me. An involuntary thought connecting them both with the dissecting-room, as it must often have been in the surgeon's time, passed across my mind in the midst of my anxiety.

"Look at the snivelling milksop!" said my uncle. "Look at the baby! This is the gentleman who, people say, is nobody's enemy but his own. This is the gentleman who can't say no. This is the gentleman who was making such large profits in his business that he must needs take a partner, t'other day. This is the gentleman who is going to marry a wife without a penny, and who falls into the hands of Jezebels who are speculating on my death!"

I knew, now, how great my uncle's rage was; for nothing short of his being almost beside himself would have induced him to utter that concluding word, which he held in such repugnance that it was never spoken or hinted at before him on any account.

"On my death," he repeated, as if he were defying me by defying his own abhorrence of the word. "On my death—death—Death! But I'll spoil the speculation. Eat your last under this roof, you feeble wretch, and may it choke you!"

You may suppose that I had not much appetite for the breakfast to which I was bidden in these terms; but I took my accustomed seat. I saw that I was repudiated henceforth by my uncle; still I could bear that very well, possessing Christiana's heart.

He emptied his basin of bread and milk as usual, only that he took it on his knees with his chair turned away from the table where I sat. When he had done, he carefully snuffed out the candle; and the cold, slate-coloured, miserable day looked in upon us.

"Now, Mr. Michael," said he, "before we part, I should like to have a word with these ladies in your presence."

"As you will, sir," I returned; "but you deceive yourself, and wrong us cruelly, if you suppose that there is any feeling at stake in this contract but pure, disinterested, faithful love."

To this, he only replied, "You lie!" and not one other word.

We went, through half-thawed snow and half-frozen rain, to the house where Christiana and her mother lived. My uncle knew them very well. They were sitting at their breakfast, and were surprised to see us at that hour.

"Your servant, ma'am," said my uncle to the mother. "You divine the purpose of my visit, I dare say, ma'am. I understand there is a world of pure, disinterested, faithful love cooped up here. I am happy to bring it all it wants, to make it complete. I bring you your son-in-law, ma'am— and you, your husband, miss. The gentleman is a perfect stranger to me, but I wish him joy of his wise bargain."

He snarled at me as he went out, and I never saw him again.

IT IS ALTOGETHER a mistake (continued the poor relation) to suppose that my dear Christiana, over-persuaded and influenced by her mother, married a rich man, the dirt from whose carriage-wheels is often, in these changed times, thrown upon me as she rides by. No, no. She married me.

The way we came to be married rather sooner than we intended was this. I took a frugal lodging and was saving and planning for her sake, when, one day, she spoke to me with great earnestness, and said:

"My dear Michael, I have given you my heart. I have said that I loved you, and I have pledged myself to be your wife. I am as much yours through all changes of good and evil as if we had been married on the day when such words passed between us. I know you well, and know that if we should be separated and our union broken off, your whole life would be shadowed, and all that might, even now, be stronger in your character for the conflict with the world would then be weakened to the shadow of what it is!"

"God help me, Christiana!" said I. "You speak the truth."

"Michael!" said she, putting her hand in mine, in all maidenly devotion, "let us keep apart no longer. It is but for me to say that I can live contented upon such means as you have, and I well know you are happy. I say so from my heart. Strive no more alone; let us strive together. My dear Michael, it is not right that I should keep secret from you what you do not suspect, but what distresses my whole life. My mother—without considering that what you have lost, you have lost for me, and on the assurance of my faith—sets her heart on riches, and urges another suit upon me, to my misery. I cannot bear this, for to bear it is to be untrue to you. I would rather share your struggles than look on. I want no better home than you can give me. I know that you will aspire and labour with a higher courage if I am wholly yours, and let it be so when you will!"

I was blest indeed, that day, and a new world opened to me. We were married in a very little while, and I took my wife to our happy home. That was the beginning of the residence I have spoken of; the Castle we have ever since inhabited together dates from that time. All our children have been born in it. Our first child—now married—was a little girl, whom we called Christiana. Her son is so like Little Frank that I hardly know which is which.

THE CURRENT impression as to my partner's dealings with me is also quite erroneous. He did not begin to treat me coldly, as a poor simpleton, when my uncle and I so fatally quarrelled; nor did he afterwards gradually possess himself of our business and edge me out. On the contrary, he behaved to me with the utmost good faith and honour.

Matters between us took this turn:—On the day of my separation from my uncle, and even before the arrival at our counting-house of my trunks (which he sent after me, *not* carriage paid), I went down to our room of business, on our little wharf, overlooking the river; and there I told John Spatter what had happened.

John did not say, in reply, that rich old relatives were palpable facts, and that love and sentiment were moonshine and fiction. He addressed me thus:

"Michael," said John, "we were at school together, and I generally had the knack of getting on better than you, and making a higher reputation."

"You had, John," I returned.

"Although," said John, "I borrowed your books and lost them; borrowed your pocket-money, and never repaid it; got you to buy my damaged knives at a higher price than I had given for them new; and to own to the windows that I had broken."

"All not worth mentioning, John Spatter," said I, "but certainly true."

"When you were first established in this infant business, which promises to thrive so well," pursued John, "I came to you, in my search for almost any employment, and you made me your clerk."

"Still not worth mentioning, my dear John Spatter," said I; "still, equally true."

"And finding that I had a good head for business, and that I was really useful *to* the business, you did not like to retain me in that capacity, and thought it an act of justice soon to make me your partner."

"Still less worth mentioning than any of those other little circumstances you have recalled, John Spatter," said I; "for I was, and am, sensible of your merits and my deficiencies."

"Now, my good friend," said John, drawing my arm through his, as he had had a habit of doing at school; while two vessels outside the windows of our counting-house—which were shaped like the stern windows of a ship—went lightly down the river with the tide, as John and I might then be sailing away in company, and in trust and confidence, on our voyage of life; "let there, under these friendly circumstances, be a right understanding between us. You are too easy, Michael. You are nobody's enemy but your own. If I were to give you that damaging character among our connection, with a shrug, and a shake of the head, and a sigh; and if I were further to abuse the trust you place in me——"

"But you never will abuse it at all, John," I observed.

"Never!" said he; "but I am putting a case—I say, and if I were further to abuse that trust by keeping this piece of our common affairs in the dark, and this other piece in the light, and again this other piece in the twilight, and so on, I should strengthen my strength, and weaken your weakness, day by day, until at last I found myself on the high road to fortune, and you left behind on some bare common, a hopeless number of miles out of the way."

"Exactly so," said I.

"To prevent this, Michael," said John Spatter, "or the remotest chance of this, there must be perfect openness between us. Nothing must be concealed, and we must have but one interest."

"My dear John Spatter," I assured him, "that is precisely what I mean."

"And when you are too easy," pursued John, his face glowing with friendship, "you must allow me to prevent that imperfection in your nature from being taken advantage of by any one; you must not expect me to humour it——"

"My dear John Spatter," I interrupted, "I *don't* expect you to humour it. I want to correct it."

"And I, too," said John.

"Exactly so!" cried I. "We both have the same end in view; and, honourably seeking it, and fully trusting one another, and having but one interest, ours will be a prosperous and happy partnership."

"I am sure of it!" returned John Spatter. And we shook hands most affectionately.

I took John home to my Castle, and we had a very happy day. Our partnership throve well. My friend and partner supplied what I wanted, as I had foreseen that he would; and by improving both the business and myself, amply acknowledged any little rise in life to which I had helped him.

I AM NOT (said the poor relation, looking at the fire as he slowly rubbed his hands) very rich, for I never cared to be that; but I have enough, and am above all moderate wants and anxieties. My Castle is not a splendid place, but it is very comfortable, and it has a warm and cheerful air, and is quite a picture of Home.

Our eldest girl, who is very like her mother, married John Spatter's eldest son. Our two families are closely united in other ties of attachment. It is very pleasant of an evening, when we are all assembled together—which frequently happens—and when John and I talk over old times, and the one interest there has always been between us.

I really do not know, in my Castle, what loneliness is. Some of our children or grandchildren are always about it, and the young voices of my descendants are delightful—oh, how delightful!—to me to hear. My dearest and most devoted wife, ever faithful, ever loving, ever helpful and sustaining and consoling, is the priceless blessing of my house; from whom all its other blessings spring. We are rather a musical family, and when Christiana sees me, at any time, a little weary or depressed, she steals to the piano and sings a gentle air she used to sing when we were first betrothed. So weak a man am I that I cannot bear to hear it from any other source. They played it once at the Theatre when I was there with Little Frank; and the child said, wondering, "Cousin Michael, whose hot tears are these that have fallen on my hand?"

Such is my Castle, and such are the real particulars of my life therein preserved. I often take Little Frank home there. He is very welcome to my grandchildren, and they play together. At this time of the year—the Christmas and New Year time—I am seldom out of my Castle. For the associations of the season seem to hold me there, and the precepts of the season seem to teach me that it is well to be there.

"AND THE CASTLE IS—" observed a grave, kind voice among the company.

"Yes. My Castle," said the poor relation, shaking his head as he still looked at the fire, "is in the Air. John our esteemed host suggests its situation accurately. My Castle is in the Air! I have done. Will you be so good as to pass the story!"

SIR ARTHUR CONAN DOYLE

1859–1930

A qualified doctor, his interests in life were far ranging. He was advocate of a Channel Tunnel, of steel helmets for soldiers and inflatable life jackets for sailors, of divorce reform, of precautions against the future horrors of U-boat warfare. He was also the author of several historical romances, books on warfare and on spiritualism; and, incidentally, the creator of Sherlock Holmes . . .

The Adventure of the Speckled Band

IN GLANCING OVER my notes of the seventy odd cases in which I have during the last eight years studied the methods of my friend Sherlock Holmes, I find many tragic, some comic, a large number merely strange, but none commonplace; for, working as he did rather for the love of his art than for the acquirement of wealth, he refused to associate himself with any investigation which did not tend towards the unusual, and even the fantastic. Of all these varied cases, however, I cannot recall any which presented more singular features than that which was associated with the well-known Surrey family of the Roylotts of Stoke Moran. The events in question occurred in the early days of my association with Holmes, when we were sharing rooms as bachelors, in Baker Street. It is possible that I might have placed them upon record before, but a promise of secrecy was made at the time, from which I have only been freed during the last month by the untimely death of the lady to whom the pledge was given. It is perhaps as well that the facts should now come to light, for I have reasons to know there are widespread rumours as to the death of Dr. Grimesby Roylott which tend to make the matter even more terrible than the truth.

It was early in April, in the year '83, that I woke one morning to find Sherlock Holmes standing, fully dressed, by the side of my bed. He was a late riser as a rule, and, as the clock on the mantelpiece showed me that it was only a quarter past seven, I blinked up at him in some surprise, and perhaps just a little resentment, for I was myself regular in my habits.

"Very sorry to knock you up, Watson," said he, "but it's the common lot this morning. Mrs. Hudson has been knocked up, she retorted upon me, and I on you."

"What is it, then? A fire?"

"No, a client. It seems that a young lady has arrived in a considerable state of excitement, who insists upon seeing me. She is waiting now in the sitting-room. Now, when young ladies wander about the Metropolis at this hour of the morning, and knock sleepy people up out of their beds, I presume that it is something very pressing which they have to communicate. Should it prove to be an interesting case, you would, I am sure, wish to follow it from the outset. I thought at any rate that I should call you, and give you the chance."

"My dear fellow, I would not miss it for anything."

I had no keener pleasure than in following Holmes in his professional investigations, and in admiring the rapid deductions, as swift as intuitions, and yet always founded on a logical basis, with which he unravelled the problems which were submitted to him. I rapidly threw on my clothes, and was ready in a few minutes to accompany my friend down to the sitting-room. A lady dressed in black and heavily veiled, who had been sitting in the window, rose as we entered.

"Good morning, madam," said Holmes cheerily. "My name is Sherlock Holmes. This is my intimate friend and associate, Dr. Watson, before whom you can speak as freely as before myself. Ha, I am glad to see that Mrs. Hudson has had the good sense to light the fire. Pray draw up to it, and I shall order you a cup of hot coffee, for I observe that you are shivering."

"It is not cold which makes me shiver," said the woman in a low voice, changing her seat as requested.

"What then?"

"It is fear, Mr. Holmes. It is terror." She raised her veil as she spoke, and we could see that she was indeed in a pitiable state of agitation, her face all drawn and grey, with restless, frightened eyes, like those of some hunted animal. Her features and figure were those of a woman of thirty, but her hair was shot with premature grey, and her expression was weary and haggard. Sherlock Holmes ran her over with one of his quick, all-comprehensive glances.

"You must not fear," said he soothingly, bending forward and patting her forearm. "We shall soon set matters right, I have no doubt. You have come in by train this morning, I see."

"You know me, then?"

"No, but I observe the second half of a return ticket in the palm of your left glove. You must have started early, and yet you had a good drive in a dog-cart, along heavy roads, before you reached the station."

The lady gave a violent start, and stared in bewilderment at my companion.

"There is no mystery, my dear madam," said he, smiling. "The left arm of your jacket is spattered with mud in no less than seven places. The marks are perfectly fresh. There is no vehicle save a dog-cart which throws up mud in that way, and then only when you sit on the left-hand side of the driver."

"Whatever your reasons may be, you are perfectly correct," said she. "I started from home before six, reached Leatherhead at twenty past, and came in by the first train to Waterloo. Sir, I can stand this strain no longer, I shall go mad if it continues. I have no one to turn to—none, save only one, who cares for me, and he, poor fellow, can be of little aid. I have heard of you, Mr. Holmes; I have heard of you from Mrs. Farintosh, whom you helped in the hour of her sore need. It was from her that I had your address. Oh, sir, do you not think you could help me too, and at least throw a little light through the dense darkness which surrounds me? At present it is out of my power to reward you for your services, but in a month or two I shall be married, with the control of my own income, and then at least you shall not find me ungrateful."

Holmes turned to his desk, and unlocking it, drew out a small case-book which he consulted.

"Farintosh," said he. "Ah, yes, I recall the case; it was concerned with an opal tiara. I think it was before your time, Watson. I can only say, madam, that I shall be happy to devote the same care to your case as I did to that of your friend. As to reward, my profession is its reward; but you are at liberty to defray whatever expenses I may be put to, at the time which suits you best. And now I beg that you will lay before us everything that may help us in forming an opinion upon the matter."

"Alas!" replied our visitor. "The very horror of my situation lies in the fact that my fears are so vague, and my suspicions depend so entirely upon small points, which might seem trivial to another, that even he to whom of all others I have a right to look for help and advice looks upon all that I tell him about it as the fancies of a nervous woman. He does not say so, but I can read it from his soothing answers and averted eyes. But I have heard, Mr. Holmes, that you can see deeply into the manifold wickedness of the human heart. You may advise me how to walk amid the dangers which encompass me."

"I am all attention, madam."

"My name is Helen Stoner, and I am living with my stepfather, who is the last survivor of one of the oldest Saxon families in England, the Roylotts of Stoke Moran, on the western border of Surrey."

Holmes nodded his head. "The name is familiar to me," said he.

"The family was at one time among the richest in England, and the estate extended over the borders into Berkshire in the north, and Hampshire in the west. In the last century, however, four successive heirs were of a dissolute and wasteful disposition, and the family ruin was eventually completed by a gambler, in the days of the Regency. Nothing was left, save a few acres of ground and the two-hundred-year-old house, which is itself crushed under a heavy mortgage. The last squire dragged out his existence there, living the horrible life of an aristocratic pauper; but his only son, my stepfather, seeing that he must adapt himself to the new conditions, obtained an advance from a relative, which enabled him to take a medical degree, and went out to Calcutta, where, by his professional skill and his force of character, he established a large practice. In a fit of anger, however, caused by some robberies which had been perpetrated in the house, he beat his native butler to death, and narrowly escaped a capital sentence. As it was, he suffered a long term of imprisonment, and afterwards returned to England a morose and disappointed man.

"When Dr. Roylott was in India he married my mother, Mrs. Stoner, the young widow of Major-General Stoner, of the Bengal Artillery. My sister Julia and I were twins, and we were only two years old at the time of my mother's re-marriage. She had a considerable sum of money, not less than a thousand a year, and this she bequeathed to Dr. Roylott entirely whilst we resided with him, with a provision that a certain annual sum should be allowed to each of us in the event of our marriage. Shortly after our return to England my mother died—she was killed eight years ago in a railway accident near Crewe. Dr. Roylott then abandoned his attempts to establish himself in practice in London, and took us to live with him in the ancestral house at Stoke Moran. The money which my mother had left was enough for all our wants, and there seemed no obstacle to our happiness.

"But a terrible change came over our stepfather about this time. Instead of making friends and exchanging visits with our neighbours, who had at first been overjoyed to see a Roylott of Stoke Moran back in the old family seat, he shut himself up in his house, and seldom came out save to indulge in ferocious quarrels with whoever might cross his path.

"Violence of temper approaching to mania has been hereditary in the men of the family, and in my stepfather's case it had, I believe, been

243

intensified by his long residence in the tropics. A series of disgraceful brawls took place, two of which ended in the police-court, until at last he became the terror of the village, and the folks would fly at his approach, for he is a man of immense strength, and absolutely uncontrollable in his anger.

"Last week he hurled the local blacksmith over a parapet into a stream, and it was only by paying over all the money that I could gather together that I was able to avert another public exposure. He had no friends at all save the wandering gipsies, and he would give these vagabonds leave to encamp upon the few acres of bramble-covered land which represent the family estate, and would accept in return the hospitality of their tents, wandering away with them sometimes for weeks on end. He has a passion also for Indian animals, which are sent over to him by a correspondent, and he has at this moment a cheetah and a baboon, which wander freely over his grounds, and are feared by the villagers almost as much as their master.

"You can imagine from what I say that my poor sister Julia and I had no great pleasure in our lives. No servant would stay with us, and for a long time we did all the work of the house. She was but thirty at the time of her death, and yet her hair had already begun to whiten, even as mine has."

"Your sister is dead, then?"

"She died just two years ago, and it is of her death that I wish to speak to you. You can understand that, living the life which I have described, we were little likely to see anyone of our own age and position. We had, however, an aunt, my mother's maiden sister, Miss Honoria Westphail, who lives near Harrow, and we were occasionally allowed to pay short visits at this lady's house. Julia went there at Christmas two years ago, and met there a half-pay Major of Marines, to whom she became engaged. My stepfather learned of the engagement when my sister returned, and offered no objection to the marriage; but within a fortnight of the day which had been fixed for the wedding, the terrible event occurred which has deprived me of my only companion."

Sherlock Holmes had been leaning back in his chair with his eyes closed, and his head sunk in a cushion, but he half-opened his lids now, and glanced across at his visitor.

"Pray be precise as to details," said he.

"It is easy for me to be so, for every event of that dreadful time is seared into my memory. The manor house is, as I have already said, very old, and only one wing is now inhabited. The bedrooms in this wing are on the ground floor, the sitting-rooms being in the central block of the buildings. Of these bedrooms, the first is Dr. Roylott's, the second my sister's, and the third my own. There is no communication between them, but they all open out into the same corridor. Do I make myself plain?"

"Perfectly so."

"The windows of the three rooms open out upon the lawn. The fatal night Dr. Roylott had gone to his room early, though we knew that he had not retired to rest, for my sister was troubled by the smell of the strong Indian cigars which it was his custom to smoke. She left her room, therefore, and came into mine, where she sat for some time, chatting about her approaching wedding. At eleven o'clock she rose to leave me, but she paused at the door and looked back.

"'Tell me, Helen,' said she, 'have you ever heard anyone whistle in the dead of the night?'

"'Never,' said I.

"'I suppose that you could not possibly whistle yourself in your sleep?'

"'Certainly not. But why?'

"'Because during the last few nights I have always, about three in the morning, heard a low clear whistle. I am a light sleeper, and it has awakened me. I cannot tell where it came from—perhaps from the next room, perhaps from the lawn. I thought that I would just ask whether you had heard it.'

"'No, I have not. It must be those wretched gipsies in the plantation.'

"'Very likely. And yet if it were on the lawn I wonder that you did not hear it also.'

"'Ah, but I sleep more heavily than you.'

"'Well, it is of no great consequence at any rate,' she smiled back at me, closed my door, and a few moments later I heard her key turn in the lock."

"Indeed," said Holmes. "Was it your custom always to lock yourselves in at night?"

"Always."

"And why?"

"I think that I mentioned to you that the Doctor kept a cheetah and a baboon. We had no feeling of security unless our doors were locked."

"Quite so. Pray proceed with your statement."

"I could not sleep that night. A vague feeling of impending misfortune impressed me. My sister and I, you will recollect, were twins, and you know how subtle are the links which bind two souls which are so closely allied. It was a wild night. The wind was howling outside, and the rain was beating and splashing against the windows. Suddenly, amidst all the hubbub of the gale, there burst forth the wild scream of a terrified woman. I knew that it was my sister's voice. I sprang from my bed, wrapped a shawl round me, and rushed into the corridor. As I opened my door I seemed to hear a low whistle, such as my sister described, and a few moments later a clanging sound, as if a mass of metal had fallen. As I ran down the passage my sister's door was unlocked, and revolved slowly upon its hinges. I stared at it horror-stricken, not knowing what was about to issue from it. By the light of the corridor lamp I saw my sister appear at the opening, her face blanched with terror, her hands groping for help, her whole figure swaying to and fro like that of a drunkard. I ran to her and threw my arms round her, but at that moment her knees seemed to give way and she fell to the ground. She writhed as one who is in terrible pain, and her limbs were dreadfully convulsed. At first I thought that she had not recognized me, but as I bent over her she suddenly shrieked out in a voice which I shall never forget, 'O, my God! Helen! It was the band! The speckled band!' There was something else which she would fain have said, and she stabbed with her finger into the air in the direction of the Doctor's room, but a fresh convulsion seized her and choked her words. I rushed out, calling loudly for my stepfather, and I met him hastening from his room in his dressing-gown. When he reached my sister's side she was unconscious, and though he poured brandy down her throat, and sent for medical aid from the village, all efforts were in vain, for she slowly sank and died without having recovered her consciousness. Such was the dreadful end of my beloved sister."

"One moment," said Holmes; "are you sure about this whistle and metallic sound? Could you swear to it?"

"That was what the county coroner asked me at the inquiry. It is my strong impression that I heard it, and yet among the crash of the gale, and the creaking of an old house, I may possibly have been deceived."

"Was your sister dressed?"

"No, she was in her nightdress. In her right hand was found the charred stump of a match, and in her left a match-box."

"Showing that she had struck a light and looked about her when the alarm took place. That is important. And what conclusions did the coroner come to?"

"He investigated the case with great care, for Dr. Roylott's conduct had long been notorious in the county, but he was unable to find any satisfactory cause of death. My evidence showed that the door had been fastened upon the inner side, and the windows were blocked by old-fashioned shutters with broad iron bars, which were secured every night. The walls were carefully sounded, and were shown to be quite solid all round, and the flooring was also thoroughly examined, with the same result. The chimney is wide, but is barred up by four large staples. It is certain, therefore, that my sister was quite alone when she met her end. Besides, there were no marks of any violence upon her."

"How about poison?"

"The doctors examined her for it, but without success."

"What do you think that this unfortunate lady died of, then?"

"It is my belief that she died of pure fear and nervous shock, though what it was which frightened her I cannot imagine."

"Were there gipsies in the plantation at the time?"

"Yes, there are nearly always some there."

"Ah, and what did you gather from this allusion to a band—a speckled band?"

"Sometimes I have thought that it was merely the wild talk of delirium, sometimes that it may have referred to some band of people, perhaps to these very gipsies in the plantation. I do not know whether the spotted handkerchiefs which so many of them wear over their heads might have suggested the strange adjective which she used."

Holmes shook his head like a man who is far from being satisfied. "These are very deep waters," said he; "pray go on with your narrative."

"Two years have passed since then, and my life has been until lately lonelier than ever. A month ago, however, a dear friend, whom I have known for many years, has done me the honour to ask my hand in marriage. His name is Armitage—Percy Armitage—the second son of Mr. Armitage, of Crane Water, near Reading. My stepfather has offered no opposition to the match, and we are to be married in the course of the spring. Two days ago some repairs were started in the west wing of the building, and my bedroom wall has been pierced, so that I have had to move into the chamber in which my sister died, and to sleep in the very bed in which she slept. Imagine, then, my thrill of terror when last night, as I lay awake, thinking over her terrible fate, I suddenly heard in the silence of the night the low whistle which had been the herald of her own death. I sprang up and lit the lamp, but nothing was to be seen in the room. I was too shaken to go to bed again, however, so I dressed, and as soon as it was daylight I slipped down, got a dog-cart at the Crown Inn, which is opposite, and drove to Leatherhead, from whence I have come on this morning, with the one object of seeing you and asking your advice."

"You have done wisely," said my friend. "But have you told me all?"

"Yes, all."

"Miss Roylott, you have not. You are screening your stepfather."

"Why, what do you mean?"

For answer Holmes pushed back the frill of black lace which fringed the hand that lay upon our visitor's knee. Five little livid spots, the marks of four fingers and a thumb, were printed upon the white wrist.

"You have been cruelly used," said Holmes.

The lady coloured deeply, and covered over her injured wrist. "He is a hard man," she said, "and perhaps he hardly knows his own strength."

There was a long silence, during which Holmes leaned his chin upon his hands and stared into the crackling fire.

"This is very deep business," he said at last. "There are a thousand details which I should desire to know before I decide upon our course of action. Yet we have not a moment to lose. If we were to come to Stoke Moran to-day, would it be possible for us to see over these rooms without the knowledge of your stepfather?"

"As it happens, he spoke of coming into town to-day upon some most important business. It is probable that he will be away all day, and that there would be nothing to disturb you. We have a housekeeper now, but she is old and foolish, and I could easily get her out of the way."

"Excellent. You are not averse to this trip, Watson?"

"By no means."

"Then we shall both come. What are you going to do yourself?"

"I have one or two things which I would wish to do now that I am in town. But I shall return by the twelve o'clock train, so as to be there in time for your coming."

"And you may expect us early in the afternoon. I have myself some small business matters to attend to. Will you not wait and breakfast?"

"No, I must go. My heart is lightened already since I have confided my trouble to you. I shall look forward to seeing you again this afternoon." She dropped her thick black veil over her face, and glided from the room.

"And what do you think of it all, Watson?" asked Sherlock Holmes, leaning back in his chair.

"It seems to me to be a most dark and sinister business."

"Dark enough and sinister enough."

"Yet if the lady is correct in saying that the flooring and walls are sound, and that the door, window and chimney are impassable, then her sister must have been undoubtedly alone when she met her mysterious end."

"What becomes, then, of these nocturnal whistles, and what of the very peculiar words of the dying woman?"

"I cannot think."

"When you combine the ideas of whistles at night, the presence of a band of gipsies who are on intimate terms with this old doctor, the fact that we have every reason to believe that the doctor has an interest in preventing his stepdaughter's marriage, the dying allusion to a band, and finally, the fact that Miss Helen Stoner heard a metallic clang, which might have been caused by one of those metal bars which secured the shutters falling back into its place, I think there is good ground to think that the mystery may be cleared along those lines."

"But what, then, did the gipsies do?"

"I cannot imagine."

"I see many objections to any such a theory."

"And so do I. It is precisely for that reason that we are going to Stoke Moran this day. I want to see whether the objections are fatal, or if they may be explained away. But what, in the name of the devil!"

The ejaculation had been drawn from my companion by the fact that our door had been suddenly dashed open, and that a huge man framed himself in the aperture. His costume was a peculiar mixture of the professional and of the agricultural, having a black top hat, a long frock-coat, and a pair of high gaiters, with a hunting-crop swinging in his hand. So tall was he that his hat actually brushed the cross-bar of the doorway, and his breadth seemed to span it across from side to side. A large face, seared with a thousand wrinkles, burned yellow with the sun and marked with every evil passion, was turned from one to the other of us, while his deep-set, bile-shot eyes, and the high, thin, fleshless nose gave him somewhat the resemblance to a fierce old bird of prey.

"Which of you is Holmes?" asked this apparition.

"My name, sir, but you have the advantage of me," said my companion quietly.

"I am Dr. Grimesby Roylott, of Stoke Moran."

"Indeed, Doctor," said Holmes blandly. "Pray take a seat."

"I will do nothing of the kind. My stepdaughter has been here. I have traced her. What has she been saying to you?"

"It is a little cold for the time of the year," said Holmes.

"What has she been saying to you?" screamed the old man furiously.

"But I have heard that the crocuses promise well," continued my companion imperturbably.

"Ha! You put me off, do you?" said our new visitor, taking a step forward, and shaking his hunting-crop. "I know you, you scoundrel! I have heard of you before. You are Holmes the meddler."

My friend smiled.

"Holmes the busybody!"

His smile broadened.

"Holmes the Scotland-Yard Jack-in-office."

Holmes chuckled heartily. "Your conversation is most entertaining," said he. "When you go out close the door, for there is a decided draught."

"I will go when I have had my say. Don't you dare to meddle with my affairs. I know that Miss Stoner has been here—I traced her! I am a dangerous man to fall foul of! See here." He stepped swiftly forward, seized the poker, and bent it into a curve with his huge brown hands.

"See that you keep yourself out of my grip," he snarled, and, hurling the twisted poker into the fireplace, he strode out of the room.

"He seems a very amiable person," said Holmes, laughing. "I am not quite so bulky, but if he had remained I might have shown him that my grip was not much more feeble than his own." As he spoke he picked up the steel poker, and with a sudden effort straightened it out again.

"Fancy his having the insolence to confound me with the official detective force! This incident gives zest to our investigation, however, and I only trust that our little friend will not suffer from her imprudence in allowing this brute to trace her. And now, Watson, we shall order breakfast, and afterwards I shall walk down to Doctors' Commons, where I hope to get some data which may help us in this matter."

It was nearly one o'clock when Sherlock Holmes returned from his excursion. He held in his hand a sheet of blue paper, scrawled over with notes and figures.

"I have seen the will of the deceased wife," said he. "To determine its exact meaning I have been obliged to work out the present prices of the investments with which it is concerned. The total income, which at the time of the wife's death was little short of £1,100 is now through the fall in agricultural prices not more than £750. Each daughter can claim an income of £250, in case of marriage. It is evident, therefore, that if both girls had married this beauty would have had a mere pittance, while even one of them would cripple him to a serious extent. My morning's work has not been wasted, since it has proved that he has the very strongest motives for standing in the way of anything of the sort. And now, Watson, this is too serious for dawdling, especially as the old man is aware that we are interesting ourselves in his affairs, so if you are ready we shall call a cab and drive to Waterloo. I should be very much obliged if you would slip your revolver into your pocket. An Eley's No. 2 is an excellent argument with gentlemen who can twist steel pokers into knots. That and a tooth-brush are, I think, all that we need."

At Waterloo we were fortunate in catching a train for Leatherhead, where we hired a trap at the station inn, and drove for four or five miles through the lovely Surrey lanes. It was a perfect day, with a bright sun, and a few fleecy clouds in the heavens. The trees and wayside hedges were just throwing out their first green shoots, and the air was full of the pleasant smell of the moist earth. To me at least there was a strange contrast between the sweet promise of the spring and this sinister quest upon which we were engaged. My companion sat in front of the trap, his arms folded, his hat pulled down over his eyes, and his chin sunk upon his breast, buried in the deepest thought. Suddenly, however, he started, tapped me on the shoulder, and pointed over the meadows.

"Look there!" said he.

A heavily-timbered park stretched up in a gentle slope, thickening into a grove at the highest point. From amidst the branches there jutted out the grey gables and high rooftree of a very old mansion.

"Stoke Moran?" said he.

"Yes, sir, that be the house of Dr. Grimesby Roylott," remarked the driver.

"There is some building going on there," said Holmes; "that is where we are going."

"There's the village," said the driver, pointing to a cluster of roofs some distance to the left; "but if you want to get to the house, you'll find it shorter to go over this stile, and so by the foot-path over the fields. There it is, where the lady is walking."

"And the lady, I fancy, is Miss Stoner," observed Holmes, shading his eyes. "Yes, I think we had better do as you suggest."

We got off, paid our fare, and the trap rattled back on its way to Leatherhead.

"I thought it as well," said Holmes, as we climbed the stile, "that this fellow should think we had come here as architects, or on some definite business. It may stop his gossip. Good afternoon, Miss Stoner. You see that we have been as good as our word."

Our client of the morning had hurried forward to meet us with a face which spoke her joy. "I have been waiting so eagerly for you," she cried, shaking hands with us warmly. "All has turned out splendidly. Dr. Roylott has gone to town, and it is unlikely that he will be back before evening."

"We have had the pleasure of making the Doctor's acquaintance," said Holmes, and in a few words he sketched out what had occurred. Miss Stoner turned white to the lips as she listened.

"Good heavens!" she cried, "he has followed me, then."

"So it appears."

"He is so cunning that I never know when I am safe from him. What will he say when he returns?"

"He must guard himself, for he may find that there is someone more cunning than himself upon his track. You must lock yourself from him to-night. If he is violent, we shall take you away to your aunt's at Harrow. Now, we must make the best use of our time, so kindly take us at once to the rooms which we are to examine."

The building was of grey, lichen-blotched stone, with a high central portion, and two curving wings, like the claws of a crab, thrown out on each side. In one of these wings the windows were broken, and blocked with wooden boards, while the roof was partly caved in, a picture of ruin. The central portion was in little better repair, but the right-hand block was comparatively modern, and the blinds in the windows, with

251

the blue smoke curling up from the chimneys, showed that this was where the family resided. Some scaffolding had been erected against the end wall, and the stonework had been broken into, but there were no signs of any workmen at the moment of our visit. Holmes walked slowly up and down the ill-trimmed lawn, and examined with deep attention the outsides of the windows.

"This, I take it, belongs to the room in which you used to sleep, the centre one to your sister's, and the one next to the main building to Dr. Roylott's chamber?"

"Exactly so. But I am now sleeping in the middle one."

"Pending the alterations, as I understand. By the way, there does not seem to be any very pressing need for repairs at that end wall."

"There were none. I believe that it was an excuse to move me from my room."

"Ah! that is suggestive. Now, on the other side of this narrow wing runs the corridor from which these three rooms open. There are windows in it, of course?"

"Yes, but very small ones. Too narrow for anyone to pass through."

"As you both locked your doors at night, your rooms were un-approachable from that side. Now, would you have the kindness to go into your room, and to bar your shutters."

Miss Stoner did so, and Holmes, after a careful examination through the open window, endeavoured in every way to force the shutter open, but without success. There was no slit through which a knife could be passed to raise the bar. Then with his lens he tested the hinges, but they were of solid iron, built firmly into the massive masonry. "Hum!" said he, scratching his chin in some perplexity, "my theory certainly presents some difficulty. No one could pass these shutters if they were bolted. Well, we shall see if the inside throws any light upon the matter."

A small side-door led into the whitewashed corridor from which the three bedrooms opened. Holmes refused to examine the third chamber, so we passed at once to the second, that in which Miss Stoner was now sleeping, and in which her sister had met her fate. It was a homely little room, with a low ceiling and a gaping fire-place, after the fashion of old country houses. A brown chest of drawers stood in one corner, a narrow white-counterpaned bed in another, and a dressing-table on the left-hand side of the window. These articles, with two small wickerwork chairs, made up all the furniture in the room, save for a square of Wilton carpet in the centre. The boards round and the panelling of the walls were brown, worm-eaten oak, so old and discoloured that it may have dated from the original building of the house. Holmes drew one of the chairs into a corner and sat silent, while his eyes travelled round and round and up and down, taking in every detail of the apartment.

"Where does that bell communicate with?" he asked at last, pointing to a thick bell-rope which hung down beside the bed, the tassel actually lying upon the pillow.

"It goes to the housekeeper's room."

"It looks newer than the other things?"

"Yes, it was only put there a couple of years ago."

"Your sister asked for it, I suppose?"

"No, I never heard of her using it. We used always to get what we wanted for ourselves."

"Indeed, it seemed unnecessary to put so nice a bell-pull there. You will excuse me for a few minutes while I satisfy myself as to this floor." He threw himself down upon his face with his lens in his hand, and crawled swiftly backwards and forwards, examining minutely the cracks between the boards. Then he did the same with the woodwork with which the chamber was panelled. Finally he walked over to the bed and spent some time in staring at it, and in running his eye up and down the wall. Finally he took the bell-rope in his hand and gave it a brisk tug.

"Why, it's a dummy," said he.

"Won't it ring?"

"No, it is not even attached to a wire. This is very interesting. You can see now that it is fastened to a hook just above where the little opening of the ventilator is."

"How very absurd! I never noticed that before."

"Very strange!" muttered Holmes, pulling at the rope. "There are one or two very singular points about this room. For example, what a fool a builder must be to open a ventilator in another room, when, with the same trouble, he might have communicated with the outside air!"

"That is also quite modern," said the lady.

"Done about the same time as the bell-rope," remarked Holmes.

"Yes, there were several little changes carried out about that time."

"They seem to have been of a most interesting character—dummy bell-ropes, and ventilators which do not ventilate. With your permission, Miss Stoner, we shall now carry our researches into the inner apartment."

Dr. Grimesby Roylott's chamber was larger than that of his step-daughter, but was as plainly furnished. A camp bed, a small wooden shelf full of books, mostly of a technical character, an arm-chair beside the bed, a plain wooden chair against the wall, a round table, and a large iron safe were the principal things which met the eye. Holmes walked slowly round and examined each and all of them with the keenest interest.

"What's in here?" he asked, tapping the safe.

"My stepfather's business papers."

"Oh! you have seen inside, then!"

"Only once, some years ago. I remember that it was full of papers."

"There isn't a cat in it, for example?"

"No. What a strange idea!"

"Well, look at this!" He took up a small saucer of milk which stood on the top of it.

"No; we don't keep a cat. But there is a cheetah and a baboon."

"Ah, yes, of course! Well, a cheetah is just a big cat, and yet a saucer of milk does not go very far in satisfying its wants, I dare say. There is one point which I should wish to determine." He squatted down in front of the wooden chair, and examined the seat of it with the greatest attention.

"Thank you. That is quite settled," said he, rising and putting his lens in his pocket. "Hullo! here is something interesting!"

The object which had caught his eye was a small dog lash hung on one corner of the bed. The lash, however, was curled upon itself, and tied so as to make a loop of whipcord.

"What do you make of that, Watson?"

"It's a common enough lash. But I don't know why it should be tied."

"That is not quite so common, is it? Ah, me! it's a wicked world, and when a clever man turns his brain to crime it is the worst of all. I think that I have seen enough now, Miss Stoner, and, with your permission, we shall walk out upon the lawn."

I had never seen my friend's face so grim, or his brow so dark, as it was when we turned from the scene of this investigation. We had walked several times up and down the lawn, neither Miss Stoner nor myself liking to break in upon his thoughts before he roused himself from his reverie.

"It is very essential, Miss Stoner," said he, "that you should absolutely follow my advice in every respect."

"I shall most certainly do so."

"The matter is too serious for any hesitation. Your life may depend upon your compliance."

"I assure you that I am in your hands."

"In the first place, both my friend and I must spend the night in your room."

Both Miss Stoner and I gazed at him in astonishment.

"Yes, it must be so. Let me explain. I believe that that is the village inn over there?"

"Yes, that is the 'Crown'."

"Very good. Your windows would be visible from there?"

"Certainly."

"You must confine yourself to your room, on pretence of a headache, when your stepfather comes back. Then when you hear him retire for the night, you must open the shutters of your window, undo the hasp, put your lamp there as a signal to us, and then withdraw with everything which you are likely to want into the room which you used to occupy. I have no doubt that, in spite of the repairs, you could manage there for one night."

"Oh, yes, easily."

"The rest you will leave in our hands."

"But what will you do?"

"We shall spend the night in your room, and we shall investigate the cause of this noise which has disturbed you."

"I believe, Mr. Holmes, that you have already made up your mind," said Miss Stoner, laying her hand upon my companion's sleeve.

"Perhaps I have."

"Then for pity's sake tell me what was the cause of my sister's death."

"I should prefer to have clearer proofs before I speak."

"You can at least tell me whether my own thought is correct, and if she died from some sudden fright."

"No, I do not think so. I think that there was probably some more tangible cause. And now, Miss Stoner, we must leave you, for if Dr. Roylott returned and saw us, our journey would be in vain. Good-bye, and be brave, for if you will do what I have told you, you may rest assured that we shall soon drive away the dangers that threaten you."

Sherlock Holmes and I had no difficulty in engaging a bedroom and sitting-room at the Crown Inn. They were on the upper floor, and from our window we could command a view of the avenue gate, and of the inhabited wing of Stoke Moran manor house. At dusk we saw Dr. Grimesby Roylott drive past, his huge form looming up beside the little figure of the lad who drove him. The boy had some little difficulty in undoing the heavy iron gates, and we heard the hoarse roar of the Doctor's voice, and saw the fury with which he shook his clenched fists at him. The trap drove on, and a few minutes later we saw a sudden light spring up among the trees as the lamp was lit in one of the sitting-rooms.

"Do you know, Watson," said Holmes, as we sat together in the gathering darkness, "I have really some scruples as to taking you to-night. There is a distinct element of danger."

"Can I be of assistance?"

"Your presence might be invaluable."

"Then I shall certainly come."

"It is very kind of you."

"You speak of danger. You have evidently seen more in these rooms than was visible to me."

"No, but I fancy that I may have deduced a little more. I imagine that you saw all that I did."

"I saw nothing remarkable save the bell-rope, and what purpose that could answer I confess is more than I can imagine."

"You saw the ventilator, too?"

"Yes, but I do not think that it is such a very unusual thing to have a small opening between two rooms. It was so small that a rat could hardly pass through."

"I knew that we should find a ventilator before ever we came to Stoke Moran."

"My dear Holmes!"

"Oh, yes, I did. You remember in her statement she said that her sister could smell Dr. Roylott's cigar. Now, of course, that suggests at once that there must be a communication between the two rooms. It could only be a small one, or it would have been remarked upon at the coroner's inquiry. I deduced a ventilator."

"But what harm can there be in that?"

"Well, there is at least a curious coincidence of dates. A ventilator is made, a cord is hung, and a lady who sleeps in the bed dies. Does not that strike you?"

"I cannot as yet see any connection."

"Did you observe anything very peculiar about that bed?"

"No."

"It was clamped to the floor. Did you ever see a bed fastened like that before?"

"I cannot say that I have."

"The lady could not move her bed. It must always be in the same relative position to the ventilator and to the rope—for so we may call it, since it was clearly never meant for a bell-pull."

"Holmes," I cried, "I seem to see dimly what you are hitting at. We are only just in time to prevent some subtle and horrible crime."

"Subtle enough and horrible enough. When a doctor does go wrong he is the first of criminals. He has nerve and he has knowledge. Palmer and Pritchard were among the heads of their profession. This man strikes even deeper, but I think, Watson, that we shall be able to strike deeper still. But we shall have horrors enough before the night is over: for goodness' sake let us have a quiet pipe, and turn our minds for a few hours to something more cheerful."

ABOUT NINE O'CLOCK the light among the trees was extinguished, and all was dark in the direction of the manor house. Two hours passed slowly away, and then suddenly, just at the stroke of eleven, a single bright light shone out right in front of us.

"That is our signal," said Holmes, springing to his feet; "it comes from the middle window."

As we passed out he exchanged a few words with the landlord, explaining that we were going on a late visit to an acquaintance, and that it was possible that we might spend the night there. A moment later we were out on the dark road, a chill wind blowing in our faces, and one yellow light twinkling in front of us through the gloom to guide us on our sombre errand.

There was little difficulty in entering the grounds, for unrepaired breaches gaped in the old park wall. Making our way among the trees, we reached the lawn, crossed it, and were about to enter through the window, when out from a clump of laurel bushes there darted what seemed to be a hideous and distorted child, who threw itself on the grass with writhing limbs, and then ran swiftly across the lawn into the darkness.

"My God!" I whispered, "did you see it?"

Holmes was for the moment as startled as I. His hand closed like a vice upon my wrist in his agitation. Then he broke into a low laugh, and put his lips to my ear.

"It is a nice household," he murmured, "that is the baboon."

I had forgotten the strange pets which the Doctor affected. There was a cheetah, too; perhaps we might find it upon our shoulders at any moment. I confess that I felt easier in my mind when, after following Holmes's example and slipping off my shoes, I found myself inside the bedroom. My companion noiselessly closed the shutters, moved the lamp on to the table, and cast his eyes round the room. All was as we had seen it in the day-time. Then, creeping up to me and making a trumpet of his hand, he whispered into my ear again so gently that it was all I could do to distinguish the words:

"The least sound would be fatal to our plans."

I nodded to show that I had heard.

"We must sit without a light. He would see it through the ventilator."

I nodded again.

"Do not go to sleep; your very life may depend upon it. Have your pistol ready in case we should need it. I will sit on the side of the bed, and you in that chair."

I took out my revolver and laid it on the corner of the table.

Holmes had brought up a long thin cane, and this he placed upon the bed beside him. By it he laid the box of matches and the stump of a candle. Then he turned down the lamp and we were left in darkness.

How shall I ever forget that dreadful vigil! I could not hear a sound, not even the drawing of a breath, and yet I knew that my companion sat open-eyed, within a few feet of me, in the same state of nervous tension in which I was myself. The shutters cut off the least ray of light, and we waited in absolute darkness. From outside came the occasional cry of a night-bird, and once at our very window a long drawn, cat-like whine, which told us that the cheetah was indeed at liberty. Far away we could hear the deep tones of the parish clock, which boomed out every quarter of an hour. How long they seemed, those quarters! Twelve o'clock, and one, and two, and three, and still we sat waiting silently for whatever might befall.

Suddenly there was the momentary gleam of a light up in the direction of the ventilator, which vanished immediately, but was succeeded by a strong smell of burning oil and heated metal. Some one in the next room had lit a dark lantern. I heard a gentle sound of movement, and then all was silent once more, though the smell grew stronger. For half an hour I sat with straining ears. Then suddenly another sound became audible —a very gentle, soothing sound, like that of a small jet of steam escaping continually from a kettle. The instant that we heard it, Holmes sprang from the bed, struck a match, and lashed furiously with his cane at the bell-pull.

"You see it, Watson?" he yelled. "You see it?"

But I saw nothing. At the moment when Holmes struck the light I heard a low, clear whistle, but the sudden glare flashing into my weary eyes made it impossible for me to tell what it was at which my friend lashed so savagely. I could, however, see that his face was deadly pale, and filled with horror and loathing.

He had ceased to strike, and was gazing up at the ventilator, when suddenly there broke from the silence of the night the most horrible cry to which I have ever listened. It swelled up louder and louder, a hoarse yell of pain and fear and anger all mingled in the one dreadful shriek. They say that away down in the village, and even in the distant parsonage, that cry raised the sleepers from their beds. It struck cold to our hearts, and I stood gazing at Holmes, and he at me, until the last echoes of it had died away into the silence from which it rose.

"What can it mean?" I gasped.

"It means that it is all over," Holmes answered. "And perhaps, after all, it is for the best. Take your pistol, and we shall enter Dr. Roylott's room."

With a grave face he lit the lamp, and led the way down the corridor. Twice he struck at the chamber door without any reply from within. Then he turned the handle and entered, I at his heels, with the cocked pistol in my hand.

It was a singular sight which met our eyes. On the table stood a dark lantern with the shutter half open, throwing a brilliant beam of light upon the iron safe, the door of which was ajar. Beside this table, on the wooden chair, sat Dr. Grimesby Roylott, clad in a long grey dressing-gown, his bare ankles protruding beneath, and his feet thrust into red heelless Turkish slippers. Across his lap lay the short stock with the long lash which we had noticed during the day. His chin was cocked upwards, and his eyes were fixed in a dreadful rigid stare at the corner of the ceiling. Round his brow he had a peculiar yellow band, with brownish speckles, which seemed to be bound tightly round his head. As we entered he made neither sound nor motion.

"The band! the speckled band!" whispered Holmes.

I took a step forward. In an instant his strange headgear began to move, and there reared itself from among his hair the squat diamond-shaped head and puffed neck of a loathsome serpent.

"It was a swamp adder!" cried Holmes—"the deadliest snake in India. He has died within ten seconds of being bitten. Violence does, in truth, recoil upon the violent, and the schemer falls into the pit which he digs for another. Let us thrust this creature back into its den, and we can then remove Miss Stoner to some place of shelter, and let the county police know what has happened."

As he spoke he drew the dog whip swiftly from the dead man's lap, and, throwing the noose round the reptile's neck, he drew it from its horrid perch, and, carrying it at arm's length, threw it into the iron safe, which he closed upon it.

SUCH ARE the true facts of the death of Dr. Grimesby Roylott, of Stoke Moran. It is not necessary that I should prolong a narrative which has already run to too great a length, by telling how we broke the sad news to the terrified girl, how we conveyed her by the morning train to the care of her good aunt at Harrow, of how the slow process of official inquiry came to the conclusion that the Doctor met his fate while indiscreetly playing with a dangerous pet. The little which I had yet to learn of the case was told me by Sherlock Holmes as we travelled back next day.

"I had," said he, "come to an entirely erroneous conclusion, which shows, my dear Watson, how dangerous it always is to reason from insufficient data. The presence of the gipsies, and the use of the word 'band', which was used by the poor girl, no doubt, to explain the appearance which she had caught a horrid glimpse of by the light of her match, were sufficient to put me upon an entirely wrong scent. I can only claim the merit that I instantly reconsidered my position when, however, it became clear to me that whatever danger threatened an occupant of the room could not come either from the window or the door. My attention was speedily drawn, as I have already remarked to you, to this ventilator, and to the bell-rope which hung down to the bed. The discovery that this was a dummy, and that the bed was clamped to the floor, instantly gave rise to the suspicion that the rope was there as a bridge for something passing through the hole, and coming to the bed. The idea of a snake instantly occurred to me, and when I coupled it with my knowledge that the Doctor was furnished with a supply of creatures from India, I felt that I was probably on the right track. The idea of using a form of poison which could not possibly be discovered by any chemical test was just such a one as would occur to a clever and ruthless man who had had an Eastern training. The rapidity with which such a poison would take effect would also, from his point of view, be an advantage. It would be a sharp-eyed coroner indeed who could distinguish the two little dark punctures which would show where the poison fangs had done their work. Then I thought of the whistle. Of course, he must recall the snake before the morning light revealed it to the victim. He had trained it, probably by the use of the milk which we saw, to return to him when summoned. He would put it through the ventilator at the hour that he thought best, with the certainty that it would crawl down the rope, and land on the bed. It might or might not bite the occupant, perhaps she might escape every night for a week, but sooner or later she must fall a victim.

"I had come to these conclusions before ever I had entered his room. An inspection of his chair showed me that he had been in the habit of standing on it, which, of course, would be necessary in order that he should reach the ventilator. The sight of the safe, the saucer of milk, and the loop of whipcord was enough to finally dispel any doubts which may have remained. The metallic clang heard by Miss Stoner was obviously caused by her father hastily closing the door of his safe upon its terrible occupant. Having once made up my mind, you know the steps which I took in order to put the matter to the proof. I heard the creature hiss, as I have no doubt that you did also, and I instantly lit the light and attacked it."

"With the result of driving it through the ventilator."

"And also with the result of causing it to turn upon its master at the other side. Some of the blows of my cane came home, and roused its snakish temper, so that it flew upon the first person it saw. In this way I am no doubt indirectly responsible for Dr. Grimesby Roylott's death, and I cannot say that it is likely to weigh very heavily upon my conscience."

MARGARET DRABBLE

b. 1939

The appearance of her first novels in the 1960s gained her
a sizeable audience among those who felt their own
dilemmas reflected in the immediacy of her writing.
Intellectually formidable she is also compassionate—except
towards the phoney, which she detests. Her short stories are
often tender, witty, precise.

The Gifts of War

Timeo Danaos et dona ferentes. Aeneid 11 1 49

WHEN SHE WOKE in the morning, she could tell at
once, as soon as she reached consciousness, that she
had some reason to feel pleased with herself, some rare
cause for satisfaction. She lay there quietly for a time,
enjoying the unfamiliar sensation, not bothering to
place it, grateful for its vague comfortable warmth. It
protected her from the disagreeable noise of her
husband's snores, from the thought of getting breakfast, from the coldness of the linoleum when she finally
dragged herself out of bed. She had to wake Kevin: he
always overslept these days, and he took so long to get dressed and get
his breakfast, she was surprised he wasn't always late for school. She
never thought of making him go to bed earlier; she hadn't the heart to
stop him watching the telly, and anyway she enjoyed his company, she
liked having him around in the evenings, laughing in his silly seven-
year-old way at jokes he didn't understand—jokes she didn't always
understand herself, and which she couldn't explain when he asked her
to. "You don't know *anything*, Mum," he would groan, but she didn't
mind his condemnations: she didn't expect to know anything, it amused
her to see him behaving like a man already, affecting superiority, harm-
lessly, helplessly, in an ignorance that was as yet so much greater than
her own—though she would have died rather than have allowed him to
suspect her amusement, her permissiveness. She grumbled at him
constantly, even while wanting to keep him there: she snapped at his
endless questions, she snubbed him, she repressed him, she provoked

261

him. And she did not suffer from doing this, because she knew that they could not hurt each other: he was a child, he wasn't a proper man yet, he couldn't inflict true pain, any more than she could truly repress him, and his teasing, obligatory conventional schoolboy complaints about her cooking and her stupidity seemed to exorcise, in a way, those other crueller onslaughts. It was as though she said to herself: if my little boy doesn't mean it when he shouts at me, perhaps my husband doesn't either: perhaps there's no more serious offence in my bruises and my greying hair than there is in those harmless childish moans. In the child, she found a way of accepting the man: she found a way of accepting, without too much submission, her lot.

She loved the child: she loved him with so much passion that a little of it spilled over generously onto the man who had misused her: in forgiving the child his dirty blazer and shirts and his dinner-covered tie, she forgave the man for his Friday nights and the childish vomit on the stairs and the bedroom floor. It never occurred to her that a grown man might resent more than hatred such second-hand forgiveness. She never thought of the man's emotions: she thought of her own, and her feelings for the child redeemed her from bitterness, and shed some light on the dark industrial terraces and the waste lands of the city's rubble. Her single-minded commitment was a wonder of the neighbourhood: she's a sour piece, the neighbours said, she keeps herself to herself a bit too much, but you've got to hand it to her, she's been a wonderful mother to that boy, she's had a hard life, but she's been a wonderful mother to that boy. And she, tightening her woolly headscarf over her aching ears as she walked down the cold steep windy street to join the queue at the post office or the butcher's, would stiffen proudly, her hard lips secretly smiling as she claimed and accepted and nodded to her role, her place, her social dignity.

This morning, as she woke Kevin, he reminded her instantly of her cause for satisfaction, bringing to the surface the pleasant knowledge that had underlain her wakening. "Hi, Mum," he said, as he opened his eyes to her, "how old am I today?"

"Seven, of course," she said, staring dourly at him, pretending to conceal her instant knowledge of the question's meaning, assuming scorn and dismissal. "Come on, get up, child, you're going to be late as usual."

"And how old am I tomorrow, Mum?" he asked, watching her like a hawk, waiting for that delayed, inevitable break.

"Come on, come on," she said crossly, affecting impatience, stripping the blankets off him, watching him writhe in the cold air, small and bony in his striped pyjamas.

"Oh, go on, Mum," he said.

"What d'you mean, 'go on'," she said, "don't be so cheeky, come on, get a move on, you'll get no breakfast if you don't get a move on."

"Just think, Mum," he said, "how old am I tomorrow?"

"I don't know what you're talking about," she said, ripping his pyjama jacket off him, wondering how long to give the game, secure in her sense of her own timing.

"Yes you do, yes you do," he yelled, his nerve beginning, very slightly, to falter. "You know what day it is tomorrow."

"Why, my goodness me," she said, judging that the moment had come, "I'd quite forgotten. Eight tomorrow. My goodness me."

And she watched him grin and wriggle, too big now for embraces, his affection clumsy and knobbly: she avoided the touch of him these days, pushing him irritably away when he leant on her chair-arm, twitching when he banged into her in the corridor or the kitchen, pulling her skirt or overall away from him when he tugged at it for attention, regretting sometimes the soft and round docile baby that he had once been, and yet proud at the same time of his gawky growing, happier, more familiar with the hostilities between them (a better cover for love) than she had been with the tender wide smiles of adoring infancy.

"What you got me for my birthday?" he asked, as he struggled out of his pyjama trousers: and she turned at the door and looked back at him, and said,

"What d'you mean, what've I got you? I've not got you anything. Only good boys get presents."

"I *am* good," he said: "I've been ever so good all week."

"Not that I noticed, you weren't," she said, knowing that too prompt an acquiescence would ruin the dangerous pleasure of doubtful anticipation.

"Go on, tell me," he said, and she could tell from his whining plea that he was almost sure that she had got what he wanted, almost sure but not quite sure, that he was, in fact, in the grip of an exactly manipulated degree of uncertainty, a torment of hope that would last him for a whole twenty-four hours, until the next birthday morning.

"I'm telling you," she said, her hand on the door, staring at him sternly, "I'm telling you, I've not got you anything." And then, magically, delightfully, she allowed herself and him that lovely moment of grace: "I've not got you anything — *yet*," she said: portentous, conspiratorial, yet very very faintly threatening.

"You're going to get it today," he shrieked, unable to restrain himself, unable to keep the rules: and as though annoyed by his exuberance she marched smartly out of the small back room, and down the narrow stairs to the kitchen, shouting at him in an excessive parade of rigour, "Come on, get moving, get your things on, you'll be late for school, you're always late—": and she stood over him while he ate his flakes, watching each spoonful disappear, heaving a great sigh of resigned fury when he spilled on the oilcloth, catching his guilty glance as he wiped it with his sleeve, not letting him off, unwilling, unable to relax into a suspect tenderness.

He went out the back way to school: she saw him through the yard and stood in the doorway watching him disappear, as she always watched him, down the narrow alley separating the two rows of back-to-back cottages, along the ancient industrial cobbles, relics of another age: as he reached the Stephensons' door she called out to him, "Eight tomorrow, then," and smiled, and waved, and he smiled back, excited, affectionate, over the ten yards' gap, grinning, his grey knee socks pulled smartly up, his short cropped hair already standing earnestly on end, resisting the violent flattening of the brush with which she thumped him each morning: he reminded her of a bird, she didn't know why, she couldn't have said why, a bird, vulnerable, clumsy, tenacious, touching. Then Bill Stephenson emerged from his back door and joined him, and they went down the alley together, excluding her, leaving her behind, kicking at pebbles and fag packets with their scuffed much-polished shoes.

She went back through the yard and into the house, and made a pot of tea, and took it up to the man in bed. She dumped it down on the corner of the dressing-table beside him, her lips tight, as though she dared not loosen them: her face had only one expression, and she used it to conceal the two major emotions of her life, resentment and love. They were so violently opposed, these passions, that she could not move from one to the other: she lacked flexibility; so she inhabited a grim inexpressive no-man's-land between them, feeling in some way that she thus achieved a kind of justice.

"I'm going up town today," she said, as the man on the bed rolled over and stared at her.

He wheezed and stared.

"I'm going to get our Kevin his birthday present," she said, her voice cold and neutral, offering justice and no more.

"What'll I do about me dinner?" he said.

"I'll be back," she said. "And if I'm not, you can get your own. It won't kill you."

He mumbled and coughed, and she left the room. When she got downstairs, she began, at last, to enter upon the day's true enjoyment: slowly she took possession of it, this day that she had waited for, and which could not now be taken from her. She'd left herself a cup of tea on the table, but before she sat down to drink it she got her zip plastic purse from behind the clock on the dresser, and opened it, and got the money out. There it was, all of it: thirty shillings, three ten-bob notes, folded tightly up in a brown envelope: twenty-nine and eleven, she needed, and a penny over. Thirty shillings, saved, unspoken for, to spend. She'd wondered, from time to time, if she ought to use it to buy him something useful, but she knew now that she wasn't going to: she was going to get him what he wanted—a grotesque, unjustifiable luxury, a pointless gift. It never occurred to her that the pleasure she took in doing things for Kevin was anything other than selfish: she felt vaguely guilty about it, she would have started furtively, like a miser, had anyone knocked on the door and interrupted her contemplation, she would bitterly have denied the intensity of her anticipation.

And when she put her overcoat on, and tied on her headsquare, and set off down the road, she tried to appear to the neighbours as though she wasn't going anywhere in particular: she nodded calmly, she stopped to gape at Mrs. Phillips' new baby (all frilled up, poor mite, in ribbons and pink crochet, a dreadful sight poor little innocent like something off an iced cake, people should know better than to do such things to their own children); she even called in at the shop for a quarter of tea as a cover for her excursion, so reluctant was she to let anyone know that she was going into town, thus unusually, on a Wednesday morning. And as she walked down the steep hillside, where the abandoned tramlines still ran, to the next fare stage of the bus, she could not have said whether she was making the extra walk to save two pence, or whether she was, more deviously, concealing her destination until the last moment from both herself and the neighbourhood.

Because she hardly ever went into town these days. In the old days she had come this way quite often, going down the hill on the tram with her girl friends, with nothing better in mind than a bit of window-shopping and a bit of a laugh and a cup of tea: penniless then as now, but still hopeful, still endowed with the touching faith that if by some miracle she could buy a pair of nylons or a particular blue lace blouse or a new brand of lipstick, then deliverance would be granted to her in the form of money, marriage, romance, the visiting prince who would glimpse her in the crowd, glorified by that seductive blouse, and carry her off to a better world. She could remember so well how hopeful they had been: even Betty Jones, fat, monstrous, ludicrous Betty Jones had cherished such rosy illusions, had gazed with them in longing at garments many sizes too small and far too expensive, somehow convinced that if she could by chance or good fortune acquire one all her flesh would melt away and reveal the lovely girl within. Time had taught Betty Jones: she shuffled now in shoes cracked and splitting beneath her own weight. Time had taught them all. The visiting prince, whom need and desire had once truly transfigured in her eyes, now lay there at

265

home in bed, stubbly, disgusting, ill, malingering, unkind: she remembered the girl who had seen such other things in him with a contemptuous yet pitying wonder. What fools they all had been, to laugh, to giggle
and point and whisper, to spend their small wages to deck themselves
for such a sacrifice. When she saw the young girls today, of the age that
she had been then, still pointing and giggling with the same knowing
ignorance, she was filled with a bitterness so acute that her teeth set
against it, and the set lines of her face stiffened to resist and endure and
conceal it. Sometimes she was possessed by a rash desire to warn them,
to lean forward and tap on their shoulders, to see their astonished vacant
faces, topped with their mad over-perfumed mounds of sticky hair, turn
upon her in alarm and disbelief. What do you think you're playing at,
she would say to them, what do you think you're at? Where do you
think it leads you, what do you think you're asking for? And they would
blink at her, uncomprehending like condemned cattle, the sacrificial
virgins, not yet made restless by the smell of blood. I could tell you a
thing or two, she wanted to say, I could tell you enough to wipe those
silly grins off your faces: but she said nothing, and she could not have
said that it was envy or a true charitable pity that most possessed and
disturbed her when she saw such innocents.

What withheld her most from envy, pure and straight and voracious,
was a sense of her own salvation. Because, amazingly, she had been
saved, against all probability: her life, which had seemed after that
bridal day of white nylon net and roses to sink deeply and almost
instantly into a mire of penury and beer and butchery, had been so
redeemed for her by her child that she could afford to smile with a kind
of superior wisdom, a higher order of knowledge, at those who had not
known her trials and her comforts. They would never attain, the silly
teenagers, her own level of consolation; they would never know what it
was like to find in an object which had at first seemed painful, ugly,
bloody and binding, which had at first appeared to her as a yet more
lasting sentence, a deathblow to the panic notions of despair and flight
—to find in such a thing love, and identity, and human warmth. When
she thought of this—which she did, often, though not clearly, having
little else to think of—she felt as though she alone, or she one of the
elected few, had been permitted to glimpse something of the very nature
of the harsh, mysterious processes of human survival; and she could
induce in herself a state of recognition that was almost visionary. It was
all she had: and being isolated by pride from more neighbourly and
everyday and diminishing attempts at commiseration, she knew it. She
fed off it: her maternal role, her joy, her sorrow. She gazed out of the
bus window now, as the bus approached the town centre and the shops,
and as she thought of the gift she was going to buy him, her eyes lit on

266

the bombed sites, and the rubble and decay of decades, and the exposed walls where dirty fading wallpapers had flapped in the wind for years, and she saw where the willowherb grew, green and purple, fields of it amongst the brick, on such thin soil, on the dust of broken bricks and stones, growing so tall in tenacious aspiration out of such shallow infertile ground. It was significant: she knew, as she looked at it, that it was significant. She herself had grown out of this landscape, she had nourished herself and her child upon it. She knew what it meant.

FRANCES JANET ASHTON HALL also knew what it meant, for she too had been born and bred there; although, being younger, she had not lived there for so long, and, having been born into a different class of society, she knew that she was not sentenced to it for life, and was indeed upon the verge of escape, for the next autumn she was to embark upon a degree in economics at a southern University. Nevertheless, she knew what it meant. She was a post-war child, but it was not for nothing that she had witnessed since infancy the red and smoking skies of the steelworks (making arms for the Arabs, for the South Africans, for all those wicked countries)—it was not for nothing that she had seen the deep scars in the city's centre, not all disguised quite comfortably as car parks. In fact, she could even claim the distinction of having lost a relative in the air-raids: her great-aunt Susan, who had refused to allow herself to be evacuated to the Lake District, had perished from a stray bomb in the midst of a highly residential suburban area. Frances was not yet old enough to speculate upon the effect that this tale, oft-repeated, and with lurid details, had had upon the development of her sensibility; naturally she ascribed her ardent pacifism and her strong political convictions to her own innate radical virtue, and when she did look for ulterior motives for her faith she was far more likely to relate them to her recent passion for a new-found friend, one Michael Swaines, than to any childhood neurosis.

She admired Michael. She also liked him for reasons that had nothing to do with admiration, and being an intelligent and scrupulous girl she would spend fruitless, anxious and enjoyable hours trying to disentangle and isolate her various emotions, and to assess their respective values. Being very young, she set a high value on disinterest: standing now, for his sake, on a windy street corner in a conspicuous position outside the biggest department store in town, carrying a banner and wearing (no less) a sandwich-board, proclaiming the necessity for Peace in Vietnam, and calling for the banning of all armaments, nuclear or otherwise, she was carrying on a highly articulate dialogue with her own conscience, by means of which she was attempting to discover whether she was truly standing there for Michael's sake alone, or whether she would

267

have stood there anyway, for the sake of the cause itself. What, she asked herself, if she had been solicited to make a fool of herself in this way merely by that disagreeable Nicholas, son of the Head of the Adult Education Centre? Would she have been prepared to oblige? No, she certainly would not, she would have laughed the idea of sandwich-boards to scorn, and would have found all sorts of convincing arguments against the kind of public display that she was now engaged in. But, on the other hand, this did not exactly invalidate her actions, for she *did* believe, with Michael, that demonstrations were necessary and useful: it was just that her natural reluctance to expose herself would have conquered her, had not Michael himself set about persuading her. So she was doing the right thing but for the wrong reason, like that man in *Murder in the Cathedral*. And perhaps it was for a *very* wrong reason, because she could not deny that she even found a sort of corrupt pleasure in doing things she didn't like doing—accosting strangers, shaking collection-boxes, being stared at—when she knew that it was being appreciated by other people: a kind of yearning for disgrace and martyrdom. Like stripping in public. Though not, surely, *quite* the same, because stripping didn't do any good, whereas telling people about the dangers of total war was a useful occupation. So doing the right thing for the wrong reason could at least be said to be better than doing the wrong thing for the wrong reason, couldn't it? Though her parents, of course, said it was the wrong thing anyway, and that one shouldn't molest innocent shoppers: Oh Lord, she thought with sudden gloom, perhaps my *only* reason for doing this is to annoy my parents: and bravely, to distract herself from the dreadful suspicion, she stepped forward and asked a scraggy thin woman in an old red velvet coat what she thought of the American policy in Vietnam.

"What's that?" said the woman, crossly, annoyed at being stopped in mid-stride, and when Frances repeated her question she gazed at her as though she were an idiot and walked on without replying. Frances, who was becoming used to such responses, was not as hurt as she had been at the beginning of the morning: she was even beginning to think it was quite funny. She wondered if she might knock off for a bit and go and look for Michael: he had gone into the store, to try to persuade the manager of the Toy Department not to sell toy machine-guns and toy bombs and toy battleships. She thought she would go and join him; and when a horrid man in a cloth cap spat on the pavement very near her left shoe and muttered something about bloody students bugger off ruining the city for decent folk, she made her mind up. So she ditched her sandwich-board and rolled her banner up, and set off through the swing doors into the cosy warmth: although it was Easter the weather was bitterly cold, spring seemed to reach them two months later than anywhere else in England. It was a pity, she thought, that there weren't any more Easter marches: she would have liked marching, it would have been more sociable; but Michael believed in isolated pockets of resistance. Really, what he meant was, he didn't like things that he wasn't organizing himself. She didn't blame him for that, he was a marvellous organizer, it was amazing the amount of enthusiasm he'd got up in the Students' Union for what was after all rather a dud project: no, not dud, she hadn't meant that, what she meant was that it was no fun, and anyone with a lower sense of social responsibility than herself couldn't have been expected to find it very interesting. Very nice green stockings on the stocking counter, she wondered if she could afford a pair. This thing that Michael had about children and violence, it really was very odd: he had a brother who was writing a thesis on violence on the television and she supposed it must have affected him. She admired his faith. Although at the same time she couldn't help remembering a short story by Saki that she had read years ago, called 'The Toys of Peace', which had been about the impossibility of making children play with anything but soldiers, or something to that effect.

When she reached the toy department, she located Michael immediately, because she could hear his voice raised in altercation. In fact, as she approached, she could see that quite a scene was going on, and if Michael hadn't looked quite so impressive when he was making a scene she would have lost nerve and fled: but as it was she approached, discreetly, and hovered on the outskirts of the centre of activity. Michael was arguing with a man in a black suit, some kind of manager figure she guessed (though what managers were or did she had no idea) and a woman in an overall: the man, she could see, was beginning to lose his patience, and was saying things like: "Now look here, young man, we're not here to tell our customers what they ought to do, we're here to sell them what they want," and Michael was producing his usual arguments about responsibility and education and having to make a start somewhere and why not here and now; he'd already flashed around his leaflets on violence and delinquency, and was now offering his catalogue of harmless constructive wooden playthings.

"Look," he was saying, "look how much more attractive these wooden animals are, I'm sure you'd find they'd sell just as well, and they're far more durable"—whereat the woman in an overall sniffed and said since when had salesmen dressed themselves up as University students, if he wanted to sell them toys he ought to do it in the proper way; an interjection which Michael ignored, as he proceeded to pick up off the counter in front of him a peculiarly nasty piece of clockwork, a kind of car-cum-aeroplane thing with real bullets and knives in the wheels and hidden bomb-carriers and God knows what, she rather thought it was a model from some television puppet programme, it was called The Desperado Destruction Machine. "I mean to say, look at this horrible thing," Michael said to the manager, pressing a knob and nearly slicing off his own finger as an extra bit of machinery jumped out at him, "whatever do you think can happen to the minds of children who play with things like this?"

"That's a very nice model," said the manager, managing to sound personally grieved and hurt, "it's a very nice model, and you've no idea how popular it's been for the price. It's not a cheap foreign thing, that, you know, it's a really well-made toy. Look—" and he grabbed it back off Michael and pulled another lever, to display the ejector-seat mechanism. The driver figure was promptly ejected with such violence that he shot right across the room, and Michael, who was quite well brought up really, dashed off to retrieve it: and by the time he got back the situation had been increasingly complicated by the arrival of a real live customer who had turned up to buy that very object. Though if it really was as popular as the manager had said, perhaps that wasn't such a coincidence. Anyway, this customer seemed very set on purchasing one, and the overalled woman detached herself from Michael's scene and started to demonstrate one for her, trying to pretend as she did so that there was no scene in progress and that nothing had been going on at all: the manager too tried to hush Michael up by engaging him in conversation and backing him away from the counter and the transaction, but Michael wasn't so easy to silence: he continued to argue in a loud voice, and stood his ground. Frances wished that he would abandon this clearly pointless attempt, and all the more as he had by now noticed her presence, and she knew that at any moment he would appeal for her support. And finally the worst happened, as she had known it might: he turned to the woman who was trying to buy The Desperado Destruction Machine, and started to appeal to her, asking her if she wouldn't like to buy something less dangerous and destructive. The woman seemed confused at first, and when he asked her for whom she was buying it, she said that it was for her little boy's birthday, and she hadn't realized it was a dangerous toy, it was just something he'd set his heart on, he'd break his heart if he didn't get it, he'd seen it on the telly and he wanted one just like that: whereupon the manager, who had quite lost his grip, intervened and started to explain to her that there was nothing dangerous about the toy at all, on the contrary it was a well-made pure British product, with no lead paint or sharp edges, and that if Michael didn't shut up he'd call the police: whereupon Michael said that there was no law to stop customers discussing products in shops with one another, and he was himself a bona-fide customer, because look, he'd got a newly-purchased pair of socks in his pocket in a Will Baines bag. The woman continued to look confused, so Frances thought that she herself ought to intervene to support Michael, who had momentarily run out of aggression: and she said to the woman, in what she thought was a very friendly and reasonable tone, that nobody was trying to stop her buying her little boy a birthday present, they just wanted to point out that with all the violence in the world today anyway it was silly to add to it by encouraging children to play at killing and exterminating and things like that, and hadn't everyone seen enough bombing, particularly here (one of Michael's favourite points, this), and why didn't she buy her boy something constructive like Meccano or a farmyard set: and as she was saying all this she glanced from time to time at the woman's face, and there was something in it, she later acknowledged, that should have warned her. She stood there, the woman, her woollen headscarf so tight round her head that it seemed to clamp her jaws together into a violently imposed silence; her face unnaturally drawn, prematurely aged; her thickly-veined hands clutching a zip plastic purse and that stupid piece of clockwork machinery: and as she listened to Frances's voice droning quietly and soothingly and placatingly away her face began to gather a glimmering of expression, from some depths of reaction too obscure to guess at: and as Frances finally ran down to a polite and only very faintly hopeful enquiring standstill, she opened her mouth and spoke. She said only one word, and it was a word that Frances had never heard before, though she had seen it in print in a once-banned book; and by some flash of insight, crossing the immeasurable gap of quality that separated their two lives, she knew that the woman herself had never before allowed it to pass her lips, that to her too it was a shocking syllable, portentous, unforgettable, not a familiar word casually dropped into the dividing spaces. Then the woman, having spoken, started to cry: incredibly, horribly, she started to cry. She dropped the clockwork toy on to the floor, and it fell so heavily that she could almost have been said to have thrown it down, and she stood there, staring at it, as the tears rolled down her face. Then she looked at them, and walked off. Nobody followed her: they stood there and let her go. They did not know how to follow her, nor what appeasement to offer for her unknown wound. So they did nothing. But Frances knew that in their innocence they had done something dreadful to her, in the light of which those long-since ended air raids and even distant Vietnam itself were an irrelevance, a triviality: but she did not know what it was, she could not know. At their feet, the Destruction Machine buzzed and whirred its way to a broken immobility, achieving a mild sensation in its death-throes by shooting a large spring coil out of its complex guts; she and Michael, after lengthy apologies, had to pay for it before they were allowed to leave the store.

DAPHNE DU MAURIER

1907–1989

Born of talented lineage—she was the granddaughter of author George du Maurier and daughter of the actor Sir Gerald du Maurier— she enhanced the family reputation by writing such famous novels as *Rebecca* and *Jamaica Inn*. She lived for many years in her much-loved home at Menabilly in Cornwall, and the darker aspects of the Cornish countryside pervade many of her most successful stories.

The Birds

ON DECEMBER THE THIRD the wind changed overnight and it was winter. Until then the autumn had been mellow, soft. The leaves had lingered on the trees, golden red, and the hedgerows were still green. The earth was rich where the plough had turned it.

Nat Hocken, because of a war-time disability, had a pension and did not work full-time at the farm. He worked three days a week, and they gave him the lighter jobs: hedging, thatching, repairs to the farm buildings.

Although he was married, with children, his was a solitary disposition; he liked best to work alone. It pleased him when he was given a bank to build up, or a gate to mend at the far end of the peninsula, where the sea surrounded the farm land on either side. Then, at midday, he would pause and eat the pasty that his wife had baked for him, and sitting on the cliff's edge would watch the birds. Autumn was best for this, better than spring. In spring the birds flew inland, purposeful, intent; they knew where they were bound, the rhythm and ritual of their life brooked no delay. In autumn those that had not migrated overseas but remained to pass the winter were caught up in the same driving urge, but because migration was denied them followed a pattern of their own. Great flocks of them came to the peninsula, restless, uneasy, spending themselves in motion; now wheeling, circling in the sky, now settling to feed on the rich new-turned soil, but even when they fed it was as though they did so without hunger, without desire. Restlessness drove them to the skies again.

Black and white, jackdaw and gull, mingled in strange partnership, seeking some sort of liberation, never satisfied, never still. Flocks of starlings, rustling like silk, flew to fresh pasture, driven by the same necessity of movement, and the smaller birds, the finches and the larks, scattered from tree to hedge as if compelled.

Nat watched them, and he watched the sea-birds too. Down in the bay they waited for the tide. They had more patience. Oyster-catchers, redshank, sanderling, and curlew watched by the water's edge; as the slow sea sucked at the shore and then withdrew, leaving the strip of seaweed bare and the shingle churned, the sea-birds raced and ran upon the beaches. Then that same impulse to flight seized upon them too. Crying, whistling, calling, they skimmed the placid sea and left the shore. Make haste, make speed, hurry and begone; yet where, and to what purpose? The restless urge of autumn, unsatisfying, sad, had put a spell upon them and they must flock, and wheel, and cry; they must spill themselves of motion before winter came.

Perhaps, thought Nat, munching his pasty by the cliff's edge, a message comes to the birds in autumn, like a warning. Winter is coming. Many of them perish. And like people who, apprehensive of death before their time, drive themselves to work or folly, the birds do likewise.

The birds had been more restless than ever this fall of the year, the agitation more marked because the days were still. As the tractor traced its path up and down the western hills, the figure of the farmer silhouetted on the driving-seat, the whole machine and the man upon it would be lost momentarily in the great cloud of wheeling, crying birds. There were many more than usual, Nat was sure of this. Always, in autumn, they followed the plough, but not in great flocks like these, nor with such clamour.

Nat remarked upon it, when hedging was finished for the day. "Yes," said the farmer, "there are more birds about than usual; I've noticed it too. And daring, some of them, taking no notice of the tractor. One or two gulls came so close to my head this afternoon I thought they'd knock my cap off! As it was, I could scarcely see what I was doing, when they were overhead and I had the sun in my eyes. I have a notion the weather will change. It will be a hard winter. That's why the birds are restless."

Nat, tramping home across the fields and down the lane to his cottage, saw the birds still flocking over the western hills, in the last glow of the sun. No wind, and the grey sea calm and full. Campion in bloom yet in the hedges, and the air mild. The farmer was right, though, and it was that night the weather turned. Nat's bedroom faced east. He woke just after two and heard the wind in the chimney. Not the storm and bluster of a sou'westerly gale, bringing the rain, but east wind, cold and dry. It sounded hollow in the chimney, and a loose slate rattled on the roof. Nat listened, and he could hear the sea roaring in the bay. Even the air in the small bedroom had turned chill: a draught came under the skirting of the door, blowing upon the bed. Nat drew the blanket round him, leant closer to the back of his sleeping wife, and stayed wakeful, watchful, aware of misgiving without cause.

Then he heard the tapping on the window. There was no creeper on the cottage walls to break loose and scratch upon the pane. He listened, and the tapping continued until, irritated by the sound, Nat got out of bed and went to the window. He opened it, and as he did so something brushed his hand, jabbing at his knuckles, grazing the skin. Then he saw the flutter of the wings and it was gone, over the roof, behind the cottage. It was a bird, what kind of bird he could not tell. The wind must have driven it to shelter on the sill.

He shut the window and went back to bed, but feeling his knuckles wet put his mouth to the scratch. The bird had drawn blood. Frightened, he supposed, and bewildered, the bird, seeking shelter, had stabbed at him in the darkness. Once more he settled himself to sleep.

Presently the tapping came again, this time more forceful, more insistent, and now his wife woke at the sound, and turning in the bed said to him, "See to the window, Nat, it's rattling."

"I've already seen to it," he told her, "there's some bird there, trying to get in. Can't you hear the wind? It's blowing from the east, driving the birds to shelter."

"Send them away," she said, "I can't sleep with that noise."

He went to the window for the second time, and now when he opened it there was not one bird upon the sill but half a dozen; they flew straight into his face, attacking him.

He shouted, striking out at them with his arms, scattering them; like the first one, they flew over the roof and disappeared. Quickly he let the window fall and latched it.

"Did you hear that?" he said. "They went for me. Tried to peck my eyes." He stood by the window, peering into the darkness, and could see nothing. His wife, heavy with sleep, murmured from the bed.

"I'm not making it up," he said, angry at her suggestion. "I tell you the birds were on the sill, trying to get into the room."

Suddenly a frightened cry came from the room across the passage where the children slept.

"It's Jill," said his wife, roused at the sound, sitting up in bed. "Go to her, see what's the matter."

Nat lit the candle, but when he opened the bedroom door to cross the passage the draught blew out the flame.

There came a second cry of terror, this time from both children, and stumbling into their room he felt the beating of wings about him in the darkness. The window was wide open. Through it came the birds, hitting first the ceiling and the walls, then swerving in mid-flight, turning to the children in their beds.

"It's all right, I'm here," shouted Nat, and the children flung themselves, screaming, upon him, while in the darkness the birds rose and dived and came for him again.

"What is it, Nat, what's happened?" his wife called from the further bedroom, and swiftly he pushed the children through the door to the passage and shut it upon them, so that he was alone now, in their bedroom, with the birds.

He seized a blanket from the nearest bed, and using it as a weapon flung it to right and left about him in the air. He felt the thud of bodies, heard the fluttering of wings, but they were not yet defeated, for again and again they returned to the assault, jabbing his hands, his head, the little stabbing beaks sharp as a pointed fork. The blanket became a weapon of defence; he wound it about his head, and then in greater darkness beat at the birds with his bare hands. He dared not stumble to the door and open it, lest in doing so the birds should follow him.

How long he fought with them in the darkness he could not tell, but at last the beating of the wings about him lessened and then withdrew, and through the density of the blanket he was aware of light. He waited, listened; there was no sound except the fretful crying of one of the children from the bedroom beyond. The fluttering, the whirring of the wings had ceased.

He took the blanket from his head and stared about him. The cold grey morning light exposed the room. Dawn, and the open window, had called the living birds; the dead lay on the floor. Nat gazed at the little corpses, shocked and horrified. They were all small birds, none of any size; there must have been fifty of them lying there upon the floor. There were robins, finches, sparrows, blue tits, larks and bramblings, birds that by nature's law kept to their own flock and their own territory, and now, joining one with another in their urge for battle, had destroyed themselves against the bedroom walls, or in the strife had been destroyed by him. Some had lost feathers in the fight, others had blood, his blood, upon their beaks.

Sickened, Nat went to the window and stared out across his patch of garden to the fields.

275

It was bitter cold, and the ground had all the hard black look of frost. Not white frost, to shine in the morning sun, but the black frost that the east wind brings. The sea, fiercer now with the turning tide, white-capped and steep, broke harshly in the bay. Of the birds there was no sign. Not a sparrow chattered in the hedge beyond the garden gate, no early missel-thrush or blackbird pecked on the grass for worms. There was no sound at all but the east wind and the sea.

Nat shut the window and the door of the small bedroom, and went back across the passage to his own. His wife sat up in bed, one child asleep beside her, the smaller in her arms, his face bandaged. The curtains were tightly drawn across the window, the candles lit. Her face looked garish in the yellow light. She shook her head for silence.

"He's sleeping now," she whispered, "but only just. Something must have cut him, there was blood at the corner of his eyes. Jill said it was the birds. She said she woke up, and the birds were in the room."

His wife looked up at Nat, searching his face for confirmation. She looked terrified, bewildered, and he did not want her to know that he was also shaken, dazed almost, by the events of the past few hours.

"There are birds in there," he said, "dead birds, nearly fifty of them. Robins, wrens, all the little birds from hereabouts. It's as though a madness seized them, with the east wind." He sat down on the bed beside his wife, and held her hand. "It's the weather," he said, "it must be that, it's the hard weather. They aren't the birds, maybe, from here around. They've been driven down, from up country."

"But Nat," whispered his wife, "it's only this night that the weather turned. There's been no snow to drive them. And they can't be hungry yet. There's food for them, out there, in the fields."

"It's the weather," repeated Nat. "I tell you, it's the weather."

His face too was drawn and tired, like hers. They stared at one another for a while without speaking.

"I'll go downstairs and make a cup of tea," he said.

The sight of the kitchen reassured him. The cups and saucers, neatly stacked upon the dresser, the table and chairs, his wife's roll of knitting on her basket chair, the children's toys in a corner cupboard.

He knelt down, raked out the old embers and relit the fire. The glowing sticks brought normality, the steaming kettle and the brown teapot comfort and security. He drank his tea, carried a cup up to his wife. Then he washed in the scullery, and, putting on his boots, opened the back door.

The sky was hard and leaden, and the brown hills that had gleamed in the sun the day before looked dark and bare. The east wind, like a razor, stripped the trees, and the leaves, crackling and dry, shivered and scattered with the wind's blast. Nat stubbed the earth with his boot.

It was frozen hard. He had never known a change so swift and sudden. Black winter had descended in a single night.

The children were awake now. Jill was chattering upstairs and young Johnny crying once again. Nat heard his wife's voice, soothing, comforting. Presently they came down. He had breakfast ready for them, and the routine of the day began.

"Did you drive away the birds?" asked Jill, restored to calm because of the kitchen fire, because of day, because of breakfast.

"Yes, they've all gone now," said Nat. "It was the east wind brought them in. They were frightened and lost, they wanted shelter."

"They tried to peck us," said Jill. "They went for Johnny's eyes."

"Fright made them do that," said Nat. "They didn't know where they were, in the dark bedroom."

"I hope they won't come again," said Jill. "Perhaps if we put bread for them outside the window they will eat that and fly away."

She finished her breakfast and then went for her coat and hood, her school books and her satchel. Nat said nothing, but his wife looked at him across the table. A silent message passed between them.

"I'll walk with her to the bus," he said, "I don't go to the farm today."

And while the child was washing in the scullery he said to his wife, "Keep all the windows closed, and the doors too. Just to be on the safe side. I'll go to the farm. Find out if they heard anything in the night." Then he walked with his small daughter up the lane. She seemed to have forgotten her experience of the night before. She danced ahead of him, chasing the leaves, her face whipped with the cold and rosy under the pixie hood.

"Is it going to snow, Dad?" she said. "It's cold enough."

He glanced up at the bleak sky, felt the wind tear at his shoulders.

"No," he said, "it's not going to snow. This is a black winter, not a white one."

All the while he searched the hedgerows for the birds, glanced over the top of them to the fields beyond, looked to the small wood above the farm where the rooks and jackdaws gathered. He saw none.

The other children waited by the bus-stop, muffled, hooded like Jill, the faces white and pinched with cold.

Jill ran to them, waving. "My Dad says it won't snow," she called, "it's going to be a black winter."

She said nothing of the birds. She began to push and struggle with another little girl. The bus came ambling up the hill. Nat saw her on to it, then turned and walked back towards the farm. It was not his day for work, but he wanted to satisfy himself that all was well. Jim, the cowman, was clattering in the yard.

"Boss around?" asked Nat.

"Gone to market," said Jim. "It's Tuesday, isn't it?"

He clumped off round the corner of a shed. He had no time for Nat. Nat was said to be superior. Read books, and the like. Nat had forgotten it was Tuesday. This showed how the events of the preceding night had shaken him. He went to the back door of the farm-house and heard Mrs. Trigg singing in the kitchen, the wireless making a background to her song.

"Are you there, missus?" called out Nat.

She came to the door, beaming, broad, a good-tempered woman.

"Hullo, Mr. Hocken," she said. "Can you tell me where this cold is coming from? Is it Russia? I've never seen such a change. And it's going on, the wireless says. Something to do with the Arctic circle."

"We didn't turn on the wireless this morning," said Nat. "Fact is, we had trouble in the night."

"Kiddies poorly?"

"No . . ." He hardly knew how to explain it. Now, in daylight, the battle of the birds would sound absurd.

He tried to tell Mrs. Trigg what had happened, but he could see from her eyes that she thought his story was the result of a nightmare.

"Sure they were real birds," she said, smiling, "with proper feathers and all? Not the funny-shaped kind, that the men see after closing hours on a Saturday night?"

"Mrs. Trigg," he said, "there are fifty dead birds, robins, wrens, and such, lying on the floor of the children's bedroom. They went for me; they tried to go for young Johnny's eyes."

Mrs. Trigg stared at him doubtfully.

"Well there, now," she answered, "I suppose the weather brought them. Once in the bedroom, they wouldn't know where they were to. Foreign birds maybe, from that Arctic circle."

"No," said Nat, "they were the birds you see about here every day."

"Funny thing," said Mrs. Trigg, "no explaining it, really. You ought to write up and ask the *Guardian*. They'd have some answer for it. Well, I must be getting on."

She nodded, smiled, and went back into the kitchen.

Nat, dissatisfied, turned to the farm-gate. Had it not been for those corpses on the bedroom floor, which he must now collect and bury somewhere, he would have considered the tale exaggeration too.

Jim was standing by the gate.

"Had any trouble with the birds?" asked Nat.

"Birds? What birds?"

"We got them up our place last night. Scores of them, came in the children's bedroom. Quite savage they were."

"Oh?" It took time for anything to penetrate Jim's head. "Never heard of birds acting savage," he said at length. "They get tame, like, sometimes. I've seen them come to the windows for crumbs."

"These birds last night weren't tame."

"No? Cold maybe. Hungry. You put out some crumbs."

Jim was no more interested than Mrs. Trigg had been. It was, Nat thought, like air-raids in the war. No one down this end of the country knew what the Plymouth folk had seen and suffered. You had to endure something yourself before it touched you. He walked back along the lane and crossed the stile to his cottage. He found his wife in the kitchen with young Johnny.

"See anyone?" she asked.

"Mrs. Trigg and Jim," he answered. "I don't think they believed me. Anyway, nothing wrong up there."

"You might take the birds away," she said. "I daren't go into the room to make the beds until you do. I'm scared."

"Nothing to scare you now," said Nat. "They're dead, aren't they?"

He went up with a sack and dropped the stiff bodies into it, one by one. Yes, there were fifty of them, all told. Just the ordinary common birds of the hedgerow, nothing as large even as a thrush. It must have been fright that made them act the way they did. Blue tits, wrens, it was incredible to think of the power of their small beaks, jabbing at his face and hands the night before. He took the sack out into the garden and was faced now with a fresh problem. The ground was too hard to dig. It was frozen solid, yet no snow had fallen, nothing had happened in the past hours but the coming of the east wind. It was unnatural, queer. The weather prophets must be right. The change was something connected with the Arctic circle.

The wind seemed to cut him to the bone as he stood there, uncertainly, holding the sack. He could see the white-capped seas breaking down under in the bay. He decided to take the birds to the shore and bury them. When he reached the beach below the headland he could scarcely stand, the force of the east wind was so strong. It hurt to draw breath, and his bare hands were blue. Never had he known such cold, not in all the bad winters he could remember. It was low tide. He crunched his way over the shingle to the softer sand and then, his back to the wind, ground a pit in the sand with his heel. He meant to drop the birds into it, but as he opened up the sack the force of the wind carried them, lifted them, as though in flight again, and they were blown away from him along the beach, tossed like feathers, spread and scattered, the bodies of the fifty frozen birds. There was something ugly in the sight. He did not like it. The dead birds were swept away from him by the wind.

"The tide will take them when it turns," he said to himself.

He looked out to sea and watched the crested breakers, combing green. They rose stiffly, curled, and broke again, and because it was ebb tide the roar was distant, more remote, lacking the sound and thunder of the flood.

Then he saw them. The gulls. Out there, riding the seas.

What he had thought at first to be the white caps of the waves were gulls. Hundreds, thousands, tens of thousands . . . They rose and fell in the trough of the seas, heads to the wind, like a mighty fleet at anchor, waiting on the tide. To eastward, and to the west, the gulls were there. They stretched as far as his eye could reach, in close formation, line upon line. Had the sea been still they would have covered the bay like a white cloud, head to head, body packed to body. Only the east wind, whipping the sea to breakers, hid them from the shore.

Nat turned, and leaving the beach climbed the steep path home. Someone should know of this. Someone should be told. Something was happening, because of the east wind and the weather, that he did not understand. He wondered if he should go to the call-box by the bus-stop and ring up the police. Yet what could they do? What could anyone do? Tens and thousands of gulls riding the sea there, in the bay, because of storm, because of hunger. The police would think him mad, or drunk, or take the statement from him with great calm. "Thank you. Yes, the matter has already been reported. The hard weather is driving the birds inland in great numbers." Nat looked about him. Still no sign of any other bird. Perhaps the cold had sent them all from up country? As he drew near to the cottage his wife came to meet him, at the door. She called to him, excited. "Nat," she said, "it's on the wireless. They've just read out a special news bulletin. I've written it down."

"What's on the wireless?" he said.

"About the birds," she said. "It's not only here, it's everywhere. In London, all over the country. Something has happened to the birds."

Together they went into the kitchen. He read the piece of paper lying on the table.

"Statement from the Home Office at eleven a.m. today. Reports from all over the country are coming in hourly about the vast quantity of birds flocking above towns, villages, and outlying districts, causing obstruction and damage and even attacking individuals. It is thought that the Arctic air stream, at present covering the British Isles, is causing birds to migrate south in immense numbers, and that intense hunger may drive these birds to attack human beings. Householders are warned to see to their windows, doors, and chimneys, and to take reasonable precautions for the safety of their children. A further statement will be issued later."

A kind of excitement seized Nat; he looked at his wife in triumph. "There you are," he said, "let's hope they'll hear that at the farm. Mrs. Trigg will know it wasn't any story. It's true. All over the country. I've been telling myself all morning there's something wrong. And just now, down on the beach, I looked out to sea and there are gulls, thousands of them, tens of thousands, you couldn't put a pin between their heads, and they're all out there, riding on the sea, waiting."

"What are they waiting for, Nat?" she asked.

He stared at her, then looked down again at the piece of paper.

"I don't know," he said slowly. "It says here the birds are hungry." He went over to the drawer where he kept his hammer and tools.

"What are you going to do, Nat?"

"See to the windows and the chimneys too, like they tell you."

"You think they would break in, with the windows shut? Those sparrows and robins and such? Why, how could they?"

He did not answer. He was not thinking of the robins and the sparrows. He was thinking of the gulls . . .

He went upstairs and worked there the rest of the morning, boarding the windows of the bedrooms, filling up the chimney bases. Good job it was his free day and he was not working at the farm. It reminded him of the old days, at the beginning of the war. He was not married then, and he had made all the blackout boards for his mother's house in Plymouth. Made the shelter too. Not that it had been of any use, when the moment came. He wondered if they would take these precautions up at the farm. He doubted it. Too easy-going, Harry Trigg and his missus. Maybe they'd laugh at the whole thing. Go off to a dance or a whist drive.

"Dinner's ready." She called him, from the kitchen.

"All right. Coming down."

He was pleased with his handiwork. The frames fitted nicely over the little panes and at the base of the chimneys.

When dinner was over and his wife was washing up, Nat switched on the one o'clock news. The same announcement was repeated, the one which she had taken down during the morning, but the news bulletin enlarged upon it. "The flocks of birds have caused dislocation in all areas," read the announcer, "and in London the sky was so dense at ten o'clock this morning that it seemed as if the city was covered by a vast black cloud.

"The birds settled on roof-tops, on window ledges and on chimneys. The species included blackbird, thrush, the common house-sparrow, and, as might be expected in the metropolis, a vast quantity of pigeons and starlings, and that frequenter of the London river, the black-headed gull. The sight has been so unusual that traffic came to a stand-still in many thoroughfares, work was abandoned in shops and offices, and the streets and pavements were crowded with people standing about to watch the birds."

Various incidents were recounted, the suspected reason of cold and hunger stated again, and warnings to householders repeated. The announcer's voice was smooth and suave. Nat had the impression that this man, in particular, treated the whole business as he would an elaborate joke. There would be others like him, hundreds of them, who did not know what it was to struggle in darkness with a flock of birds. There would be parties tonight in London, like the ones they gave on election nights. People standing about, shouting and laughing, getting drunk. "Come and watch the birds!"

Nat switched off the wireless. He got up and started work on the kitchen windows. His wife watched him, young Johnny at her heels.

"What, boards for down here too?" she said. "Why, I'll have to light up before three o'clock. I see no call for boards down here."

"Better be sure than sorry," answered Nat. "I'm not going to take any chances."

"What they ought to do," she said, "is to call the army out and shoot the birds. That would soon scare them off."

"Let them try," said Nat. "How'd they set about it?"

"They have the army to the docks," she answered, "when the dockers strike. The soldiers go down and unload the ships."

"Yes," said Nat, "and the population of London is eight million or more. Think of all the buildings, all the flats, and houses. Do you think they've enough soldiers to go round shooting birds from every roof?"

"I don't know. But something should be done. They ought to do something."

Nat thought to himself that 'they' were no doubt considering the problem at that very moment, but whatever 'they' decided to do in London and the big cities would not help the people here, three hundred miles away. Each householder must look after his own.

"How are we off for food?" he said.

"Now, Nat, whatever next?"

"Never mind. What have you got in the larder?"

"It's shopping day tomorrow, you know that. I don't keep uncooked food hanging about, it goes off. Butcher doesn't call till the day after. But I can bring back something when I go in tomorrow."

Nat did not want to scare her. He thought it possible that she might not go to town tomorrow. He looked in the larder for himself, and in the cupboard where she kept her tins. They would do, for a couple of days. Bread was low.

"What about the baker?"

"He comes tomorrow too."

He saw she had flour. If the baker did not call she had enough to bake one loaf.

"We'd be better off in the old days," he said, "when the women baked twice a week, and had pilchards salted, and there was food for a family to last a siege, if need be."

"I've tried the children with tinned fish, they don't like it," she said.

Nat went on hammering the boards across the kitchen windows. Candles. They were low in candles too. That must be another thing she meant to buy tomorrow. Well, it could not be helped. They must go early to bed tonight. That was, if . . .

He got up and went out of the back door and stood in the garden, looking down towards the sea. There had been no sun all day, and now, at barely three o'clock, a kind of darkness had already come, the sky sullen, heavy, colourless like salt. He could hear the vicious sea drumming on the rocks. He walked down the path, half-way to the beach. And then he stopped. He could see the tide had turned. The rock that had shown in mid-morning was now covered, but it was not the sea that held his eyes. The gulls had risen. They were circling, hundreds of them, thousands of them, lifting their wings against the wind. It was the gulls that made the darkening of the sky. And they were silent. They made not a sound. They just went on soaring and circling, rising, falling, trying their strength against the wind.

Nat turned. He ran up the path, back to the cottage.

"I'm going for Jill," he said. "I'll wait for her, at the bus-stop."

"What's the matter?" asked his wife. "You've gone quite white."

"Keep Johnny inside," he said. "Keep the door shut. Light up now, and draw the curtains."

"It's only just gone three," she said.

"Never mind. Do what I tell you."

He looked inside the toolshed, outside the back door. Nothing there of much use. A spade was too heavy, and a fork no good. He took the hoe. It was the only possible tool, and light enough to carry.

He started walking up the lane to the bus-stop, and now and again glanced back over his shoulder.

The gulls had risen higher now, their circles were broader, wider, they were spreading out in huge formation across the sky.

He hurried on; although he knew the bus would not come to the top of the hill before four o'clock he had to hurry. He passed no one on the way. He was glad of this. No time to stop and chatter.

At the top of the hill he waited. He was much too soon. There was half an hour still to go. The east wind came whipping across the fields from the higher ground. He stamped his feet and blew upon his hands. In the distance he could see the clay hills, white and clean, against the heavy pallor of the sky. Something black rose from behind them, like a smudge at first, then widening, becoming deeper, and the smudge became a cloud, and the cloud divided again into five other clouds, spreading north, east, south and west, and they were not clouds at all; they were birds. He watched them travel across the sky, and as one section passed overhead, within two or three hundred feet of him, he knew, from their speed, they were bound inland, up country, they had no business with the people here on the peninsula. They were rooks, crows, jackdaws, magpies, jays, all birds that usually preyed upon the smaller species; but this afternoon they were bound on some other mission.

"They've been given the towns," thought Nat, "they know what they have to do. We don't matter so much here. The gulls will serve for us. The others go to the towns."

He went to the call-box, stepped inside and lifted the receiver. The exchange would do. They would pass the message on.

"I'm speaking from Highway," he said, "by the bus-stop. I want to report large formations of birds travelling up country. The gulls are also forming in the bay."

"All right," answered the voice, laconic, weary.

"You'll be sure and pass this message on to the proper quarter?"

"Yes . . . yes . . ." Impatient now, fed-up. The buzzing note resumed.

"She's another," thought Nat, "she doesn't care. Maybe she's had to answer calls all day. She hopes to go to the pictures tonight. She'll squeeze some fellow's hand, and point up at the sky, and 'look at all them birds!' She doesn't care."

The bus came lumbering up the hill. Jill climbed out and three or four other children. The bus went on towards the town.

"What's the hoe for, Dad?"

They crowded around him, laughing, pointing.

"I just brought it along," he said. "Come on now, let's get home. It's cold, no hanging about. Here, you. I'll watch you across the fields, see how fast you can run." He was speaking to Jill's companions who came from different families, living in the council houses. A short cut would take them to the cottages.

"We want to play a bit in the lane," said one of them.

"No, you don't. You go off home, or I'll tell your mammy."

They whispered to one another, round-eyed, then scuttled off across the fields. Jill stared at her father, her mouth sullen.

284

"We always play in the lane," she said.

"Not tonight, you don't," he said: "Come on now, no dawdling."

He could see the gulls now, circling the fields, coming in towards the land. Still silent. Still no sound.

"Look, Dad, look over there, look at all the gulls."

"Yes. Hurry, now."

"Where are they flying to? Where are they going?"

"Up country, I dare say. Where it's warmer."

He seized her hand and dragged her after him along the lane.

"Don't go so fast. I can't keep up."

The gulls were copying the rooks and crows. They were spreading out in formation across the sky. They headed, in bands of thousands, to the four compass points.

"Dad, what is it? What are the gulls doing?"

They were not intent upon their flight, as the crows, as the jackdaws had been. They still circled overhead. Nor did they fly so high. It was as though they waited upon some signal. As though some decision had yet to be given. The order was not clear.

"Do you want me to carry you, Jill? Here, come pick-a-back."

This way he might put on speed; but he was wrong. Jill was heavy. She kept slipping. And she was crying too. His sense of urgency, of fear, had communicated itself to the child.

"I wish the gulls would go away. I don't like them. They're coming closer to the lane."

He put her down again. He started running, swinging Jill after him. As they went past the farm turning he saw the farmer backing his car out of the garage. Nat called to him.

"Can you give us a lift?" he said.

"What's that?"

Mr. Trigg turned in the driving seat and stared at them. Then a smile came to his cheerful, rubicund face.

"It looks as though we're in for some fun," he said. "Have you seen the gulls? Jim and I are going to take a crack at them. Everyone's gone bird crazy, talking of nothing else. I hear you were troubled in the night. Want a gun?"

Nat shook his head.

The small car was packed. There was just room for Jill, if she crouched on top of petrol tins on the back seat.

"I don't want a gun," said Nat, "but I'd be obliged if you'd run Jill home. She's scared of the birds."

He spoke briefly. He did not want to talk in front of Jill.

"O.K.," said the farmer, "I'll take her home. Why don't you stop behind and join the shooting match? We'll make the feathers fly."

Jill climbed in, and turning the car the driver sped up the lane. Nat followed after. Trigg must be crazy. What use was a gun against a sky of birds?

Now Nat was not responsible for Jill he had time to look about him. The birds were circling still, above the fields. Mostly herring gull, but the black-backed gull amongst them. Usually they kept apart. Now they were united. Some bond had brought them together. It was the black-backed gull that attacked the smaller birds, and even new-born lambs, so he'd heard. He'd never seen it done. He remembered this now, though, looking above him in the sky. They were coming in towards the farm. They were circling lower in the sky, and the black-backed gulls were to the front, the black-backed gulls were leading. The farm, then, was their target. They were making for the farm.

Nat increased his pace towards his own cottage. He saw the farmer's car turn and come back along the lane. It drew up beside him with a jerk.

"The kid has run inside," said the farmer. "Your wife was watching for her. Well, what do you make of it? They're saying in town the Russians have done it. The Russians have poisoned the birds."

"How could they do that?" asked Nat.

"Don't ask me. You know how stories get around. Will you join my shooting match?"

"No, I'll get along home. The wife will be worried else."

"My missus says if you could eat gull, there'd be some sense in it," said Trigg, "we'd have roast gull, baked gull, and pickle 'em into the bargain. You wait until I let off a few barrels into the brutes. That'll scare 'em."

"Have you boarded your windows?" asked Nat.

"No. Lot of nonsense. They like to scare you on the wireless. I've had more to do today than to go round boarding up my windows."

"I'd board them now, if I were you."

"Garn. You're windy. Like to come to our place to sleep?"

"No, thanks all the same."

"All right. See you in the morning. Give you a gull breakfast."

The farmer grinned and turned his car to the farm entrance.

Nat hurried on. Past the little wood, past the old barn, and then across the stile to the remaining field.

As he jumped the stile he heard the whirr of wings. A black-backed gull dived down at him from the sky, missed, swerved in flight, and rose to dive again. In a moment it was joined by others, six, seven, a dozen, black-backed and herring mixed. Nat dropped his hoe. The hoe was useless. Covering his head with his arms he ran towards the cottage. They kept coming at him from the air, silent save for the beating wings. The terrible, fluttering wings. He could feel the blood on his hands, his wrists, his neck. Each stab of a swooping beak tore his flesh. If only he could keep them from his eyes. Nothing else mattered. He must keep them from his eyes. They had not learnt yet how to cling to a shoulder, how to rip clothing, how to dive in mass upon the head, upon the body. But with each dive, with each attack, they became bolder. And they had no thought for themselves. When they dived low and missed, they crashed, bruised and broken, on the ground. As Nat ran he stumbled, kicking their spent bodies in front of him.

He found the door, he hammered upon it with his bleeding hands. Because of the boarded windows no light shone. Everything was dark.

"Let me in," he shouted, "it's Nat. Let me in."

He shouted loud to make himself heard above the whirr of the gulls' wings.

Then he saw the gannet, poised for the dive, above him in the sky. The gulls circled, retired, soared, one with another, against the wind. Only the gannet remained. One single gannet, above him in the sky. The wings folded suddenly to its body. It dropped, like a stone. Nat screamed, and the door opened. He stumbled across the threshold, and his wife threw her weight against the door.

They heard the thud of the gannet as it fell.

HIS WIFE dressed his wounds. They were not deep. The backs of his hands had suffered most, and his wrists. Had he not worn a cap they would have reached his head. As to the gannet . . . the gannet could have split his skull.

The children were crying, of course. They had seen the blood on their father's hands.

"It's all right now," he told them. "I'm not hurt. Just a few scratches. You play with Johnny, Jill. Mammy will wash these cuts."

He half shut the door to the scullery, so that they could not see. His wife was ashen. She began running water from the sink.

"I saw them overhead," she whispered. "They began collecting just as Jill ran in with Mr. Trigg. I shut the door fast, and it jammed. That's why I couldn't open it at once, when you came."

"Thank God they waited for me," he said. "Jill would have fallen at once. One bird alone would have done it."

Furtively, so as not to alarm the children, they whispered together, as she bandaged his hands and the back of his neck. "They're flying inland," he said, "thousands of them. Rooks, crows, all the bigger birds. I saw them from the bus-stop. They're making for the towns."

"But what can they do, Nat?"

"They'll attack. Go for everyone out in the streets. Then they'll try the windows, the chimneys."

287

"Why don't the authorities do something? Why don't they get the army, get machine-guns, anything?"

"There's been no time. Nobody's prepared. We'll hear what they have to say on the six o'clock news."

Nat went back into the kitchen, followed by his wife. Johnny was playing quietly on the floor. Only Jill looked anxious.

"I can hear the birds," she said. "Listen, Dad."

Nat listened. Muffled sounds came from the windows, from the door. Wings brushing the surface, sliding, scraping, seeking a way of entry. The sound of many bodies, pressed together, shuffling on the sills. Now and again came a thud, a crash, as some bird dived and fell. "Some of them will kill themselves that way," he thought, "but not enough. Never enough."

"All right," he said aloud, "I've got boards over the windows, Jill. The birds can't get in."

He went and examined all the windows. His work had been thorough. Every gap was closed. He would make extra certain, however. He found wedges, pieces of old tin, strips of wood and metal, and fastened them at the sides to reinforce the boards. His hammering helped to deafen the sound of the birds, the shuffling, the tapping, and more ominous— he did not want his wife or the children to hear it—the splinter of cracked glass.

"Turn on the wireless," he said, "let's have the wireless."

This would drown the sound also. He went upstairs to the bedrooms and reinforced the windows there. Now he could hear the birds on the roof, the scraping of claws, a sliding, jostling sound.

He decided they must sleep in the kitchen, keep up the fire, bring down the mattresses and lay them out on the floor. He was afraid of the bedroom chimneys. The boards he had placed at the chimney bases might give way. In the kitchen they would be safe, because of the fire. He would have to make a joke of it. Pretend to the children they were playing at camp. If the worst happened, and the birds forced an entry down the bedroom chimneys, it would be hours, days perhaps, before they could break down the doors. The birds would be imprisoned in the bedrooms. They could do no harm there. Crowded together, they would stifle and die.

He began to bring the mattresses downstairs. At sight of them his wife's eyes widened in apprehension. She thought the birds had already broken in upstairs.

"All right," he said cheerfully, "we'll all sleep together in the kitchen tonight. More cosy here by the fire. Then we shan't be worried by those silly old birds tapping at the windows."

He made the children help him rearrange the furniture, and he took the precaution of moving the dresser, with his wife's help, across the window. It fitted well. It was an added safeguard. The mattresses could now be lain, one beside the other, against the wall where the dresser had stood.

"We're safe enough now," he thought, "we're snug and tight, like an air-raid shelter. We can hold out. It's just the food that worries me. Food, and coal for the fire. We've enough for two or three days, not more. By that time . . ."

No use thinking ahead as far as that. And they'd be giving directions on the wireless. People would be told what to do. And now, in the midst of many problems, he realized that it was dance music only coming over the air. Not Children's Hour, as it should have been. He glanced at the dial. Yes, they were on the Home Service all right. Dance records. He switched to the Light programme. He knew the reason. The usual programmes had been abandoned. This only happened at exceptional times. Elections, and such. He tried to remember if it had happened in the war, during the heavy raids on London. But of course. The B.B.C. was not stationed in London during the war. The programmes were broadcast from other, temporary quarters. "We're better off here," he thought, "we're better off here in the kitchen, with the windows and the doors boarded, than they are up in the towns. Thank God we're not in the towns."

At six o'clock the records ceased. The time signal was given. No matter if it scared the children, he must hear the news. There was a pause after the pips. Then the announcer spoke. His voice was solemn, grave. Quite different from midday.

"This is London," he said. "A National Emergency was proclaimed at four o'clock this afternoon. Measures are being taken to safeguard the lives and property of the population, but it must be understood that these are not easy to effect immediately, owing to the unforeseen and unparalleled nature of the present crisis. Every householder must take precautions to his own building, and where several people live together, as in flats and apartments, they must unite to do the utmost they can to prevent entry. It is absolutely imperative that every individual stays indoors tonight, and that no one at all remains on the streets, or roads, or anywhere without doors. The birds, in vast numbers, are attacking anyone on sight, and have already begun an assault upon buildings; but these, with due care, should be impenetrable. The population is asked to remain calm, and not to panic. Owing to the exceptional nature of the emergency, there will be no further transmission from any broadcasting station until seven a.m. tomorrow."

They played the National Anthem. Nothing more happened. Nat switched off the set. He looked at his wife. She stared back at him.

289

"What's it mean?" said Jill: "What did the news say?"

"There won't be any more programmes tonight," said Nat. "There's been a breakdown at the B.B.C."

"Is it the birds?" asked Jill. "Have the birds done it?"

"No," said Nat, "it's just that everyone's very busy, and then of course they have to get rid of the birds, messing everything up, in the towns. Well, we can manage without the wireless for one evening."

"I wish we had a gramophone," said Jill, "that would be better than nothing."

She had her face turned to the dresser, backed against the windows. Try as they did to ignore it, they were all aware of the shuffling, the stabbing, the persistent beating and sweeping of wings.

"We'll have supper early," suggested Nat, "something for a treat. Ask Mammy. Toasted cheese, eh? Something we all like?"

He winked and nodded at his wife. He wanted the look of dread, of apprehension, to go from Jill's face.

He helped with the supper, whistling, singing, making as much clatter as he could, and it seemed to him that the shuffling and the tapping were not so intense as they had been at first. Presently he went up to the bedrooms and listened, and he no longer heard the jostling for place upon the roof.

"They've got reasoning powers," he thought, "they know it's hard to break in here. They'll try elsewhere. They won't waste their time with us."

Supper passed without incident, and then, when they were clearing away, they heard a new sound, droning, familiar, a sound they all knew and understood.

His wife looked up at him, her face alight. "It's planes," she said, "they're sending out planes after the birds. That's what I said they ought to do, all along. That will get them. Isn't that gun-fire? Can't you hear guns?"

It might be gun-fire, out at sea. Nat could not tell. Big naval guns might have an effect upon the gulls out at sea, but the gulls were inland now. The guns couldn't shell the shore, because of the population.

"It's good, isn't it," said his wife, "to hear the planes?"

And Jill, catching her enthusiasm, jumped up and down with Johnny. "The planes will get the birds. The planes will shoot them."

Just then they heard a crash about two miles distant, followed by a second, then a third. The droning became more distant, passed away out to sea.

"What was that?" asked his wife. "Were they dropping bombs on the birds?"

"I don't know," answered Nat, "I don't think so."

He did not want to tell her that the sound they had heard was the crashing of aircraft. It was, he had no doubt, a venture on the part of the authorities to send out reconnaissance forces, but they might have known the venture was suicidal. What could aircraft do against birds that flung themselves to death against propeller and fuselage, but hurtle to the ground themselves? This was being tried now, he supposed, over the whole country. And at a cost. Someone high up had lost his head.

"Where have the planes gone, Dad?" asked Jill.

"Back to base," he said. "Come on, now, time to tuck down for bed."

It kept his wife occupied, undressing the children before the fire, seeing to the bedding, one thing and another, while he went round the cottage again, making sure that nothing had worked loose. There was no further drone of aircraft, and the naval guns had ceased. "Waste of life and effort," Nat said to himself. "We can't destroy enough of them that way. Cost too heavy. There's always gas. Maybe they'll try spraying with gas, mustard gas. We'll be warned first, of course, if they do. There's one thing, the best brains of the country will be on to it tonight."

Somehow the thought reassured him. He had a picture of scientists, naturalists, technicians, and all those chaps they called the back-room boys, summoned to a council; they'd be working on the problem now. This was not a job for the government, for the chiefs-of-staff—they would merely carry out the orders of the scientists.

"They'll have to be ruthless," he thought. "Where the trouble's worst they'll have to risk more lives, if they use gas. All the livestock, too, and the soil—all contaminated. As long as everyone doesn't panic. That's the trouble. People panicking, losing their heads. The B.B.C. was right to warn us of that."

Upstairs in the bedrooms all was quiet. No further scraping and stabbing at the windows. A lull in battle. Forces regrouping. Wasn't that what they called it, in the old war-time bulletins? The wind hadn't dropped, though. He could still hear it, roaring in the chimneys. And the sea breaking down on the shore. Then he remembered the tide. The tide would be on the turn. Maybe the lull in battle was because of the tide. There was some law the birds obeyed, and it was all to do with the east wind and the tide.

He glanced at his watch. Nearly eight o'clock. It must have gone high water an hour ago. That explained the lull: the birds attacked with the flood tide. It might not work that way inland, up country, but it seemed as if it was so this way on the coast. He reckoned the time limit in his head. They had six hours to go, without attack. When the tide turned again, around one-twenty in the morning, the birds would come back . . .

There were two things he could do. The first to rest, with his wife and the children, and all of them snatch what sleep they could, until the small hours. The second to go out, see how they were faring at the farm, see if the telephone was still working there, so that they might get news from the exchange.

He called softly to his wife, who had just settled the children. She came half-way up the stairs and he whispered to her.

"You're not to go," she said at once, "you're not to go and leave me alone with the children. I can't stand it."

Her voice rose hysterically. He hushed her, calmed her.

"All right," he said, "all right. I'll wait till morning. And we'll get the wireless bulletin then too, at seven. But in the morning, when the tide ebbs again, I'll try for the farm, and they may let us have bread and potatoes, and milk too."

His mind was busy again, planning against emergency. They would not have milked, of course, this evening. The cows would be standing by the gate, waiting in the yard, with the household inside, battened behind boards, as they were here at the cottage. That is, if they had time to take precautions. He thought of the farmer, Trigg, smiling at him from the car. There would have been no shooting party, not tonight.

The children were asleep. His wife, still clothed, was sitting on her mattress. She watched him, her eyes nervous.

"What are you going to do?" she whispered.

He shook his head for silence. Softly, stealthily, he opened the back door and looked outside.

It was pitch dark. The wind was blowing harder than ever, coming in steady gusts, icy, from the sea. He kicked at the step outside the door. It was heaped with birds. There were dead birds everywhere. Under the windows, against the walls. These were the suicides, the divers, the ones with broken necks. Wherever he looked he saw dead birds. No trace of the living. The living had flown seaward with the turn of the tide. The gulls would be riding the seas now, as they had done in the forenoon.

In the far distance, on the hill where the tractor had been two days before, something was burning. One of the aircraft that had crashed; the fire, fanned by the wind, had set light to a stack.

He looked at the bodies of the birds, and he had a notion that if he heaped them, one upon the other, on the window sills they would make added protection for the next attack. Not much, perhaps, but something. The bodies would have to be clawed at, pecked, and dragged aside, before the living birds gained purchase on the sills and attacked the panes. He set to work in the darkness. It was queer; he hated touching them. The bodies were still warm and bloody. The blood matted their feathers. He felt his stomach turn, but he went on with his work. He noticed, grimly, that every window-pane was shattered. Only the boards had kept the birds from breaking in. He stuffed the cracked panes with the bleeding bodies of the birds.

When he had finished he went back into the cottage. He barricaded the kitchen door, made it doubly secure. He took off his bandages, sticky with the birds' blood, not with his own cuts, and put on fresh plaster.

His wife had made him cocoa and he drank it thirstily. He was very tired.

"All right," he said, smiling, "don't worry. We'll get through."

He lay down on his mattress and closed his eyes. He slept at once. He dreamt uneasily, because through his dreams there ran a thread of something forgotten. Some piece of work, neglected, that he should have done. Some precaution that he had known well but had not taken, and he could not put a name to it in his dreams. It was connected in some way with the burning aircraft and the stack upon the hill. He went on sleeping, though; he did not awake. It was his wife shaking his shoulder that awoke him finally.

"They've begun," she sobbed, "they've started this last hour, I can't listen to it any longer, alone. There's something smelling bad too, something burning."

Then he remembered. He had forgotten to make up the fire. It was smouldering, nearly out. He got up swiftly and lit the lamp. The hammering had started at the windows and the doors, but it was not that he minded now. It was the smell of singed feathers. The smell filled the kitchen. He knew at once what it was. The birds were coming down the chimney, squeezing their way down to the kitchen range.

He got sticks and paper and put them on the embers, then reached for the can of paraffin.

"Stand back," he shouted to his wife, "we've got to risk this."

He threw the paraffin on to the fire. The flame roared up the pipe, and down upon the fire fell the scorched, blackened bodies of the birds.

The children woke, crying. "What is it?" said Jill. "What's happened?"

Nat had no time to answer. He was raking the bodies from the chimney, clawing them out on to the floor. The flames still roared, and the danger of the chimney catching fire was one he had to take. The flames would send away the living birds from the chimney top. The lower joint was the difficulty, though. This was choked with the smouldering helpless bodies of the birds caught by fire. He scarcely heeded the attack on the windows and the door; let them beat their wings, break their beaks, lose their lives, in the attempt to force an entry into his home. They would not break in. He thanked God he had one of the old cottages, with small windows, stout walls. Not like the new council houses. Heaven help them up the lane, in the new council houses.

"Stop crying," he called to the children. "There's nothing to be afraid of, stop crying."

He went on raking at the burning, smouldering bodies as they fell into the fire.

"This'll fetch them," he said to himself, "the draught and the flames together. We're all right, as long as the chimney doesn't catch. I ought to be shot for this. It's my fault. Last thing I should have made up the fire. I knew there was something."

Amid the scratching and tearing at the window boards came the sudden homely striking of the kitchen clock. Three a.m. A little more than four hours yet to go. He could not be sure of the exact time of high water. He reckoned it would not turn much before half past seven, twenty to eight.

"Light up the primus," he said to his wife. "Make us some tea, and the kids some cocoa. No use sitting around doing nothing."

That was the line. Keep her busy, and the children too. Move about, eat, drink; always best to be on the go.

He waited by the range. The flames were dying. But no more blackened bodies fell from the chimney. He thrust his poker up as far as it could go and found nothing. It was clear. The chimney was clear. He wiped the sweat from his forehead.

"Come on now, Jill," he said, "bring me some more sticks. We'll have a good fire going directly." She wouldn't come near him, though. She was staring at the heaped singed bodies of the birds.

"Never mind them," he said, "we'll put those in the passage when I've got the fire steady."

The danger of the chimney was over. It could not happen again, not if the fire was kept burning day and night.

"I'll have to get more fuel from the farm tomorrow," he thought. "This will never last. I'll manage, though. I can do all that with the ebb tide. It can be worked, fetching what we need, when the tide's turned. We've just got to adapt ourselves, that's all."

They drank tea and cocoa and ate slices of bread and Bovril. Only half a loaf left, Nat noticed. Never mind though, they'd get by.

"Stop it," said young Johnny, pointing to the windows with his spoon, "stop it, you old birds."

"That's right," said Nat, smiling, "we don't want the old beggars, do we? Had enough of 'em."

They began to cheer when they heard the thud of the suicide birds.

"There's another, Dad," cried Jill, "he's done for."

"He's had it," said Nat, "there he goes, the blighter."

This was the way to face up to it. This was the spirit. If they could keep this up, hang on like this until seven, when the first news bulletin came through, they would not have done too badly.

"Give us a fag," he said to his wife. "A bit of a smoke will clear away the smell of the scorched feathers."

"There's only two left in the packet," she said. "I was going to buy you some from the Co-op."

"I'll have one," he said, "t'other will keep for a rainy day."

No sense trying to make the children rest. There was no rest to be got while the tapping and the scratching went on at the windows. He sat with one arm round his wife and the other round Jill, with Johnny on his mother's lap and the blankets heaped about them on the mattress.

"You can't help admiring the beggars," he said, "they've got persistence. You'd think they'd tire of the game, but not a bit of it."

Admiration was hard to sustain. The tapping went on and on and a new rasping note struck Nat's ear, as though a sharper beak than any hitherto had come to take over from its fellows. He tried to remember the names of birds, he tried to think which species would go for this particular job. It was not the tap of the woodpecker. That would be light and frequent. This was more serious, because if it continued long the wood would splinter as the glass had done. Then he remembered the hawks. Could the hawks have taken over from the gulls? Were there buzzards now upon the sills, using talons as well as beaks? Hawks, buzzards, kestrels, falcons—he had forgotten the birds of prey. He had forgotten the gripping power of the birds of prey. Three hours to go, and while they waited the sound of the splintering wood, the talons tearing at the wood.

Nat looked about him, seeing what furniture he could destroy to fortify the door. The windows were safe, because of the dresser. He was not certain of the door. He went upstairs, but when he reached the landing he paused and listened. There was a soft spatter on the floor of the children's bedroom. The birds had broken through . . . He put his ear to the door. No mistake. He could hear the rustle of wings, and the light patter as they searched the floor. The other bedroom was still clear. He went into it and began bringing out the furniture, to pile at the head of the stairs should the door of the children's bedroom go. It was a preparation. It might never be needed. He could not stack the furniture against the door, because it opened inward. The only possible thing was to have it at the top of the stairs.

"Come down, Nat, what are you doing?" called his wife.

"I won't be long," he shouted. "Just making everything shipshape up here."

He did not want her to come; he did not want her to hear the pattering of the feet in the children's bedroom, the brushing of those wings against the door.

At five-thirty he suggested breakfast, bacon and fried bread, if only to stop the growing look of panic in his wife's eyes and to calm the fretful children. She did not know about the birds upstairs. The bedroom, luckily, was not over the kitchen. Had it been so she could not have failed to hear the sound of them, up there, tapping the boards. And the silly, senseless thud of the suicide birds, the death-and-glory boys, who flew into the bedroom, smashing their heads against the walls. He knew them of old, the herring gulls. They had no brains. The black-backs were different, they knew what they were doing. So did the buzzards, the hawks . . .

He found himself watching the clock, gazing at the hands that went so slowly round the dial. If his theory was not correct, if the attack did not cease with the turn of the tide, he knew they were beaten. They could not continue through the long day without air, without rest, without more fuel, without . . . his mind raced. He knew there were so many things they needed to withstand siege. They were not fully prepared. They were not ready. It might be that it would be safer in the towns after all. If he could get a message through, on the farm telephone, to his cousin, only a short journey by train up country, they might be able to hire a car. That would be quicker—hire a car between tides . . .

His wife's voice, calling his name, drove away the sudden, desperate desire for sleep.

"What is it? What now?" he said sharply.

"The wireless," said his wife. "I've been watching the clock. It's nearly seven."

"Don't twist the knob," he said, impatient for the first time, "it's on the Home where it is. They'll speak from the Home."

They waited. The kitchen clock struck seven. There was no sound. No chimes, no music. They waited until a quarter past, switching to the Light. The result was the same. No news bulletin came through.

"We've heard wrong," he said, "they won't be broadcasting until eight o'clock." They left it switched on, and Nat thought of the battery, wondered how much power was left in it. It was generally recharged when his wife went shopping in the town. If the battery failed they would not hear the instructions.

"It's getting light," whispered his wife, "I can't see it, but I can feel it. And the birds aren't hammering so loud."

She was right. The rasping, tearing sound grew fainter every moment. So did the shuffling, the jostling for place upon the step, upon the sills. The tide was on the turn. By eight there was no sound at all. Only the wind. The children, lulled at last by the stillness, fell asleep. At half past eight Nat switched the wireless off.

"What are you doing? We'll miss the news," said his wife.

"There isn't going to be any news," said Nat. "We've got to depend upon ourselves."

He went to the door and slowly pulled away the barricades. He drew the bolts, and kicking the bodies from the step outside the door breathed the cold air. He had six working hours before him, and he knew he must reserve his strength for the right things, not waste it in any way. Food, and light, and fuel; these were the necessary things. If he could get them in sufficiency, they could endure another night.

He stepped into the garden, and as he did so he saw the living birds. The gulls had gone to ride the sea, as they had done before; they sought sea food, and the buoyancy of the tide, before they returned to the attack. Not so the land birds. They waited and watched. Nat saw them, on the hedgerows, on the soil, crowded in the trees, outside in the field, line upon line of birds, all still, doing nothing.

He went to the end of his small garden. The birds did not move. They went on watching him.

"I've got to get food," said Nat to himself, "I've got to go to the farm to find food."

He went back to the cottage. He saw to the windows and the doors. He went upstairs and opened the children's bedroom. It was empty, except for the dead birds on the floor. The living were out there, in the garden, in the fields. He went downstairs.

"I'm going to the farm," he said. His wife clung to him. She had seen the living birds from the open door.

"Take us with you," she begged, "we can't stay here alone. I'd rather die than stay here alone."

He considered the matter. He nodded. "Come on, then," he said, "bring baskets, and Johnny's pram. We can load up the pram."

They dressed against the biting wind, wore gloves and scarves. His wife put Johnny in the pram. Nat took Jill's hand.

"The birds," she whimpered, "they're all out there, in the fields."

"They won't hurt us," he said, "not in the light."

They started walking across the field towards the stile, and the birds did not move. They waited, their heads turned to the wind.

WHEN THEY reached the turning to the farm, Nat stopped and told his wife to wait in the shelter of the hedge with the two children.

"But I want to see Mrs. Trigg," she protested. "There are lots of things we can borrow, if they went to market yesterday; not only bread, and . . ."

"Wait here," Nat interrupted. "I'll be back in a moment."

The cows were lowing, moving restlessly in the yard, and he could see a gap in the fence where the sheep had knocked their way through, to roam unchecked in the front garden before the farm-house. No smoke came from the chimneys. He was filled with misgiving. He did not want his wife or the children to go down to the farm.

"Don't jib now," said Nat, harshly, "do what I say."

She withdrew with the pram into the hedge, screening herself and the children from the wind.

He went down alone to the farm. He pushed his way through the herd of bellowing cows, which turned this way and that, distressed, their udders full. He saw the car standing by the gate, not put away in the garage. The windows of the farm-house were smashed. There were many dead gulls lying in the yard and around the house. The living birds perched on the group of trees behind the farm and on the roof of the house. They were quite still. They watched him.

Jim's body lay in the yard . . . what was left of it. When the birds had finished, the cows had trampled him. His gun was beside him. The door of the house was shut and bolted, but as the windows were smashed it was easy to lift them and climb through. Trigg's body was close to the telephone. He must have been trying to get through to the exchange when the birds came for him. The receiver was hanging loose, the instrument torn from the wall. No sign of Mrs. Trigg. She would be upstairs. Was it any use going up? Sickened, Nat knew what he would find.

"Thank God," he said to himself, "there were no children."

He forced himself to climb the stairs, but half-way he turned and descended again. He could see her legs, protruding from the open bedroom door. Beside her were the bodies of the black-backed gulls, and an umbrella, broken.

"It's no use," thought Nat, "doing anything. I've only got five hours, less than that. The Triggs would understand. I must load up with what I can find."

He tramped back to his wife and children.

"I'm going to fill up the car with stuff," he said. "I'll put coal in it, and paraffin for the primus. We'll take it home and return for a fresh load."

"What about the Triggs?" asked his wife.

"They must have gone to friends," he said.

"Shall I come and help you, then?"

"No; there's a mess down there. Cows and sheep all over the place. Wait, I'll get the car. You can sit in it."

Clumsily he backed the car out of the yard and into the lane. His wife and the children could not see Jim's body from there.

"Stay here," he said, "never mind the pram. The pram can be fetched later. I'm going to load the car." Her eyes watched his all the time. He believed she understood, otherwise she would have suggested helping him to find the bread and groceries.

They made three journeys altogether, backwards and forwards between their cottage and the farm, before he was satisfied they had everything they needed. It was surprising, once he started thinking, how many things were necessary. Almost the most important of all was planking for the windows. He had to go round searching for timber. He wanted to renew the boards on all the windows at the cottage. Candles, paraffin, nails, tinned stuff; the list was endless. Besides all that, he milked three of the cows. The rest, poor brutes, would have to go on bellowing.

On the final journey he drove the car to the bus-stop, got out, and went to the telephone box. He waited a few minutes, jangling the receiver. No good, though. The line was dead. He climbed on to a bank and looked over the countryside, but there was no sign of life at all, nothing in the fields but the waiting, watching birds. Some of them slept—he could see the beaks tucked into the feathers.

"You'd think they'd be feeding," he said to himself, "not just standing in that way."

Then he remembered. They were gorged with food. They had eaten their fill during the night. That was why they did not move this morning . . .

No smoke came from the chimneys of the council houses. He thought of the children who had run across the fields the night before.

"I should have known," he thought, "I ought to have taken them home with me."

He lifted his face to the sky. It was colourless and grey. The bare trees on the landscape looked bent and blackened by the east wind. The cold did not affect the living birds, waiting out there in the fields.

"This is the time they ought to get them," said Nat, "they're a sitting target now. They must be doing this all over the country. Why don't our aircraft take off now and spray them with mustard gas? What are all our chaps doing? They must know, they must see for themselves."

He went back to the car and got into the driver's seat.

"Go quickly past that second gate," whispered his wife. "The postman's lying there. I don't want Jill to see."

He accelerated. The little Morris bumped and rattled along the lane. The children shrieked with laughter.

"Up-a-down, up-a-down," shouted young Johnny.

It was a quarter to one by the time they reached the cottage. Only an hour to go.

"Better have cold dinner," said Nat. "Hot up something for yourself and the children, some of that soup. I've no time to eat now. I've got to unload all this stuff."

He got everything inside the cottage. It could be sorted later. Give them all something to do during the long hours ahead. First he must see to the windows and the doors.

He went round the cottage methodically, testing every window, every door. He climbed on to the roof also, and fixed boards across every chimney, except the kitchen. The cold was so intense he could hardly bear it, but the job had to be done. Now and again he would look up, searching the sky for aircraft. None came. As he worked he cursed the inefficiency of the authorities.

"It's always the same," he muttered, "they always let us down. Muddle, muddle, from the start. No plan, no real organization. And we don't matter, down here. That's what it is. The people up country have priority. They're using gas up there, no doubt, and all the aircraft. We've got to wait and take what comes."

He paused, his work on the bedroom chimney finished, and looked out to sea. Something was moving out there. Something grey and white amongst the breakers.

"Good old Navy," he said, "they never let us down. They're coming down channel, they're turning in the bay."

He waited, straining his eyes, watering in the wind, towards the sea. He was wrong, though. It was not ships. The Navy was not there. The gulls were rising from the sea. The massed flocks in the fields, with ruffled feathers, rose in formation from the ground, and wing to wing soared upwards to the sky.

The tide had turned again.

Nat climbed down the ladder and went inside the kitchen. The family were at dinner. It was a little after two. He bolted the door, put up the barricade, and lit the lamp.

"It's night-time," said young Johnny.

His wife had switched on the wireless once again, but no sound came from it.

"I've been all round the dial," she said, "foreign stations, and that lot. I can't get anything."

"Maybe they have the same trouble," he said, "maybe it's the same right through Europe."

She poured out a plateful of the Triggs' soup, cut him a large slice of the Triggs' bread, and spread their dripping upon it.

They ate in silence. A piece of the dripping ran down young Johnny's chin and fell on to the table.

"Manners, Johnny," said Jill, "you should learn to wipe your mouth."

The tapping began at the windows, at the door. The rustling, the jostling, the pushing for position on the sills. The first thud of the suicide gulls upon the step.

"Won't America do something?" said his wife. "They've always been our allies, haven't they? Surely America will do something?"

Nat did not answer. The boards were strong against the windows, and on the chimneys too. The cottage was filled with stores, with fuel, with all they needed for the next few days. When he had finished dinner he would put the stuff away, stack it neatly, get everything shipshape, handy-like. His wife could help him, and the children too. They'd tire themselves out, between now and a quarter to nine, when the tide would ebb; then he'd tuck them down on their mattresses, see that they slept good and sound until three in the morning.

He had a new scheme for the windows, which was to fix barbed wire in front of the boards. He had brought a great roll of it from the farm. The nuisance was, he'd have to work at this in the dark, when the lull came between nine and three. Pity he had not thought of it before. Still, as long as the wife slept, and the kids, that was the main thing.

The smaller birds were at the window now. He recognized the light tap-tapping of their beaks, and the soft brush of their wings. The hawks ignored the windows. They concentrated their attack upon the door. Nat listened to the tearing sound of splintering wood, and wondered how many million years of memory were stored in those little brains, behind the stabbing beaks, the piercing eyes, now giving them this instinct to destroy mankind with all the deft precision of machines.

"I'll smoke that last fag," he said to his wife. "Stupid of me, it was the one thing I forgot to bring back from the farm."

He reached for it, switched on the silent wireless. He threw the empty packet on the fire, and watched it burn.

RUMER GODDEN

b. 1907

A gentle, intensely alive person, she spent much of her
life in India. A devout Roman Catholic and mother of
two devoted children, she now lives in Scotland. Her
deep interest in religion and her sympathetic
understanding of young people are often reflected in the
stories she writes. She was awarded the OBE in 1993.

Fireworks for Elspeth

WHEN ELSPETH woke on the last morning she
was visited by a feeling of extraordinary sim-
plicity; everything she had to do was done;
there was nothing now but to go. She felt as
if the doors and windows of the house were
already wide open, with the sun shining on its
white walls, on the lawns and the lavender
bushes; the sun seemed to make a path from
her own window over the lawn and the tops
of the trees, over the copse to the wood and
the sky; yes, it looked like a path. I have only
to go, thought Elspeth blissfully. Roderick, her
black cocker spaniel, lay at the foot of her bed; there was, it was true, a
gap in her mind where she must say goodbye to Roderick—but that was
legitimate grief, thought Elspeth, nothing disturbing. Nothing disturbing, she thought and stretched herself on the bed; then she remembered
the lunch party.

How she had pleaded with Mother! "A lunch party! Oh *Mother*, no!
Please no."

"Why not?"

"It wouldn't be—suitable," Elspeth had said, with temerity.

"Elspeth, do I or do I not know what is suitable? *Not* a party! Just
the family and a few intimate friends."

"But they are the worst."

"Elspeth!"

Elspeth would have liked to have said, it's the questions and the looks. I feel the looks, Mother. I know I shouldn't feel them but—but I do and they talk so much. They—they prise everything open. Aunt Euphrosyne and Morna and Jean, Lady Bannerman, all of them. They know me so well they take it for granted they can ask things but . . . they have such picking eyes, thought Elspeth in despair. They pick everything to pieces, into little little pieces; this is whole, in me, but they tatter it to pieces. I know it is my fault to let them, but they do. "Mother," she had begun aloud but Mother was saying, "Just Aunt Euphrosyne and Uncle Arthur and Morna and Jean. Major Fitzgerald, of course . . ."

"And the Baldocks and Lady Bannerman and Larry and Colin Crump," said Elspeth bitterly.

"They are exactly whom I thought of asking," said Mother; then she had looked at Elspeth and her face hardened. "Well, Elspeth, why not?"

Elspeth could never say things to Mother; she could have talked to Aunt Bevis but that would have made Mother worse. "Bevis is *not* your mother," Mother often said.

"It—it will all be so complicated," Elspeth had said, about the lunch party, stumbling over the words. "I—I wanted it simple, quiet and—kind of—usual, Mother." She picked up Roderick and held him tightly to give herself courage while Mother tapped with a pencil on the blotter. "Don't you understand, Mother?"

"No," said Mother.

"I thought—if I could leave, just simply, as if it were everyday . . ."

"You *cannot* pretend," said Mother, "that this kind of thing is everyday."

That had stopped Elspeth, and she could not bear to have this same scene again; instead she had said desperately, "Think of the washing-up. Father and I shall have to leave at half-past two. I shan't be here to help Marlowe."

"We shall have to get used to that," Mother's voice had been cold. "I shall get Mrs. Paget from the village," and she had picked up her pen. "It will be easiest for everybody. If you thought at all, Elspeth, you would know what these last few hours will be like for us; for your father and me, though I must say Father doesn't seem to feel it; *if* you thought, but of course you don't think, if you did, you couldn't do this."

"Oh *Mother!*" Elspeth had pleaded once again but Mother held up her hand for silence, that thin white peremptory hand that looked fragile and was strong—strong as iron. Elspeth knew how strong it was and her nerves tingled. It was almost time to go but she had not gone yet; she could still be stopped. The hand was heavy with rings; Mother always wore her rings; diamonds, rubies, sapphires. Her hand must be strong to bear those rings, thought Elspeth, and she wondered idly what

303

she herself would have done with them when, as Mother had often said they should, they came to her. Now they won't, Elspeth had thought, with relief. No rings, no Lady Bannerman's emeralds, none of the family silver and pictures and china. Daphne will have them all. I—I have escaped, thought Elspeth and her face glowed; she was filled with this inner contentment, this feeling of rightness that was hers now by right— or almost hers—as if it had been given to me, thought Elspeth, and she thought, it is my gift from God, my jewels and money, my family.

Mother had returned to the subject of the luncheon party. "It will be best," she said, "no matter what I feel—and it doesn't matter what I feel—be quiet, Elspeth. I won't have people saying we're bundling you off. They might think there was something wrong, a family rift—or that there was an unhappy love affair."

"Couldn't they think it was choice?" asked Elspeth. At that, Mother had bowed her head and her neck stiffened as it did when she was mortally displeased; she pulled her chair into the writing table and began to write the notes, but her hand trembled on the paper and Elspeth, watching, was smitten. Once again she had hurt Mother—for —for nothing, thought Elspeth. When I'm so happy why can't I be generous? Why must I always do it? she thought in despair; do what Sister Monica so often said she must not, seek her own way? Trying to impose her own will, instead of accepting? "In these last few days try to do, to be, everything your parents want," Sister Monica had said. "Show them how you love them . . ." and I can't be five minutes with Mother before we begin . . . No wonder they wonder at me, thought Elspeth. This rebellious and unpleasant girl to make a nun!

She had looked helplessly across the room at Aunt Bevis who had been sewing in the window and Aunt Bevis had looked back at her and smiled. Never, thought Elspeth, had anyone as clear eyes as Aunt Bevis —they were set a little tilted as if, for all her quietness, Aunt Bevis had an extra private and particular view of the world. Is that what makes her so—large? thought Elspeth now, so without walls? She can see over the wall—but then Mother had caught the look and asked sharply, "Bevis, where's the list? You took it when you went to the telephone. Now it's *lost*."

"It's under the blotter on the right hand side," said Aunt Bevis. "Thursday, 2nd April, at a quarter to one," Mother had written in her clear, pointed hand. On Thursday, 2nd April, today thought Elspeth in bed, she, Elspeth Catherine Mary Erskine, was to enter the Order of the Sisters of Mary at their Convent of St. Faith at Chiswick where she had already spent two retreats. She was very happy about it; very shy, but no one seemed to grasp that she was either of these things.

"What are you going to be called?" her cousin Morna had asked.

"Reverend Mother has agreed that I shall be Catherine Mary," said Elspeth. "They are saints' names as well as my own."

"Sister Catherine Mary." Morna tried it, and relapsed into helpless giggles.

"Shut up, Morna!" said her sister Jean but Morna could not shut up. Soon Jean and then Elspeth herself were giggling too, as they had always giggled all their short lives when they were together.

"Really! You girls are too silly," Aunt Euphrosyne always said, but the silliness broke out as soon as they met, though Morna was twenty to Elspeth's and Jean's nineteen.

"But a nun *isn't* funny," Elspeth had protested, shaking helplessly.

"Of c-course not," said Jean. "It's just—you—one of us—as a n-nun!"

The giggling had been all right, it was silly but easy; it was the questions, the—feeling against her, that Elspeth could not face. I wish I belonged to another family, she thought that often in these days, one of those families, in Ireland or America, where it's part of family life for a daughter or a sister or cousin to enter an Order. In ours you would think no one in the world had ever joined an Order before. "They make it seem so extraordinary," she said bitterly to Sister Monica, who was Mistress of the Novices. "If only I could *tell* them, Sister. If only I could explain."

"Wait," said Sister Monica. "Wait and they will see."

For a long time now people had been exhorting Elspeth to wait. "Sixteen is too young. Don't be ridiculous." "Seventeen's too young." Elspeth had retorted with St. Thérèse of Lisieux, as young girls wanting to marry have retorted with Juliet. "St. Thérèse was a case apart," she was told, "Wait," and, "Eighteen is too young. Wait."

She had, of course, needed her parents' consent and at one time it seemed that Mother, and Father led on by Mother, never would consent. Then at long last there was hope, but she still had to wait. "If, at the end of a year you still want it . . ."

"I shall still want it," said Elspeth.

"You always were obstinate," said Mother. "Even as a little thing you would rather be sent to bed or shut up in the cloakroom than give in."

The trouble is, thought Elspeth, that I have always given in—except over this. Now I can't. She did not understand how she managed to be so steady but, when the year was up, they had given their consent—if Mother's could be called a consent. Even when it was decided, Mother never left Elspeth alone. "Robert killed, Daphne gone, one might think you would realise that you are all we have left."

"But Mother, you didn't mind when Daphne went away to be married. Hong Kong is the other side of the world!"

"That was *quite* different," said Mother. "Marriage is a woman's destiny."

"But Mother . . ."

"I hope I should never be so selfish as to stand between my child and *that*," said Mother.

"But Mother . . ."

"If only I could have seen you happily married," said Mother.

"But Mother, there are other . . ."

"Husband, home, children," said Mother.

"Mother, if I were marrying a king or a prince . . . !"

It was of no use. Mother would not listen and if she had, Elspeth could not have explained.

The news had burst suddenly on the family and the family friends. Usually, over any happening or idea, Mother took Aunt Euphrosyne and most of the neighbourhood into her strict confidence—how often had Robert and Daphne and Elspeth writhed when their most private doings and feelings were made discreetly and unfailingly public. Now, until the ultimate decision was taken, Mother had not breathed a word. I suppose she thought it would spoil my chances, thought Elspeth. Young men would shy off me if they knew. I mightn't get all my dances! Now young men, dances, chances, did not matter. The news was out and everyone seemed bewildered.

"But how did it happen?" asked Mr. Baldock.

"It began when she went on that wretched French family exchange holiday," said Mother. "The daughter . . ."

Yes, there, with Jeanne Marie, thought Elspeth. Dear, dear Jeanne Marie.

"In Paris, that's where she got the idea," Mother complained.

"What a place to go to and get the idea of being a nun," said Mr. Baldock.

Mr. Baldock, a mild little man who grew violets, was Elspeth's godfather and now he looked at her as if he had been given a little seedling to cherish and it had suddenly grown into a rampant vine. "Can't *you* get this nonsense out of her head?" Elspeth had heard him ask Aunt Bevis.

"Is nonsense the right word?" asked Aunt Bevis.

"Well, no," said Mr. Baldock. "But Elspeth! Our pretty little girl!"

"She's not a little girl," said Aunt Bevis.

"It seems so unnatural," said Mr. Baldock. "Elspeth dear, are you sure?"

The family were more definite.

"She's out of her mind!" said Uncle Arthur.

"Girls get like this," said Aunt Euphrosyne. "It's usually anaemia."

"Elspeth is not the *least* anaemic," said Mother. "She has a lovely colour," and she began to cry. "She's serious, Euphy."

"I can't believe it," said Aunt Euphrosyne, "Elspeth! Not *Elspeth*! Why, she was always the naughty disobedient one."

"Euphy is glad, of course," said Mother afterwards. "She was always jealous because you were by far the prettiest."

"Mother, don't, don't say things like that!"

"It's true. At least you'll be out of the way," said Mother vindictively, "I expect she thinks that now Larry will marry Jean."

There had been something a little sadistic about the cousins.

"They give you all the worst things to do when you're a novice," said Morna. "You scrub floors and clean lavatories and shovel coal. You do all the rough work."

"And you won't like that," said Aunt Euphrosyne. "You were always what Nanny calls backward in coming forward to help."

"Was I?" asked Elspeth. She did not really, fairly think she was.

"Last time you stayed with us," said Morna, "you left your towel on the bathroom floor and the tiles were all over powder and you never even turned down your bed."

"They bully you and humiliate you to find out what you're made of. I have read about it," said Jean and she added, "If you like one thing more than another, it's taken away."

"Life does that to you as well," said Aunt Bevis. "As you will find out."

Elspeth had looked at Aunt Bevis in surprise. Aunt Bevis's cheeks had been quite pink.

The whole neighbourhood was roused.

"A well plucked girl like that!" said Major Fitzgerald. "You should have seen the way she rode that mare of mine in the Dunbar Hunt Cup, not anyone's ride, I can tell you."

Colin Crump had blinked at Elspeth from behind his glasses and something seemed to boil up in him as if he wanted to speak; of course, no one counted Colin Crump, but there was trouble with Larry.

"I thought you were going to marry Larry," said Lady Bannerman in her gruff voice and she said, as Elspeth thought she would, "I meant to give you my emeralds."

Elspeth was touched and went to kiss her but Lady Bannerman held her off. "Don't kiss me," she said; there was a harshness in her voice that smote Elspeth. "You hurt Larry," said Lady Bannerman, her lips trembling, "You led him on, you little—vixen!"

"I didn't," Elspeth had said before she could stop herself. "Don't answer. Be quiet. Submit," said Sister Monica, but Elspeth was cut. Led Larry on! She might have said, "He was there before I led him," but that would have been to hurt him more. She had picked up Roderick and hid her face against him and immediately all thought of Larry was wiped away. Soon, soon, Elspeth had thought, I shall have to say good-bye to you, Roddy. Roddy's small black spaniel body was warm, silky, firm in her arms. He licked her neck and his eyes, between his absurd down-hanging ears, looked into her face. Her own eyes swam in sudden tears. She dared not keep Roderick in her arms; hastily she put him down.

"You're not listening to me," Lady Bannerman had said. "Hard as nails. You young things don't care how you hurt."

They all said that but, willy nilly, thought Elspeth, she had to put on this front of hardness with them, or give way completely. "She has grown so hard," they said.

"Father is twelve years older than I," said Mother. "When he goes, I shall be left alone. If I get ill . . ."

"Mother, why should you get ill? You're awfully strong."

"You're like marble," said Mother, "like marble."

I'm not. I'm not. If only I were! thought Elspeth, and she had thought of Jeanne Marie who was already professed and of Jeanne Marie's father and mother and brother who were so glad. Elspeth had borrowed the old Rover from Father and gone over to Chiswick to find Sister Monica. "Sister, ought I to give it all up?"

"You must ask yourself that," said Sister Monica. All the Sisters were the same; when you asked them, implored them, knelt to them, they put you gently back on your own feet.

Elspeth had looked up at Sister Monica's calm face. Sister Monica was sorting beans into bags for the kindergarten school; the infants used them for counting and Elspeth watched her fingers, picking the beans up in twenties, never making a mistake and slipping them into bags and tying the strings with a firm knot.

"Sister, help me," said Elspeth.

"Dear child, I can't help you," but perhaps Sister Monica had spoken to Mother Dorothea because the Reverend Mother had sent for Elspeth.

"If you have the least doubt, Elspeth . . ."

"I haven't, Reverend Mother." There Elspeth was firm; then the firm clearness clouded. "It's not my doubts, it's theirs. They make me wonder if I'm selfish. Mother, what should I do?"

"I think you should read the Commandments," said Mother Dorothea.

"The—the Commandments?"

"Yes. They are in the right order."

Now Elspeth understood. Her firmness shone but she cried, "If only I could *explain* to them, Mother. If I could make them see. I—I'm so dumb!"

Reverend Mother was silent for a few moments and then she said, "Perhaps you are given no words because there is no need for words. The action speaks, Elspeth," and she asked, her face serious, "Isn't that the way of the Cross?"

"But—but mine is such a little thing," said Elspeth, slightly shocked.

"A little thing but it makes you suffer. I think you have to consent to suffer, Elspeth. If Our Lord had not consented, He would have spoiled God's plan; have you thought of that? On the Cross He did simply what was asked of Him. He did not try and improve on the work of the Master. He used no fireworks," brought out Mother Dorothea after a hesitation.

Fireworks. That was a funny word for Reverend Mother to use, Elspeth had thought. It seemed almost irreverent. She sat silent, thinking, then she said, "But . . ." and remembered it was not customary to argue with Reverend Mother.

"But what? You may speak, Elspeth."

"The sky darkened," pleaded Elspeth, "the veil was—rent."

Reverend Mother was adamant. "That was given Him," said Reverend Mother. "Sometimes things are given; it's not for us to expect or ask. No. He did not use His power." Her voice grew deep with feeling. "They taunted Him and crowned Him with thorns. They told Him to come down off the Cross and prove Himself God and how did He answer? He let them win; hung there and died." Reverend Mother's face became marvellously kind and she put her hand on Elspeth's head. "He didn't ask for vindication but suffered and died—and lived. That proved Him God."

As Elspeth drove home it had stayed in her mind; she had thought about it every day since.

The second of April remained fixed. Mother's invitations went out and were accepted and the time went quickly till it came to the last day and Elspeth woke now to that sensation of emptiness and space, the windows and doors open and the sun streaming in. On the borderland of her sleep the birds sounded like the Convent choir where the children chirruped in an unconscious cherubic singing; she opened her eyes and looked along the sun's path that seemed to go from her bed, across the garden and the tops of the trees, across the copse where she used to play with Robert, to the woods and the far sky. The path might, she thought, have been a vision, only it was the sun; the singing might have been cherubs, only it was the birds; and suddenly, feeling completely happy and rational, she sat up in bed.

Aunt Bevis came in with two cups of tea. In her old Paisley dressing-gown she sat down on the bed. "Well, I must say," said Aunt Bevis, "it's refreshing to go away without packing."

In the past weeks Elspeth had given all her things away; her books in the white bookcase, the doll Mignonette she had had since she was five, and Dinah, her old rubbed velvet piccaninny; all her clothes, shoes, ornaments, treasures, had gone. The gardener's children had some of her things, the cousins some. "Would Morna like my pink net dress?" "Jean, my tennis racquet's for you. What a pity you can't get into my boots." The riding boots were new, glossy, black on their trees. Major Fitzgerald had given them to Elspeth for her birthday. "Fifty-six guineas," the Major said, mournfully.

"I couldn't warn him," said Elspeth. "Mother wouldn't let me."

As she gave away her things, her happiness mounted—until other people came in. "Mother, would you and Father mind if I gave my brushes to Marlowe? I mean—she's been with us so long and she thinks they're lovely."

"You thought them lovely once," said Mother.

"I—I do now. Of course I do. I love them but I won't need them," said Elspeth.

I won't need anything, I shall be free. That was all done. This heavenly morning she was empty of things and she lay back in bed as she thought; no more fittings and bringing things back on approval and thinking what I shall wear: and my face, with its horrible freckles, won't matter: my hair and Mother wanting it to be waved and having it cut only by Mr. Charles: and not wearing the same dress twice in the same place—and new hats and having things shortened and taken in and cleaned, and washing out gloves and handkerchiefs . . . "No, not even packing," said Elspeth aloud. The new life was breaking through the old but for this last day it had to be an admixture; in each thing, in each thought, there was both old and new.

After Aunt Bevis had gone, Elspeth dressed. It was the last time she would put on these clothes, usual clothes; a grey skirt, grey blouse, pale pink jersey, stockings, grey shoes. They would do for the lunch party. At the Convent she would take them off and pack them in a cardboard box and give it to Sister Monica.

"What will you wear?" Morna had asked. Morna and Jean were terribly curious about every detail. The Order wore a plain black habit, "Like a rather full black dress but long," said Elspeth, "and black stockings and shoes."

"Wool stockings, flat shoes?" asked Morna.

"Yes," said Elspeth and Morna made a face. "Go on," said Morna. "Tell some more."

"We wear a white toque."

"Is that the head thing?"

"Yes. For six months I'm on probation. Then I am a novice for two years. Then I change the white veil for a black and am a Junior for three more. I'm given a black cord with a crucifix," said Elspeth.

"What will you wear at night?" asked Jean.

"A nightgown, I suppose," said Elspeth.

"Don't you know?"

"I didn't ask," said Elspeth, suddenly shy.

"She took it for granted, I expect," said Aunt Bevis and she rounded on Jean, "What do you think she will wear? A black shroud?"

Aunt Bevis had promised to take Elspeth's few remaining things and send them away with her Relief Committee box.

"You had better wait six months, Bevis," Mother had said. "She has six months in which to change her mind."

"Mother, I shan't change my mind."

"No, you won't," said Mother and she said bitingly, "What is the use of hoping when there isn't any hope?"

That was one of the times when Elspeth had timidly approached her.

"Mother, if only you could be glad!"

"Glad!" and for the first time she had said to Elspeth, "What *is* it that draws you, Elspeth? What is it you see? I wish I could understand."

Elspeth took heart and cast about for words. "It's as if instead of being blown about with life, with all the days and years," Elspeth said or tried to say, "you were rooted whole in a whole place."

"But you have a place, a good home," said Mother.

"Yes, but . . . ." "There are pieces in a kaleidoscope, bits of paper and rag; you twist the glass and they are whole in a whole pattern." She might have used that symbol, or "It's like finding yourself on a map, knowing where you are, and then you know the direction," but Elspeth could only twist her hands helplessly.

"It was that horrid little Jeanne Marie," said Mother.

"It wasn't," said Elspeth hotly. Then she tried painfully for the exact truth. "It wasn't only Jeanne Marie. She was only a little part. Why, it was always," said Elspeth with sudden light. "Why, Mother, you taught me. Think. Think of hymns," said Elspeth.

"Hymns?"

"Don't you remember how you used to play and we sang?"

"Oh yes," said Mother, softening, "on Sunday evenings."

They both remembered those mild evenings.

"There was that one," said Elspeth, "'Loving Shepherd of Thy Sheep'."

Mother's eyes filled with tears. "It was Robert's favourite hymn."

"But think of what it meant," said Elspeth impatiently, "what it said. Didn't you *mean* us to take it seriously?"

Mother's eyes had flickered. "Seriously but not too seriously,"

311

Mother would have said, if she were truthful but she could not very well say that; instead she had said bitterly, "I never thought I should have to suffer by your being good!" and Elspeth had sighed. All the scenes ended like that.

There were sausages for breakfast. The table was laid with a white cloth, blue and white china, silver, a bowl of primroses. The coffee bubbled gently in the Cona; there was a smell of coffee, hot milk, sausages, toast, marmalade and apples. "What will they give you to eat in that place?" Marlowe had often asked. Marlowe was worried about that; she had wanted Elspeth to take a bottle of malt and cod-liver oil. "But I couldn't, Marlowe dear." At any rate Marlowe was determined that Elspeth should eat one last good breakfast. Morna and Jean too, often talked about the food.

"You'll have lentils," said Morna, "and fish. Ugh!"

"Bread and water on Fridays," said Jean.

"No, on Fridays you'll fast, and what about Lent?"

"Listen," said Aunt Bevis, "Have you ever seen a nun who didn't look perfectly well fed?" When they came to think about it, as a matter of fact, they had not.

Mother's breakfast tray was there. "I'll take it up," said Elspeth and Aunt Bevis did not interfere.

Mother was sitting up in bed reading her letters.

"Your breakfast, Mother."

"Why didn't you let Marlowe bring it?"

"I wanted to," said Elspeth and kissed her. Mother did not say anything sharp and by her bed, on the table, was Elspeth's miniature Dresden cup and saucer. Elspeth had brought it to her, the last of her things. Never, thought Elspeth, had she loved people as much, as—as compassionately as when she gave away her possessions. "Mother, will you have this?" and she put the little rosy cup, with its shepherds and shepherdesses, down at Mother's side.

Mother had not answered but now she had it by her bed, and again Elspeth felt that trembling love. She bent down and kissed her mother. "Remember I—I love you just as much," she whispered.

Mother sighed. "That's some consolation." They were, in that moment, closer than they had ever been; then Mother put up her hand to Elspeth's cheek, the rings felt cold and hard. Mother sighed again, then she said, turning over her letters, "Will they let you have your own post?"

Elspeth was startled. "I—I don't know, Mother. I never asked. I don't see why not."

"Those places are full of taboos," said Mother. "I'm not going to write letters and have them pruned by the Sister Superior."

"I suppose they know best for us, Mother." Elspeth said that tact-lessly, but she was trying to convince herself. Mother flushed and said something that linked straight with what Mother Dorothea had said, though Mother would have hated to know that.

"Honouring your father and mother is a commandment," said Mother and she gave a harsh laugh, "but of course it's a long way down the list."

Things are made clear at last, thought Elspeth, quite and horridly clear, but she could not bear it; she said as she had often said when she had had to go back to school, "Mother, don't. Don't. Not on my last day."

After a moment Mother said in a normal every-day voice, "What are you going to do this morning?" and Elspeth answered as she had answered a thousand times, "Oh, all the usual things."

But that was not quite true; after she had helped with the work, she planned to go all round the house and garden and into the copse, with Father perhaps, and take Roderick for a last scamper in the woods. That's what I want to do, thought Elspeth. I want to see the house for the last time, the old white walls, the flagged path, the lavender bushes, the slated roof brooding among the trees. I shall see it again, of course, but I shall be separated, not quite as I am now. She had meant to go all over it, inside as well as out, touch each window-sill, see it all: the gleam of silver and copper and brass, the polished mahogany, the white sheepskin rug in front of the drawing-room fire: the crystal vases of cut daffodils, the books and papers, *Punch* and *The Times* folded in the paper-rack: the worn red brocade on the seats of the chairs: the pat-terned staircarpet, the wallpaper in the bedrooms, the Peter Rabbit frieze in the nursery and its window bars and high fender; she had meant to go into the copse and see if the wild hyacinths, that she used to pick with Robert, were out; she had meant to walk down the wood paths with Roderick, but there was the lunch party, of course.

Elspeth dusted the drawing-room and put out extra ashtrays and then helped Aunt Bevis with the flowers. Mother was even more fussy than usual about the flowers.

"What would *you* like on the table, Elspeth? It's your party." That had become true. Mysteriously it had become Elspeth's party. "Of course I would do anything for you children," Mother said, pushing back her hair and smoothing her forehead where, obviously, she had a headache, "but these days the work *is* heavy. I had thought of prim-roses," said Mother, returning to the flowers.

"Primroses would be lovely," but when the primroses were done, Mother remembered the pudding was white and the whole effect would be pale. "It will look hideous, quite hideous in this dark room; you must get brightly coloured primulas." Elspeth picked them, orange and rust primulas, dark crimson, vivid blue and magenta, and arranged them in a great bowl.

There were the best table-mats to get out, the lace in one was creased and had to be ironed; there were finger bowls to wash; she had to go down to the village for cigarettes, though she would have liked to keep out of the village. "You go off today then, Miss Elspeth," and when Elspeth said, "Yes," they all avoided her eyes and looked embarrassed; all except the postmistress, Mrs. Cox, who was jauntily confident she would come back. The Post Office was also the village shop. Elspeth had to face Mrs. Cox. "You will soon have enough of it," she told Elspeth as she handed her the cigarettes. "We shall soon have you back." Elspeth did not argue as she did with Mother; she knew she was a nine days' wonder in the village and she hastily made her escape.

When she came in, the telephone was ringing and she went to answer it. "Hallo," said Elspeth and the voice at the other end paused before it spoke. "Is that—you Elspeth?" it said, uncertainly. "Could I speak to your mother?" Since they heard that Elspeth was going to be a nun, their friends seemed to doubt that she could answer the telephone; but nuns telephone, thought Elspeth in irritation; they use typewriters and vacuum cleaners and go in cars and aeroplanes. They drive cars; I have even seen a nun driving a buggy very fast; they are not medieval idiots, thought Elspeth.

Everybody's nerves were getting overtaxed. Mother went to lie down, even Aunt Bevis was cross and Marlowe, in the kitchen, was unapproachable. I didn't mean it to be like this, thought Elspeth unhappily; she looked across the lawn, where the daffodils were bending and bobbing along the hedge by the wicket-gate that led into the copse; she could see the tops of the birch trees, the milk gleam of their stems, but time was getting short and she had to help Marlowe make the pudding. It was one of Mother's favourites, mushrooms in grass; the mushrooms were meringue shells, lined with chocolate and turned upside down on fondant stems; they stood on a base of chocolate mousse decorated with fronds of angelica grass. While Elspeth was arranging them in the pantry her father came and stood by her. He watched while she cut the angelica grass and wearily stuck it in. "Damned flummery," said Father suddenly.

"Dad, I wanted to come with you and see what they are doing in the copse," said Elspeth miserably.

He jingled his keys and the silver in his pockets. "The heavy timber's gone," he said, "except the big beech. It took two days to get that down. I should like you to have seen it. Fine tree!" then he added, "Better do as your Mother wants."

Father never made an outcry. "Your Mother's a very emotional

314

woman," he had often said to his children. "She feels." Her feelings were so strong that no one paid much attention to his. When Robert was killed, Mother collapsed but Father only seemed more silent, to grow a little smaller, a little balder; he began to have indigestion, but he was as quiet and gentle as before. Daphne was his favourite but when she married Cyril, and that had meant Hong Kong, he had only been anxious about her settlement; he had had to sell some of the land, some of his first editions, and take off some of the timber as he was doing now in the copse, but he never spoke of bills or worries, except perhaps about the bullfinches that had invaded the fruit last summer; he only took more soda mints. Nowadays, thought Elspeth, he always smelled of soda mints.

When Elspeth had made her decision, he had said, "You really want to do this, Kitten?"

"Yes, Dad."

He had looked at her more seriously than she had known that he could look. "You know what it means?"

"Yes."

"The privations, Elspeth, and the—deprivations."

"Yes. Reverend Mother has explained them clearly,"—Elspeth might have said, "terribly clearly"—"to me."

"I shall have to sell out some shares," said Father. Elspeth was smitten and he said, "Don't look worried. If you had married, you would have had to have a settlement," and he put his hand on her shoulder and said what none of them had said, "This calls for something handsome."

Elspeth, flushed and incoherent with gratitude and tears, had only been able to stammer again, "If—if I were marrying a prince or a duke . . . Oh Dad!"

Now he stayed by her in the pantry, looking at the mushrooms and jingling his keys. "I suppose your Mother wants all that," and he sighed and went away.

There was one thing that Elspeth was determined to do that morning and that was to give Roderick a good brush, leave him clean, fresh and ordered. As soon as she had finished the mushrooms she whistled him up and took him into the cloakroom.

"From the moment you come to St. Faith's," Sister Monica had said, "you will own nothing in the world. Here we don't say 'my cell', 'my bed'; everything belongs to the Order and is lent to you. Not even the handkerchief you use is yours, you understand?"

"Yes, Sister."

"That isn't hard," said Sister Monica, "It's surprisingly easy. You will see. It will come quite naturally."

That had been true of most things, Elspeth might almost say of everything—except Roderick.

"You will remember his water, Aunt Bevis?"

"I shall remember."

But who will take him for long walks in the woods? Who will understand him? Roderick was not anybody's dog, not like most spaniels; his moods were as dark as his coat; sometimes Elspeth would think there was a being shut up in Roderick, a captured beast, who looked out of his eyes and wrung his heart and made him disagreeable.

"He doesn't mean to be cross. He needs understanding, Aunt Bevis."

"I shall try and understand him."

"When he gets a stick and puts his paw on it, it means he only wants you to pretend to take it; he wants to bounce away with it himself, and when he growls and lies by himself, he's unhappy and then you must leave him and only show you love him very much—and remember he's an actor, Aunt Bevis. When he pretends he doesn't want his food, he wants it very much . . ."

Not even Aunt Bevis could have patience for that! If—if I had known what it was like to leave Roderick, perhaps I shouldn't have gone, thought Elspeth, but that's *disgraceful*! What, mind more about a spaniel than Father, more than Mother or Aunt Bevis! How can I? thought Elspeth, but she could. A dog cannot stand in the way of humans, it is not fitting, but, "He's so innocent, Aunt Bevis." Now, as she brushed him, Elspeth saw that it was dangerous to go near Roderick that morning; she could not trust herself and tears fell on his head and ran, shining, down his black coat, helpless warm tears.

"Elspeth!"

She whipped round. It was Larry Bannerman. Larry arrived early. He was standing in the doorway of the cloakroom, looking at her with an expression on his face that made her turn back quickly to Roderick; even Roderick was safer than that look on Larry's face. Roderick pierced her, but she pierced Larry. Oh, how silly everything is, thought Elspeth.

"Why do you let them make you go?" said Larry. His voice was angry.

"No one's making me go. I want to go," said Elspeth.

"Then why are you crying?" said Larry.

"Don't you expect me to feel it?" said Elspeth angrily too.

They hurled these angry questions at each other.

"Do you think I'm made of stone?" cried Elspeth.

"Yes," said Larry tersely.

Stone! Marble! Hard as nails! Oh, I'm not. I'm not. She began to cry again.

Larry took one step nearer. "Elspeth, Elspeth! My little love!" His voice shook with feeling.

"Larry, *please* go away."

He came nearer. "You don't want to go."

"I do! I do!"

"It's an idea that's got hold of you."

"No, Larry! No!" said Elspeth breathlessly between the pent up sobs that shook her. "It's—it's my life." She might have said, "Don't you see, I'm fighting for my life."

"Elspeth, I love you." He stood there just above her, his eyes pleading, very much as Roderick's eyes pleaded when they looked up at her, only Larry's looked down. Elspeth did not know herself what it was in her that made her able to harden her heart, even against these two; that gave her strength to do it. "Elspeth."

She whispered, "Larry, couldn't you love Jean?"

His eyes blazed and he said, "You're not the only one who can fix their heart on something." At that Elspeth burst into sobs, crying aloud, "Oh Larry! Go aw-a-ay!" He turned on his heel and went. Elspeth could hear his steps ringing on the tiles of the back passage and she cried helplessly, her sobs stifled against Roderick's coat.

"Elspeth! El-speth! Lady Bannerman is here, and Co-lin."

Let me run away, thought Elspeth. She felt hunted. I shall go now. Say goodbye to Roderick and leave him in the kitchen with Marlowe and get my coat and bag and get on a bus and go there by myself. I can't stand it, thought Elspeth. I can't stand any more.

There were only minutes more, not many minutes, an hour or two, before that door in Chiswick would shut on her, before the calm, the peace and sanctity would ring her round and she would be safe, attained, achieved. It was near but it seemed far away with these minutes that lay between, these painful pricking minutes. She shut her eyes and the tears ran out under her lids. I can't stand—all the—pricks.

"Elspeth, your mother's calling you." Elspeth's eyes flew open and her chin went up. It was Larry's voice again but mercifully he did not come in. He spoke from the passage outside and, again, she heard his steps going away. She heard the front door bell ring, Marlowe's steps in the hall; then Aunt Euphrosyne's voice shrilled with Mother's. She heard Uncle Arthur's boom and Roderick struggled to get down. He had a passion for Uncle Arthur. Elspeth put him down on the floor and he tore out. She heard Uncle Arthur's "*Hullo* little dog!" and Mother's "Get down, Roddy. Down!" and then "Elspeth! Elspeth!"

"Just getting tidy," called Elspeth in a loud voice and began splashing her face with cold water, trying to cool her red eyes. Then she heard Mother's quick pattering steps, her high heels on the passage outside.

"Elspeth, what are you doing in there?"

"I have been brushing Roddy."

"Brushing Roddy! Everyone's here."

"I'm just coming, Mother."

"You know the men want the cloakroom for washing their hands." Mother sounded cross.

"Yes, Mother."

"Come along. It looks so rude."

Elspeth combed her hair with Father's old comb, rolled down her sleeves; she would have to leave her face and hope no one would notice. "Now for it," said Elspeth and she dug her nails into her palms. She saw Mother's slight, tall form in the grey pleated dress at the door of the drawing-room; "Tchk!" said Mother and bent down to pick a thread off the carpet. Then she went in. Elspeth heard her voice saying, "Of course, the poor child has had a great deal to do." Elspeth flinched but she had to go in. Swiftly, breathlessly, she crossed the hall and in a moment she found herself taking round glasses on a little tray, handing cigarettes in the silver box as she had a hundred times before; this—this is what I have been bred to do, thought Elspeth, but after a little while she saw that everything was different; different in the way their eyes looked at her; the contrast in their voices as they greeted her; they seemed to edge away from her, draw together against her. Am I imagining it? thought Elspeth. Then she found herself talking to Colin Crump.

Colin Crump had always been a joke to them; he had been asked to every party she could remember, usually to make the numbers even or because boys were short. "What happens to him in between?" asked Jean. "Perhaps he only comes to life for parties," said Morna. As long as they could remember, he had been there: first as a little boy with eyes in owlish glasses and sticking-out teeth, who stammered, then as a large boy with even thicker glasses and a gold plate and a voice that went up and down; and latterly as this young man, Colin Crump, whose teeth were straight, whose stammer was fixed, but whose glasses were thicker than ever. His eyes looked owlish still as they glowed into Elspeth's. She and her cousins had always run away from him, tried to skip his dances, particularly Elspeth; now she could not escape. "I—I think this is splendid of you, El-Elspeth," said Colin Crump confidentially, and Elspeth was startled into looking at him. "I d-don't know how you found the c-courage to st-ick out for your own way . . ." he was saying, "but of c-course you always d-did."

"Did I?" asked Elspeth uncertainly.

"That's what always made me admire you so t-t-tremendously," said Colin.

She had never known that Colin Crump admired her, or that he could do anything as positive as admire. She felt she should say something. "Did you?" or, "How kind of you," but she could not say that. She could only smile; the smile did not feel real, it felt like a faked simper. She thought everyone in the room was watching her; ostensibly they were talking to one another, laughing, but they never took their eyes off her; they were aware of her. How strange that, in all the familiar gathering, Colin Crump, whom she had never thought of except as a joke, should be the only one to understand her. Colin and, perhaps, Aunt Bevis. She began to feel hotly rebellious, as if something were rising in her under all these eyes, these looks, these thoughts that were completely out of sympathy with her. At the least little signal I shall break, thought Elspeth.

She could see through the door, across the hall to the dining-room; the table gleamed with its silver, lace and the colours of the primulas. She thought of the morning's hurry and fuss and she had a sudden vision of the refectory at St. Faith's, the empty clean room, no curtains, only windows, the tables laid out with a bowl and cup for each Sister, who brought her own fork and knife and spoon and helped herself from a side table. She remembered the quiet eating while a young novice, perhaps herself soon, stood and read aloud. She saw the colours of the flowers under the statue of the Virgin; the flowers came in their seasons for Her, those that grew in the Convent garden, they did not have to match the pudding. That's not fair of me, thought Elspeth, then she cried, but there one isn't interfered with, broken up; there one can remember, be whole, be the whole of yourself because you are allowed to lose yourself. A longing swept over Elspeth; she felt she could not wait.

The guests had fallen into three circles. The young ones were in the window—except Larry, who kept by his mother, tossing down drink after drink. Lady Bannerman was silent but her eyes kept looking from Elspeth to Jean and back to Elspeth. Jean was looking pretty in her new tweed suit. "Is it tomato colour?" asked Elspeth.

"They call it spring red," said Jean.

"It's bright tomato," said Elspeth derisively and then remembered Sister Monica and said, "It suits you." Jean did not hear her. All of them were listening to their elders.

The men were by the fire, talking jerkily. "That damned bullfinch," said Father.

"There's a spring trap on the market now," said Uncle Arthur.

"Herring nets," that was Major Fitzgerald. "They will have every plum if you don't stop 'em; darned little robbers," and they began to talk about apples—a glut of cider apples—and of Major Fitzgerald's Worcester Permains. That was harmless but on the sofa there was the sound of whispers. In spite of the forbidding silence of Larry and his mother, the women were on the topic of Elspeth. It was Aunt Euphrosyne who whispered. Mrs. Baldock leaned forward to hear; her blue straw with the white bow met Aunt Euphrosyne's feathers; Mother's head was in between. "Utterly, utterly, selfish," Elspeth heard; and Jean heard and Morna and Larry and Colin Crump, the whole room, and Elspeth felt a burning colour flood her neck.

"Ribston Pippins," said Father loudly.

"Can't beat 'em," said Major Fitzgerald.

After all it was Aunt Bevis who precipitated it. Aunt Bevis had been sitting with an expression on her face that showed, Elspeth thought, that she was worrying over the food. She had argued with Mother that there was not enough chicken; "We should have had three from the farm, not two," said Aunt Bevis; now, suddenly, she spoke; perhaps if she had not been worrying over the chicken she would not have spoken as bluntly. "How dare you badger the child," said Aunt Bevis. "Yes, how dare you!" Elspeth began to tremble and Colin turned. To her horror Colin joined in. "You—you shouldn't," said Colin Crump, stuttering and swallowing. "D-do you remember," he said and the words seemed to swell with the difficulty he had to get them out—as words are difficult for me, thought Elspeth, wishing he would be silent, but he was determined to go on. "Do you re-member, Mrs. Ersk-kine, when they c-came to C-Christ and said His mother and His brethren were st-standing without . . .?" He could not go on, he was as scarlet as Elspeth, but, "Yes," said Aunt Bevis furiously and loudly. "Do you remember what Christ said?"

"I remember, Bevis," said Mother, her voice high. "I remember and I have always thought it was heartless. Heartless!"

There was such a silence that if Roderick had shed one hair on the carpet it would have been heard. Every eye in the room, whether it looked at her or not, was turned on Elspeth. She had never felt as exposed. Sister Monica had told her not to speak but now it was as if, willy nilly, through Colin and Aunt Bevis she had spoken, as if she had been given a voice. Then justify it, thought Elspeth in agony.

St. Elizabeth found her apron full of roses. St. Teresa had levitation. The wind changed for St. Joan. "Oh God!" prayed Elspeth, her lips silent, her hands sticky.

If, through the open window, a wind had swept in and filled all the room with sound; if she, Elspeth, could have been lifted up, even two feet from the carpet, lifted without a hand touching her; if roses had fallen or their scent perfumed the room, even one or two roses, but she was left. There was no help, no vindication.

She had to stand there before them all, helpless and silent. She could feel her heart beating hurtfully; for a moment she could only feel the hurt, the smart, and then it became a tiny echo, echoing down two thousand years—no, nineteen hundred and sixty, thought Elspeth. The drawing-room seemed to swim round her and she heard Reverend Mother Dorothea's words; those near voices faded and Mother Dorothea's calm, authoritative, directed her, "No fireworks."

Elspeth's hands unclenched and, as if she had broken the tension, everyone relaxed. The clock ticked, Uncle Arthur cleared his throat, Roderick stretched and sighed blissfully at Uncle Arthur's feet; Mother gave a quick little sob and dabbed her eyes. Everywhere conversation broke out.

"Ribston Pippins? Yes, nothing to beat them," said Mr. Baldock.

"They had a nice brown corduroy skirt with a little checked coat, but I chose this," said Jean.

"Have you heard the S-Simmons are having a band for their d-dance?" asked Colin Crump of Morna.

"From the Crane Club. It will cost a fortune; quite ridiculous!" called Aunt Euphrosyne.

Lady Bannerman passed her drink to Larry. Larry drank it.

"Bevis, it's a quarter past. Don't you think . . .?" said Mother, but just then Marlowe sounded the gong.

GRAHAM GREENE

1904–1991

"A desire to reduce a chaos of experience to some sort of order . . ."
This motive lies behind more than a dozen novels (including
"entertainments" like *Brighton Rock* and serious studies
of moral crisis like *The Heart of the Matter*) and numerous
short stories, the best of which often evoke the
terrors of a vividly remembered childhood.

The End of the Party

PETER MORTON woke with a start to face the
first light. Through the window he could see
a bare bough dropping across a frame of silver.
Rain tapped against the glass. It was January
the fifth.

He looked across a table, on which a nightlight had guttered into a pool of water, at the
other bed. Francis Morton was still asleep, and
Peter lay down again with his eyes on his
brother. It amused him to imagine that it was
himself whom he watched, the same hair, the
same eyes, the same lips and line of cheek. But
the thought soon palled, and the mind went back to the fact which lent
the day importance. It was the fifth of January. He could hardly believe
that a year had passed since Mrs. Henne-Falcon had given her last
children's party.

Francis turned suddenly upon his back and threw an arm across his
face, blocking his mouth. Peter's heart began to beat fast, not with
pleasure now but with uneasiness. He sat up and called across the
table, "Wake up." Francis's shoulders shook and he waved a clenched
fist in the air, but his eyes remained closed. To Peter Morton the whole
room seemed suddenly to darken, and he had the impression of a great
bird swooping. He cried again, "Wake up," and once more there was
silver light and the touch of rain on the windows. Francis rubbed his
eyes. "Did you call out?" he asked.

"You are having a bad dream," Peter said with confidence. Already experience had taught him how far their minds reflected each other. But he was the elder, by a matter of minutes, and that brief extra interval of light, while his brother still struggled in pain and darkness, had given him self-reliance and an instinct of protection towards the other who was afraid of so many things.

"I dreamed that I was dead," Francis said.

"What was it like?" Peter asked with curiosity.

"I can't remember," Francis said, and his eyes turned with relief to the silver of day, as he allowed the fragmentary memories to fade.

"You dreamed of a big bird."

"Did I?" Francis accepted his brother's knowledge without question, and for a little the two lay silent in bed facing each other, the same green eyes, the same nose tilting at the tip, the same firm lips parted, and the same premature modelling of the chin. The fifth of January, Peter thought again, his mind drifting idly from the image of cakes to the prizes which might be won. Egg-and-spoon races, spearing apples in basins of water, blind man's buff.

"I don't want to go," Francis said suddenly. "I suppose Joyce will be there . . . Mabel Warren." Hateful to him, the thought of a party shared with those two. They were older than he. Joyce was eleven and Mabel Warren thirteen. Their long pigtails swung superciliously to a masculine stride. Their sex humiliated him, as they watched him fumble with his egg, from under lowered scornful lids. And last year . . . he turned his face away from Peter, his cheeks scarlet.

"What's the matter?" Peter asked.

"Oh, nothing. I don't think I'm well. I've got a cold. I oughtn't to go to the party." Peter was puzzled. "But, Francis, is it a bad cold?"

"It will be a bad cold if I go to the party. Perhaps I shall die."

"Then you mustn't go," Peter said with decision, prepared to solve all difficulties with one plain sentence, and Francis let his nerves relax in a delicious relief, ready to leave everything to Peter. But though he was grateful he did not turn his face towards his brother. His cheeks still bore the badge of a shameful memory, of the game of hide and seek last year in the darkened house, and of how he had screamed when Mabel Warren put her hand suddenly upon his arm. He had not heard her coming. Girls were like that. Their shoes never squeaked. No boards whined under their tread. They slunk like cats on padded claws.

When the nurse came in with hot water Francis lay tranquil leaving everything to Peter. Peter said, "Nurse, Francis has got a cold."

The tall starched woman laid the towels across the cans and said, without turning, "The washing won't be back till to-morrow. You must lend him some of your handkerchiefs."

"But, Nurse," Peter asked, "hadn't he better stay in bed?"

"We'll take him for a good walk this morning," the nurse said. "Wind'll blow away the germs. Get up now, both of you," and she closed the door behind her.

"I'm sorry," Peter said, and then, worried at the sight of a face creased again by misery and foreboding, "Why don't you just stay in bed? I'll tell mother you felt too ill to get up." But such a rebellion against destiny was not in Francis's power. Besides, if he stayed in bed they would come up and tap his chest and put a thermometer in his mouth and look at his tongue, and they would discover that he was malingering. It was true that he felt ill, a sick empty sensation in his stomach and a rapidly beating heart, but he knew that the cause was only fear, fear of the party, fear of being made to hide by himself in the dark, uncompanioned by Peter and with no nightlight to make a blessed breach.

"No, I'll get up," he said, and then with sudden desperation, "But I won't go to Mrs. Henne-Falcon's party. I swear on the Bible I won't." Now surely all would be well, he thought. God would not allow him to break so solemn an oath. He would show him a way. There was all the morning before him and all the afternoon until four o'clock. No need to worry now when the grass was still crisp with the early frost. Anything might happen. He might cut himself or break his leg or really catch a bad cold. God would manage somehow.

He had such confidence in God that when at breakfast his mother said, "I hear you have a cold, Francis," he made light of it. "We should have heard more about it," his mother said with irony, "if there was not a party this evening," and Francis smiled uneasily, amazed and daunted by her ignorance of him. His happiness would have lasted longer if, out for a walk that morning, he had not met Joyce. He was alone with his nurse, for Peter had leave to finish a rabbit-hutch in the woodshed. If Peter had been there he would have cared less; the nurse was Peter's nurse also, but now it was as though she was employed only for his sake, because he could not be trusted to go for a walk alone. Joyce was only two years older and she was by herself.

She came striding towards them, pigtails flapping. She glanced scornfully at Francis and spoke with ostentation to the nurse. "Hello, Nurse. Are you bringing Francis to the party this evening? Mabel and I are coming." And she was off again down the street in the direction of Mabel Warren's home, consciously alone and self-sufficient in the long empty road. "Such a nice girl," the nurse said. But Francis was silent, feeling again the jump-jump of his heart, realising how soon the hour of the party would arrive. God had done nothing for him, and the minutes flew.

They flew too quickly to plan any evasion, or even to prepare his heart for the coming ordeal. Panic nearly overcame him when, all unready, he found himself standing on the doorstep, with coat-collar turned up against a cold wind, and the nurse's electric torch making a short luminous trail through the darkness. Behind him were the lights of the hall and the sound of a servant laying the table for dinner, which his mother and father would eat alone. He was nearly overcome by a desire to run back into the house and call out to his mother that he would not go the party, that he dared not go. They could not make him go. He could almost hear himself saying those final words, breaking down for ever, as he knew instinctively, the barrier of ignorance that saved his mind from his parents' knowledge. "I'm afraid of going. I won't go. I daren't go. They'll make me hide in the dark, and I'm afraid of the dark. I'll scream and scream and scream." He could see the expression of amazement on his mother's face, and then the cold confidence of a grown-up's retort.

"Don't be silly. You must go. We've accepted Mrs. Henne-Falcon's invitation." But they couldn't make him go; hesitating on the doorstep while the nurse's feet crunched across the frost-covered grass to the gate, he knew that. He would answer: "You can say I'm ill. I won't go. I'm afraid of the dark." And his mother: "Don't be silly. You know there's nothing to be afraid of in the dark." But he knew the falsity of that reasoning; he knew how they taught also that there was nothing to fear in death, and how fearfully they avoided the idea of it. But they couldn't make him go the party. "I'll scream. I'll scream."

"Francis, come along." He heard the nurse's·voice across the dimly phosphorescent lawn and saw the small yellow circle of her torch wheel from tree to shrub and back to tree again. "I'm coming," he called with despair, leaving the lighted doorway of the house; he couldn't bring himself to lay bare his last secrets and end reserve between his mother and himself, for there was still in the last resort a further appeal possible to Mrs. Henne-Falcon. He comforted himself with that, as he advanced steadily across the hall, very small, towards her enormous bulk. His heart beat unevenly, but he had control now over his voice, as he said with meticulous accent, "Good evening, Mrs. Henne-Falcon. It was very good of you to ask me to your party." With his strained face lifted towards the curve of her breasts, and his polite set speech, he was like an old withered man. For Francis mixed very little with other children. As a twin he was in many ways an only child. To address Peter was to speak to his own image in a mirror, an image a little altered by a flaw in the glass, so as to throw back less a likeness of what he was than of what he wished to be, what he would be without his unreasoning fear of darkness, footsteps of strangers, the flight of bats in dusk-filled gardens.

"Sweet child," said Mrs. Henne-Falcon absent-mindedly, before, with a wave of her arms, as though the children were a flock of chickens, she whirled them into her set programme of entertainments: egg-and-spoon races, three-legged races, the spearing of apples, games which held for Francis nothing worse than humiliation. And in the frequent intervals when nothing was required of him and he could stand alone in corners as far removed as possible from Mabel Warren's scornful gaze, he was able to plan how he might avoid the approaching terror of the dark. He knew there was nothing to fear until after tea, and not until he was sitting down in a pool of yellow radiance cast by the ten candles on Colin Henne-Falcon's birthday cake did he become fully conscious of the imminence of what he feared. Through the confusion of his brain, now assailed suddenly by a dozen contradictory plans, he heard Joyce's high voice down the table. "After tea we are going to play hide and seek in the dark."

"Oh, no," Peter said, watching Francis's troubled face with pity and an imperfect understanding, "don't let's. We play that every year."

"But it's in the programme," cried Mabel Warren. "I saw it myself. I looked over Mrs. Henne-Falcon's shoulder. Five o'clock, tea. A quarter to six to half-past, hide and seek in the dark. It's all written down in the programme."

Peter did not argue, for if hide and seek had been inserted in Mrs. Henne-Falcon's programme, nothing which he could say would avert it. He asked for another piece of birthday cake and sipped his tea slowly. Perhaps it might be possible to delay the game for a quarter of an hour, allow Francis at least a few extra minutes to form a plan, but even in that Peter failed, for children were already leaving the table in twos and threes. It was his third failure, and again, the reflection of an image in another's mind, he saw a great bird darken his brother's face with its wings. But he upbraided himself silently for his folly, and finished his cake encouraged by the memory of that adult refrain, "There's nothing to fear in the dark." The last to leave the table, the brothers came together to the hall to meet the mustering and impatient eyes of Mrs. Henne-Falcon.

"And now," she said, "we will play hide and seek in the dark."

Peter watched his brother and saw, as he had expected, the lips tighten. Francis, he knew, had feared this moment from the beginning of the party, had tried to meet it with courage and had abandoned the attempt. He must have prayed desperately for cunning to evade the game, which was now welcomed with cries of excitement by all the other children. "Oh, do let's." "We must pick sides." "Is any of the house out of bounds?" "Where shall home be?"

"I think," said Francis Morton, approaching Mrs. Henne-Falcon,

326

his eyes focused unwaveringly on her exuberant breasts, "it will be no use my playing. My nurse will be calling for me very soon."

"Oh, but your nurse can wait, Francis," said Mrs. Henne-Falcon absent-mindedly, while she clapped her hands together to summon to her side a few children who were already straying up the wide staircase to upper floors. "Your mother will never mind."

That had been the limit of Francis's cunning. He had refused to believe that so well-prepared an excuse could fail. All that he could say now, still in the precise tone which other children hated, thinking it a symbol of conceit, was, "I think I had better not play." He stood motionless, retaining, though afraid, unmoved features. But the knowledge of his terror, or the reflection of the terror itself, reached his brother's brain. For the moment, Peter Morton could have cried aloud with the fear of bright lights going out, leaving him alone in an island of dark surrounded by the gentle lapping of strange footsteps. Then he remembered that the fear was not his own, but his brother's. He said impulsively to Mrs. Henne-Falcon, "Please, I don't think Francis should play. The dark makes him jump so." They were the wrong words. Six children began to sing, "Cowardy cowardy custard," turning torturing faces with the vacancy of wide sunflowers towards Francis Morton.

Without looking at his brother, Francis said, "Of course I'll play. I'm not afraid, I only thought . . ." But he was already forgotten by his human tormentors and was able in loneliness to contemplate the approach of the spiritual, the more unbounded torture. The children scrambled round Mrs. Henne-Falcon, their shrill voices pecking at her with questions and suggestions. "Yes, anywhere in the house. We will turn out all the lights. Yes, you can hide in the cupboards. You must stay hidden as long as you can. There will be no home."

Peter, too, stood apart, ashamed of the clumsy manner in which he had tried to help his brother. Now he could feel, creeping in at the corners of his brain, all Francis's resentment of his championing. Several children ran upstairs, and the lights on the top floor went out. Then darkness came down like the wings of a bat and settled on the landing. Others began to put out the lights at the edge of the hall, till the children were all gathered in the central radiance of the chandelier, while the bats squatted round on hooded wings and waited for that, too, to be extinguished.

"You and Francis are on the hiding side," a tall girl said, and then the light was gone, and the carpet wavered under his feet with the sibilance of footfalls, like small cold draughts, creeping away into corners.

"Where's Francis?" he wondered. "If I join him he'll be less

327

frightened of all these sounds." "These sounds" were the casing of
silence: the squeak of a loose board, the cautious closing of a cupboard
door, the whine of a finger drawn along polished wood.

Peter stood in the centre of the dark deserted floor, not listening but
waiting for the idea of his brother's whereabouts to enter his brain.
But Francis crouched with fingers on his ears, eyes uselessly closed,
mind numbed against impressions, and only a sense of strain could
cross the gap of dark. Then a voice called "Coming", and as though his
brother's self-possession had been shattered by the sudden cry, Peter
Morton jumped with his fear. But it was not his own fear. What in his
brother was a burning panic, admitting no ideas except those which
added to the flame, was in him an altruistic emotion that left the reason
unimpaired. "Where, if I were Francis, should I hide?" Such, roughly,
was his thought. And because he was, if not Francis himself, at least a
mirror to him, the answer was immediate. "Between the oak bookcase
on the left of the study door, and the leather settee." Peter Morton was
unsurprised by the swiftness of the response. Between the twins there
could be no jargon of telepathy. They had been together in the womb,
and they could not be parted.

Peter Morton tiptoed towards Francis's hiding place. Occasionally a
board rattled, and because he feared to be caught by one of the soft
questers through the dark, he bent and untied his laces. A tag struck the
floor and the metallic sound set a host of cautious feet moving in his
direction. But by that time he was in his stockings and would have
laughed inwardly at the pursuit had not the noise of someone stumbling
on his abandoned shoes made his heart trip in the reflection of another's
surprise. No more boards revealed Peter Morton's progress. On stock-
inged feet he moved silently and unerringly towards his object. Instinct
told him that he was near the wall, and, extending a hand, he laid the
fingers across his brother's face.

Francis did not cry out, but the leap of his own heart revealed to
Peter a proportion of Francis's terror. "It's all right," he whispered,
feeling down the squatting figure until he captured a clenched hand.
"It's only me. I'll stay with you." And grasping the other tightly, he
listened to the cascade of whispers his utterance had caused to fall. A
hand touched the bookcase close to Peter's head and he was aware of
how Francis's fear continued in spite of his presence. It was less intense,
more bearable, he hoped, but it remained. He knew that it was his
brother's fear and not his own that he experienced. The dark to him
was only an absence of light; the groping hand that of a familiar child.
Patiently he waited to be found.

He did not speak again, for between Francis and himself touch was
the most intimate communion. By way of joined hands thought could

328

flow more swiftly than lips could shape themselves round words. He could experience the whole progress of his brother's emotion, from the leap of panic at the unexpected contact to the steady pulse of fear, which now went on and on with the regularity of a heart-beat. Peter Morton thought with intensity, "I am here. You needn't be afraid. The lights will go on again soon. That rustle, that movement is nothing to fear. Only Joyce, only Mabel Warren." He bombarded the drooping form with thoughts of safety, but he was conscious that the fear continued. "They are beginning to whisper together. They are tired of looking for us. The lights will go on soon. We shall have won. Don't be afraid. That was only someone on the stairs. I believe it's Mrs. Henne-Falcon. Listen. They are feeling for the lights." Feet moving on a carpet, hands brushing a wall, a curtain pulled apart, a clicking handle, the opening of a cupboard door. In the case above their heads a loose book shifted under a touch. "Only Joyce, only Mabel Warren, only Mrs. Henne-Falcon," a crescendo of reassuring thought before the chandelier burst, like a fruit tree, into bloom.

The voices of the children rose shrilly into the radiance. "Where's Peter?" "Have you looked upstairs?" "Where's Francis?" but they were silenced again by Mrs. Henne-Falcon's scream. But she was not the first to notice Francis Morton's stillness, where he had collapsed against the wall at the touch of his brother's hand. Peter continued to hold the clenched fingers in an arid and puzzled grief. It was not merely that his brother was dead. His brain, too young to realise the full paradox, yet wondered with an obscure self-pity why it was that the pulse of his brother's fear went on and on, when Francis was now where he had been always told there was no more terror and no more darkness.

NEIL M. GUNN

1891–1973

This Scottish fisherman's son, who towered above his fellow men both physically and mentally, became one of the Scottish Highland's greatest writers. Although he served for many years in the Civil Service, in both England and Scotland, he was something of a mystic. He is at his best when describing the ordinary life of the Highland fishing and crofting communities, interpreting in simple prose the complex character of the Celt.

The Sea

 HIS EYES CAME staring out of sleep . . . his flushed cheeks paled.

"Mither!"

She stood beside him in her nightdress, a candle in her hand, tall and listening. About her ghost-like presence he heard the moaning of the wind.

"Do you hear it?" Her uplifted solemn voice spoke as to the night itself. Every now and then the moan rose to a shriek. Terror dissolved his breast. "I'm frightened," she said to herself.

"Why—Mither——" He gulped, his eyes round and listening.

"I'm frightened," she repeated, in the same toneless voice, and slowly turned her face to the little window.

Through the ravening devilry of the wind they could hear, soft as the thud of blood in the ears, the faint far booming of the sea. "It started about one o'clock," she said. "For hours it's been like that."

He could not find a word. His heart was beating up into his throat. His eyes were on his mother, his own kind mother, standing there so still, wrapped in her dreadful thought. The wind caught the house and shook it and snarled over it. The candle trembled in her hand.

"Oh!" broke from her.

"Never mind, Mither! Never mind!" he cried.

"I couldn't stay alone," she communed. "I don't know what to do."

"All right, Mither!" His eager voice firmed in a desperate effort to inspire confidence, to keep her from giving way. He had never seen her give way, never seen her quiet wisdom tested to breaking point. His own mother . . .

Nor would she give way now. Only she had no one to turn to, and the agony of listening to the winter storm with his father and brother at sea, caught in it, with nowhere to run for but the little creek, the rock-bound creek—it could not be borne lying in bed. The wind was on the front of the house. That meant it was smashing the great seas into the little creek. One could hear the far faint boom-oom. Desperate apprehension drove her about the house, drove her to wake her twelve-year-old son.

"They must have gone to the far ground," she said. "If they had shot out off the Height they would have been in and home long ago."

He sat up in bed, gone very pale, his eyes on his mother. He heard the storm, its demoniac clutch and howl. He watched his mother. She was standing listening, her head half turned. A sudden runnel of hot candle-grease spilled over on to her hand. She looked down at it with a little start and the remoteness in her eyes filled with a momentary hot welling-up of emotion. He felt tears surge, unmanly tears, and his heart cried, "Mither! Mither!" but he was silent.

"We have no one to send to see," she said, her emotion quietly strangled.

That was what was troubling her, too. The others of the crews would have some of their kin about the shore, waiting; while from this house would be no one, as though all through the storm the house lay in the sin of sleep. And if news had to be brought it would have to be brought by strangers. There would be no deep-speaking eyes of the same blood. He understood all this. Through the storm came a sudden crashing from down below in the tree plantation. He threw the clothes off his legs.

"I'll go down, Mither," he said.

She started; looked at his slim little form, his white boy's body. But something stood in his face, and his eyes no longer looked at her; they were the eyes of one going about a man's business. He lifted his diminutive trousers from the floor.

"Oh, I cannot let you go."

He slipped the braces up over his shoulders. "Ould John will be down," he said. "He'll be at the harbour office. I'll go there."

She had not thought of the harbour office nor of Ould John, the last of the harbourmasters—his post, in fact, having long fallen into disuse. Now before she was done thinking of them he was ready, all except his stockings and boots, which were drying before the smoored peat fire on the kitchen hearth.

"Yes, I'll go, Mither. Don't be frightened." And he went before

331

her to the kitchen, where he soon got into his stockings and boots. He stood up. "Where's my bonnet?" She got a great woollen scarf and twisted it twice round his neck and crossed it over his breast, tucking the ends inside his jacket, but saying nothing. "That's all right," he muttered, acknowledging the care, but implying man-like that it was hardly needed. "Where's my bonnet?" It was time he was off. She got him into a cut-down oilskin ulster and tied it round his middle. "Here's your bonnet," she said at last. He pulled it down on his head firmly and started for the door.

She could not find a word. When the key was turned the door smashed open, choking her. She put out her hand but already he was over the doorstep. She called to him urgently, called to him to come back. His voice answered from the night, "All right, Mither. Don't be frightened!" The blackness of his small body dwindled uncertainly and was gone.

She got the door shut and came into the kitchen where the oil lamp burned, turned low. She stood by the table listening, her eyes round and her breath held, as though some voice might cry out of the night to her. At last she was physically frightened. Over her body went a tremor; the ravening wind clutched her body, shook it; her eyes beheld the dark road where her young son battled; her young son going the way they all went, the dread way of the sea. Her womanhood came over her, her motherhood, and a sound like a stifled whine broke from her; she took a few quick uncertain steps, like an animal turning in a circle, then stumbled to her knees at the chair by the bedside and prayed, a prayer of no words, a desperate linking of God, O God, to those at sea and to the little figure battling through the heaving plantation down to the steep harbour walls; the little figure hardly severed from her body— become man at a stroke.

And he held by his gruff manliness as he went down the pitch-black avenue of trees. They interlaced above the roadway. He could not see his own hands before his eyes as he sent them groping in front of him, waggling and swimming, so as to touch, to ward off, until his neck got sore holding his head back from what at any moment might hit it. He tripped over a broken tree branch and screamed. Then he gathered himself by the little wall that bordered the road and crept along it. While yet he trembled with fear, he was ashamed of that treacherous scream; while every hand-thrust and foot-thrust might hit into Something, while all the ghosts and demons of story and dream shrieked around and above him, he was yet ashamed of his treachery to himself.

He emerged from the avenue breathing in gulps and set off hurriedly on the just discernible greyness of the road. Throwing back a look at the trees, he heard their fierce black roar and imagined he saw their inter-writhing serpent bodies. Heartened, he went on. A little gust of assurance spouted to his head. A smile that was a crinkling shiver passed over him in the faintest elation. He was here alone. He was not frightened. He was out in this night alone, going on, with things around him in the mysterious, black, fierce world. . . Then he heard the sea.

It came right at him in a giant heave, cleansed of the mufflng roar of the trees. He quivered under it and almost stopped. The earth trembled under his feet, though the beach was nearly half a mile away. The sound of it seemed to stand up over the earth, as in great oncoming billows, vast towering waves, onrushing, obliterating. He felt himself walking nearer it like a quivering spot of fear walking towards immense doom. There could be no resistances, no sense of fighting back in his twelve-year-old body. Then suddenly he saw in his mind great green billows, a boat heeled and spun and plunging down, his brother's face and his father's, heeled and tossed and clutching desperately, their faces—oh, their faces—their brave faces . . .

A cold shiver swept his skin and tears stuck in his throat. His steps quickened as though something had tautened inside him. He did not think of the things about him any more. They were suddenly nothing—compared with the thing in front. He licked his lips. Already they were salt. The salty tang tautened him still more.

He kept well back from the harbour wall, its yawning chasm affrighting him dreadfully, so that he almost mistrusted the broad gravelled surface, which he knew intimately, and clung to the inner grassy verge. The creaking and clanking of cordage and boats and gear came up over the wall. The tide must be well in. He thought he heard human voices, but could see nothing. The wind buffeted him mercilessly, sometimes throwing him back a step or two. At the end of this long stone wall, he caught against the horizon the harbourmaster's stone hut. From below the hut and at an obtuse angle to the stone wall ran out a concrete jetty called the 'quay'. Over the outer point of this quay, where high in its iron cage the lantern stood, the sea broke in solid white water.

After leaning against the wind, the sudden suction of the lee of the harbourmaster's hut brought him almost in a run against the legs of Ould John, the ancient and bearded harbourmaster, who cried in a loud startled voice, "God bless me!" then fumbled with his hands about the little body at his knees. "God bless me, boy, who are you?" He stooped down and shouted above the storm, "Eh? Who are you?"

"I'm Hugh."

"What's that?"

"I'm Hugh Miller."

"Hugh Miller! God bless me, boy, what are you doing here?" He was astounded.

"My mother——" But the boy stopped and started again, shouting back, "I came to see if there's any word of the boats."

"You did! God bless me! You're not frightened?"

"No."

"What! Well, well. Eh!" He took Hugh's hands and rubbed them. "You're not cold, are you?"

"No."

"That's you!" His breezy old voice was warm with admiration, and the warmth went about Hugh's heart. The whiskers swept Hugh's face as the antique head went erect. Hugh had a sudden strange intuition of being admitted to the valhallas of men.

He had played pranks on Ould John, had been inclined with other boys to mimic his whiskered mannerisms and agedness. Now as the old man went to the gable corner and stuck his beard in the weather, Hugh seemed to hear in his voice something wild and defiant, something splendid and terrible.

"No, sir!" he shouted, choked back by the wind, "no, sir; there's no sign of them yet." And he began stamping up and down the few feet of shelter.

Hugh cowered to the wall, his teeth chattering a little though he did not feel cold. The harbour lay below him, dark and swaying. On the other side, directly opposite, ran the black face of the breakwater with foam seething through its teeth. Ominous it looked, deathly cold, mercilessly gluttonous. Its slanting piles, starting opposite the quay-end, ran inward to a strip of beach which was backed by a few fishermen's cottages. The incoming waves, hitting first the quay-end, smashed clean over it, then swung across the few yards of harbour entrance and, meeting the piles, hissed through them in a racing line of white froth. Inward, the harbour basin undulated and swung in dark unbroken water, in safety. Any boat that was still alive had to make that narrow entrance between the quay-end and the smoking piles.

"Yes, sir; a stormy morning!" sang out Ould John. "It's ten years this winter fishing since they were caught as complete!" So he bespoke Hugh, companionably, shouting down the night and his own anxiety. Hugh sensed him and glowed and feared. The cold and the excitement made his teeth rattle for seconds on end. Ould John sheltered a match. "It must be lightening soon."

"I think I can see a little better," cried Hugh.

"Yes, sir; it's about due!" stamped John.

Hugh stole to the corner and put his head round. He cowered back. A tumultuous ocean of fury, grey-black, upheaving. Nothing could live in that. Nothing . . . Nothing but brave men, who always lived. Hugh had never known death. Fear had him now, but not death. And through his fear ran a thin excitement which made his teeth rattle. They would come, his father in one boat, his brother in another. There were three boats.

Three small boats, with five men to each, for the most part skippers of the bigger boats that lay hauled inward beyond the breakwater awaiting the summer herring fishings in various ports; now clubbed together to make what they could in their own decaying creek out of the winter fishing.

A dimness began to infuse the black. There could no longer be any doubting. Out of that ocean of unleashed fury pale morning was sending a grey forebreath, was struggling to slow, wan birth.

"If they're coming, they'll soon be now," shouted Ould John.

If they're coming! Surely they were coming.

"They couldn't run anywhere else?" Their boats had been known to make across for Cromarty.

"No, not anywhere else!" reckoned Ould John. "Hardly—against that!" But his irony was subdued and manly and Hugh did not feel hurt.

And now Ould John hung about the corner, and at last his voice broke in a great cry: "There she comes!"

It was still dark and only fugitively could Hugh get a glimpse of the tossing, oncoming craft. And not for long did either of them glimpse her. One moment she lived fair in the entrance way, neither his father's boat nor his brother's; the next moment, and the sea in a yawing lift had carried her clean across it and piled her up against the outside of the breakwater. Voices cried through the gloom. Cry and counter-cry, commanding and urgent, echoing doomed and forlorn. "Look!" cried Hugh. "Look, there's someone creeping out on the piles!" A black splayed figure could be discerned breaking the straight line of the slippery pile-tops.

"That'll be young Jimmy Mackay going out with a life rope," declared Ould John, triumph in his voice. Hugh glowed and shivered, and about his lungs gathered a queer constriction. Then his brother's boat came.

He saw her for an instant half-slewed round in the trough of a wave, then as she was about to straighten up and rise, the sea smashed over the quay-head, caught her and swept her like a bit of dead planking through spindrift smoke on to the outside of the breakwater. The cries were renewed. The sinister piles came alive and spouted foam through their black teeth.

"Will they?—will they——?" choked Hugh.

"Yes, sir!" answered Ould John. "They should take them off. They'll keep their heads. They'll beach before they smash altogether. Ay, ay!" Unless, he could have added, they smashed in the first impact—which

335

was not unlikely, no, not at all unlikely. "But we can do nothing. And there's no sign of your father." He drew his head back a moment. "No, sir; there's no sign of him. But he'll come," he added. "And," he cried, stamping mightily, "and it's himself that'll be at the tillie!" In his voice was a brave agony of helplessness and ardour. And suddenly through it all the thought of his father at the tiller thrilled Hugh. It was not his place, because he was not the oldest skipper aboard; but at times of crisis, when extraordinary seamanship was needed, they always put his father to the helm. That was known. He thrilled now so that the cold shivers rayed all over his skin and the thing in his throat stuck in an unswallowable lump.

Peering round Ould John's body, he was first to catch sight of his father's boat. A ghostly wraith of a craft, she came tossing out of, and vanishing into, that grey-dark tumultuous sea, but with nose ever searching out the quay-head. Nearer and nearer, yawing and slipping and plunging, but with nose persistently seeking out the solid wall-end. Nearer still, and nearer, until at last Ould John's voice uprose, "My God, you'll smash her to atoms!" And little Hugh began to feel it coming, the crisis and smash of it in his body, and to crash on that quay-head in that boiling hell of a sea meant instant and absolute annihilation. With the sea running inward there was a slim chance on the sloping piles of the breakwater, but on the concrete quay-head, none. And now, yard after yard, when his father, for pride in whose seamanship he could have died, could still have sheered off . . . came the moment of tense agonizing awaiting as she took the wave in the final headlong onslaught . . . and she was shot through the harbour entrance and half-way up the basin before the two by the hut drew breath. Then Ould John turned to the little fellow by his side, his whiskers jutting wildly at the elements, and cried, "That's your father for you!" The wave that, unknown to his father, had swept the others on the break-water, his father had had the skill to time to his own use, come how it would.

For the first time that night tears found the way to his eyes unguarded, and came streaming down his face, but noiselessly. The tears swept everything out of their way, even thought of his brother they momentarily swept, leaving only pride and exultation. He ran after Ould John, followed him down the steep slimy stone steps in the harbour wall— until he was observed and ordered back.

Presently the crew came up talking in quiet earnestness to Ould John. Then his father saw Hugh, stopped abruptly, and into his face came a glimmering white look that remained in the inmost places of Hugh's mind for ever after like a vision.

When they had crossed the river above the harbour and gone down the other side, they found the inhabitants of the cottages clustered about the beach. In a miraculous and heroic way the ten men had won clear, some with minor injuries and some exhausted. Their two boats were smashed to matchwood.

Hugh saw his mother's face as they came round the corner of the house. His father said:

"Well, Mither, we've got back," and his voice was kind and smiling.

She looked over all three of them. They stood a moment. Then she turned into the kitchen where the table was laid.

"You'll go up and change your clothes," she said to her older son. Hugh went with him, and after a little began to laugh uncertainly.

"Boy, weren't the waves in it?" he chuckled.

"Ay," said his brother, stretching his almost full-grown body and smiling lazily.

"Yon one fairly got ye!"

"Ay," said his brother, yawning. Then he looked at Hugh amusedly. "If Jimmy hadn't climbed out with the rope I'd have been a gonner."

"Did you hang on?"

"Yes, with my body swinging away in between the piles." He rubbed a hip. "That was the stuff for you, boy! If you'd seen me do the acrobatic feat—like the mannie in the circus!" He looked amusedly at Hugh. "Give's a pull."

Hugh, by hanging on to the blue jersey, skinned it over his brother's head.

"It's all wet. But you should have seen father taking the harbour! He went through it like a rocket!"

"Did he?"

"Ay. But at first he was gripping at the quay-head and Ould John got excited! He thought he was going to smash on the point!" He laughed.

"What did he say?"

"He shouted at father so that you could have heard him a mile off—'My God, you'll smash her to atoms!'"

"What words are these I hear you saying?" asked his mother quietly, as she walked in.

Hugh wriggled away shamefacedly. "Nothing," he mumbled. She turned to her other son.

"Here's a dry shirt for you. Put it on you at once. It's warm. And don't be long. The tea is ready."

When she had gone out, Hugh looked up, his face red.

"Man, you were fairly copped!" scoffed his brother.

"She was frightened herself," retaliated Hugh. Then thinking of what he said he grew more shamefaced than ever. His brother laughed.

L. P. HARTLEY

1895–1972

Educated at Harrow and Balliol, a member of the Athenaeum,
he epitomized the English literary gentleman. The countryhouse
society between the wars, which he knew and observed so well,
formed the setting not only for his most successful novels
such as *The Go-Between* and *The Hireling* but also
for some of his most nightmarish short stories.

The Cotillon

"BUT," protested Marion Lane, "you
don't mean that we've all got to dance the
cotillon in masks? Won't that be terribly
hot?"

"My dear," Jane Manning, her friend
and hostess, reminded her, "this is
December, not July. Look!" She pointed
to the window, their only protection against
a soft bombardment of snowflakes.

Marion moved across from the fireplace
where they were sitting and looked out.
The seasonable snow had just begun to fall,
as though in confirmation of Mrs. Manning's words. Here and there the
gravel still showed black under its powdery coating, and on the wing of
the house which faced east the shiny foliage of the magnolia, pitted with
pockets of snow, seemed nearly black too. The trees of the park which
yesterday, when Marion arrived, were so distinct against the afternoon
sky that you could see their twigs, were almost invisible now, agitated
shapes dim in the slanting snow. She turned back to the room.

"I think the cotillon's a good idea, and I don't want to make difficulties," she said. "I'm not an obstructionist by nature, am I? Tell me
if I am."

"My dear, of course you're not."

"Well, I was thinking, wouldn't half the fun of the cotillon be gone
if you didn't know who was who? I mean, in those figures when the

338

women powder the men's faces, and rub their reflections off the looking-glass, and so on. There doesn't seem much point in powdering a mask."

"My darling Marion, the mask's only a bit of black silk that covers the top part of one's face; you don't imagine we shan't recognize each other?"

"You may," said Marion, "find it difficult to recognize the largest, barest face. I often cut my best friends in the street. They needn't put on a disguise for me not to know them."

"But you can tell them by their voices."

"Supposing they won't speak?"

"Then you must ask questions."

"But I shan't know half the people here."

"You'll know all of us in the house," her friend said; "that's sixteen to start with. And you know the Grays and the Fosters and the Boltons. We shall only be about eighty, if as many."

"Counting gate-crashers?"

"There won't be any."

"But how will you be able to tell, if they wear masks?"

"I shall know the exact numbers, for one thing, and for another, at midnight, when the cotillon stops, everyone can take their masks off—must, in fact."

"I see."

The room was suddenly filled with light. A servant had come in to draw the curtains. They sat in silence until he had finished the last of the windows; there were five of them in a row.

"I had forgotten how long this room was," Marion said. "You'll have the cotillon here, I suppose?"

"It's the only possible place. I wish it were a little longer, then we could have a cushion race. But I'm afraid we shall have to forgo that. It would be over as soon as it began."

The servant arranged the tea-table in front of them and went away.

"Darling," said Jane suddenly, "before Jack comes in from shooting with his tired but noisy friends, I want to say what a joy it is to have you here. I'm glad the others aren't coming till Christmas Eve. You'll have time to tell me all about yourself."

"Myself?" repeated Marion. She stirred in her chair. "There's nothing to tell."

"Dearest, I can't believe it! There must be, after all these months. My life is dull, you know—no, not dull, quiet. And yours is always so *mouvementée*."

"It used to be," admitted Marion. "It used to be; but now I——"

There was a sound of footsteps and laughter at the door, and a voice cried "Jenny, Jenny, have you some tea for us?"

"You shall have it in a moment," Mrs. Manning called back. Sighing, she turned to her friend.

"We must postpone our little séance."

FIVE DAYS had gone by—it was the evening of the twenty-seventh, the night of the ball. Marion went up to her room to rest. Dinner was at half-past eight, so she had nearly two hours' respite. She lay down on the bed and turned out all the lights except the one near her head. She felt very tired. She had talked so much during the past few days that even her thoughts had become articulate; they would not stay in her mind; they rose automatically to her lips, or it seemed to her that they did. "I am glad I did not tell Jenny," she soliloquized; "it would only have made her think worse of me, and done no good. What a wretched business." She extinguished the light, but the gramophone within her went on more persistently than ever. It was a familiar record; she knew every word of it: it might have been called *The Witness for the Defence*. "He had no reason to take me so seriously," announced the machine in self-excusatory accents. "I only wanted to amuse him. It was Hugh Travers who introduced us: he knows what I am like; he must have told Harry; men always talk these things over among themselves. Hugh had a grievance against me, too, once; but he got over it; I have never known a man who didn't." For a moment Marion's thoughts broke free from their bondage to the turning wheel and hovered over her past life. Yes, more or less, they had all got over it. "I never made him any promise," pursued the record, inexorably taking up its tale: "what right had he to think he could coerce me? Hugh ought not to have let us meet, knowing the kind of man he was—and—and the kind of woman I was. I was very fond of him, of course; but he would have been so exacting, he *was* so exacting. All the same," continued the record—sliding a moment into the major key only to relapse into the minor—"left to myself I could have managed it all right, as I always have. It was pure bad luck that he found me that night with the other Harry. That was a dreadful affair." At this point the record, as always, wobbled and scratched: Marion had to improvise something less painful to bridge over the gap. Her thoughts flew to the other Harry and dwelt on him tenderly; he would never have made a scene if he could have helped it; he had been so sweet to her afterwards. "It was just bad luck," the record resumed; "I didn't want to blast his happiness and wreck his life, or whatever he says I did."

What had he actually said? There was an ominous movement in Marion's mind. The mechanism was being wound up, was going through the whole dreary performance again. Anything rather than that! She turned on the light, jumped off the bed, and searched among her letters. The moment she had it in her hand, she realized that she knew it by heart.

DEAR MARION,

After what has happened I don't suppose you will want to see me again, and though I want to see you, I think it better for us both that I shouldn't. I know it sounds melodramatic to say it, but you have spoilt my life, you have killed something inside me. I never much valued Truth for its own sake, and I am grateful to Chance for affording me that peep behind the scenes last night. I am more grateful to you for keeping up the disguise as long as you did. But though you have taken away so much, you have left me one flicker of curiosity: before I die (or after, it doesn't much matter!) I should like to see you (forgive the expression) unmasked, so that for a moment I can compare the reality with the illusion I used to cherish. Perhaps I shall. Meanwhile good-bye.

Yours once, and in a sense still yours,

HENRY CHICHESTER.

Marion's eyes slid from the letter to the chair beside her where lay mask and domino, ready to put on. She did not feel the irony of their presence; she did not think about them; she was experiencing an immense relief—a relief that always came after reading Harry's letter. When she thought about it it appalled her; when she read it it seemed much less hostile, flattering almost; a testimonial from a wounded and disappointed but still adoring man. She lay down again, and in a moment was asleep.

Soon after ten o'clock the gentlemen followed the ladies into the long drawing-room; it looked unfamiliar even to Jack Manning, stripped of furniture except for a thin lining of gilt chairs. So far everything had gone off splendidly; dinner, augmented by the presence of half a dozen neighbours, had been a great success; but now everyone, including the host and hostess, was a little uncertain what to do next. The zero hour was approaching; the cotillon was supposed to start at eleven and go on till twelve, when the serious dancing would begin; but guests motoring from a distance might arrive at any time. It would spoil the fun of the thing to let the masked and the unmasked meet before the cotillon started; but how could they be kept apart? To preserve the illusion of secrecy Mrs. Manning had asked them to announce themselves at the head of the staircase, in tones sufficiently discreet to be heard by her alone. Knowing how fallible are human plans, she had left in the cloakroom a small supply of masks for those men who, she knew, would forget to bring them. She thought her arrangements were proof against mischance, but she was by no means sure; and as she looked about the room and saw the members of the dinner-party stealing furtive glances at the clock, or plunging into frantic and short-lived conversations, she began to share their uneasiness.

"I think," she said, after one or two unsuccessful efforts to gain the ear of the company, "I think you had all better go and disguise yourselves, before anyone comes and finds you in your natural state." The guests tittered nervously at this pleasantry, then with signs of relief upon their faces they began to file out, some by one door, some by the other, according as the direction of their own rooms took them. The long gallery (as it was sometimes magniloquently described) stood empty and expectant.

"THERE," breathed Mrs. Manning, "would you have recognized that parlour bandit as Sir Joseph Dickinson?"

"No," said her husband, "I wouldn't have believed a mask and a domino could make such a difference. Except for a few of the men, I hardly recognized anyone."

"You're like Marion; she told me 'she often cuts her best friends in the street."

"I dare say that's a gift she's grateful for."

"Jack! You really mustn't. Didn't she look lovely to-night! What a pity she has to wear a mask, even for an hour!"

Her husband grunted.

"I told Colin Chillingworth she was to be here: you know he's always wanted to see her. He is such a nice old man, so considerate—the manners of the older generation."

"Why, because he wants to see Marion?"

"No, idiot! But he had asked me if he might bring a guest——"

"Who?"

"I don't remember the man's name, but he has a bilious attack or something, and can't come, and Colin apologized profusely for not letting us know: his telephone is out of order, he said."

"Very civil of him. How many are we then, all told?"

"Seventy-eight; we should have been seventy-nine."

"Anyone else to come?"

"I'll just ask Jackson." The butler was standing half-way down the stairs. He confirmed Mrs. Manning's estimate. "That's right, Madam; there were twenty-two at dinner and fifty-six have come in since."

"Good staff-work," said her husband. "Now we must dash off and put on our little masks."

They were hurrying away when Mrs. Manning called over her shoulder: "You'll see that the fires are kept up, Jackson?"

"Oh, yes, Madam," he replied. "It's very warm in there."

IT WAS. Marion, coming into the ballroom about eleven o'clock was met by a wave of heat, comforting and sustaining. She moved about among the throng, slightly dazed, it is true, but self-confident and elated. As she expected, she could not put a name to many of the people who kept crossing her restricted line of vision, but she was intensely aware of their eyes—dark, watchful but otherwise expressionless eyes, framed in black. She welcomed their direct regard. On all sides she heard conversation and laughter, especially laughter; little trills and screams of delight at identities disclosed; voices expressing bewilderment and polite despair—"I'm very stupid, I really cannot imagine who you are," gruff rumbling voices, and high falsetto squeaks, obviously disguised. Marion found herself a little impatient of this childishness. When people recognized her, as they often did (her mask was as much a decoration as a concealment) she smiled with her lips but did not try to identify them in return. She felt faintly scornful of the women who were only interesting provided you did not know who they were. She looked forward to the moment when the real business of the evening would begin.

But now the band in the alcove between the two doors had struck up, and a touch on her arm warned her that she was wanted for a figure. Her partner was a raw youth, nice enough in his way, eager, good-natured and jaunty, like a terrier dog. He was not a type she cared for, and she longed to give him the slip.

The opportunity came. Standing on a chair, rather like the Statue of Liberty in New York Harbour, she held aloft a lighted candle. Below her seethed a small group of masked males, leaping like salmon, for the first to blow the candle out would have the privilege of dancing with the torch-bearer. Among them was her partner; he jumped higher than the rest, as she feared he would; but each time she saw his Triton-like mouth soaring up she forestalled his agility and moved the candle out of his reach. Her arm began to tire; and the pack, foiled so often, began to relax their efforts. She must do something quickly. Espying her host among the competitors, she shamelessly brought the candle down to the level of his mouth.

"Nice of you," he said, when, having danced a few turns, they were sitting side by side. "I was glad of that bit of exercise."

"Why, do you feel cold?"

"A little. Don't you?"

Marion considered. "Perhaps I do."

"Funny thing," said her host, "fires seem to be blazing away all right, and it was too hot ten minutes ago."

Their eyes travelled inquiringly round the room. "Why," exclaimed Manning, "no wonder we're cold; there's a window open."

As he spoke, a gust of wind blew the heavy curtains inwards, and a drift of snow came after them.

"Excuse me a moment," he said. "I'll soon stop that."

She heard the sash slam, and in a few moments he was back at her side.

"Now who on earth can have done it?" he demanded, still gasping from contact with the cold air. "The window was wide open!"

"Wide enough to let anyone in?"

"Quite."

"How many of us ought there to be?" asked Marion. "I'm sure you don't know."

"I do—there are——"

"Don't tell me, let's count. I'll race you."

They were both so absorbed in their calculations that the leaders of the cotillon, coming round armed with favours for the next figure, dropped into their laps a fan and a pocket book and passed on unnoticed.

"Well, what do you make it?" they cried almost in unison.

"Seventy-nine," said Marion. "And you?"

"Seventy-nine, too."

"And how many ought there to be?"

"Seventy-eight."

"That's a rum go," said Manning. "We can't both be mistaken. I suppose someone came in afterwards. When I get a chance I'll talk to Jackson."

"It can't be a burglar," said Marion, "a burglar wouldn't have chosen that way of getting in."

"Besides, we should have seen him. No, a hundred to one it was just somebody who was feeling the heat and needed air. I don't blame them, but they needn't have blown us away. Anyhow, if there is a stranger among us he'll soon have to show up, for in half an hour's time we can take off these confounded masks. I wouldn't say it of everyone, but I like you better without yours."

"Do you?" smiled Marion.

"Meanwhile, we must do something about these favours. The next figure's beginning. I say, a fur rug would be more suitable, but may I give this fan to you?"

"And will you accept this useful pocket book?"

They smiled and began to dance.

Ten minutes passed; the fires were heaped up, but the rubbing of hands and hunching of shoulders which had followed the inrush of cold air did not cease. Marion, awaiting her turn to hold the looking-glass, shivered slightly. She watched her predecessor on the chair. Armed with a handkerchief, she was gazing intently into the mirror while each in his turn the men stole up behind her, filling the glass with their successive reflections; one after another she rubbed the images out. Marion was wondering idly whether she would wait too long and find the candidates exhausted when she jumped up from her chair, handed the looking-glass to the leader of the cotillon, and danced away with the man of her choice. Marion took the mirror and sat down. A feeling of unreality oppressed her. How was she to choose between these grotesque faces? One after another they loomed up, dream-like, in the glass, their intense, almost hypnotic eyes searching hers. She could not tell whether they were smiling, they gave so little indication of expression. She remembered how the other women had paused, peered into the glass, and seemed to consider; rubbing away this one at sight, with affected horror, lingering over that one as though sorely tempted, only erasing him after a show of reluctance. She had fancied that some of the men looked piqued when they were rejected; they walked off with a toss of the head; others had seemed frankly pleased to be chosen. She was not indifferent to the mimic drama of the figure, but she couldn't contribute to it. The chill she still felt numbed her mind, and made it drowsy; her gestures seemed automatic, outside the control of her will. Mechanically she rubbed away the reflection of the first candidate, of the second, of the third. But when the fourth presented himself, and hung over her chair till his mask was within a few inches of her hair, the onlookers saw her pause; the hand with the handkerchief lay motionless in her lap, her eyes were fixed upon the mirror. So she sat for a full minute, while the man at the back, never shifting his position, drooped over her like an earring.

"She's taking a good look this time," said a bystander at last, and the remark seemed to pierce her reverie—she turned round slowly and then gave a tremendous start; she was on her feet in a moment. "I'm so sorry," someone heard her say as she gave the man her hand, "I never saw you. I had no idea that anyone was there."

A few minutes later Jane Manning, who had taken as much share in the proceedings as a hostess can, felt a touch upon her arm. It was Marion.

"Well, my dear," she said. "Are you enjoying yourself?"

Marion's voice shook a little. "Marvellously!" She added in an amused tone:

"Queer fellow I got hold of just now."

"Queer-looking, do you mean?"

"Really I don't know; he was wearing a sort of death-mask that covered him almost completely, and he was made up as well, I thought, with French chalk."

"What else was queer about him?"

"He didn't talk. I couldn't get a word out of him."

"Perhaps he was deaf."

"That occurred to me. But he heard the music all right; he danced beautifully."

"Show him to me."

Marion's eyes hovered round the room without catching sight of her late partner.

"He doesn't seem to be here."

"Perhaps he's our uninvited guest," said Jane, laughing. "Jack told me there was an extra person who couldn't be accounted for. Now, darling, you mustn't miss this figure: it's the most amusing of them all. After that, there are some favours to be given, and then supper. I long for it."

"But don't we take off our masks first?"

"Yes, of course, I'd forgotten that."

THE FIGURE described by Mrs. Manning as being the most amusing of all would have been much more amusing, Marion thought, if they had played it without masks. If the dancers did not recognize each other, it lost a great deal of its point. Its success depended on surprise. A space had been cleared in the middle of the room, an oblong space like a badminton court, divided into two, not by a net but by a large white sheet supported at either end by the leaders of the cotillon, and held nearly at arm's length above their heads. On one side were grouped the men, on the other the women, theoretically invisible to each other; but Marion noticed that they moved about and took furtive peeps at each other round the sides, a form of cheating which, in the interludes, the leaders tried to forestall by rushing the sheet across to intercept the view. But most of the time these stolen glimpses went on unchecked, to the accompaniment of a good deal of laughter; for while the figure was in progress the leaders were perforce stationary. One by one the men came up from behind and clasped the top edge of the sheet, so that their gloved fingers, and nothing else, were visible the farther side. With becoming hesitation a woman would advance and take these anonymous fingers in her own; then the sheet was suddenly lowered and the dancers stood face to face, or rather mask to mask. Sometimes there were cries of recognition, sometimes silence, the masks were as impenetrable as the sheet had been.

It was Marion's turn. As she walked forward she saw that the gloved hands were not resting on the sheet like the rest; they were clutching it so tightly that the linen was caught up in creases between the fingers and crumpled round their tips. For a moment they did not respond to her touch, then they gripped with surprising force. Down went the leader's arms, down went the corners of the sheet. But Marion's unknown partner did not take his cue. He forgot to release the sheet, and she remained with her arms held immovably aloft, the sheet falling in folds about her and almost covering her head. "An unrehearsed effect, jolly good, I call it," said somebody. At last, in response to playful tugs and twitches from the leaders, the man let the sheet go and discovered himself to the humiliated Marion. It was her partner of the previous figure, that uncommunicative man. His hands, that still held hers, felt cold through their kid covering.

"Oh," she cried, "I can't understand it—I feel so cold. Let's dance."

They danced for a little and then sat down. Marion felt chillier than ever, and she heard her neighbours on either side complaining of the temperature. Suddenly she made a decision and rose to her feet.

"Do take me somewhere where it's warmer," she said. "I'm perished here."

The man led the way out of the ballroom, through the ante-room at the end where one or two couples were sitting, across the corridor into a little room where a good fire was burning, throwing every now and then a ruddy gleam on china ornaments and silver photograph frames. It was Mrs. Manning's sitting-room.

"We don't need a light, do we?" said her companion. "Let's sit as we are."

It was the first time he had volunteered a remark. His voice was somehow familiar to Marion, yet she couldn't place it; it had an alien quality that made it unrecognizable, like one's own dress worn by someone else.

"With pleasure," she said. "But we mustn't stay long, must we? It's only a few minutes to twelve. Can we hear the music from here?"

They sat in silence, listening. There was no sound.

"Don't think me fussy," Marion said. "I'm enjoying this tremendously, but Jenny would be disappointed if we missed the last figure. If you don't mind opening the door, we should hear the music begin."

As he did not offer to move, she got up to open it herself, but before she reached the door she heard her name called.

"Marion!"

"Who said that, you?" she cried, suddenly very nervous.

"Don't you know who I am?"

"Harry!"

Her voice shook and she sank back into her chair, trembling violently.

"How was it I didn't recognize you? I'm—I'm so glad to see you."

"You haven't seen me yet," said he. It was like him to say that, playfully grim. His words reassured her, but his tone left her still in doubt.

She did not know how to start the conversation, what effect to aim at, what note to strike; so much depended on divining his mood and playing up to it. If she could have seen his face, if she could even have caught a glimpse of the poise of his head, it would have given her a cue; in the dark like this, hardly certain of his whereabouts in the room, she felt hopelessly at a disadvantage.

"It was nice of you to come and see me—if you did come to see me," she ventured at last.

"I heard you were to be here." Again that non-committal tone! Trying to probe him she said:

"Would you have come otherwise? It's rather a childish entertainment, isn't it?"

"I should have come," he answered, "but it would have been in—in a different spirit."

She could make nothing of this.

"I didn't know the Mannings were friends of yours," she told him. "He's rather a dear, married to a dull woman, if I must be really truthful."

"I don't know them," said he.

"Then you gate-crashed?"

"I suppose I did."

"I take that as a compliment," said Marion after a pause. "But—forgive me—I must be very slow—I don't understand. You said you were coming in any case."

"Some friends of mine called Chillingworth offered to bring me."

"How lucky I was! So you came with them?"

"Not with them, after them."

"How odd. Wasn't there room for you in their car? How did you get here so quickly?"

"The dead travel fast." His irony baffled her. But her thoughts flew to his letter, in which he accused her of having killed something in him; he must be referring to that.

"Darling Hal," she said. "Believe me, I'm sorry to have hurt you. What can I do to—to——"

There was a sound of voices calling, and her attention thus awakened caught the strains of music, muffled and remote.

"They want us for the next figure. We must go," she cried, thankful that the difficult interview was nearly over. She was colder than ever, and could hardly keep her teeth from chattering audibly.

"What is the next figure?" he asked, without appearing to move.

"Oh, you know—we've had it before—we give each other favours, then we unmask ourselves. Hal, we really ought to go! Listen! Isn't that midnight beginning to strike?"

Unable to control her agitation, aggravated by the strain of the encounter, the deadly sensation of cold within her, and a presentiment of disaster for which she could not account, she rushed towards the door and her outstretched left hand, finding the switch, flooded the room with light. Mechanically she turned her head to the room; it was empty. Bewildered she looked back over her left shoulder, and there, within a foot of her, stood Harry Chichester, his arms stretched across the door.

"Harry," she cried, "don't be silly! Come out or let me out!"

"You must give me a favour first," he said sombrely.

"Of course I will, but I haven't got one here."

"I thought you always had favours to give away."

"Harry, what do you mean?"

"You came unprovided?"

She was silent.

"*I* did not. I have something here to give you—a small token. Only I must have a *quid pro quo*."

He's mad, thought Marion. I must humour him as far as I can.

"Very well," she said, looking around the room. Jenny would forgive her—it was an emergency. "May I give you this silver pencil?"

He shook his head.

"Or this little vase?"

Still he refused.

"Or this calendar?"

"The flight of time doesn't interest me."

"Then what can I tempt you with?"

"Something that is really your own—a kiss."

"My dear," said Marion, trembling, "you needn't have asked for it."

"Thank you," he said. "And to prove I don't want something for nothing, here is your favour."

He felt in his pocket. Marion saw a dark silvery gleam; she held her hand out for the gift.

It was a revolver.

"What am I to do with this?" she asked.

"You are the best judge of that," he replied. "Only one cartridge has been used."

Without taking her eyes from his face she laid down the revolver among the bric-à-brac on the table by her side.

"And now your gift to me."

"But what about our masks?" said Marion.

"Take yours off," he commanded.

"Mine doesn't matter," said Marion, removing as she spoke the silken visor. "But you are wearing an entirely false face."

349

"Do you know why?" he asked, gazing at her fixedly through the slits in the mask.

She didn't answer.

"I was always an empty-headed fellow," he went on, tapping the waxed covering with his gloved forefinger, so that it gave out a wooden hollow sound—"there's nothing much behind this. No brains to speak of, I mean. Less than I used to have, in fact."

Marion stared at him in horror.

"Would you like to see? Would you like to look right into my mind?"

"No! No!" she cried wildly.

"But I think you ought to," he said, coming a step nearer and raising his hands to his head.

"HAVE YOU seen Marion?" said Jane Manning to her husband. "I've a notion she hasn't been enjoying herself. This was in a sense her party, you know. We made a mistake to give her Tommy Cardew as a partner; he doesn't carry heavy enough guns for her."

"Why, does she want shooting?" inquired her husband.

"Idiot! But I could see they didn't get on. I wonder where she's got to—I'm afraid she may be bored."

"Perhaps she's having a quiet talk with a howitzer," her husband suggested.

Jane ignored him. "Darling, it's nearly twelve. Run into the ante-room and fetch her; I don't want her to miss the final figure."

In a few seconds he returned. "Not there," he said. "Not there, my child. Sunk by a twelve-inch shell, probably."

"She may be sitting out in the corridor."

"Hardly, after a direct hit."

"We'll look." They went away and returned with blank faces. The guests were standing about talking; the members of the band, their hands ready on their instruments, looked up inquiringly.

"We shall have to begin without her," Mrs. Manning reluctantly decided. "We shan't have time to finish as it is."

The hands of the clock showed five minutes to twelve.

The band played as though inspired, and many said afterwards that the cotillon never got really going, properly warmed up, till those last five minutes. All the fun of the evening seemed to come to a head, as though the spirit of the dance, mistrustful of its latter-day devotees, had withheld its benison till the final moments. Everyone was too excited to notice, as they whirled past that the butler was standing in one of the doorways with a white and anxious face. Even Mrs. Manning, when at last she saw him, called out cheerfully, almost without pausing for an answer:

350

"Well, Jackson, everything all right, I hope?"

"Can I speak to you a moment, Madam?" he said. "Or perhaps Mr. Manning would be better."

Mrs. Manning's heart sank. Did he want to leave?

"Oh, I expect I shall do, shan't I? I hope it's nothing serious."

"I'm afraid it is, Madam, very serious."

"All right, I'll come." She followed him on to the landing.

A MINUTE LATER her husband saw her threading her way towards him.

"Jack! Just a moment."

He was dancing and affected not to hear. His partner's eyes looked surprised and almost resentful, Mrs. Manning thought; but she persisted none the less.

"I know I'm a bore and I'm sorry, but I really can't help myself."

This brought them to a stand.

"Why, Jane, has the boiler burst?"

"No, it's more serious than that, Jack," she said, as he disengaged himself from his partner with an apology. "There's been a dreadful accident or something at the Chillingworths. That guest of theirs, do you remember, whom they were to have brought and didn't——"

"Yes, he stayed behind with a headache—rotten excuse—"

"Well, he's shot himself."

"Good God! When?"

"They found him half an hour ago, apparently, but they couldn't telephone because the machine was out of order, and had to send."

"Is he dead?"

"Yes, he blew his brains out."

"Do you remember his name?"

"The man told me. He was called Chichester."

They were standing at the side of the room, partly to avoid the dancers, partly to be out of earshot. The latter consideration need not have troubled them, however. The band, which for some time past had been playing nineteenth-century waltzes, now burst into the strains of *John Peel*. There was a tremendous sense of excitement and climax. The dancers galloped by at break-neck speed; the band played fortissimo; the volume of sound was terrific. But above the din—the music, the laughter and the thud of feet—they could just hear the clock striking twelve.

Jack Manning looked doubtfully at his wife. "Should I go and tell Chillingworth now? What do you think?"

"Perhaps you'd better—it seems so heartless not to. Break it to him as gently as you can, and don't let the others know if you can help it."

351

Jack Manning's task was neither easy nor agreeable, and he was a born bungler. Despairing of making himself heard, he raised his hand and cried out, "Wait a moment!" Some of the company stood still and, imagining it was a signal to take off their masks, began to do so; others went on dancing; others stopped and stared. He was the centre of attention; and before he had got his message fairly delivered, it had reached other ears than those for which it was intended. An excited whispering went round the room: "What is it? What is it?" Men and women stood about with their masks in their hands, and faces blanker than before they were uncovered. Others looked terrified and incredulous. A woman came up to Jane Manning and said:

"What a dreadful thing for Marion Lane."

"Why?" Jane asked.

"Didn't you know? She and Harry Chichester were the greatest friends. At one time it was thought—"

"I live out of the world, I had no idea," said Jane quickly. Even in the presence of calamity, she felt a pang that her friend had not confided in her.

Her interlocutor persisted: "It was talked about a great deal. Some people said—you know how they chatter—that she didn't treat him quite fairly. I hate to make myself a busybody, Mrs. Manning, but I do think you ought to tell her; she ought to be prepared."

"But I don't know where she is!" cried Jane, from whose mind all thought of her friend had been banished. "Have you seen her?"

"Not since the sheet incident."

"Nor have I."

Nor, it seemed, had anyone. Disturbed by this new misadventure far more than its trivial nature seemed to warrant, Jane hastened in turn to such of her guests as might be able to enlighten her as to Marion's whereabouts. Some of them greeted her inquiry with a lift of the eyebrows but none of them could help her in her quest. Nor could she persuade them to take much interest in it. They seemed to have forgotten that they were at a party, and owed a duty of responsiveness to their hostess. Their eyes did not light up when she came near. One and all they were discussing the suicide, and suggesting its possible motive. The room rustled with their whispering, with the soft hissing sound of 'Chichester' and the succeeding 'Hush!' which was meant to stifle but only multiplied and prolonged it. Jane felt that she must scream.

All at once there was silence. Had she screamed? No, for the noise they had all heard came from somewhere inside the house. The room seemed to hold its breath. There it was again, and coming closer; a cry, a shriek, the shrill tones of terror alternating in a dreadful rhythm with a throaty, choking sound like whooping-cough. No one could have recognized it as Marion Lane's voice, and few could have told for Marion Lane the dishevelled figure, mask in hand, that lurched through the ballroom doorway and with quick stumbling steps, before which the onlookers fell back, zigzagged into the middle of the room.

"Stop him!" she gasped. "Don't let him do it!" Jane Manning ran to her.

"Dearest, what is it?"

"It's Harry Chichester," sobbed Marion, her head rolling about on her shoulders as if it had come loose. "He's in there. He wants to take his mask off, but I can't bear it! It would be awful! Oh, do take him away!"

"Where is he?" someone asked.

"Oh, I don't know! In Jane's sitting room, I think. He wouldn't let me go. He's so cold, so dreadfully cold."

"Look after her, Jane," said Jack Manning. "Get her out of here. Anyone coming with me?" he asked, looking round. "I'm going to investigate."

Marion caught the last words. "Don't go," she implored. "He'll hurt you." But her voice was drowned in the scurry and stampede of feet. The whole company was following their host. In a few moments the ballroom was empty.

FIVE MINUTES LATER there were voices in the ante-room. It was Manning leading back his troops. "Barring, of course, the revolver," he was saying, "and the few things that had been knocked over, and those scratches on the door, there wasn't a trace. Hullo!" he added, crossing the threshold, "what's this?"

The ballroom window was open again; the curtains fluttered wildly inwards; on the boards lay a patch of nearly melted snow.

Jack Manning walked up to it. Just within the further edge, near the window, was a kind of smear, darker than the toffee-coloured mess around it, and roughly oval in shape.

"Do you think that's a footmark?" he asked of the company in general.

No one could say.

W. F. HARVEY

1885–1937

A doctor by profession and a Quaker, his lungs were
permanently damaged while he was operating on a stoker
trapped in a smoke-filled engine room during the First World War.
The action earned him the Albert Medal but the gentle hero was
an invalid the rest of his days, occasionally writing tales
as violent as his own nature was peaceable.

August Heat

PENISTONE ROAD, CLAPHAM,
20th August, 190–.

I HAVE HAD WHAT I believe to
be the most remarkable day in
my life, and while the events are
still in my mind, I wish to put
them down on paper as clearly as
possible.

Let me say at the outset that
my name is James Clarence Withencroft. I am forty years old, in perfect
health, never having known a day's illness. By profession I am an artist,
not a very successful one, but I earn enough money by my black-and-
white work to satisfy my necessary wants. My only near relative, a
sister, died five years ago, so that I am independent.

I breakfasted this morning at nine, and after glancing through the
morning paper I lighted my pipe and proceeded to let my mind wander
in the hope that I might chance upon some subject for my pencil.

The room, though door and windows were open, was oppressively
hot, and I had just made up my mind that the coolest and most comfortable place in the neighbourhood would be the deep end of the public
swimming-bath, when the idea came.

I began to draw. So intent was I on my work that I left my lunch
untouched, only stopping work when the clock of St. Jude's struck four.

The final result, for a hurried sketch, was, I felt sure, the best thing

I had done. It showed a criminal in the dock immediately after the judge had pronounced sentence. The man was fat—enormously fat. The flesh hung in rolls about his chin; it creased his huge, stumpy neck. He was clean-shaven (perhaps I should say a few days before he must have been clean-shaven) and almost bald. He stood in the dock, his short, clumsy fingers clasping the rail, looking straight in front of him. The feeling that his expression conveyed was not so much one of horror as of utter, absolute collapse.

There seemed nothing in the man strong enough to sustain that mountain of flesh.

I rolled up the sketch, and without quite knowing why, placed it in my pocket. Then with the rare sense of happiness which the knowledge of a good thing well done gives, I left the house.

I believe that I set out with the idea of calling upon Trenton, for I remember walking along Lytton Street and turning to the right along Gilchrist Road at the bottom of the hill where the men were at work on the new tram lines.

From there onwards I have only the vaguest recollection of where I went. The one thing of which I was fully conscious was the awful heat, that came up from the dusty asphalt pavement as an almost palpable wave. I longed for the thunder promised by the great banks of copper-coloured cloud that hung low over the western sky.

I must have walked five or six miles, when a small boy roused me from my reverie by asking the time.

It was twenty minutes to seven.

When he left me I began to take stock of my bearings. I found myself standing before a gate that led into a yard bordered by a strip of thirsty earth, where there were flowers, purple stock and scarlet geranium. Above the entrance was a board with the inscription:

CHS. ATKINSON.   MONUMENTAL MASON.
WORKER IN ENGLISH AND ITALIAN MARBLES.

From the yard itself came a cheery whistle, the noise of hammer blows, and the cold sound of steel meeting stone.

A sudden impulse made me enter.

A man was sitting with his back towards me, busy at work on a slab of curiously veined marble. He turned round as he heard my steps and I stopped short.

It was the man I had been drawing, whose portrait lay in my pocket.

He sat there, huge and elephantine, the sweat pouring from his scalp, which he wiped with a red silk handkerchief. But though the face was the same, the expression was absolutely different.

He greeted me smiling, as if we were old friends, and shook my hand.

I apologized for my intrusion.

"Everything is hot and glary outside," I said. "This seems an oasis in the wilderness."

"I don't know about the oasis," he replied, "but it certainly is hot, as hot as hell. Take a seat, sir!"

He pointed to the end of the gravestone on which he was at work, and I sat down.

"That's a beautiful piece of stone you've got hold of," I said.

He shook his head. "In a way it is," he answered; "the surface here is as fine as anything you could wish, but there's a big flaw at the back, though I don't expect you'd ever notice it. I could never make really a good job of a bit of marble like that. It would be all right in a summer like this; it wouldn't mind the blasted heat. But wait till the winter comes. There's nothing quite like frost to find out the weak points in stone."

"Then what's it for?" I asked.

The man burst out laughing.

"You'd hardly believe me if I was to tell you it's for an exhibition, but it's the truth. Artists have exhibitions: so do grocers and butchers; we have them too. All the latest little things in headstones, you know."

He went on to talk of marbles, which sort best withstood wind and rain, and which were easiest to work; then of his garden and a new sort of carnation he had bought. At the end of every other minute he would drop his tools, wipe his shining head, and curse the heat.

I said little, for I felt uneasy. There was something unnatural, uncanny, in meeting this man.

I tried at first to persuade myself that I had seen him before, that his face, unknown to me, had found a place in some out-of-the-way corner of my memory, but I knew that I was practising little more than a plausible piece of self-deception.

Mr. Atkinson finished his work, spat on the ground, and got up with a sigh of relief.

"There! what do you think of that?" he said, with an air of evident pride.

The inscription which I read for the first time was this:

SACRED TO THE MEMORY

OF

JAMES CLARENCE WITHENCROFT.

BORN JAN. 18TH, 1860.

HE PASSED AWAY VERY SUDDENLY

ON AUGUST 20TH, 190–

"In the midst of life we are in death"

For some time I sat in silence. Then a cold shudder ran down my spine. I asked him where he had seen the name.

"Oh, I didn't see it anywhere," replied Mr. Atkinson. "I wanted some name, and I put down the first that came into my head. Why do you want to know?"

"It's a strange coincidence, but it happens to be mine."

He gave a long, low whistle. "And the dates?"

"I can only answer for one of them, and that's correct."

"It's a rum go!" he said.

But he knew less than I did. I told him of my morning's work. I took the sketch from my pocket and showed it to him. As he looked, the expression of his face altered until it became more and more like that of the man I had drawn.

"And it was only the day before yesterday," he said, "that I told Maria there were no such things as ghosts!"

Neither of us had seen a ghost, but I knew what he meant.

"You probably heard my name," I said.

"And you must have seen me somewhere and have forgotten it! Were you at Clacton-on-Sea last July?"

I had never been to Clacton in my life. We were silent for some time. We were both looking at the same thing, the two dates on the gravestone, and one was right.

"Come inside and have some supper," said Mr. Atkinson.

His wife is a cheerful little woman, with the flaky red cheeks of the country-bred. Her husband introduced me as a friend of his who was an artist. The result was unfortunate, for after the sardines and watercress had been removed, she brought out a Doré Bible, and I had to sit and express my admiration for nearly half an hour.

I went outside, and found Atkinson sitting on the gravestone smoking. We resumed the conversation at the point we had left off.

"You must excuse my asking," I said, "but do you know of anything you've done for which you could be put on trial?"

He shook his head.

"I'm not a bankrupt, the business is prosperous enough. Three years ago I gave turkeys to some of the guardians at Christmas, but that's all I can think of. And they were small ones, too," he added as an afterthought.

He got up, fetched a can from the porch, and began to water the flowers. "Twice a day regular in the hot weather," he said, "and then the heat sometimes gets the better of the delicate ones. And ferns, good Lord! they could never stand it. Where do you live?"

I told him my address. It would take an hour's quick walk to get back home.

"It's like this," he said. "We'll look at the matter straight. If you go back home to-night, you take your chance of accidents. A cart may run over you, and there's always banana skins and orange peel, to say nothing of falling ladders."

He spoke of the improbable with an intense seriousness that would have been laughable six hours before. But I did not laugh.

"The best thing we can do," he continued, "is for you to stay here till twelve o'clock. We'll go upstairs and smoke; it may be cooler inside." To my surprise I agreed.

WE ARE SITTING now in a long, low room beneath the eaves. Atkinson has sent his wife to bed. He himself is busy sharpening some tools at a little oilstone, smoking one of my cigars the while.

The air seems charged with thunder. I am writing this at a shaky table before the open window. The leg is cracked, and Atkinson, who seems a handy man with his tools, is going to mend it as soon as he has finished putting an edge on his chisel.

It is after eleven now. I shall be gone in less than an hour.

But the heat is stifling.

It is enough to send a man mad.

SUSAN HILL

b. 1942

Born in Yorkshire, she began writing in her late teens and in a few prolific years captured many of Britain's most coveted literary prizes. Unlike the confused and tortured characters of some of her novels and short stories, she leads a fulfilling life as a writer, broadcaster and mother of two daughters. Married to the Shakespearian scholar, Stanley Wells, she lives in Oxford.

How Soon Can I Leave?

THE TWO LADIES who lived together were called Miss Bartlett and Miss Roscommon.

Miss Roscommon, the older and stouter of the two, concealed her fear of life behind frank reference to babies and lavatories and the sexing of day-old chicks. It was well known that she had travelled widely as a girl, she told of her walking tours in Greece, and how she had driven an ambulance during the Spanish Civil War.

Miss Bartlett, who was only forty, cultivated shyness and self-effacement, out of which arose her way of leaving muttered sentences to trail off into the air, unfinished. Oh, do not take any notice of anything *I* may say, she meant, it is of no consequence, I am sorry to have spoken . . . But the sentences drew attention to her, nevertheless.

"What was that?" people said, "I beg your pardon, I didn't quite catch . . . Do speak up . . ." And so, she was forced to repeat herself and they, having brought it upon themselves, were forced to listen. She also protested helplessness in the face of everyday tools. It was Miss Roscommon who peeled all the potatoes and defrosted the refrigerator and opened the tins.

Their house, one of two white bungalows overlooking the bay, was called Tuscany. When Miss Bartlett had finally come to live with Miss

Roscommon, seven years before, each one believed that the step was taken for the good of the other. Miss Bartlett had been living in one of the little stone cottages, opposite the harbour, working through the winter on the stock that she sold, from her front room and on a trestle outside, in summer. From November until March, there were no visitors to Mountsea. Winds and rain scoured the surface of the cliffs and only the lifeboat put out to sea. Miss Roscommon had taken to inviting Miss Bartlett up to the bungalow for meals.

"You should have a shop," she had begun by saying, loading Miss Bartlett's plate with scones and home-made ginger jam, "properly equipped and converted. It cannot be satisfactory having to display goods in your living-room. Why have you not thought of taking a shop?"

Miss Bartlett made marquetry pictures of the church, the lighthouse and the harbour, table-lamps out of lobster pots and rock worked over with shells. She also imported Italian straw baskets and did a little pewter work. The idea of a shop had come to her, and been at once dismissed, in the first weeks after her coming to Mountsea. She was too timid to take any so definite a step, for, by establishing herself in a shop, with her name written up on a board outside, was she not establishing herself in the minds of others, as a shop*keeper*? As a girl, she had been impressed by her mother's constant references to her as dreamy and artistic, so that she could not possibly now see herself in the role of shopkeeper. Also, by having her name written up on that board, she felt that she would somehow be committing herself to Mountsea, and by doing that, finally abandoning all her hopes of a future in some other place. As a girl, she had looked out at the world, and seen a signpost, with arms pointing in numerous different directions, roads leading here, or here, or there. She had been quite unable to choose which road to take for, having once set out upon any of them, she would thereby be denying herself all the others. And what might I lose, she had thought, what opportunities shall I miss if I make the wrong choice?

So that, in the end, she had never chosen, only drifted through her life from this to that, waking every morning to the expectation of some momentous good fortune dropped in her lap.

"That cottage is damp," said Miss Roscommon, allowing her persuasions to take on a more personal note, as they got to know one another better. "I do not think you look after yourself properly. And a place of business should not have to double as a home."

At first, Miss Bartlett shrank from the hints and persuasions, knowing herself to be easily swayed, fearful of being swept along on the tide of Miss Roscommon's decision. I am only forty years old, she said, there is plenty of opportunity left for me, I do not have to abandon hope by retreating into middle age, and life with another woman. Though certainly she enjoyed the meals the other cooked, the taste of home-baked pasties and stews and herb-flavoured vegetables.

"I'm afraid that I cannot cook," she said, "I live on milk and cheese and oven-baked potatoes. I would not know where to begin in the kitchen." It did not occur to her that this was any cause for shame, and Miss Roscommon tut-tutted and floured the pastry-board, relieved to have, once again, a sense of purpose brought into her life.

"There were nine of us in the family," she said, "and I was the only girl. At the age of seven, I knew how to bake a perfect loaf of bread. I am quite content to be one of the Marthas of this world."

But I will not go and *live* there, Miss Bartlett told herself, towards the end of that summer. I am determined to remain independent, my plans are fluid, I have my work, and besides, it would never do, we might not get on well together and then it would be embarrassing for me to have to leave. And people might talk.

Though she knew that they would not, and that it was of her own judgement that she was most afraid, for Mountsea was full of ladies of indeterminate age, sharing houses together.

The winter came, and the cottage was indeed damp. The stone walls struck cold all day and all night, in spite of expensive electric heaters, and Miss Bartlett spent longer and longer afternoons at Tuscany, even taking some of her work up there, from time to time.

At the beginning of December, the first of the bad storms sent waves crashing up over the quayside into the front room.

Of course, Miss Roscommon is lonely, she said now, she has need of me, I should have realized. That type of woman, who appears to be so competent and strong, feels the onset of old age and infirmity more than most, but she cannot say so, cannot give way and confess to human weakness. She bakes me cakes and worries about the dampness in my house because she needs my company and concern for herself.

And so, on Christmas Eve, when the second storm filled Miss Bartlett's living-room with water up to the level of the window seat, she allowed herself to be evacuated by the capable Miss Roscommon up to the white bungalow.

"It will not be for good," she said anxiously, "when the weather improves, I shall have to go back, there is the business to be thought of."

"We shall make plans for a proper shop," said Miss Roscommon firmly, "I have a little money . . ."

She filled up a pottery bowl with leek soup, having acquired her faith in its restorative powers when she had set up a canteen at the scene of a mining disaster in the nineteen-twenties.

Miss Bartlett accepted the soup and a chair close to the fire and an electric blanket for her bed, thereby setting the seal on the future pattern of their relationship. By the beginning of February, plans for the shop were made, by mid-March, the work was in hand. There was no longer any talk of her moving, she would sell her goods from the new shop during the summer days, but she would live at Tuscany. The garage was fitted with light, heat and two extra windows, and made into a studio.

"This is quite the best arrangement," said Miss Roscommon, "here, you will be properly fed and looked after, I shall see to that."

Over the seven years that followed, Miss Bartlett came to rely upon her for many more things than the comforts of a well-kept home. It was Miss Roscommon who made all the business arrangements for the new shop, who saw the bank manager, the estate agent and the builder, Miss Roscommon who advised with the orders and the accounts. During the summer seasons, the shop did well, and after three years, at her friend's suggestion, Miss Bartlett started to make pink raffia angels and pot-pourri jars, for the Christmas postal market.

She relaxed, ceased to feel uneasy, and if, from time to time, she did experience a sudden shot of alarm, at seeing herself so well and truly settled, she said, not, "Where else would I go?" but, "I am needed here. However would she manage without me? It would be cruel to go." All the decisions were left to Miss Roscommon. "You are so much better at these things . . ." Miss Bartlett said, and drifted away to her studio, a small woman with pastel-coloured flesh.

Perhaps it was her forty-seventh birthday that jolted her into a renewed awareness of her situation. She looked into the mirror on that morning, and saw middle-age settled irrevocably over her features. She was reminded of her dependence upon Miss Roscommon.

I said I would not stay here, she thought, would never have my name written up above a permanent shop, for my plans were to remain fluid. And now it is seven years, and how many opportunities have I missed? How many roads are closed to me?

Or perhaps it was the visit of Miss Roscommon's niece Angela, and her husband of only seven days, one weekend in early September.

"I shall do a great deal of baking," Miss Roscommon said, "for they will certainly stay to tea. We shall have cheese scones and preserves and a layer cake."

"I did not realize that you had a niece."

Miss Roscommon rose from the table heavily, for she had put on weight, over the seven years. There had also been some suspicion about a cataract in her left eye, another reason why Miss Bartlett told herself she could not leave her.

"She is my youngest brother's child. I haven't seen her since she was a baby."

Miss Bartlett nodded and wandered away from the breakfast table, not liking to ask why there had been no wedding invitation. Even after seven years, Miss Roscommon kept some of her secrets, there were subjects upon which she simply did not speak, though Miss Bartlett had long ago bared her own soul.

The niece Angela, and her new husband, brought a slab of wedding cake, which was put to grace the centre of the table, on a porcelain stand.

"And this," said Miss Roscommon triumphantly, "*this* is my friend, Miss Mary Bartlett." For Miss Bartlett had hung behind in the studio for ten minutes after their arrival, out of courtesy and because it was always something of a strain for her to meet new people.

"Mary is very shy, very retiring," her own mother had always said, "she is artistic you see, she lives in her own world." Her tone had always been proud and Miss Bartlett had therefore come to see her own failure to make human relationships as a mark of distinction. Her shyness had been cultivated, readily admitted to.

The niece and her husband sat together on the sofa, a little flushed and self-conscious in new clothes. Seeing them there, Miss Bartlett realized for the first time that no young people had ever been inside the bungalow, since her arrival. But it was more than their youthfulness which struck her, there was an air of suppressed excitement about them, a glitter, they emanated pride in the satisfactions of the flesh.

Miss Roscommon presided over a laden tea-table, her face still flushed from the oven. "And Miss Bartlett is very clever," she told them, "she makes beautiful things. You must go down to the shop and see them, buy something for your new home."

"You make things?" said Angela, through a mouthful of shortbread, "what sort of things?"

Miss Bartlett made a little gesture of dismissal with her hand. "Oh, not very much really, nothing at all exciting. Just a few little . . . I'm sure you wouldn't . . ." She let her voice trail off, but it was Miss Roscommon and not the niece Angela who took her up on it.

"Now that is just nonsense," she said firmly. "There is no virtue in this false modesty, I have told you before. Of course Angela will like your things, why should she not? Plenty of visitors do, and there is nothing to be ashamed of in having a talent."

"I wore a hand-embroidered dress," said the niece Angela, "for my wedding."

Miss Bartlett watched her, and watched the new husband, whose eyes followed Angela's slim hand as it moved over to the cake plate and back, and up into her mouth. Their eyes met and shone with secrets, across the table. Miss Bartlett's stomach moved a little, with fear and excitement. She felt herself to be within touching distance of some very important piece of knowledge.

"Do you help with this shop, then—?" asked the husband, though without interest.

"Oh, no! Well, here and there with the accounts and so forth, because Mary doesn't understand any of that, she is such a dreamer! No, no, that is not my job, that is not what keeps me so busy. My job is to look after Mary, of course. I took that upon myself quite some time ago, when I saw that I was needed. She is such a silly girl, she lives in a world of her own and if I were not here to worry about her meals and her comforts, she would starve, I assure you, simply starve."

"Oh, I don't think I really . . ."

"Of course you would," said Miss Roscommon. "Now let me have your cup to be filled."

The young couple exchanged another glance, of comprehension and amusement. How dare you, thought Miss Bartlett, almost in tears with anger and frustration, at being so looked upon and judged and misunderstood. What do you know of it, how can you sit there so smugly? It is because you are young and know nothing. It is all very well for you.

"All the same," said the niece Angela, sitting back in her chair, "it's very nice to be looked after. I must say."

She smiled like a cat.

"Yes, that has always been my role in life, that is *my* talent," said Miss Roscommon, "to do all the looking after." She leaned over and patted Miss Bartlett on the hand. "She is my responsibility now, you see," she told them confidently. "My little pussy-cat."

Miss Bartlett pushed the hand away and got to her feet, her face flushed with shame and annoyance. "What a foolish thing to say! Of course I am not, how very silly you make me look. I am a grown woman, I am quite capable of looking after myself."

Miss Roscommon, not in the least discomfited, only began to pour the tea dregs into a slop basin, smiling.

When they were about to leave, Miss Bartlett said, "I will walk down the hill with you, and we shall drop in for a minute at the shop. Yes, I insist . . . But not for you to buy anything. You must choose a wedding present from my stock, it is the very least I can do." For she wanted to keep them with her longer, to be seen walking in their company down the hill away from the bungalow, wanted to be on their side.

"You will need a warm coat, it is autumn now, the evenings are drawing in. Take your mohair."

"Oh, leave me, leave me, do not *fuss*." And Miss Bartlett walked to the end of the gravelled drive, while the niece and her new husband made their good-byes.

"I am afraid it is all she has to worry over nowadays," she said hastily, the moment they had joined her. "It gives her pleasure, I suppose, to do all that clucking round and I have not the heart to do anything but play along, keep up appearances. If it were not for me, she would be so lonely. Of course, I have had to give up a good deal of my own life, on that account."

The niece Angela took her husband's arm. "It must be very nice and comfortable for you there," she said, "all the same." Miss Bartlett turned her face away and looked out to sea. Another winter, she thought, and I am now forty-seven years old. You do not understand.

She detained them in the shop for as long as possible, fetching out special items from the stock room and taking time over the wrapping paper. Let me be with you, she wanted to say, let me be on your side, for do you not see that I still have many opportunities left, I am not an old woman, I know about the world and the ways of modern life. Take me with you.

But when they had gone she stood in the darkening shop and saw that they had already placed and dismissed her, that she did not belong with them and there was no hope left. She sat on the stool beside the till and wept, for the injustice of the world and the weakness of her own nature. I have become what I always dreaded becoming, she said, everything has slipped through my fingers.

And for all of it, after a short time, she began to blame Miss Roscommon. She has stifled me, she thought, she preys upon me, I am treated as her child, her toy, her *pussy-cat*, she has humiliated me and fed off my dependence and the fact that I have always been so sensitive. She is a wicked woman. And then she said, *but I do not have to stay with her*. Fortified by the truth of this new realization, Miss Bartlett blew her nose, and walked back up the hill to Tuscany.

"YOU CANNOT LEAVE," said Miss Roscommon, "what nonsense, of course you cannot. You have nowhere else to go and besides, in ten days' time we set off for our holiday in Florence."

"You will set off. I am afraid my plans have now changed." Miss Bartlett could not now bear the thought of being seen with her friend in all the museums and art galleries of Florence, discussing the paintings in loud, knowledgeable voices and eating wholemeal sandwiches out of neat little greaseproof bags, speaking very slowly to the Italians. This year Miss Roscommon must go alone. She did not allow herself to think of how, or whether she would enjoy herself. We are always hearing of how intrepid she was as a girl, she thought. Then let her be intrepid again. Aloud, she said, "I am going back to live at the cottage." For she had kept it on, and rented it to summer visitors.

365

Miss Roscommon turned herself, and her darning, a little more towards the light.

"You are being very foolish," she said mildly. "But I understand why, it is your age, of course."

Appalled, Miss Bartlett went through to her room, and began to throw things furiously, haphazardly, into a suitcase. I am my own mistress, she said, a grown-up woman with years ahead of me, it is time for me to be firm. I have pandered to her long enough.

The following day, watched by Miss Roscommon, she moved back down the hill to the cottage. She would, she decided, stay there for a while, give herself time to get accustomed, and to gather all of her things around her again, and then she would look out and make plans, take steps towards her new life.

That evening, hearing the wind around her own four walls, she said, I have escaped. Though she woke in the night and was aware of being entirely alone in the cottage, of not being able to hear the loud breathing of Miss Roscommon in the room next door.

She expected the Italian holiday to be cancelled, on some pretext, and was astonished when Miss Roscommon left, on the appointed day and alone. Miss Bartlett took the opportunity of going up to Tuscany and fetching some more of her things down, work from the studio to keep her busy in the evening, and during the days, too, for now it was October and few people came into the shop.

Here I am, she said, twisting the raffia angels and winding ribbon around the pot-pourris, etching her gift cards, here I am, living my own life and making my own decisions. She wanted to invite someone down to stay, someone young, so that she could be seen and approved of, but there was no one. A search through all the drawers and cupboards at the bungalow did not yield her the address of the niece Angela. She would have sent a little note, with a Christmas gift, to tell of her removal, prove her independence.

Miss Roscommon returned from Italy, looking rather tired and not very suntanned. She came in with a miniature plaster copy of a Donatello statue, and some fine art postcards. Miss Bartlett made tea, and the conversation was very stilted.

"You are not warm enough here," said Miss Roscommon, "I will send down some extra blankets."

"Oh no, thank you. Please don't do that."

But the following day the blankets, and a Dutch apple pie, arrived with the butcher's boy.

Miss Bartlett bought huge slabs of cheese and eggs, which she could boil quite well, and many potatoes, and ate them off her knee while she read detective stories through the long evenings. She thought that she might buy a television set for company, though she was busy too, with the postal orders for Christmas. When all this is over, she told herself, that is when I shall start looking about me and making my plans. She thought of all the things she might have done as a girl, the studio in London and the woodblock engravings for the poetry press, the ballet company for whom she might have been asked to do some ethereal costume designs. She read in a newspaper of a woman who had started her own firm, specializing in computer management, at the age of fifty and was now rather wealthy, wholly respected in a man's world. Miss Bartlett looked at herself in the mirror. I am only forty-seven, she said.

In her white bungalow, lonely and lacking a sense of purpose, Miss Roscommon waited.

On November the seventh, the first of the storms came, and Miss Bartlett sat in her back room and heard the wind and the crashing of the sea, terrified. The next morning, she saw that part of the pierhead had broken away. Miss Roscommon sent down a note, with a meat pasty, via the butcher's boy.

"I am worried about you," she wrote, "you cannot be looking after yourself, and I know that it is damp in that cottage. Your room here is ready for you at any time."

Miss Bartlett tore the note up and threw the pasty away, but she thought of the warm bed, the fires and soft sofas at Tuscany.

Two days later, when the gales began again, Miss Roscommon came herself, and hammered at the door of the cottage, but Miss Bartlett hid upstairs, behind a cheval mirror, until she went away. This time, there was no note, only a thermos flask of lentil soup on the doorstep.

She is suffocating me, thought Miss Bartlett, I cannot bear all these unwanted attentions, I only wish to be left alone. It is a poor thing if a woman of her age and resources can find nothing else to occupy her, nothing else to live for. But in spite of herself, she drank the soup, and the taste of it, the smell of the steam rising up into her face, reminded her of all the meals at Tuscany, the winter evenings spent happily sitting beside the fire.

When the storms came again, another section of the pier broke away, the lifeboat put out to sea and sank with all hands, and the front room of Miss Bartlett's cottage was flooded, rain broke in through a rent in the roof. She lay all night, too terrified by the roaring of the wind and seas, to get out of bed and do anything about it, only whimpering a little with cold and fright, remembering how close the cottage came to the water, how vulnerable she was.

As a child, she had been afraid of all storms, gales and thunder and cloudbursts drumming on the roof, and her mother had understood, wrapped her in a blanket and taken her into her own bed.

"It is because you have such a vivid imagination," she had said, "you feel things that the other, ordinary little children, cannot ever feel." And so, nothing had been done to conquer this praiseworthy fear of storms.

Now, I am alone, thought Miss Bartlett, there is no one, my mother is dead, and who is there to shelter and understand me? A flare rocket, sent up from the sinking lifeboat, lit up the room faintly for a second, and then she knew who there was, and that everything would be all right. On the stormy nights, Miss Roscommon always got up and made sandwiches and milky hot drinks, brought them to her as she lay awake in bed, and they would sit reading nice magazines, in the gentle circle of the bedside lamp.

I have been very foolish, Miss Bartlett thought, and heard herself saying it aloud, humbly, to Miss Roscommon. A very foolish, selfish woman, I do not deserve to have you as a friend.

She did not take very much with her up the hill on the following morning, only a little handcase and some raffia work. The rest could follow later, and it would be better to arrive like that, it would be a real indication of her helplessness.

The landscape was washed very clean and bare and pale, but the sea churned and moved within itself, angry and battleship grey. In the summer, Miss Bartlett thought, refreshed again by the short walk, it will be time to think again, for I am not committing myself to any permanent arrangement and things will have to be rather different now, I will not allow myself to be treated as a pet plaything, that must be understood. For she had forgotten, in the cold, clear morning, the terrors of the previous night.

She wondered what to do, ring the bell or knock or simply open the back door into the kitchen, where Miss Roscommon would be working, and stand there, case in hand, waiting to be forgiven. Her heart beat a little faster. Tuscany was very settled and reassuring in its low, four-square whiteness on top of the hill. Miss Bartlett knocked timidly at the blue kitchen door.

It was some time before she gave up knocking and ringing, and simply went in. Tuscany was very quiet.

She found her in the living-room, lying crumpled up awkwardly on the floor, one of her legs twisted underneath her. Her face was a curious, flat colour, like the inside of a raw potato. Miss Bartlett drew back the curtains. The clock had stopped just before midnight, almost twelve hours ago.

For a moment, she stood there, still holding her little case, in the comfortable, chintzy room, and then she dropped down on to her knees, and took the head of Miss Roscommon into her lap and, rocking and rocking, cradling it like a child, Miss Bartlett wept.

Acknowledgments

EVIDENCE IN CAMERA, from *The Allingham Casebook* 1969, is reprinted by permission of P.&M. Youngman Carter Ltd.

PATIENCE, © copyright Nigel Balchin, is reprinted by permission of Peters Fraser & Dunlop Group Ltd.

THE LITTLE FISHES, copyright H. E. Bates, is from *Sugar for the Horse*. Reprinted by permission of Michael Joseph Ltd. and the Estate of H. E. Bates.

THE APPRENTICE, copyright Hilaire Belloc, is from *Belloc's Stories, Essays and Poems*. Reprinted by permission of the Peters Fraser & Dunlop Group Ltd.

THE AVENGING CHANCE by Anthony Berkeley, © The Society of Authors 1928 is reprinted by permission of The Society of Authors.

RUNNING WOLF by Algernon Blackwood, copyright Garnstone Press, is reprinted by permission of A. P. Watt Ltd. on behalf of Sheila Reeves.

THE DEMON LOVER, first published 1945, copyright the Estate of Elizabeth Bowen, is from *The Demon Lover* by Elizabeth Bowen. Reprinted by permission of the Estate of Elizabeth Bowen and Jonathan Cape Ltd.

THE HIGGLER, © 1972 The Estate of the late A. E. Coppard, is reprinted by permission of the author's representatives and Jonathan Cape Ltd.

PARSON'S PLEASURE, © 1958 Roald Dahl, is from *Kiss, Kiss* by Roald Dahl. Reprinted by permission of Michael Joseph Ltd. and Penguin Books Ltd.

WINTER'S MORNING, © 1971 Len Deighton, is from *Declarations of War* by Len Deighton. Reprinted by permission of the publishers Jonathan Cape Ltd.

PHYSIC by Walter de la Mare is reprinted by permission of The Literary Trustees of Walter de la Mare, and The Society of Authors as their representative.

THE GIFTS OF WAR, © 1969 Margaret Drabble, is reprinted by permission of the Peters Fraser & Dunlop Group Ltd.

THE BIRDS, copyright Daphne du Maurier 1952, is from *The Apple Tree*. Reprinted by permission of Curtis Brown Ltd., London, on behalf of The Chichester Partnership.

FIREWORKS FOR ELSPETH, copyright 1953 by Rumer Godden, is from *Gone: A Thread of Stories* by Rumer Godden. Reprinted by permission of Curtis Brown Ltd., London, on behalf of Rumer Godden.

THE END OF THE PARTY is from *Collected Stories of Graham Greene*. Reprinted by permission of The Bodley Head Ltd. and the Estate of Graham Greene.

THE COTILLON, copyright © 1951, 1973 by the Estate of L. P. Hartley, is from *The Complete Short Stories of L. P. Hartley*, Hamish Hamilton 1973, first published in *The Travelling Grave*. Reprinted by permission of Hamish Hamilton Ltd.

The publishers have made all possible efforts to trace copyright holders but if any omissions have occurred, please let us know.

THE ILLUSTRATIONS were by

The portrait of J. B. Priestley was drawn by Carol Binch after a photograph by Mark Gerson